# Lilith

### by J. R. Salamanca

WELCOME RAIN PUBLISHERS
NEW YORK

*For Mimi*

*who makes them possible,
this, and all my books,*

*with love*

O *what can ail thee, knight-at-arms,*
  *Alone and palely loitering?*
*The sedge has withered from the lake,*
  *And no birds sing. . . .*

*I met a lady in the meads,*
  *Full beautiful—a fairy's child,*
*Her hair was long, her foot was light,*
  *And her eyes were wild. . . .*

—JOHN KEATS, *La Belle Dame Sans Merci*

# Lilith

$J$ GREW UP in a small Southern town which was different from most other towns because it contained an insane asylum. At the time I was growing up there, however, I did not think of this as a distinction. As we had been aware of it from birth, it had for us who lived there no aspect of novelty; it was simply one of the facts of our existence, and belonged, with the fire station, the clinic, the schoolhouse and the granary, among those elemental institutions by which life is both sustained and interpreted. I thought all towns had asylums. With the equanimity of a child I accepted the fact that there was madness everywhere, just as there were conflagration, illness, ignorance and hunger. I can, indeed, remember being disconcerted, somewhere around the age of twelve, by the discovery that other towns did not have asylums, and engaging in much troubled speculation as to how the insane people of these communities were disposed of.

So that, although there was mania somewhere beyond the shadows of its quiet elms and the shop windows of its main street, our town was not compromised in its pleasantness. It was a clean, pretty, leisurely town in central Maryland, with wide streets and two-story frame houses with great cool, awning-shaded porches. For subsistence it depended mainly upon the grain and dairy products of the rolling grassy farmland which surrounded it. The wheat was sacked and shipped from a large commercial grain elevator at the edge of the city; a spur line ran into it from the Baltimore & Ohio Railway, and one of the delights of my boyhood was to compile the names of roadbeds from the boxcars standing in the yards. I remember how bright the rails were in the sun, the sprinkle of brass-colored wheat and grain dust that blew about in the cinders, the silent yawning vastness of the empty cars with their steel-bound planks and hieroglyphic inscriptions of tonnage, load weight, cubic content and so forth; and the beauty and mystery of their names—to an inland boy as beautiful as the names of ships to a coastal dweller—Wabash, Santa Fé, Great Northern, Seaboard Air Line. And I can remember yet the quick bright thrill of excitement on seeing for the first time a legend unknown to me: The Hiawatha, Route of the Buffaloes.

Our district was also famous for its fruit, and at harvest time I would often work as a picker in the apple and peach orchards of the countryside. For this work I was paid a dollar a day, a great deal of money for a boy in those times; but I should rather —for the memories it has given me of long September days, standing on my ladder waist-deep in sweet-scented oceans of Elberta leaves, of heavy yellow peaches, hot with sunlight, softly furred and blushed with bluish crimson, and of country girls with brown arms and blowing hair, half hidden by the branches, singing ballads in the tops of apple trees—for these memories I should rather have paid the owners of those enchanted orchards.

Our town, which is called Stonemont, was the county seat. Its main street was laid out in an inverted L, like the move of a knight on a chessboard. On its shorter, lower, segment, set far back from the street on a high lawn to which a flight of five stone steps ascended from the sidewalk, stood the county courthouse, an old building of rose-colored brick, its two-columned portico paved with foot-worn stone and shadowed by giant elms. Directly in front of it the main street was divided by a narrow island on which, facing the courthouse, stood the statue of a Confederate soldier, his arms crossed upon his breast, his face shadowed by a slouch hat, one foot placed forward with a look of noble resolution which gained in pathos from the shabbiness of his tattered uniform and the empty scabbard that hung against his thigh. Beneath him, on the tall granite pedestal, was inscribed a legend which I never failed to reread when I passed and which never failed to give me the same warm glow of tragic pride:

TO OUR HEROES OF POPE COUNTY
*That We Through Life May Not Forget To Love*
*The Thin Gray Line*

The upper segment of the street was perhaps five blocks in length, and lined with the establishments familiar to all small towns: a barbershop; a small, false-fronted motion-picture house; the United States Post Office, before which an American flag hung over the sidewalk, casting, on windy days, its writhing, tormented shadow—a convulsive ghost—upon the pavement; a hardware store; an independent grocery and a two-story stuccoed office building with worn wooden corridors, open at either end to the afternoon sunlight. The doors of the offices were always propped open with rubber wedges, so that, walking through the corridors—as I did every Thursday afternoon to deliver magazines—one could look into the old-fashioned, high-ceilinged rooms, where the town's realtors, lawyers and insurance agents, big red-faced men in shirt sleeves and suspenders, lounged in swivel chairs, chuckling and drawling into telephones, looking up, as one walked by, to wink or toss a stick of chewing gum from the littered desk top through the open door. At the end of that street, as if its commerce faded into fantasy, was a music shop, always locked and silent, in whose sunny window a dulcimer lay forever, its strings furred with dust, its warm, wine-colored wood glowing softly. I can never remember that shop being open, and the dulcimer was never moved. Every year the dust grew heavier upon it, and the faded page of sheet music which lay beside it in the window grew paler with age, so that one could barely read the dying letters: I'll Take You Home Again, Kathleen. That locked shop, with its hushed and sunlit window, is for me still full of its strange, soundless music.

Stonemont was the site of the annual county fair, and for this event a permanent fairground had been built at the outskirts of the city, just beyond the cemetery, on a sloping hillside wooded thinly with fine old shade trees, white oaks and hickories. Among this grove were built the exhibition halls for domestic arts, farm produce and machinery, and the many long, low-gabled barns for livestock. The yearly fair is one of the most pleasant memories of my youth. It was held in late summer, on five blue days of August, when the apples on the hills were ripening and there were great golden, burnished pumpkins glowing in the stubble of the mown fields. How I loved the fair and the clear, late-August days! The air had the first faint winey reek of autumn and there were sudden fresh gusts of wind that made the pennants snap on the tent tops; the Ferris wheel turned slowly against the hard, blue, burning sky; there was the pungent, resiny smell of sawdust from the soft carpet of tanbark with which the grounds were scattered, the rich, wry, dusty scent of alfalfa and the royal smell of animals from the barns; the lowing of cattle and the droll bleating of sheep, blended with the murmur and milling of the crowds, the shouting of pitch-men, the soft footfalls in the sawdust, and the pennants snapping in the wind.

At the edge of the fairgrounds was a picnic grove where, in the early afternoons, people sat with spread blankets and open hampers in the shade of the gray oaks. One could look down from there, as I often did, and see, far below on the hillside beyond the brightness and clamor of the fair, the cemetery—silent in the sunlight, with its bleached headstones and tall, still cedars— where my mother lay buried, all her yellow ribbons extinguished by the rain.

Have I said enough about this town? It was, as you see, an ordinary provincial place, sunny, pleasant, unhurried. The insane asylum we seldom saw, as it was in a secluded residential area, considerably apart from the town's commercial district.

During my last year of high school, however, I saw it much more frequently, as at that time I began to work as delivery boy on a grocery truck. It was my job to assemble the orders in cardboard cartons in the stock room of the market, load them into the truck and then to accompany the driver on his rounds through the residential area, carrying the cartons, when he stopped to make a delivery, from truck to kitchen. It was one of the most satisfying jobs I have ever had. I do not know exactly what there was about it that I found so pleasant, but there was something gravely rewarding, almost revelatory, to me about handling food. Packing the boxes and bags of provisions, effecting and accompanying their course from market to table, gave me an intimate and fundamental sense of labor, as if I were working directly at the very sources of life.

It seems to me now as if those Saturday mornings were invariably warm and sunny, and I can remember sitting beside the driver, a cheerful contented man named Charlie, as we drove through the quiet shaded streets under the great elms, smiling dreamily, comforted by the closeness of sacks of clean white flour, melons, scarlet onions in string bags, moist, dripping packages of meat. Let me remember more closely: once a squirrel fell—the only time in my life I have seen it happen. Somehow it misjudged its leap in the branches that arched across the street and plunged down, twisting in its fall, from a great height, striking the stone heavily just in front of our truck, where it lay shivering.

We often made deliveries in that part of the town where the asylum was situated. It was in the "fashionable" part of Stonemont, a district of large old-fashioned houses with stained-glass attic windows of vivid red and blue and front walks paved with polished fragments of bright-colored stone. Several of these houses, to which we delivered regularly, were on the same street

15

as the asylum, so that I had the frequent opportunity of surveying it in the course of our rounds.

The building itself was difficult to see. It was set far back, perhaps fifty yards, from the street, behind beautifully landscaped grounds. There were avenues of arbor vitae, several magnificent poplar trees, from which the Lodge took its name, and a group of tall, low-hanging willows, under which a pair of Grecian stone benches glowed in the shadow. The driveway was bordered with privet and wound in a graceful curve from the street between the boles of the poplars. At the back of these grounds, thickly planted at its base with rose-of-Sharon bushes, stood the main building. It was actually a converted mansion (although I did not learn this until many years later), three stories in height, with a wide screened porch surrounding it on three sides, from which a set of broad wooden steps descended to the drive. It was an old Gothic building, typical of the early part of the century, full of bays and towers and long dormers, surmounted by a slate mansard roof, through which five ivy-covered chimneys, their moist bricks showing between the leaves, projected comfortably. All of its many windows were barred with heavy diagonal wire netting. (To the side were several small auxiliary buildings which I never noticed in very great detail: a small cottage, a shed, and a kind of converted loft with a flight of outside stairs ascending to it.)

It was always very quiet. In the late afternoons the blend of sunlight and shadow lying on the soft lawns and the ivied walls was calm and lovely. There was nothing grim or terrible about it; never were there faces peering from the high barred windows, or the sound of screams or violence within. With its elaborate and spacious grounds and its air of age and dignity, it had, indeed, a peaceful, almost an idyllic, aspect. And yet, standing in the sunny street to look at it, as I so often did, I would feel my mind shadowed and solemnized for a moment with a sudden delicate pall of awe, for children are moved by the mystery of madness, as they are moved by the other mysteries of life.

There is one picture of the place which I must set down here:

the most enduring which I have of it. When I think of the Lodge this is the way I always see it, in a sudden wan, bright image, apparently preserved forever, which is projected somewhere in my mind.

I shall have to regress a little in order to reconstruct it fully, for I feel that the picture for some reason would not be complete unless it were presented together with—framed by, as it were— the event which immediately preceded it. Nothing ever is seen clearly; always the pathos of the perceiver helps to create the thing perceived, as the image of water in sunlight is illumined by the thirst of the observer. In some such way, I believe, the event of which I speak helped to color and create this image of the Lodge which was to become so important for me, whose magic was to cast so deep a spell upon my life.

A short time earlier I had delivered a box of groceries to a Mrs. Hallworth. Her house was in the close neighborhood of the Lodge, a prosperous, well-kept place with a gardener usually busy in the front yard, mowing the lawn or kneeling at the walk to clip the edges. She was a regular customer of ours; and this was the fourth consecutive week that I had delivered her order, although I had never seen her. Ordinarily I was admitted to the kitchen by the maid, a sullen young Negress who opened the door silently with an expression of great suspicion and dislike. On this morning, however, she did not appear. No one answered my tapping against the light frame of the screen door which opened onto the back porch. I pressed my face against it and called, "Groceries!"

From a small high window in the side wall of the house a petulant female voice shouted, "What is it?"

"Groceries, ma'am," I repeated.

"Well, the door is open. Bring them in and set them on the kitchen table."

"Yes, ma'am."

I opened the door toward me and, holding it with my shoulders, carried the box up the steps and across the back porch into the kitchen. I put it on the large porcelain-topped table in the center of the floor, pushing aside several unwashed dinner plates on which a coating of orange-colored sauce had hardened and a slim-stemmed glass, still beaded with sweat and cool to my hand. From the hall which entered into the kitchen I heard the muted cascade of a water closet, a sound which suddenly increased in volume as a door was opened into the hallway and a middle-aged woman appeared, buttoning the front of a light summer dress. She held crumpled under her arm a garment of some type—another dress, apparently—of pale-blue silk, which she made a perfunctory attempt to conceal against her body.

"Here are your groceries, ma'am," I said with some embarrassment.

She came into the kitchen, her hands lingering upon, and then abandoning, the upper button of her dress, looking at me longer and more reflectively, I felt, than was required by the casualness of the circumstance. She was perhaps fifty, with graying hair and a round, soft, still pretty face, oddly combining a middle-aged, maternal benevolence with something avid, a look of candid, unquenched sensuality in her very pale-blue eyes. Her heavy-breasted, still vigorous-looking body was voluptuous in a plump, matronly way, and obviously uncorseted under her light cotton dress.

"Oh, thank you, young man," she said. "I'm just all at odds and ends this morning because that damn maid didn't show up."

"Yes, ma'am," I said.

"You just cannot depend on these nigras. She claimed to have a toothache, but you know how they are."

She smiled at me and lifted one hand to brush back with a movement of artificial, somehow unpleasant delicacy a strand of loose pale hair that had fallen across her forehead.

I murmured, "Yes, ma'am," again and stood for a moment looking into her eyes, held in some kind of a profound, spontaneous communication with her. It seems almost absurd in transcribing the event, but I felt that quick, impulsive, strangely zealous contact of my look flower suddenly, not beautifully or rarely, perhaps (but there are common flowers), into a relationship. My gaze was a moment too long. There was an instant when I knew I should have turned away toward the door, and, having done so, would have successfully dismissed another of those experiences from which the profound convention of modesty protects us; but I did not, and, having delayed that instant, I felt myself compromised, drawn with her into a covenant of confidence, both primitive and very subtle, from which I could not now, without dishonesty, renege. When I did break our gaze and make my belated movement toward the door I was not surprised, therefore, to hear her say, "I think perhaps you had better wait just a minute, young man. I just want to check this order and make sure everything has been sent."

"Yes, ma'am," I said, turning again toward her.

She dropped the crumpled dress she had been carrying onto a chair and began to rummage with assumed concern among the groceries.

"Isn't there an order sheet in here? There ought to be."

"Yes, ma'am, it's there somewhere," I said.

"I'm just entirely at a loss this morning. I was so upset about that maid that I had to have a cocktail to quiet my nerves. Can you imagine that! A cocktail for breakfast!"

She lifted her head toward me with an expression of spurious, gay vitality that made her pleasant maternal face almost ugly with imposture. "I wonder if you could help me find it?"

"Yes, ma'am," I murmured. "I know it's there, because I put it in myself."

I moved toward the table and bent above the carton to search with her. From her body there came a warm, strong smell of flesh, undisguised by perfume or cosmetics, moist and earthlike, which I could not escape. I knew that she leaned forward purposely to expose, beneath the fallen front of her dress, her heavy naked breasts, and I lowered my eyes quickly, shifting my hands among the groceries. I found the order slip and gave it to her, relinquishing it hastily to avoid the touch of her hands.

"Here it is, ma'am."

"Oh, yes. Thank you. Now, let me see."

She studied the slip of paper for a moment, frowning and shaking her head. "I just can't make out a thing without my glasses. I wonder if you'd read it off to me. I know you won't have any trouble reading it, with those lovely big brown eyes."

I murmured with embarrassment. She turned her back against me, her body touching mine, and held the slip for me to read across her shoulder. I stood cringing from the contact of her body, staring at her hands in a kind of grief. They were still firm and strong enough to be womanly, but they were aging hands, the skin dry and freckled with pale-brown patches of pigment, the fingers slightly swollen, puffed about her rings, the veins corded and blue—my grandmother's hands, as I had watched them sewing so many times. When she lifted one suddenly to clasp my chin in it I felt strengthless with shame, but out of some obscure, fierce sense of charity or dignity, I did not flinch. I smiled at her, my face flaming, while she squeezed my cheek and jaw lightly and said in a voice of dreadful, sweetened fondness, "My, they certainly do have handsome young grocery men these days. I can just see I'm going to have to let Dora off every Saturday morning."

I could not move or speak. She held my chin for a moment, smiling at me with heavy, suddenly undisguised concupiscence, while I stared beyond her, my eyes moving in idle, random desperation about the room. I do not know what I should have done—perhaps I should have yielded to her—if I had not chanced to see in that moment the dress which she had dropped into a chair. I realized suddenly that she had just exchanged it, as I was entering the house, for the one she was now wearing—and on the pale-blue silk, exposed as she had dropped it carelessly, I could see a dark-edged, scarlet stain of menstrual blood.

There was a convulsion of disgust in my throat, and I turned quickly, mumbling some absurd apology, and left the house, lurching against the door frame in my haste and barely controlling an hysterical desire to run as I went down the back steps and along the stone walk to the street. I do not know how I managed to conceal my feelings from Charlie—perhaps his cheerful simplicity made him oblivious to them—but he said nothing. I sat beside him, burning-faced and tremulous, in the truck while we drove through the suddenly oppressive sunlight and parked directly opposite the Lodge. I was, for once, far too distracted to glance in its direction, even to think of it. My hands were still trembling as I opened the rear door of the van to remove the box of groceries, and in my agitation I dropped the carton. A box of eggs fell open and smashed upon the pavement. I stood, staring down at them bleakly: bright-yellow, shining, naked yolks, some of them broken and oozing in livid rivulets, embedded in a pool of glittering colorless slime.

There came, from across the street, a sprinkle of cool, delightful laughter. I lifted my head and looked across the pavement and the low barberry hedge which bordered it, to the asylum lawn. A girl in a white dress stood watching me in the broken shadow of a willow. Her long yellow hair, very pale and radiant, like sunlight through honey, lay softly on her shoulders, stirring a little in a breath of air which swung the willow trailers gracefully in front of her. She held them apart with her hand, looking through at me. I shall say her face was slender and white, with great violet eyes and a bright, tender mouth, cleft with a hint of cruelty, but merry in that moment, lifted in laughter from her moist teeth; yet nothing I put down here can convey her inexpressible strangeness and beauty. She laughed again—a sound like the crystal prisms of a wind-chime blown together in a breeze of cool, perfumed air—and, while I watched her raptly, lifted one hand, as pale and fragile as a branch of coral, and hid her eyes with it in a shy, alluring gesture, both timid and wanton, letting the willows fall together like a veil. Was she alone? I can never quite remember. Sometimes it seems that there was an attendant, a dark-haired woman in a matron's uniform, standing a little away from her, but the image fades into nebulosity at its edges, and I cannot quite recall. All that I see clearly is the girl in her white gown, the cruel and tender beauty of her face before she covers it with her hand, the slenderness and pallor of her throat and arms, all softly diffused and delicately shadowed by the sunlight falling through the willows, casting a radiance like golden frost upon her hair; and behind her, rising distantly and mistily with a look of enchantment through the summer haze, the Palace of Fantasy from which she had strayed.

$\mathcal{T}$HAT WAS the last time I was to see the Lodge as a boy; I was eighteen that summer—the summer I went away to war. It was four years before I returned, and when I looked upon the Lodge again my childhood was past. But I must leave this to be told later, in its place; I must say first a little more about myself and my life in this town before the war.

I was often alone as a boy. My childhood was not entirely un-happy—it was often far from so—and yet I felt subtly distinguished from my companions, and from the life of our town, by the circumstances of my birth. What those circumstances were I never learned exactly in my youth, for they were never spoken of at home, although they seem to me now fairly certain, and simple enough to be assumed with confidence. But then they were only a haunting source of isolation that made my early life lonely and sometimes very painful. I remember that, on entering the grocery store or Wingate's Pharmacy to make a purchase for my grandmother, there would be sometimes a moment of silent attentive interest from the townspeople gathered there, while, with burning self-consciousness, I would stand reading the labels of packaged merchandise behind the counter as I waited to be served. Often, coming home from school in the afternoon, kicking a stone ahead of me along the sidewalk in some solitary, smiling game—it might be a racing car whose driver, if he ran off the track onto the grass edges of the sidewalk, would be killed—I would pass a pair of ladies chatting on a front walk and become suddenly aware of their suspended conversation, perhaps hearing scraps of their hushed, quickly resumed talk as I passed:

"That's the Robinson girl's child, you know."

"Yes, I thought it was. He looks like her, doesn't he?"

"Oh, I think he looks more like *him*."

"Yes, he *does*. Now that you mention it, why, he *does*."

I do not know by what manner I learned to interpret the difference in attitude which was expressed by the omission of my mother's first name when she was spoken of; but slowly, and profoundly, I became aware of it. Other women were Amy Pritchard, or June Hogan, or Belle King; but my mother was always "the Robinson girl"—a kind of formal, habitual opprobrium which made me feel all the more keenly a sense of warm, bewildered indignation in that the speakers themselves were hardly aware of casting it. My grandparents are the only people I have ever heard call my mother by her beautiful name.

"Beth, your dress is soiled, dear. Right there on the collar."

"Oh, is it? Thank you, Mother Bruce." (Lifting her hand to the litter of yellow ribbons woven into the lace collar of her blouse.) "Do you think I ought to change it?"

"I think it might be better, dear."

She died when I was eight, and I was brought up by my grandparents. My mother and I had lived with them for many years before her death—I think almost from the time that I was born—although they were not her parents. They were my father's people, but they loved my mother and cared for her as devotedly as if she had been their own child, although her gentle, distracted efforts to "pay her way" by helping my grandmother with the housework were generally more troublesome than helpful.

My father I never saw. So far as I can understand it now, I believe that his marriage to my mother was enforced—brought about, I am more than certain, by my grandfather's unobstructable sense of moral duty—and that, soon after it, he deserted her. Her own parents were dead, and her single close relative, the maiden aunt by whom she had been raised, had grown senile and was now a county ward. Although there was a little property in her name, including her family house, it was falling to ruin and was almost "eaten up," as they say, by unpaid taxes, so that she was very nearly destitute. My grandparents, not only to redress their son's abuse of her, but out of their own great natural compassion and affection for my mother and me, had taken us in to live with them.

All this I have pieced together mostly by silence and by sorrow, for, as I say, my father was never spoken of in our house, and nothing was kept in his memory; there was none of his toys or childhood possessions, no pictures, no clothing, no souvenirs— nothing to indicate that he had ever existed, or that my grandparents had ever had a son, except myself. Only my mother kept, in secret, a relic of him: a small, oval, sepia-colored photograph in a silver frame, which she kept hidden in a drawer of her dressing table. One of the last and most vivid memories I have of her was the discovery of that photograph.

She had sent me to fetch her manicure scissors from the dressing table, and, rummaging in the drawer, I had discovered the picture, wrapped lightly in a lilac-colored cambric handkerchief. Whatever scruples a child of eight may have had (they must have been small) as to his elders' privacy, they were immediately overcome by the burning sudden crisis of years of lonely curiosity; I could tell from the shape and weight of the object that it was a photograph, and almost before unwrapping it I was certain of its identity. I lifted off the handkerchief and stood staring with a kind of mournful fascination at the darkly handsome face in the old photograph. Although I never saw it again, I can remember the features very vividly: large somber eyes with fine, highly arched brows; a sullen, sensitive mouth, almost as beautiful as a woman's; very small, delicate ears; and a mass of black curls fallen over the high forehead. There was something very unpleasant about the face, and yet it resembled my own enough for me to feel a melancholy pride. As I stood staring at it I heard someone enter the room and, looking up quickly into the mirror, saw my mother standing behind me at the door. I watched her for a moment, flushing, and dropped my eyes.

"That is your father, Vincent," she said after a considerable pause.

I murmured, "Yes'm."

"It is not a very good picture of him; but it was taken before our marriage, and I'm very fond of it."

"Yes, ma'am."

There was another moment of silence, and she lifted her hands and held them close to her breast with the tips of her fingers pressed together as if she were praying, looking down closely at her bitten nails.

"He could be very tender," she said. "I want you to know he was often very tender with me, no matter what . . . you may learn of him. And he had the most beautiful hands I have ever seen."

I murmured again, watching her lowered face in the mirror in a sudden trembling rush of grief. She stood for a moment looking down at the tips of her fingers in a humble, anxious way, and then turned suddenly and left the room. I folded the photograph into the lilac handkerchief as I had found it and went after her. She had gone out onto the front porch and was leaning against one of the white posts, her lips sucked in between her teeth, staring out at the street and crying softly. I stood behind her for a moment, staring at the fallen ribbons hanging untied from her sleeves, trying desperately to think of something that would comfort or divert her; but all that I could find to say was "What do you want for Christmas this year, Mama?" I burst into tears as I said it, and buried my face against the curve of her hip, hugging her slender waist against me fiercely. We clung together, weeping, while yellow poplar leaves fell down slowly through the afternoon sunlight.

In a moment she quieted her breathing and placed her hand on my hair, saying in a cool, precise voice, "Your father was the only love of my life. I want you to believe that, Vincent."

That was the only direct knowledge I ever had of him, and afterward I began to hate my unknown sire, whose profligacy had brought me into the world and caused my mother so much anguish. I believe her pathetic devotion to him made me despise him even more. Every year she used to write to him, although she never knew his whereabouts. I learned this only a few weeks before she died, when she had gone to bed with the illness from which she never recovered. It was in November. She called me into her room one cold bright morning and held my hand for a moment while I sat on the edge of her bed. She was sitting up, propped against her pillows, with a litter of stationery on the bedclothes in front of her.

"I want you to do an errand for me, Vincent," she said.

"Yes, Mama."

"I'd like you to mail this letter for me, dear. I would do it myself, but I'm afraid I simply could not get as far as the post office this morning. I feel a little weak today."

She put the envelope into my hand and I glanced at it involuntarily, for I had never known her to write to anyone. She waited for a moment, watching me, and dropped her head.

"It is to your father," she said. "Today is our anniversary, Vincent. I write to him every year on our anniversary." I did not answer her, but sat staring at the envelope in my hands. She said softly, "I wish I had not had to ask you. I always mail it myself, but I'm afraid I can't, today. I did get up, to get the stationery, and it made me feel quite faint."

"You didn't put any return address on it, Mama," I said.

"I know," she said. "You see, I don't know where he is, but I like to feel that he gets them. So I just send them out like this, and when they don't come back to me I feel that he does, somehow."

"Yes'm," I murmured.

"I'm sending it to Capri this year. I think that would be such a lovely place for him to be. That's in Italy, Vincent; a lovely, sunny island." She blushed faintly through her pallor and lowered her eyes again. "I know it's a silly thing to do; but it does make me feel as if I can still reach him, in some way."

"I think it's a real nice idea, Mama," I said.

She laid her hand on my hair and smiled at me. "And you won't say anything to Grandma and Grandpa about it, will you? I'm afraid they would think it was very foolish."

"No, ma'am."

She died three weeks later. On the morning of her death I went again, as I had every morning of her illness, to her bedside. She was very weak, and I could see that it was an effort for her to open her eyes. When she did so she lay for a long time, smiling at me while she moved her fingers gently in my hair.

"You are a beautiful boy, Vincent," she said at last. "And you have a beautiful name. I have named you for the gentlest and kindest of all the saints. He loved all the poor and the destitute, and he cared for them and gave his life to them. I think that is the finest thing a man can do, and I would like you to try to be like him all your life. Will you do that for me, Vincent?"

"Yes'm," I murmured, clutching her hand against my face and adding in a trembling voice, "Get well, please, won't you, Mama?"

"I will try," she said. "But if I shouldn't, I want you not to cry too much. You must turn your tears into something finer, as St. Vincent did. There are too many tears in the world." She closed her eyes and lay smiling, her fingers stirring my hair.

That was the last thing she said to me. She died during the night. There must have been a crisis of some kind in her illness, for I was awakened by the hall light shining through my half-opened door and the sudden commotion in the house. I remember running out into the hall in my pajamas and struggling hysterically with the doctor, a stout old man in a dark suit who was hurrying up the stairs with my grandmother—beating at him frantically with my fists and breaking the gold chain that stretched across his vest. Its bright links fell sprinkling onto the carpet like a serpent's shattered, golden spine. He held me away with mild astonishment while I kicked and shrieked at him: "Get out of our house! She doesn't need you! My mother is all well, and she doesn't need any doctor, or anybody! Go away from our house! Please, please, *please!*"

$A$FTER HER DEATH, as I had promised her, I did not often cry; but I was silent, with that terrible silence of children who have been touched too soon by tragedy. I recovered very slowly from her death—perhaps it would be truer to say that I became very slowly the person whom her death had created from my earlier self —and when I did, the world was changed for me. It was still a place of beauty, pleasure, and often of happiness, but that deep mine of peace and perpetuity which I had known to exist at its core was no longer there for me, or held another kind of ore. "There had passed away a glory from the earth," although the rainbow came and went, and the rose was as lovely as before. Yet, as I say, there was much pleasure and happiness, for children heal readily, and grow, and are endowed with an infinite will to survive. Nor was I ever wholly destitute, for I was always aware of the abiding love and kindness of my grandparents. My devotion turned entirely to them and was fulfilled.

I used, at fair time, to help my grandmother in the kitchen, preparing the chutney and chili sauce and mint jelly which she exhibited every year. She was a stout, strong, handsome woman with very soft silver hair which she pinned up carefully every morning in the same pompadour style she had worn since she was a girl in England. I loved to see her bustling about the huge old kitchen over her steaming pots, slicing tomatoes and bright crimson peppers, chattering to me in her cheerful Midland accent while I sat crushing herbs with a china pestle in a wooden bowl: "Have them good and fine, Sonny, as we did last year. There's a good lad." When I think of her now I remember the little yellow horn combs in her silver hair and the ancient bittersweet pungence of bay and rosemary. I remember also her smiling, carefully controlled pride when she won, as she invariably did, red or blue ribbons for her sauces, and, one year, the Grand Award in Home Arts—a great purple rosette—for a tatted counterpane on which she had worked for many years.

My grandfather had brought her to America as his bride at the turn of the century and had invested the proceeds of his share of the family business in a printing shop. He had prospered at this trade until 1930, when the drastically reduced activity of the Depression had revealed the long-standing malpractices of his partner. He had managed, through his great industry and integrity, to salvage the reputation of his small company and had later opened a restaurant in an abandoned Colonial tavern which stood at the outskirts of the town. This building he had devotedly reconstructed, furnishing it with early-American antiques, restoring its huge old fieldstone hearths and furbishing it with iron foundry ware, gleaming copper bed-warmers, skillets and horse-brasses. I think he was always at heart an English innkeeper; his tavern appealed profoundly to some old racial instinct of his. He loved it, and flourished.

In spite of his being an immigrant in a community of old, often rancorous ante-bellum families, he had won, by his dignity and temperance, a position of great respect in Stonemont and had held, since before I can remember, a seat on the town council. He was a very short man with a plump, firm belly and a stern but sensitive big-featured face. He used to walk about the streets of Stonemont, winter and summer, in a black serge suit and a faded and fraying Panama hat, carrying an old-fashioned Malacca cane with a gold head.

He loved horses. I can remember, with a sudden warm pang of affection, his face as he sat beside me in the show pavilion at the county fair when the draft horses were being judged, watching the huge old Percheron stallions with that humble, radiant look, so selfless and genuine, of a man absorbed in something he loves. As a boy he had worked in his father's rendering concern in Liverpool, and in those days, long before automobiles, their delivery wagons had been drawn by teams of Clydesdales. It had been his job to care for them. "I groomed them night and morning," he told me countless times, "and kept their manes and tails braided up in red ribbons the year round. It was a job, too—Liverpool is a dirty city. Ah, you should have seen them—stepping along over the cobbles with their great feet, all the brass shining on their harnesses. It was a lovely sight!"

He taught me to love them, too; perhaps the capacity to love them was there already, but he showed me what was beautiful in them, and he taught me, most important of all, the great patience with which one must learn to love things truly. On my twelfth birthday he bought me one of my own, a little strawberry mare which he managed to buy very cheaply, because of a blind eye, at a county auction. I think that was the happiest birthday of my life. I stabled her at a farm just outside the town and paid for her keep with money that I earned delivering magazines, mowing lawns and fruit picking. I became a fine rider, and from that birthday onward I entered the jousting championships every year at the county fair.

Jousting is a very popular rural sport in Maryland, and tournaments are held throughout the summer months in the farm country. Although many of the old elements of chivalry are preserved, the tournaments are no longer a contest between mounted knights, having become a demonstration of skill in riding and accuracy with the lance. A course is laid out under a series of wooden arches—three or more of them—from each of which a steel ring, bound in white cord to make it more easily visible, is suspended in a metal clip. As these rings are no larger than the diameter of a coffee cup, and must be taken at full gallop with a fifteen-foot lance, it is a truly stirring exhibition of horsemanship and poise. The riders are designated, according to the household, village or locality which they represent, as "The Knight of Boyds," "The Knight of Gaitherburg," "The Knight of Longview Farm" or—a particularly appropriate one, which always made me smile with romantic delight—"The Knight of Damascus"; and each wears, fluttering from his sleeve or basted to his jersey, the colors of his patron. How clearly I can see the summer sunlight falling among the elms, the railed wooden platform where the four-man band, in vests and shirt sleeves, sit on folding chairs, their brass horns glinting in the shadow as they raise them to sound a flourish for each champion, the line of wooden benches behind the roped boundaries of the course where elderly ladies in bright straw hats and cotton dresses sit holding a chicken leg in one hand, a sheet of waxed paper spread out in their laps, and the dogs and children running among the standing crowd of country people in their Sunday clothes!

I shall never forget the year—it was my fourteenth—when I took forty-six out of fifty rings to win the Junior Championship at the county fair. It was a victory for which I had long prepared. Every weekend, during the school term, and almost every day throughout the summer, I would walk along the cool streets to the edge of town and then for a mile along the highway in the sun, to practice target riding. My grandfather bought me a lance, made out of hickory, with a steel-tipped point, and came with me, as often as he could, to help me train. I would gallop the length of a course I had laid out under a row of shade oaks at the edge of a meadow, tilting at metal washers which I had hung from the lower branches, while he stood in the center of the field with his short, stout arms folded across his chest and his Panama hat pulled down to his thick gray eyebrows, watching my progress like a general deploying troops from a hillside. Sometimes in his excitement he would run along beside me as I rode, brandishing his cane and very often his hat as well, while he shouted instructions and encouragement: "Up out of the saddle, Lad! Up in the stirrups—keep a straight back—that's a good boy! Now then, elbow up—up higher—level with the lance—head over—give her the rein—good lad! Good lad!"

He had my grandmother make a banner for the tournament, a copy of the faded coat-of-arms that hung above the parlor sofa, which she embroidered beautifully, in colored thread, on a pennant of scarlet silk. It was run up above the judges' stand for my victory, and I shall never forget with what pride I watched it drifting, nobly and idly, in the mild breeze as I rode back down the list in triumph from my final trial, escorted by the pages—two very pretty, grinning girls in jodhpurs, mounted on bay mares—to accept my trophy from the Tribune, while the trumpets blared in tribute to my victory. I looked across to where my grandfather stood inside the gallery ropes nodding at me gently, unable to speak, his eyes shining with tears, clutching against his plump English belly his crushed and ruined Panama hat. I think I restored for him in that moment something that his son had once destroyed.

I do not believe I ever realized, until the tournament, the fierceness of my grandfather's pride, or the depth to which it had been wounded by my father's dishonor; although in looking back, now, upon my childhood, I can remember many earlier incidents which might have illustrated it. One of these I recall—perhaps because I was only ten years old at the time—with particular clarity. This took place one evening when, walking with my grandfather on one of the pleasant strolls which we invariably took together before dinner, I was harried by a group of schoolboys sitting on the retaining wall of the courthouse lawn as we walked by. There was one considerably older boy among them, the privilege of whose company they were conspicuously aware of, and feeling, I suppose, that anxiety to distinguish themselves in the presence of a senior which is so common to small boys, they called after me a series of faintly disguised allusions to my ancestry, in a tone of voice very cunningly calculated to sound impressively defiant to the larger boy among them and yet not quite loud enough to be heard by, or to offend, my grandfather (who was after all a very old man, probably with imperfect hearing and obviously absorbed deeply in his thoughts). My grandfather did hear them, however, and, turning upon me a look of such pale and violent fury that I was astonished and alarmed—for I had never seen such passion in his face before— he drove me back with threatening gestures of his cane and the command to challenge and engage them. One of the bolder boys accepted my very tentative demand for satisfaction, and after struggling for a few minutes on the courthouse lawn we fell off the wall onto the sidewalk, so that my opponent banged his skull painfully on the stone and fled sobbing—a very dubious victory which I was nevertheless happy to appropriate as entirely of my own design. My grandfather stood by throughout without once offering his assistance; but when I returned, very shaken and unsteady, he leaned down and laid his hands on my shoulders, smiling at me with a tenderness quite as intense as his anger of the moment before, and said gently, "Good lad. Well done. You have a good name, Sonny, and it's up to you to prove it. There'll be no one but you to defend it, soon." I mumbled, "Yes, sir," feeling pleased with my fortuitous success, and with the obvious pride he took in it, but entirely mystified by the intensity of his feelings. It was only in the light of my later understanding of his nature that I was able to interpret it—and with a regret for which I have never found assuagement.

$B$ECAUSE OF the solitariness of my nature and the fewness of my friends I was painfully inept at social events; although I was an active and enthusiastic member of the high-school debating and dramatic clubs, I was never asked to join a fraternity, I never learned to dance, avoided the school proms, and seldom attended parties. One year, however, in the fall of my junior year of high school, I did attend the annual class picnic; and it was there that I met Laura, who is of such importance to this story.

The combined junior-and-senior-class picnic was held at the beginning of each school year on Sugar Loaf Mountain, about fifteen miles from Stonemont, at the northern end of the Blue Ridge. It is, I think, the highest place in eastern Maryland—a blunt blue mountain, rising above the rolling fields of Montgomery and Frederick and Pope counties. We drove here in a school bus on a fine Saturday in mid-September. It is very beautiful in the fall, when the gum trees have turned the moist red of fresh blood and the few silver leaves of the tall aspens shimmer in the wind on the high slopes. There is a paved road that winds to within five hundred yards of the summit; here, among the great gray boulders and laurel thickets of a small plateau, there are stone barbecue pits and heavy wooden picnic tables. There is also a lookout, as it is called—an imitation Gothic castle with a battlemented parapet, built of the stones and boulders of the slopes. There is a splendid view: one looks out over vast blue distances, westward to the gentle peaks of the Blue Ridge Mountains in Virginia, southward over the coastal plain, sunken and glimmering, almost to Washington, and northward to the green, softly heaving farmlands of Pennsylvania. Beyond the lookout there is a footpath leading to the very summit of the mountain, a rough, laborious trail cut through dense thickets and with steps hewn almost vertically in places out of the granite cliffs of the mountain peak. The prospect of gaining this further, consummate, height and the unimpeded view which one must have from the summit was almost magically urgent to me. I could hardly wait to complete my hasty share of the preparations—gathering a few armloads of dead branches for a pit fire—before separating myself as unobtrusively as I could from the party and starting up the trail toward the peak.

It was a very steep and difficult climb of forty minutes, and I often had to stop, gasping, my heart pounding dully in my ears, to rest before going on; but it was more than worth the effort. From the top the view was truly magnificent. Below and around me lay a huge unbroken panorama of hills, farmland and forests; thin, glittering streams; the far-off, silent Potomac winding between its forested shores; tiny villages and homesteads, looking like pieces on a game board, all bathed in a soft violet mist and full of the tranquil and transcendant charm which great perspective gives to things. I fell down at full length in the grass at the bole of one of the small wind-warped pines that grow on the upper slopes and lay looking out over the distant, blue, beautiful earth with a curious sense of triumph. Far below me I could hear still the voices of my schoolmates, ringing, faint with distance, through the pines: the thin, pretty shrieking and laughter of the girls and the coarse exuberant shouting of the boys. The sound made me smile gently.

My reverie was disturbed very shortly by Laura, whom I saw walking toward me through the stony grass. She was a short, plain but pleasant-looking girl whom I had seen often about the school but whom I did not know well, as she was in a different class from myself. My dismay at her intrusion was so great that for a moment I considered fleeing, with only a perfunctory pretense of not having seen her, to some other portion of the small circular plateau of the mountain peak; but her approach toward me was so determined and candid that I was forced to abandon the impulse. I sat up as she came near me, clasping my knees and nodding in a pretense of friendly composure. She came and stood immediately beside me, smiling and lifting both hands to brush back her short dark hair, disheveled from the climb.

"Well, this is where you are," she said.

"Yes." My voice was somewhat hesitant with surprise at the unexpectedness of the greeting. "Were you looking for me?"

"Yes."

"Oh."

I could think of nothing else to say; and in the silence she seated herself beside me in the grass, dropping down heavily with exaggerated fatigue and drawing a great sighing breath which she expelled slowly with a humorously weary sound.

"It's a pretty steep climb, isn't it?" I said.

"My goodness, yes. My legs are all twittery."

I had never before seen her so closely or at such length. Although she was not actually stout, her body had a heavy, graceless look; her wrists, ankles and waist were too thick, and—a thing which has always distressed me in women—her bosom too full. Her hands were appealing in motion and full of vitality, but broad and blunt-fingered and, in repose, not pleasant to watch. There was something curious about her features which it took me several moments to discover: although her face gave a simple, not ugly, but undistinguished general impression, her eyes and lips were truly beautiful. Her mouth was warm, full and sensitive, and I had the impression that she had constantly to exercise control over her lips to keep them from betraying her. Her eyes were a deep, pure brown, as brilliant and profound as a certain type of quartz which is common in our county and which, as a boy, I used to shatter sometimes with a hammer so that I might see the sheer, glittering facets of dark-chocolate-colored, liquid-looking stone; they had a wide, vulnerable look which combined oddly with the strength and simplicity of her appearance. She smiled at me pleasantly; and, becoming suddenly aware of the length of my gaze, I looked hastily away.

"How did you know I was up here?" I asked.

"I saw you slip away and start up the path."

"Oh. I didn't know anybody was watching me."

"I was, though. I was watching you on the bus, too. Didn't you know that?"

"No. Why?"

"Because I think you're very handsome," she said. "I like to look at you."

I turned away in embarrassment and stared out for a moment at the valley, murmuring, "It's a wonderful view up here, isn't it?"

"Yes." She looked out briefly, her head moving in a rapid, cursory arc, and pointed to the distant river, glinting in the hollows of the hills. "What's that river you can see down there? The Potomac?"

"Yes."

"I didn't know it came up this way."

"Yes, it does."

She turned her head to watch me for a moment. "Is that what you came up here for—to look at the view?"

"Yes, I guess so," I said; and then, aware of the oddness of the question, I added, "Why did you think?"

"I thought you might just have wanted to get away from us. I could tell you didn't like the picnic very much."

"I did. I liked it very much."

"Why didn't you wait and get something to eat, then? There won't be anything left by the time you get back."

"I wasn't very hungry." I looked at her fully for a moment, feeling suddenly rather indignant. "That seems like a pretty funny question to ask anybody."

She returned my gaze steadily, not in a challenging way, but simply, studiously and gently; and it was I who had to look away.

"I don't think that's really a very nice impulse," she said. "To run away from people like that, just because you feel uncomfortable."

"What do you mean?"

"I think you came up here because you like to feel superior. You don't feel as if you were really *among* us, so you like to feel above us. But I don't think that really solves anything."

"That isn't true," I murmured. "I don't feel like that at all."

"Well, I wish you'd come back down and have some hamburgers, or something. They'll all be gone soon. And I'm terribly hungry."

I sat still for a moment, staring away at the distant hills and plucking at the grass with my fingers.

"What did you follow me up here for, anyway?" I asked.

"I just wanted to get you to come back and have some fun. It isn't very nice when you see people being so lonely." She laid her hand over my own, stilling my fingers. "Vincent, come back down with me."

"All right," I said, feeling suddenly quietly delighted by the invitation. "I was coming down in a minute, anyway."

We walked back between the boulders and laurel to the edge of the plateau, where the trail descended. She kept purposefully ahead of me, and as I followed her I watched the pleasant resolute movements of her body: the firm, alternate placement of her heavy-calved legs, the shifting of her broad hips under her woolen skirt and the serene carriage of her shoulders—movements not dainty or graceful, but vigorous and appealing in a womanly way. At the bottom of the first long flight of stone steps she turned and looked up at me, standing two levels above her. We were in the shadow of the granite cliff we had just descended.

"Are you tired?" I asked.

"No. Do you know my name?"

"No."

"It's Laura." She looked into my eyes for a moment. "Do you have a girl friend?"

I murmured in embarrassment that I did not.

"I think you ought to," she said. "I could be your girl friend, if you like. I mean, we don't have to say we love each other, or swear eternal devotion, or anything like that; but it's nice to have somebody to do things with, and to talk to about your troubles, and everything. I'd like to, if you would. We could stop any time you wanted."

I looked down at her silently, both confused and moved by her candor, and feeling in myself a flowering of startling affection. But I was disturbed by a subtle complexity of emotion: there is often, in the relationships of lonely people, a kind of gentle bitterness. They will not, out of pride, permit themselves too easily to accept affection. From secure people, there is always the fear of condescension in such an overture; and if it is made by people equally as lonely as themselves, there is a kind of shared shame, as if two diseased and outcast persons had applied to each other for comfort. Since they are aware of this essentially negative and ignoble nature of their relationship, there very often exists between them a deeply buried, mutual disrespect. My sensitivity to such things made me recoil for a moment with the swift instinct of caution and alarm that people like myself feel at a proposal of such intimacy. I do not mean that Laura was such a person, but I feared it. I could find in neither her eyes nor manner, however, either condescension or this kind of shyly desperate appeal. She watched me steadily and serenely, with a look of frank and simple equanimity that I found strangely touching.

"Do you want to?" she asked. "I think we could have fun. I'm not jealous, either, so you don't have to worry about that."

"Well, I don't know how to dance, or anything," I said softly.

"We don't have to dance, if you don't want to. But I think I could teach you. I'm a very good dancer. You just have to have confidence."

I felt the light stir of a falling leaf in my hair. She raised her hand to pick it away, and through the short sleeve of her blouse

I could see the unshaven soft brown hair of her armpit. She held the leaf by its stem, a pale golden poplar leaf, like a blunt star.

"Isn't it pretty?"

"Yes."

I put my hands lightly on her shoulders and we looked into each other's eyes for a moment before I kissed her—timidly at first, and then with considerable passion, for she was the first girl I had ever kissed, and there was in my embrace many years of loneliness and the longing of boyish fantasies.

It was in this way that Laura and I became sweethearts. We "went together" throughout that and my final year of high school; and although it gave to both of us much comfort, companionship, and a kind of formal tenderness, it was also, in many ways, an unfortunate alliance. I write these sentences with great deliberation, for I feel it is extremely important that I be completely just in describing our relationship; but I must be honest as well. Laura was kind, intelligent and generous in many things; but there was about her a quality—not of coldness, but a kind of wry aplomb—as if, at the center of herself, something was withheld, as if something had been sacrificed to a social image which she held of herself and which she was determined to preserve and to confirm. There are people who move among us with all the forms of liberal living—with poise and charity and principle— who yet, although they have established an identity for themselves by these virtues and conventions, are somehow stunted by them, too, who remain somehow aloof, eternally virgin, spiritually amateur. For Laura, I think, this was the penalty of convention; whatever she gained by it must be measured against what was lost: the exercise of the great insight and compassion of which I felt that she was capable, and the flowering of that rare and delicate contact of our natures for which I always longed and which I never knew. If I had not thought her capable of it I should not consider this tragic; but there are very few persons with whom one feels it to be possible, and when one sees the possible aborted one cannot but mourn. She seemed to have mastered the techniques of living, and in this achievement to have somehow stifled and deformed her talent for it. I know that this is a crucial, and perhaps a querulous, premise, and I hope that Laura will forgive me for these words. I know, too, that they may be written out of the bitterness which was created by what occurred between us later; and if this is so, Laura, be as charitable with me as you can allow yourself to be, for I have need of charity today.

*A* FEW MILES from Stonemont there was a turf farm with a large artificial lake, whose owners permitted the townspeople to use it as a park. It was a lovely lake, surrounded by willows and water maples and bordered with soft green turf which grew to the water's edge. We went there often, in the summer to swim and in the winter to ice skate. Laura was not graceful or particularly expert at either of these sports, but I liked to watch her. She swam and skated with a stubborn methodical competence which, to someone like myself who does not have it, is strangely comforting. And yet I disliked intensely her appearance as she came out of the water and can still, in remembering it, feel my eyes clench slightly closed against the image, as they did then: plump, pale, dripping body, large breasts bouncing heavily under the drenched wool of her swimming suit, short stout thighs, white as lard, glittering with water, thick fingers plucking at the wet wool, stretching it away from the contours of her body.

She taught me to dance on summer nights in her living room, with a phonograph playing on the dining table, the windows open onto the front porch and the curtains blowing softly in the warm night air. She danced beautifully, with a lyric lightness and skill and with something as near to total joy as I ever saw in her. I do not understand how someone who performed all other things with such mechanical earnestness could, in dancing, become suddenly so subtle, graceful and grave. It delighted me to watch her eyes while we danced; they were always turned away, gazing softly and sightlessly, filled and welling with that tender awareness of something other than reality which I always longed and rejoiced to see in them. She had a way, when I faltered or became confused, of stopping suddenly, taking my hand very gently and pressing it against her hip, leaning and swaying her body in a slowly and luxuriously accelerating motion, drawing me with her into the trance of the rhythm and murmuring to me softly, "Slowly, Vincent. Slowly. It's like dreaming. You have to let yourself dream." Is it poor comfort, Laura, to know that if I ever loved you truly it was when we danced together?

Afterward we would sit together on her porch swing in the summer darkness, hearing the shrill of insects in the trees and the soft mutter of quiet talk from neighboring porches. Patting her moist temples and her plump white throat with a linen handkerchief, speaking in her composed and solemn way about the school events and daily trivia which made up most of our conversation—how different she seemed from the flowing, fervent being who had guided me about the parlor a few minutes before! And however much I longed to restore or preserve the feeling which had animated her while we were dancing—this profound, spontaneous joy—however much I wished it to warm and illumine all of our intercourse, I could not; for only in dancing would she yield herself to it. Our conversation lapsed into banalities; our relationship was not the constant quiet rapture of communion for which I longed but an exchange of miscellanea, opinions and advice:

"You did awfully well tonight, Vincent. You'll be a good dancer."

42

"No, I don't think so. I just can't do it. I make a mistake and then go all to pieces."

"It's just learning the steps. When you know the steps you'll feel safe, and you won't get lost like that."

"No, that isn't it. I know the steps, but I just can't do it. You can't learn to dance the way you do, Laura, by just learning the steps; you've got to have some kind of music inside you. And I don't have it."

"You're too impatient, Vincent. You've got to be patient about things."

Sometimes her father would call her from inside the house, and she would excuse herself and go upstairs to take care of him. He was an invalid who had been increasingly bedridden for the last two years. During the day, while Laura was in school, her mother took care of him, and in the evenings, to relieve her, Laura attended to him. Looking in through the open windows, I would see her leading him along the upstairs hall to the bathroom—a frail old man with a sunken chest and a stubble of gray beard, shuffling along the hall in a stained woolen bathrobe while he clutched at her tremblingly. He looked unclean and— quite irrationally—evil to me, and it made me cringe to see Laura's physical closeness to him, his bent body in the dirty robe pressing against her, his dark blotched hands fumbling at her arms and shoulders for support. Sometimes she would carry a bedpan from his room, clutching the rim of the white enamel basin firmly in her strong hands as she went quickly down the hall toward the bathroom. I would turn my head away with revulsion at the sight.

"What's the matter with him, Laura?" I asked her once.

"He has some kind of a blood disease. Nobody seems to really know what it is."

"He doesn't seem to be getting much better, does he?"

"No, he's getting worse all the time; he's in bed most of the time now. I think he'll die before next spring."

I sat silently for a few moments in deference to this impending tragedy, feeling oddly oppressed by the matter-of-factness of her tone.

"What will you do then, Laura?"

"Oh, Mother and I will stay on here. She'll have money enough to last until she dies, I think, with her dressmaking—and if we take in roomers. We'll have two extra bedrooms after Father dies. We're going to try and save up enough for me to go to business college in Baltimore for two years; I can get a much better job that way."

"Oh. What kind of work are you going to do, Laura?"

"Well, if I can go to business college I can get a junior-executive job, I think. It's certainly worth the investment, if we can manage it. If not, I'll just do stenography or secretarial work. Of course, what I really want to do is get married. I want very much to have children. But you have to plan for everything."

"Yes, I guess so."

She lifted her handkerchief and fluttered it before her face to drive away the midges and in a moment said, "What are you going to do, Vincent?"

"What am I going to do?"

"Yes. I mean, have you decided what you would like to do in life?"

It was a question I dreaded, for I did not have the slightest idea. Whenever I was so challenged—as I had been several times by my grandfather—I would sit staring wanly, my mind accelerating in a desperate effort of concentration, as if by an act of will I might somehow invoke an inspiration. On one occasion, when he had questioned me with more than usual insistence, I had tried holding my breath and narrowing my eyes, hoping to achieve some mystic and spontaneous state of insight in which all my instincts, energies and aptitudes would flower forth suddenly in a revelation of my true vocation. How I longed for some specific, cherished ambition to declare! How I should have liked to announce my devotion to some ancient, honorable institution which my grandfather, and all men, would commend! But how-

44

ever much I wished—and often tried, sincerely—to consider my destiny in transcendental terms, in sober academic generalities, I could produce only the most vivid and vagabond particulars: What would I like to do? Why, I would like to make Laura gasp with passion. I would like to be able to play "Greensleeves" and "Can Ye Sew Cushions?" on the dulcimer. I would like to win the senior jousting tournament at the county fair. I would like, some afternoon, to kiss Mrs. Murchison as she stepped out of the drugstore with the wind blowing her red hair. I would like to steal into the cemetery at night with a chisel and chip the terrible graven dates and the terrible words THY WILL IS OUR PEACE from my mother's headstone.

And yet—as appealing and significant as these things seemed to me—I recognized, with humiliation and a great sense of inadequacy, the hopelessness of producing them as evidence of a firm and zealous purpose in life.

"I really think you ought to start planning your life, Vincent. You're a junior already, and you'll be out of school next year."

I ran my fingers through my hair and said uncertainly, "I know. I think I'd like to do some kind of charity work, or something like that, if I could."

"Some kind of charity work?"

"Yes. I promised my mother I'd do something like that. She wanted me to do something that would help poor people, and destitute people, if I could."

"Is that what you really want to do?"

"Well, I don't really know. Sometimes I think I'd like to play a musical instrument of some kind. You know that shop at the end of Main Street?"

"Which one? Oh, the one that's always closed. Yes."

"Well, did you ever notice that dulcimer in the window? I'd love to know how to play a dulcimer. I've never heard one; have you?"

"No. Why do you want to play something that you've never even heard?"

45

"I don't know. I just like the way it looks. It looks like it would make a wonderful sound."

She was silent, lifting her handkerchief to pat her throat thoughtfully.

"I don't think there's very much opportunity for musicians of any kind," she said after a moment. "They have a very hard time finding work. And I never even heard of a dulcimer player. I don't think there'd be any demand for them at all."

"No, I guess not," I said. "I haven't really thought very much about what I want to do. I think my grandfather would like me to go into the restaurant with him. But I promised my mother I'd help people somehow."

"Well, what would that mean? Wouldn't you have to study social work, or something like that?"

"I don't know. I guess so."

"It seems to me that social work is very highly specialized; I think you'd have to have a master's degree, at least, to get anywhere. And that's six years of college. Do you think you could afford to study that long?"

"No, I don't think so. I couldn't ask my grandfather for that much money. Maybe I could work my way through, or something. I'm not sure yet."

When I left her in the evenings we would stand on the front steps in the shadow of the wistaria vine and kiss, shyly and tentatively, holding each other's arms, but never with the whole-hearted passion of our first embrace. I say that our relationship was banal and obtuse, and yet I can remember very clearly the immediate loneliness for her that I used to feel, walking home through the quiet dark streets, and the sense of peace and compensation that the knowledge of her affection for me, and her quiet competence, and our few fumbling moments of passion gave to me.

Yet sometimes I would become fiercely indignant at what I considered the ignominy of our relationship. I was shamed by the lack of vitality of her feelings and because the compassion in which our friendship was founded was not as profound as I felt that it might and should have been. I would not tolerate an intimacy with anyone which was fatuous and conventional.

I broke out in exasperation at her once: "Laura, look at my face—you say you like to look at me."

"I do. It's very handsome. Is that what you want to hear? You're very handsome, Vincent." She smiled and brushed my lips with a shaft of wheat that she had plucked.

"No, be serious, Laura. Nothing ever seems to—well, to *move* you. I want you to be moved by something. Look at my hands, then. Watch when I move my fingers. Don't you see? Doesn't anything ever move you?"

"What's the matter, Vincent? Are you angry?"

"No. It's just that I don't want us to be—well, ridiculous. Can't you understand that? If we go on . . . courting, or whatever it is that we're doing, just because we happened to meet each other, and not to be in love with anybody else—well, then it's ridiculous. Don't you understand that?"

"No. I think you're angry. You're too intense, Vincent. You've been alone for such a long time that you've been dreaming about girls. But girls aren't the way you dream about them."

"What are they like, then?"

She dropped her head for a moment and clasped the back of one hand with the other. I waited for her to answer, but she did not.

"What are they like, then?" I asked her almost angrily. "Are they like you?"

"Some of them are. I am, Vincent."

It was a cool fall evening, and we were sitting under naked trees beside a stony spring to which we often walked. We had built a fire of oak twigs, and it was dying, the embers glowing bitterly, like a heap of rubies, under the gray ash. I stirred them with a branch, watching the exposed coals bloom into a livid incandescence. She watched the fire for a moment and said, "Do you want to stop, then?"

"No."

"Why?"

"Because I think it can be different than this. I think we can feel really close to each other. I want us to be really in love, Laura."

I looked up at her face, which was flushed from the heat of the fire, her brown eyes shining darkly, the glow of the coals buried deeply in them. "Your eyes are so different from the rest of you," I said. "You seem as if you had somebody else's eyes."

"I think you resent me," Laura said, "because I'm not like the girl you always dreamed you would have. I'm not very beautiful, or talented, or witty, and you resent me for that. You feel as if you'd been cheated."

I stared into the fire, flushing, for I think, with a sudden pang of remorse, I may have recognized the partial truth, at least, of what she said; and it made my protest and dissatisfaction seem suddenly ignoble and vindictive. And in the spasm of humility which followed this acknowledgment I saw also, with suddenly humbled vision, the vanity of my appeal for love, for a profundity of feeling that could be made to grow—slowly and surely, as it must grow—only by patience, devotion and selflessness.

"Well, I'm sorry you feel like that," I said. "I don't think it's so, Laura; I certainly hope it isn't."

She leaned toward me and laid her hand on my shoulder. "I think it's very nice, the way we are now," she said. "I don't want you to be all wild and impetuous and everything. I just want to make you calm, and more sure about things, and more peaceful. I think that's what you need, Vincent."

"I don't want to be all wild, Laura. I only want us to feel really close to each other. I want us to be really in love. I think that's the only way you *can* feel peaceful."

"And then what would happen?"

"What do you mean?"

"What would happen if we were really in love?"

"I don't know. We would be in love, that's all. It would mean much more to us that way."

She took the stalk of wheat from between her teeth and tossed it, like a little spear, onto the coals, watching it flare for a moment and then curl and blacken convulsively, almost instantly carbonized by the heat.

"I have to be the way I am, Vincent," she said. "If it isn't enough for you, I don't know what to do. I said we could stop any time you wanted to."

"I don't want to stop," I said. "I want to be in love with you, Laura. I have to be in love with somebody."

"Does it have to be me?"

"I want it to be you. I couldn't be in love with any of those other girls. They don't think about anything but fraternity pins, and dances, and records, and things like that. I think you know more than they do, and I think you could give somebody more than they could. I guess it's silly to say these things out loud, though. I guess it isn't something you can ask for."

She stood up, brushing her skirt with her palms, and stared into the fire for a moment, her hands laid still against her thighs. "We'll just have to wait and see," she said.

What Laura meant by this I did not inquire, for I felt, as always, chastened by her sobriety and also—perhaps more significantly—alarmed by the prospect of surrendering what we had, however insufficient it might seem; for hers was the single relationship I had, outside of my grandparents', which was not merely social or conventional. And so our friendship continued in its muted, passionless way.

$\mathcal{J}$ CAN REMEMBER only one other instance of quarreling, or of open discontent between us; but it was far more distressing, far more crucial than this. It is, indeed, one of the bitterest memories of my life. It began with the terrible accident to my horse.

I have never forgotten the beauty of that day, for it was so in contrast to all that happened on it; perhaps it is for this reason that I still very often, on a day of brilliant sunlight, feel a sense of dread come over me, falling lightly and coldly, like a web woven of threads of ice. This was in the early spring of our last year together, a few months before I went away to war. It was a cool April day, very still, with a clear vivid blue sky, almost violet-colored, and pale, intense sunlight which made shadows of extraordinary sharpness, the color of steel. I took my horse out in the midafternoon and rode until evening through the rolling country north of Stonemont. The mare was eight years old at that time and tired easily if ridden hard; but she loved to ramble. I would drop the reins and let her wander at whatever pace she chose down country roads barred with shadow from the rows of tall cedars that lined them and along dirt lanes bordered with fences buried and sagging under clumps of matted honeysuckle.

On the way back I turned off the lane we had been following into open country so that the mare might drink from one of the shallow stony streams that run through the center of the gently sloped valleys between each pair of hills. I could see the water below us, glinting in the sunlight, between the thin poplars of the hillside. The mare stepped down daintily with nervous caution over the stony soil, lurching sometimes from the roughness of the inclined ground. It is excruciating to confess, but I think I was to blame for the dreadful thing that followed; I should have tightened the reins and guided her down the uneven slope, for she was always uncertain of footing on rough ground because of her blind eye. But I did not; I leaned back in the saddle, letting the reins fall loosely, and looked up, smiling, because the maple trees were budding. All above us they spread out a delicate pattern of scarlet buds, like a lady's hat veil dotted with tiny balls of plush, exquisitely fragile against the clear blue sky. I reached up to touch one as the mare stumbled: a blood-colored, sticky, tender embryo, unclenching slowly in the spring sunlight. A patch of stony rubble slid under her rear hoofs; she lurched forward, stepped on a loose rock that rolled with her weight, and fell heavily sideways. As I hurtled out of the saddle I saw with horror, in that moment of brilliant vision which so often occurs in an emergency, that directly beneath her falling body there was a jaggedly pointed stump of poplar, as thick as a man's arm and two feet tall, which would impale her. I struck the ground heavily, spinning violently across the stony soil, hearing the sickening blunt thud of the horse's belly as it plunged down upon the pointed stump, and then, as I leapt to my feet, a second, intolerable sound: the animal's long, ecstatic, quivering scream of pain. I shall never in my life hear such a sound again. I staggered about among the bare trees, cringing from the cry, my palms pressed hard against my ears to shut it out, running a few steps away from, and then back toward, the writhing, screaming mare in an anguish of shock and indecision. I wanted to run as quickly and as far as possible from that terrible sound, but I knew that I could not leave the horse to suffer. It would take me an hour, at least, to reach the town, and perhaps another half hour to return, by car or bicycle, with a rifle.

Let me recount this as quickly as possible: I found a heavy, jagged rock and bludgeoned the horse to death, crushing her skull until she lay shiveringly still. Then I rose and stood for a moment, shuddering, staring softly into the sunlight.

I began to walk away in stiff, lunging, automatic steps, then more and more quickly as my numbness passed, until finally I was running frantically as I entered the first streets of the town. I went immediately to Laura's house. It was almost dusk, and I remember that, because of the warmth of the day, she had brought several pots of geraniums up from the cellar, where they were kept "sleeping" through the winter; she was carrying one up the front steps as I came into her walk, and, hearing my steps, she turned, clutching the heavy earthenware pot against her apron, staring at me with a look of growing bewilderment.

"Vincent, what on earth has happened to you?" she whispered.

"I killed my horse, Laura."

"Oh, my goodness. You're covered with blood."

"I know. I had to kill my horse," I said. "She fell down and got terribly hurt, and I had to kill her, because she was screaming."

She set the pot down on the steps and came a little toward me down the walk. "I don't know what to do. I guess you'd better come in and get washed off. Do you feel all right?"

"I guess so. I feel kind of trembly, though."

"Do you want some brandy? We have some brandy that Daddy takes."

"I don't know. I never had any."

"Well, come on in the house."

"All right."

I followed her in through the front door and up the stairs toward the bathroom.

"Don't touch the banisters."

"No."

In the bathroom I closed the toilet and sat down on it with my head in my hands.

"You look awfully pale," Laura said.

"I know. My hands are all cold. I feel kind of sick."

"Well, just wait a minute, and I'll get you some brandy. I think it'll make you feel better."

"All right. Thank you."

I sat with my face in my hands, fighting to suppress the waves of nausea that swept over me, until Laura returned. She brought me in a moment a clean cotton shirt and a tumbler of brandy which I held in trembling hands and drank without pausing. It made me gasp.

"Do you feel any better?" Laura said.

"I think so, yes. It certainly is hot."

"I brought you one of Father's shirts. You'd better take that one off; it's all spattered with blood."

"All right. Thank you."

I unbuttoned and removed the blood-soaked shirt, which she dropped into the bathtub.

"I'll wash it out and you can get it the next time you come," she said.

"No, I don't want it. Just throw it away, Laura."

"All right. Let me wash you off a little. It's all in your hair and everything. You'd better lean over the basin."

She soaked a washcloth in hot water and, while I leaned over the white enamel bowl, bathed my arms, neck and shoulders gently, squeezing the cloth sometimes to let the water run in warm rivulets across my flesh. She bent a little over me while she did so, speaking with a softness that I had never heard in her voice before, her hands, when they touched me, expressing an intense and unfamiliar gentleness. I sat leaning across the basin, my arms resting on its edge, my eyes closed, drowsy with comfort, infinitely soothed by the cleanliness and coolness of the sparkling white enamel, the steam, the hot cloth upon my skin, the strong and tender touch of her hands and the nearness of her body. I had never felt such a physical attraction for her before. I was intensely aware of her loose fragrant hair and the warm redolence of her white flesh beneath her clean cotton dress. This idle, languorous sense of comfort grew slowly, then more swiftly, then with startling fierceness, into a passion such as I had never known. I was suddenly possessed with a flaming, trembling, almost demented desire for Laura that made my whole body ache, as if with fever, for contact with her. I raised my head from the basin and took her arm in my hand, pressing my face against the cool white flesh of her forearm. She stood very still.

"Do you feel any better?"

"Yes. It feels wonderful."

"Do you want any more brandy?"

"No, thank you."

"Vincent, what's the matter?"

"Nothing. I just want to hold you. You feel so wonderful, Laura."

I put my arms around her waist and drew her body against me. She yielded stilly for a moment, and then I felt her lean away from me, her body tensing in withdrawal.

"You're all wet, Vincent. It'll ruin my dress."

"Please, let me just hold you for a minute." I clenched her suddenly close in my arms and pressed my face, still stained with watery blood, against her waist. "Laura, I want to love you," I whispered hoarsely. "Please. Please let me love you."

She put her hands on my shoulders and twisted her body in my arms. "No. Don't, Vincent. Don't."

"Please. I want to love you. I have to, Laura. Let me, please."

"No. Let me go."

I dropped down onto my knees before her on the bathroom floor, my arms locked fiercely about her, burying my face against the cleft of her groin, breathing the buried musk of her body through the crushed cotton of her skirt.

"No. Don't, Vincent. Stop. I won't. It isn't decent. I won't ever do that until I'm married. It isn't decent."

She took my wrists in her hands, twisting and wrenching them until she had broken free, and backed away from me against the wall.

"Why did you have to do that?" she said. "It's just horrible. I never thought you'd do anything like that."

I knelt in front of her, naked from the waist up, my hair still dripping with watery gore, my face flushed with the intensity of shame into which my violent feeling had been suddenly transposed by her revulsion, watching her gather her skirt away from me in very formal, involuntary, clutching movements of her hands, like the oppressed heroines of silent movies. From the end of the hall her father began to call with feeble impatience in his old, trembling voice: "Laura . . . Laura . . . *Laura* . . ." She turned away from me quickly and went out of the bathroom. I snatched up the clean shirt she had brought me and left the house, thrusting my arms into the sleeves as I ran down the stairs and out the front door into the quiet evening.

I have as much need for dignity as anyone, and I should like to understand better why I was led in such a wanton manner to bring that ugly day to its even uglier conclusion by an act of savage mortification with a woman who was perhaps as old as my grandmother. Because that is what I did. Hardly pausing in my flight from Laura's house, I set out down the darkening streets toward the house of the Mrs. Hallworth to whom, a week before, I had delivered a box of groceries. I walked quickly, my jaws clenched with bitter resolution.

The sky had gone scarlet behind the black elms and rooftops of the street when I reached the front walk that led up to the dark veranda of her handsome clapboard house. Behind the glider and the white wicker rocking chairs of the front porch there was lamplight inside the windows of the living room. I went up the walk without pausing, mounted the wide steps to the veranda and tapped with the brass knocker on the paneled white door. The fanlight above the door cast a faint downward glow in which I spread my hands while I stood waiting with a fierce impatience. There was still blood between my fingers. I scrubbed the back of my hand across my thigh and knocked again.

In a moment the door opened and Mrs. Hallworth, clad in a blue silk negligee that was stained with scattered red spots, peered out at me. She stood unsteadily, her greying hair astray, peering out at me with a look of confusion that changed slowly to one of faintly amused congeniality.

"Well, my goodness," she said. "It's the *grocery* boy! If this isn't a pleasant surprise." She smiled at me, lifting her hand to brush back from her forehead the stray strands of her hair. "Now what could bring you here at this time of night? I don't suppose you've got any more *potatoes* for me?"

"No, ma'am," I said, my resolution faltering suddenly. "I was wondering—I was wondering if maybe I made a mistake on your order the other day. I was wondering if you still had your order slip."

"Well, I don't know," she said. "Why don't you come in, and I'll see if I can find it somewhere." She opened the door wider, clutching the knob to steady herself as she held it aside for me to enter. I went into the house and stood in the small foyer while she closed the door and stood for a moment with her laced hands dangling in front of her, regarding me with a look of curious, genial, concern.

"My goodness," she said. "You look like you're upset about something. You've got blood on your hands. Did you know that?"

I nodded abjectly. "I killed my horse," I said. "He broke his leg and I had to kill him with a rock."

"Oh, my Lord!" She clicked her tongue with dismay. "Oh, that must make you feel terrible! Why don't you come on back in the kitchen and let me wash them off? It'll make you feel a little better."

"No, that's okay," I said. I looked down at my hands and rubbed the bloodstain between my fingers with my thumb. "I'm sorry to trouble you like this. Maybe I ought to come back some other time."

"It's no trouble at all," she said. "You come on here in the living room and sit down for a minute while I look for that order slip." She laid her hand gently against my back and guided me

into the living room. On a side table beside one of the overstuffed dark armchairs there was a decanter of wine and a half-
empty glass.

"You sit right down there," she said. "And I'll just see if I can
find that order slip." She moved across the room to a mahogany
secretary that stood against the wall and tugged open a drawer.
"I keep most of my records in here. Let me just see now." She
took a sheaf of papers from the drawer and turned back to me.
"What is your name, young man?"

"Vincent," I said.

"Vincent. Oh, that's a lovely name. You have the name of a
saint, did you know that?"

"Yes, ma'am," I said.

"And I suppose you have a saintly nature, isn't that right?"

"No, ma'am," I said.

"You *don't*? Well, I'm surprised to hear that. When you were
here the other day you certainly *behaved* like a saint. I was
afraid I might have offended you, the way you took off from
here."

"No, ma'am, you didn't offend me."

"Well, I'm glad to hear that. Because I think what might do
you a lot of good right now is a little glass of wine. Being as
upset as you are about your horse."

"I don't drink wine, ma'am," I said.

"You mean you never *have* drunk wine, or you don't *intend* to
drink wine, *ever*?"

"I never have drunk any," I said.

"Well, why don't you have just a little sip of it, right now, to
sort of steady your nerves? I think you might like it."

She came across the room toward me, shoving the file of papers into the picket of her negligee and bending down to take
hold of the neck of the decanter.

"I'm afraid I only have this one glass, but why don't we share
it?" she said. "We can have a little loving cup." She poured the

57

glass full and handed it to me. "Now, you try that. I think it'll make you feel a lot better. Go ahead, take just a little sip. It's zinfandel, a very sweet wine. I think you'll like it."

I took the glass from her hand and after staring into the pale red wine for a moment I sipped it uncertainly, then tilted back my head and drank the wine to the bottom of the glass with a defiant, desperate haste. It was cool and sweet, and almost instantly I felt the glow of it in my belly.

"Now, isn't that better?" she said. She took the glass from me and poured it full again, gazing solemnly into the wine for a moment.

"I know how you must feel," she said. "Having to do such a terrible thing. When I was a little girl I had a little dog that I loved more than anything in the world, and he ran out into the street one day and got hit by a car. I just didn't think I'd ever get over it. I don't think I ever *have* got over it. I know how much children suffer. And I know much their suffering is misunderstood, or dismissed, by others. I know how sensitive they are." She sipped from her glass and gazed at me over the rim of it. "I have a very great love of children," she said. "They are the purest and finest members of the human race. I would do anything in the world to ease the suffering of young people. There is nothing in the world I wouldn't do to ease their pain." She put out her hand and laid it against my cheek. "And I think you have suffered greatly," she said. "I think you're a very sensitive young man, and it grieves me to know that you've been introduced to sorrow so soon in your life. I wish there was something I could do to ease your pain."

Moved by some monstrous, inexorable impulse that was composed, I suppose, partly of indignation toward Laura, partly of gratitude toward this wonderfully sympathetic woman, partly of raw desire, I lunged out of the chair and found myself kneeling at her feet clutching her to me, as half an hour before I had knelt before Laura and clutched her rigidly unwilling

58

body to my face. She set down the wine glass and stroked my hair.

"Now, don't grieve, Vincent," she said. "You're such a beautiful boy. It's just not right that such a beautiful young man should be so unhappy. Why don't you come upstairs with me and I'll see if I can ease your suffering a little. I think you deserve a little comfort. Now you get up and take my hand, and I'll try to prove to you that the world is not full of only terrible things. Now get up, sweetheart."

I stood up and took her hand, gazing down with a kind of strengthless submission at the flowered carpet. I took her hand and she led me gently through the arch of the living room and up the carpeted stairs to the open door of her bedroom, where she turned to put her arms around me and kiss me on the mouth.

I remember that as I left her house, carrying with me indelibly its odors of wine, furniture polish, perfumed sheets, and Mrs. Hallworth's moist and powdered flesh, I was, for the first time since my mother's death, crying softly and soundlessly. I don't think I would have been aware of my tears but for the sudden coolness of the evening air against my wet cheeks.

But however bewildered, however confusedly vindictive I may have felt toward Laura at that moment, it was not for that reason that the bitterness of which I've spoken earlier grew between us. After a period of reasonable reflection I could understand the revulsion she must have felt at the suddenness, shamelessness, and violence of my behavior, and I felt a growingly urgent obligation to apologize for it. But the thing for which I've never been able to forgive her, the thing whose peculiar and subtle cruelty I've brooded on for years, is what she said to me a few days later when I went again to her house to apologize.

I have said a few days—I think it must have been nearer to a few weeks, for I remember that as the weather was much warmer we sat in the steel-and-canvased glider in her back yard and that the wistaria tree above us had begun to bloom, opening its great purple blossoms softly and standing in that dark and mournful beauty which only these trees have. In all this time I had seen Laura only occasionally and distantly at school; she had not telephoned, or made any effort to see me, and I had begun to miss her greatly. In addition, I was beset with a growing feeling of remorse: I became convinced that I had shocked and offended her acutely and that I must make some effort to repair her wounded sensibilities. But however distressed Laura may have been at my behavior, she gave no indication of it; she greeted me with her usual composure at the front door and suggested that we sit out in the glider because it was such a nice evening. She had, in spite of my protest, washed out and ironed my soiled shirt, and she said that it was all ready, if I had changed my mind about accepting it.

"It would be a terrible waste to throw away a perfectly good shirt like that," she said.

"All right. Thank you very much, Laura."

"I was going to give it to the Salvation Army if you didn't come back to get it."

I stared at the ground for a moment and then said, "I guess you didn't care whether I came back or not, after the way I acted."

"I thought you might," she said. "So I saved it for a while."

There was a breath of evening breeze that made the big tree stir softly, and I looked up and watched the white curtains blowing out into the yard from the open windows of the upstairs bedrooms—a clean, blithe, gentle billowing which I have always loved for the sense of purification which it suggests: the cleansing out of old, fraught, winter-stale houses in a sweet, cool, vernal bath of air.

"How is your father, Laura?" I asked.

"Oh, he's getting weaker all the time. I guess we just have to expect the worst."

"Oh, I'm sorry to hear that."

"He had another attack this morning. Mother's upstairs with him right now."

"That certainly is too bad."

"It's such an awful strain on her; that's the worst part."

"Yes."

There was a long pause, during which I gathered the determination to make my apology.

"The main reason I came back, Laura," I said, "was that I wanted to tell you I was very sorry for the way I acted the last time I was here. I'm very sorry about it, and I hope I didn't hurt your feelings, or anything."

"Thank you, Vincent. It's nice of you to say that."

"I don't know why I did it, but I hope you don't feel too— well, too disgusted with me."

"No, I don't, Vincent. I know you were very upset about your horse, and people do all kinds of things when they get very upset like that."

"Yes." I felt a vague sense of chagrin at the ease with which she apparently forgave me, and wondered, with a swiftly growing apprehension, whether I had really expected or desired it. The sense of guilt which my adventure had created in me lay like a monstrous weight on my heart, and I bore it with the terrible sensitivity of which only a boy of that age is capable. I felt unclean and vicious, and I think for this reason I experienced my sudden doubt as to whether I could ever decently resume my relationship with Laura: I was not worthy of her; I could no longer honorably enjoy her affection and companionship with so foul a secret on my conscience. I almost wished that she would refuse to accept my apology, or ever to see me again, and thus relieve me of the imposture—the feigned respectability— that I would otherwise have to make.

"My father says that one of a Christian's chief duties is to forgive people, no matter what they do to him, and no matter whether he understands it or not," Laura said. "And I believe that. So I don't think we have to talk about it any more, Vincent. I think we ought to just pretend it never happened."

I stared wretchedly at the shadowed lawn, feeling a growing constriction of my breath and blood at the suddenly imminent necessity of my confession. I saw that there was no way to avoid making it.

"I don't think we can, Laura," I said.

"What do you mean?"

"Well, sometimes people do things that nobody would ever think they were capable of. I don't think people ever really understand each other. I don't even think they understand themselves a lot of times."

"You don't have to understand people in order to forgive them," Laura said. "That's what I just said. It shouldn't make any difference."

"I know, but you don't know the worst of it. You don't know what else I did; and you wouldn't want to have anything to do with me any more if you did."

"What do you mean? What else did you do, Vincent?"

She turned to face me and I stared into her eyes with a look of desperate resolution.

"I hate to tell you this, Laura, but I have to, because I just don't think it would be right for you not to know about it. I'm not asking you to forgive me, or anything, but I have to tell you. You don't have to listen if you won't want to; you can just leave now, and then we won't have to see each other again."

"No. I want to know." She made a slight negative motion of her head and watched me calmly and alertly.

"Well, when I left here the other evening, I didn't go right home. I went to see . . . someone else. And—well, you know what I wanted you to do—I did it with her, Laura." I stared at the ground, speaking slowly and miserably. Laura sat silently for a moment and then said with a soft bitterness which I had never heard in her voice before, "I thought you didn't like any of those other girls. I thought you weren't interested in any of the things they liked. Well, it looks as if you're interested in *some* of the things they like."

"No, it wasn't any of those other girls at school," I said. "It was—well, somebody you don't know at all, Laura."

She pressed her lips together tightly with emotion. "And I guess that's where you've been all this time. All this time I've been waiting for you to come back. I guess that's why you don't come to see me any more. I guess you think you're in love with her or something, don't you?"

"Oh, no, Laura. It wasn't anything like that. I thought you wouldn't want to see *me*; that's why I didn't come back."

She turned again to face me and asked with steady, quiet intensity, "Do you love her, Vincent?"

"No. Oh, my gosh. It wasn't a *girl* at all, Laura. It was a woman. A woman I used to deliver groceries to."

"A *woman?*"

"Yes. I went back to her house after I left here, and I did it with her. I mean I didn't force her to, or anything. I could tell she wanted me to. And she's pretty old. Maybe as old as my grandmother. That's what I had to tell you. That's why I said I couldn't see you any more."

I sat silently, clenching my laced fingers together, waiting for her to revile me. But Laura expressed neither the outrage nor disgust which I expected; she sat quietly, and after a pause in which she seemed to have regained her composure completely she lifted her hand to brush her hair back thoughtfully and said, "Well, that's different, then. As long as you don't love her, I don't really think it matters. I don't see why we can't just go on the way we were."

This seemed to me so insensitive, so harrowingly equivocal a thing to say that I could not reply (I have never been able to reply to it), but sat in a kind of afflicted silence. This was broken in a moment by the voice of Laura's mother. She leaned out of the upstairs window, her face contorted with grief, and called down shrilly, "Laura—Laura, come up right away, please! I just can't make him answer me. I'm afraid—I'm afraid he's gone."

Laura was out of the glider in an instant, murmuring a swift apology to me as she ran across the lawn toward the steps. I did not leave immediately; when she had gone I sat for some time in the glider and looked up at the open window of the old man's room, watching the white curtains blow out into the yard gently, jubilantly, from the soiled sills.




$\mathcal{A}$FTER THIS my feelings toward Laura were never the same. Whatever intimacy or ardor may have existed between us was almost entirely extinguished, and I no longer held any hope for its development into the profound and meaningful attachment which I had once thought possible. I still saw her occasionally; I would walk home from school with her sometimes, and I think we went once or twice to a motion picture together, sitting on her front porch afterward and talking for a while in a constrained and artificial way. But the only moment of anything like true feeling that I experienced with her again was on the morning, a few months later, when I left Stonemont to join the army. Laura came to the station to see me off and brought me a box lunch which she had packed for me to eat on the train. My grandparents were there also—both with wet eyes, looking suddenly terribly small and old—so that it was possible for us to speak only in the most inane and formal manner. She gave the box to me, still holding it by the string after she had placed it in my hands, as if in a final, fugitive contact with me, and said with a curious shy smile, "There's half a fried chicken and a piece of pumpkin pie that I just made this morning. You like pumpkin pie, don't you, Vincent?"

"Yes. Thank you very much, Laura."

We stood uncomfortably, shifting our feet on the stone of the station platform; and then she looked up into my face and said quite gently, "I had to come down, because I wanted to say that I'm so proud of you, Vincent, for enlisting; and I know you'll do something wonderful, and then everybody in Stonemont will know what you're really like."

I shook my head, smiling painfully.

"And please take care of yourself, because we want you to come back to us."

"Yes, I will, Laura."

I was strangely affected by the incident. Whether it was due to the compassion which, mistakenly or not, I sensed in Laura's gesture, or to the natural pathos of the situation, I do not know; but at any rate I carried away with me a fond final memory of her which seemed to supersede all the other, less fortunate, ones, and on the strength of it I exchanged letters with her throughout the war—something which, considering how perfunctory our relationship had become since that day of her father's death, I should surely not otherwise have done. Was this what Laura intended? It is difficult to know, and perhaps not charitable to speculate; but I do know that her letters—all but the final one— were a source of much pleasure and comfort to me during the long two years that I was overseas.

I have never been sure whether my enlistment was not partially due, at least, to the deterioration of my affair with her; but my more conscious motives were simple expediency, a nebulous but rather moving concept of soldiery which I had as a boy and a revelatory, deeply disturbing speech of my grandfather's which he delivered as we walked out under the elms to the end of Frederick Avenue one evening after having a soda together at the corner drugstore. That was in the summer of 1942—the summer during which I worked as delivery boy on the grocery truck—and Stonemont, like the rest of the world, was infected with the excitement, the dark vitality, of war. I had graduated from high school in the spring of that year and had just turned eighteen. The world which lay before me, the world which had seemed so remote, so pleasantly vague and fabulous until the moment when I walked down from the bunting-draped commencement platform in my cap and gown, clutching the fragile wand of my maturity —the ribbonbound parchment scroll of my diploma—had become suddenly a shadowed and rather ominous region whose unknown and unavoidable terrain filled me with a vague sense of alarm. We passed the statue of the Confederate soldier, blue with evening and seeming more poignant, more full of brave significance than ever, so that I looked at it with even more than ordinary thoughtfulness.

There was for me at that time something peculiarly inspiring in the image of a soldier. I do not mean by this that I felt any of the usual romantic or chauvinistic sentiments about warfare, for I think that even as a boy I was aware, with the casual irony of youth, that God is on the side of all armies in all battles and that the principles for which men die in one season will be archaic by the next; it was not the nation, the principles or the institutions they defended which made soldiers seem glorious in my eyes (for any of these, from another point of view, might be considered absurd or infamous), but their simple act of sacrifice itself, the blind submission of their lives and fortunes to something greater than themselves, their beautiful obedience. Perhaps it was for me an image of life, in which, in very much the same way—fighting for principles which are never really understood, against odds they do not know and enemies whom they might love, serving captains they may despise and distrust, in a cause which may be hopeless —men nevertheless go on, struggling, suffering, killing, obeying their humanity in a blind and valiant act of sacrifice. I think it was this that moved me; for people who are subtly estranged from their environment, their institutions and companions, both by temperament and fortune, as I was in my youth, are apt to be more keenly and more wistfully sensitive to such a concept than are others. Feeling their separateness, and the unaccountable guilt of loneliness, they feel the need, perhaps, to redeem it by an act of service or sacrifice, in the company of comrades. It is a way for them to rejoin humanity.

Perhaps it was this. Or perhaps it was the fact that the warrior whom our town commemorated and for whom I felt such reverence was a Rebel, disarmed, defeated, and eternally, magnificently defiant. I have never known, really. That bronze statue was one of the chief poems of my youth and, like all poems, full of mystery.

All of these emotions and speculations were made peculiarly relevant by my grandfather's conversation on that evening. He strolled with his arms clasped behind him in the small of his back in a habitual European manner, his cane held between them, straight up and down his back like a poker, removing it occasionally to touch the brim of his Panama hat with its gold head in salute to an acquaintance or to point out to me some object about which he held an unusual or amusing scrap of information.

"Look at that bird, Sonny, on the lawn there. It has golden eyes, do you see? That's a Brewer's Blackbird. It's the only blackbird that has golden eyes."

"Yes, sir. That certainly is interesting."

My grandfather was an inveterate reader of encyclopedias; he had very little formal education and, like many such men, a passion for miscellanea, which he innocently expected others to construe as erudition. One of his most touching pretensions was to illustrate, every time we went walking together, the universality of his interests and learning by delivering a constant stream of lore on every possible topic of art or science which might be represented on the way.

"Do you see those columns, on the courthouse? They're Doric. Doric columns always have acacia leaves at the top; that's called the lintel." (His acquaintance with many subjects was as imperfect as it was unfailingly enthusiastic.)

"Where does it get the name, Grandpa?" I asked, indulging his authority.

"Doric. Why, that's taken from the people who first designed them: the Dorians. A Middle Eastern people." He paused for a moment with a look of some disconcertion, having apparently exhausted his information on the subject, and then went on with a marvelous imposture of benignity, "I'd like to go into it further with you, Sonny, but I really prefer that you look it up for yourself. A thing that's looked up like that, out of genuine interest, is never forgotten. Never."

"Yes, sir."

Although he had managed to meet the occasion with this splendid piece of improvisation, I felt that I had caused him some embarrassment, and resolved to limit my responses in the future to a murmur of pleasurable enlightenment. We walked on through the quiet dusk, watching the golden twilight flooding the widow's-walks and wind vanes of the tall old wooden houses and glittering on the attic windows. Anyone who loves small towns as I do (I would have a world of small towns if I could) will understand the strange, sweet melancholy that falls upon them in the evening when the elms are still, the long shadows dying on the lawns, the porches vacant and the stir of supper not yet started in the kitchen windows. Oppressed by the gentle sadness of this atmosphere and my sudden somber awareness of the world's vast incumbency, I fell into silence as we walked. After a while my grandfather said, "Have you something on your mind, Sonny?"

"Oh. No, sir. I was just thinking about that soldier, mostly, I guess."

"Yes," he said. "It's in the air."

We had come abreast of Poplar Lodge, and my grandfather

nodded at the great dark slope of mansard roof behind the spruce and poplars of the drive.

"Fine old place," he said. "Most beautiful old house in town. There's a bit of irony in that, Sonny, if you want to look for it."

"Yes, sir, I guess there is."

I looked in at the quiet darkening grounds as we walked past and felt blow across my heart a breath of the mysterious delight which had possessed me, only a week or two before, when I had looked across the barberry hedge into the eyes of the graceful, haunting creature who stood laughing at me from the shadow of the willows.

"I wonder what they're doing in there right now?" I said musingly.

"Dreaming their poor, mad dreams," my grandfather said. "Poor souls. Lost souls."

We walked on to the end of the avenue and at the edge of the town stood looking out across the blue, rolling hills of the Upper County. There were lights on in the distant barns for milking, and shadowy herds of Holsteins standing mournfully at pasture gates.

"It's a beautiful country," my grandfather said. "A chosen land. But it's changing, Sonny. All those cigar-box suburbs creeping out from Washington. They're a blight on the face of the earth." He tapped a fallen log beside the road with his cane and said, "Let's sit down here, Lad, till I get the gimp out of my leg."

"Yes, sir."

He sat with his hands resting on the head of his cane and his chin on the backs of them, staring at the fading landscape while he spoke mildly:

"When I first came to this town, forty years ago, people resented me. They used to write things on my shop window sometimes with soap—ugly things. They were suspicious and hostile. They had a right to be. Now I feel the same way about newcomers— can't stand them. We have a right to feel that way—to resent the strangers, the unknown, unproven people. It's part of human

69

nature; no use denying it." He turned to regard me solemnly. "Nothing has any value unless it's hard earned. Friendship, wealth, fame. Nothing."

"No, sir."

He nodded, looking into my eyes intently, and laid his hand on my knee.

"Your Grandma and I love you very much," he said. "You know that, don't you, Sonny?"

"Yes, sir."

"Well, I want to say that at the outset, so you won't be offended by what I have to say. We've watched you grow up, Vincent my boy, from the day you were born. You've been like a son to us, and we love you. We've seen you grow into a fine, strong, honest lad. We know all your good points, and we thank God for them; but we'd not be doing our duty if we didn't point out your faults now and again, too—as we see them. We've all got faults, you know."

"Yes, sir," I murmured.

"Now, I'll tell you how I've always thought about you, Vincent: as a sort of knight without a cause. You've got great capabilities, Sonny; you've got intelligence and imagination, and those are the things that make men a success in all the higher pursuits of life. But they've got to be harnessed to something. Intelligence and imagination, unless they're harnessed to a fine and useful cause, can come to very sad ends, believe me. I've seen it happen, my boy." I knew, from the thoughtful sadness with which he said the words, that he was thinking of my father, and I felt the quick faint throe of mingled regret and shame which always accompanied his memory.

"Life is a complicated business, at the best of times," he went on; and, as if to illustrate the fact, he lifted one hand and regarded the back of it earnestly while he flexed his fingers, studying all the intricate movements of bone and muscle and scowling softly, as if chagrined at its complexity. "And you've been born into especially difficult ones, Sonny. These are hard days for a man to settle his mind and plan a life for himself; but it's something every man must do. Now, we've never had a really determined talk about your future, and I think it's time we did. You're out of high school now, and you must be thinking about it seriously."

"Yes, sir, I know."

"Well, these are very competitive days, Sonny; you realize that, I'm sure. It used to be possible, forty years ago, for a man to make his own way with no education but what he'd given himself, as I did. But not any more. Today there are half a dozen young fellows with college degrees waiting for every opening. A man must be educated or he hasn't a chance. And he must have the other things he gets from college, too: the associations he makes, the ability to deal with people easily and confidently, like an equal. The whole background."

"Yes, sir, those are very important things. I realize that."

"Well now, I'm not a rich man, as you know, Vincent; but those are advantages I want you to have, Lad. It's a thing I've always hoped to be able to do—send you to college and give you a decent start in life. I haven't spoken of it before because I've never been sure, until now, that I'd be able to afford it, and I didn't want to disappoint you. But I think now—with careful managing, and a lot of hard effort on your part—I think I can manage it." He nodded, smiling with pride, and grasped my knee, giving it a vigorous, cordial shake. I was truly awed with gratitude, and felt a warm flood of affection for him.

"That certainly is nice of you, Grandpa," I said. "I don't know how to thank you, sir."

"It's no more than I want to do, Lad. I wouldn't want it said that any flesh of mine had gone down in the struggle without making his mark. It means a lot to me, Lad—your success."

"Yes, sir."

He watched my eyes intently for a moment and then, as if reassured of the genuineness of my enthusiasm, nodded slightly and turned his head, lifting his hand and pinching together the center of his lower lip in a reflective way.

"Now, there's only one thing that troubles me, Lad; and I feel I must speak of it. It's this . . . aimlessness of yours, Sonny; this lack of purpose that I've spoken of. I wonder if you're really ready to take advantage of a college education yet. I wonder if you shouldn't be a bit more mature first—a bit more sober in your mind. I'd hate to think of you frittering away all those years and coming out of it no better off than you went in, or even flunking out, perhaps, and making a disgrace of yourself."

"I don't know, sir; maybe so."

"It's a thing to consider, Vincent. Now, it just occurred to me—I know you won't be offended at my mentioning it—that a period of service of some kind—like the army, say—hard, useful, disciplined service, might give you a greater sense of reality, of purpose about life. I think you might be better prepared to buckle down and get the most out of your education afterwards." He paused for a moment and watched me silently, as if to determine the success of this suggestion. "You said just now you'd been thinking about the soldier back there: the monument. Well, I don't know what you had in mind, Lad; but it occurred to me you might be considering something of the kind yourself."

"Well, I don't know, sir." As he did not answer, I added in a moment, "I'll probably be drafted pretty soon, anyway."

"Ah, that's it exactly," he said with fresh enthusiasm. "If you were to start college now you'd have your work interrupted, at any rate, and it would be all that much harder to take it up again afterwards. There'd be such a lot you would have forgotten. Now, if you've got it to do anyway, mightn't it be better to enlist and get it over with? There's so much more honor in it that way, Lad." His voice dropped slightly and took on a hushed and intense quality. "Think of the source of pride it would be to you, Sonny —to all of us. I don't mind telling you, Lad, it would mean a great deal to me to have my own grandson—my own flesh and blood—

one of the first to enlist in the service of his country. That's something a man could talk about with pride. Something to make him walk with his head up, I can tell you."

"Yes, sir."

He laid his hand on my knee and went on in the same urgent way. "Life isn't all pleasure and dreams, you know, Lad. And it isn't all taking, either—not by a long shot. We have to pay our way, you know. We have obligations—to our country, our family—every step of the way. There are duties we have to face and debts we have to pay." I nodded, feeling increasingly uncomfortable and, for some reason, ashamed. He removed his hand and, as if somewhat chastened by his own intensity, went on more mildly. "Then, too, there's the business of finding yourself, as I say. There's nothing that gives a man such a feeling of belonging to things—to his time, his country, his fellow men—as serving them, bravely and unselfishly."

"Yes, sir, I think that's very true."

"Well, then, we'll say no more about it, for the time. It's a thing you'll want to think over, at any rate, Lad. P'raps in a day or two we can have a chat about it."

But I did not need so long. After dinner that evening (at which I had been very silent), I followed him into the parlor and stood for a moment beside his armchair. He held a folded newspaper in one hand and was leaning forward over a military map of Europe which was spread out on the hassock in front of him. From the day's dispatches he was marking very meticulously with a red pencil the current positions of the opposed forces. When he raised his head inquiringly I said. "I'm going to join the army, Grandpa." He looked into my eyes with a growingly humble gaze and then lowered his head suddenly and turned his face away from me. "Will you tell Grandma for me? I just don't like to." He nodded. "Good night," I said and turned toward the stairs.

When I had reached them he called brokenly, "Just a minute, Sonny." I stood with my hand on the newel post, watching him rise and come toward me, all the muscles of his face slackened in a quivering and ruinous look of great emotion and his eyes streaming behind his steel-rimmed glasses. "I just want to tell you that this is the proudest moment of my life, Lad," he said, and put his large hands on my shoulders, drawing me against his chest; but I could not return his embrace. I stood stiffly, staring beyond him at the framed coat-of-arms above the sofa while he clutched my shoulders.

It was a beautiful summer night, and I sat for a short while by the open window of my bedroom, staring out at the moonlit roofs of the town, before I went to bed. A slanted square of yellow light lay on the mown grass of the back yard, and I could see my grandmother's plump shadow washing dishes in the kitchen window. It was joined in a moment by the shadow of my grandfather, and the two dark figures for a moment faced each other in an oddly formal way, framed in the square of light like an old-fashioned paper silhouette, and then were suddenly merged as my grandmother moved into his arms, her own form losing all of its identity in his. There was something strangely passionate and sordid about this mime of shadows—in the way my grandfather's image extended its dark arms in a swift voracious gesture of affection, enfolding and seeming to consume that of my grandmother, becoming transformed, as it did so, into one great bloated shape, as if gorged on the victim of its tenderness. I left the window and lay down on the bed without removing my clothes, staring up at the ceiling for a long while and breaking at last into violent stifled sobs as I felt sweep over me in a vast, empty, almost annihilating tide the greatest loneliness I have ever known.

So it was that I came to stand that morning, a few days later, on the platform of our railway station, where my grandparents and Laura, with her box lunch, waited to see me off. I shook hands with my grandfather and he stood smiling and nodding at me through his tears, his lips compressed in an effort to control his feeling. I saw with a clarity that I had never known before the aged roundness of his shoulders and the sagging gray flesh of his jowls; he seemed suddenly piteous to me, and I felt a strange and generous elation, as if all that he had said to me on the evening of our walk were transcended by the fineness of the act that had proceeded from it. I felt for a moment truly glad to be going away to war, convinced of my own valor and full of a glowing sense of chivalry which shed upon the world and all of its events a warm, apocalyptic light of beauty and benevolence. My grandmother embraced me tremulously—a warm little woman who smelled of wax and soap and the great cool kitchen of the house where I was raised—murmuring, "God bless you, Sonny," while I patted her plump rounded back. I held Laura's hand for a moment, looking smilingly into her eyes, and went away to war.

$\mathcal{T}$HIS IS the last picture of my childhood. Of the war, which follows, I shall say little, for all this which occurs before my return to Stonemont is, in a certain sense, a prelude; and feeling that both my time and determination for the telling of this story are limited, I must hurry on to what is perhaps more properly its beginning.

I do not know exactly how long that sudden luminous sense of dedication which I had felt on leaving Stonemont endured, but as a conscious sensation it was very soon diminished by a succession of training camps in the desert heat of Utah and California and the bitter cold of a Dakota winter, and then dispelled entirely by the realities of combat duty in the South Pacific. I was assigned to the Air Corps, trained as a radio operator and attached to a bomber squadron of the 13th Air Force, which was stationed at that time on the island of Espiritu Santo in the New Hebrides.

Yet there must have been a period, early in the war, when I was still responsive to that glowing sense of chivalry with which I had departed, for I remember experiencing, when the name of my first station was disclosed, not the irony which I should surely have felt at a later period of the war but a kind of mystic delight at its significance. It seemed to me that there was something unmistakably providential and symbolic in my having been sent forth to defend the Holy Spirit. This was an illusion which was soon dispelled, as I have said, by years of tedium, dirt, brutality, fatigue and fear.

Over the next two years we moved, as the Japanese retreated, to Guadalcanal, Hollandia, Biak, Leyte and Tacloban, through steaming muddy jungle stations, blasted coral atolls and the shattered, stinking, misery-laden cities of the Philippines. There were alternate periods of degrading, slothful idleness and, when the heavy offensives were in progress, of exhausting, concentrated duty, during which we flew missions almost around the clock, snatching a few hours of sleep in the shelter of a wing while our bomb bays were reloaded. There were also occasional furloughs in Australia, which I remember with almost equal abhorrence for the savage recklessness with which they were spent—the primitive drunken violence, the bitter lovemaking with prostitutes or avid, pathetic children barely into their teens and full of the hysteria of war, who used to roam the streets of Sydney in search of "Yanks"—and for the remorse and self-disgust which followed them.

This whole period of my life has about it the quality of a dream, lurid and grotesque, whose bizarre intensity has nevertheless a kind of demented splendor, like a heap of shattered stained glass from a ruined cathedral window which I saw once in the rubble of a Manila street: broken images in livid, leprous colors, the fragments, once holy, profaned by mutilation, insanely and obscenely juxtaposed. It is a dream which recurs yet; as lately as two nights ago, when I fell asleep with the window open beside my bed and the curtains blowing across my face and shoulders with a fragrant softness which, in the narcotic moment between consciousness and sleep, I imagined to be the touch of Lilith's hair, it returned to abrade my mind with images like these: a hand, severed neatly at the wrist with the horrifying fastidiousness with which high explosive sometimes separates the human body, lying pale and bloodless on a doily of moist fern as if placed very carefully on display, like one of those morbidly tempting exhibits —a lifeless flounder on a bed of parsley—that decorate the windows of sea-food restaurants. Or the eyes of the American civilians who had been imprisoned for three years in the Walled City before we arrived to liberate them—even more pitiable than their wasted bodies and shrunken, skeletal faces—so shy, so tragically, irremediably shy, their ruined spirits peering through with the heartbreaking humility of those who have been mortally violated. Or the dreadful antic quality of the scene that ensued one evening when a Japanese soldier, either abandoned as his unit had retreated from the island or left behind on the suicidal sniping duty for which they sometimes volunteered, had crept down from the hillside jungle where, for the three months since our occupation, he had managed to survive, and, after watching the feature almost entirely through, flung four hand grenades in rapid succession into the amphitheater of log benches where a hundred airmen of our group sat watching a motion picture projected on an outdoor screen: four huge scarlet roses opening suddenly in the velvet darkness, each one accompanied by a paean of anguished wonder, while above the carnival of screaming, stumbling, maimed young men a gigantic Rita Hayworth, oblivious in the throes of her libido, writhed and whimpered in the arms of her seducer in a ghastly parody of their agony.

Yet the war had a single compensation for me, in that I made the first close and genuine friend of my life. He was a hut-mate of mine, another radio operator, who had also trained at Sioux Falls and been assigned, a few months before me, to the same squadron. His name was Eric Sladek. He was a huge Texan, very nearly seven feet tall, of Czechoslovakian descent, with bright red hair and a broad, gentle, jolly face. When he smiled, two gold teeth were revealed in the very center of his mouth. He had a charming, robust and very nimble personality, being able to assume, for social purposes, the callous self-sufficiency which was the conventional military attitude without having it impair or displace in the slightest degree the perceptive and generous serenity of his nature.

I do not know on what our friendship was based, for we were really very different; but we fell easily into that happy bantering masculine intimacy which I had so often envied in the relations of my schoolmates, and I learned for the first time in my life the delightful and surprising manner in which the spirit grows in the sunlight of friendship. My nature seemed to enlarge and include his own; I had his strength, his wit, his poise to defend me; I became less tense and painfully sensitive; I even found an unsuspected element of gaiety in myself; indeed, I think it was largely by virtue of Eric's friendship that I was able to endure the war.

Although he came from a very thinly populated and provincial part of the Panhandle and spoke with a deep, indestructible (and, I thought, fascinating) vernacular, he was in fact one of the few educated men in our squadron. He had gone for three years to Texas A. & M., where he was taking a degree in Agriculture and minoring in English literature, but had left, before his graduation, to join the army. It was Eric who taught me the joy of reading. My exposure to literature in high school had been so desultory and academic that I had never afterward been stimulated to pursue it of my own accord; but I learned from him that it was something very different from the store of abstract rhetorical luxury which I was accustomed to consider it. The first time he made me aware of this was on a hilltop at Wau, New Guinea, where we had landed with both our planes damaged on a small emergency strip after a daylight raid in support of infantry action on the slopes below. While we waited for the ground crews to repair our planes we sat on a gasoline drum and watched the fighting in the hillside jungles beneath us. Half a mile to the south troops of an Australian Commando division were attempting to take a Japanese-held plateau, to which the only passable approach was a narrow trail, cut out of the banyan jungles of the hillside. On this trail the Japanese had zeroed in 38-millimeter guns, withholding their fire until our troops were halfway up—after which they proceeded systematically to decimate them. Eric watched this carnage in silence for about ten minutes; then, staring down at the black-and-scarlet shell bursts among the shattered trees, he said softly, more to himself than to me, a few lines from a poem by Wilfred Owen:

> "What passing-bells for these that die as cattle?
> Only the monstrous anger of the guns.
> Only the stuttering rifles' rapid rattle
> Can patter out their hasty orisons.
> No mockeries for them from prayers or bells,
> Nor any voice of mourning save the choirs—
> The shrill, demented choirs of wailing shells;
> And bugles calling for them from sad shires."

"What does 'orisons' mean?" I asked him.

"Prayers, kid."

"That's a pretty good poem, isn't it?" I said after a moment of revelatory consideration.

"Boy, it's better than pretty good," Eric said.

Fortunately, there was ample sustenance for the passion for literature that he created in me. During the war the government printed and distributed through the U.S.O., the Red Cross and other service agencies an extensive library of popular novels, modern and classical, which I read, I think, almost in its entirety. They were printed on "pulp," bound in paper covers, and were small enough to fit into a pocket, so that I was literally never without one. How well I remember those plump narrow booklets, bulging snugly and promisingly against the breast pocket of my fatigues or flying suit, through whose pages I came to know Ethan Frome, Lt. Henry and his doomed Catharine, Rima the Bird Girl, and poor, reckless Madame Bovary. Most of the books Eric had read before, but those which he had not we had the pleasure of discovering and discussing together, and he taught me many things about them of which I should never have been aware without his guidance. (I remember, for example, when I was reading *A Passage to India*, his pointing out to me the beauty of Forster's description of the Marabar Caves, a passage which was one of his great favorites and whose many pages he could recite entirely by heart. I had read it with only cursory attention, but Eric's interpretation revealed it to me—I still believe it to be so—as one of the most beautiful prose-poems of modern literature.)

It was my growing interest in literature that led me, while on leave with Eric once in Sydney, to formulate the plan which represented the first truly constructive and enthusiastic effort I had ever made to solve the problem of my destiny. This was, in partnership with him, to open and operate a book shop in Stonemont after the war. The government was at this time offering loans to ex-servicemen with which to start small businesses, and it was our intention to pool the resources, after our discharge, to which we might be entitled by this provision. We chose Stonemont for our location because of its proximity to Washington and the number of highly literate people—college students, high-level government employees and retired people of means and culture—who might be expected to make up our patronage—Eric's home town of Blackwater being excluded by its provinciality from any of these assets.

That it was an essentially realistic plan is confirmed, I think, by the fact that it not only survived repeated discussion and examination but grew in exuberance upon it. It seemed to me that nothing could have come closer to the requirements of my temperament or so perfectly have satisfied the searching of my imagination: handling, examining, displaying (and inveterately perusing!) the things I most loved and respected in the world, with the one close companion of my life, in the quiet town where I was born. Knowing the limitations of my own practicality, I do not think I would ever have considered entering into such an enterprise by myself, but I felt that with Eric's assistance I would be able, by my enthusiasm and my love and growing knowledge of books, to make a real contribution to its success. I was quite transformed by the prospect. I went so far as to announce my intentions to Laura in a long and garrulous letter and even to begin speculating as to the most appropriate site for our venture—perhaps the empty candy store next to Davidson's market, or even the abandoned music shop at the end of Main Street! This state of felicitous anticipation was as short lived as it was remarkable, for less than two months after the conception of our plan Eric disappeared forever into the Philippine Sea.

The last time I spoke to him it was in code, with a telegraph key, from the radio compartment of a grounded B-24, during the fighting for Manila in the winter of 1945. We had been forced down onto an emergency strip by bad weather after a low-altitude napalm attack on Japanese gun positions in the Zambales foothills. Eric's plane had left the engagement half an hour before the rest of our squadron with one of its port engines shot out, heading for our home base on Leyte. We had been threatened all morning with a rain front from the south, and by the time our own bomb bays were empty and the mission completed, the weather had deteriorated so badly that we were forced to land at Murphy Field, a small, hastily patched runway a few miles from Manila. When we had landed I sat in the parked plane and tuned my liaison radio until I had managed to pick up the sound of Eric's transmitter.

It was very difficult to hear, because the headphones were full of a crashing roar of static from the storm and there was heavy traffic on the frequency; but very faintly, distorted by the static and feeble with distance, I heard the sound of his key. An operator's "fist"—the style and rhythm of his code—is very nearly as individual as his voice, so that, although his call letters were indistinct, I could recognize his signal instantly. It was hurried and erratic, as if the plane were lurching violently in bad weather, causing his hand to stumble on the key. He was transmitting V's with very long final dashes, alternating with his call letters—a procedure used only to enable a ground station to take radio bearings—and from this I knew that he was lost. When he had finished sending I heard the ground operator at Samar acknowledge his transmission and ask him to stand by. In the interval I began to call Eric myself, sending our call letters repeatedly until, many minutes later, I heard him answer, his signal now barely audible above the roar: "Lost, Vince."

"Over land?" I asked him. (We spoke in Q-signals, three-letter code groups, each standing for a phrase or sentence, so that it was possible to express a great deal of information very briefly and swiftly.)

"Over water. Two engines inoperative. Fuel low."

"Radio compass operative?"

"Negative."

"Celestial navigation?"

"No visibility."

"How much fuel?"

"Twenty minutes."

There was a long interval, during which his signal blew away entirely in the noise and distance, and then, even more faintly, I heard the end of a message he was sending in uncoded English: ". . . give Moose my guitar. You keep the Oxford book. Good luck, kid."

After a short silence in which I tried very hard to think of what to say I sent back to him: "We need the Oxford book to start the shop. Get the hell back here." I waited for a moment, but he did not reply. Hoping that I had missed hearing his acknowledgment, I went on sending: "Ditch and sit tight. Samar has fix on you. Light flares when you hear motors. Stay with it."

There were then many minutes of silence in which I retuned

the whole frequency area without hearing Eric's call again. I heard the base operator at Samar sending his position, and copied the figures in my log. Eric did not acknowledge the bearing. About five minutes later I heard his last transmission. He began sending very rapidly and erratically, as if the plane were now entirely out of control, so that I had automatically to correct the errors in his code: "Samar Base from 416. Samar Base from 416. I have a message for you . . ." His key sputtered for a moment and then stopped suddenly. There was a long pause, after which the Samar operator sent: "Proceed with message." He repeated this many times, waiting after each transmission for Eric to reply, but there was no answer. I sat listening for a long while, until well past the time that he had estimated their fuel would last; but I never heard him again.

Finally I switched off the radio and climbed out of the plane, jumping down onto the crushed coral of the runway.

I sat for some time under the wing, staring off at the great dark thunderheads above the hills in the north and listening to the distant bumping sound of the Japanese guns. In my breast pocket was a letter I had received from Laura three days before, and I took it out and reread it for the fifth or sixth time, not with any real interest or feeling but in a rather idle and abstracted way, as if in an effort to engage my mind with something:

DEAR VINCENT:

*I have felt for some time that your letters to me did not really express any real affection for me in a romantic sense, but were more like letters that you might write to a very good friend, and when I received your last letter in which you wrote about your plan to open a book shop after the war with your friend, and did not refer to me in any way in writing about your plans for your future life, I decided that I was right about this. So I don't think that what I have to say will come as any real surprise to you, or that you will be very much affected by it.*

*In my last letter I told you about the boarder who had been stay-*

*ing in Daddy's old room leaving, and that Mr. Ashcott had moved into the room and seemed to be very nice. I think I mentioned that he was always very eager to help in any way that he could, and that he even used to help Mother with the cooking on weekends and things of that kind. Since that time my affection and respect for him have increased to the point where we have become quite intimate, and developed a very sincere and wonderful affection for each other. In fact he has asked me to marry him, and as he is a very sincere and wonderful person with very good prospects I think it would be foolish of me to refuse.*

*We are going to be married next week, and I look forward to a very happy and contented life with him. As I say, I do not think that you will be very much affected by this news, and I do not feel that I have been untrue to you in any respect, as we have never really had any understanding of a romantic nature, which I think you will agree. I hope that we can continue to be very good friends, as I have a very sincere respect for you, which I am sure I will always have. I hope when you return to Stonemont you will come to visit us. Norman joins me in expressing our very best wishes for whatever you decide to do in the future, and says that he is looking forward to meeting you some day.*

*With very best wishes for your future life,*

LAURA

I crumpled the letter in my hand and tossed it out onto the coral, watching it blow away in the rainy wind. At the edge of the airstrip I could see a huge water pipe stretching away across the flat grassland toward Manila. It was about four feet in diameter and supported by heavy concrete abutments at intervals of a thousand yards. Feeling a sudden restless desire to follow it, I climbed one of the concrete supports and walked along the top of the pipe for a mile or two in the rain. It passed over fields of swamp water, rice paddies, jungle scrub and, finally, a narrow muddy river at the outskirts of the city. There were cheap wooden buildings clustered around the riverbank, most of them burned out or blasted by shells, with heaps of rubble strewn about them: the twisted frames of brass beds, disemboweled mattresses, shards of pottery, calendars with charred and fluttering leaves. There was a road beside the river, pitted with shell craters, and along it a line of refugees was moving slowly through the yellow mud toward the capital. Many of them had crouched at the riverbank to rest and sat huddled in the rain beside their shabby bundles of clothing, pots and pans, sullen, soaked chickens, their legs bound together with twine, oil lamps and water jugs. There was a sour smell, like stale garbage, from the riverbank, and a choppy, high-pitched babble of Tagalog. Beneath the water pipe I saw an old man kneeling and sobbing beside his wife, whom he had been pushing along the road in a home-made two-wheeled wooden cart. Both her knees were bound with dirty bandages, and I guessed that she had had the backs of them seared by the Japanese—a form of punishment which they inflicted commonly upon hostile Filipinos and a particularly brutal one in that, even when the burns were healed, the victims were permanently crippled. The woman had died, or was dying, and the old man knelt beside her in the mud, holding her face in his hands and trying to brush the rain out of her eyes, rocking slowly back and forth from his hips and crooning softly, his face contorted with grief. I stood watching them for a moment and then walked back along the water pipe toward the airfield, staring sightlessly into the gray cloud masses above the hills and murmuring across the thousands of miles that separated us, "Not this, either, Grandfather."

A short time after this I was wounded by anti-aircraft fire during a raid on a Japanese base at Lifu. A flak fragment hit me in the lower part of the abdomen, chipping off a piece of my left hip bone and leaving a dark-blue, wedge-shaped scar, like a half-closed jackknife. I was sent back to a general hospital at New Caledonia and after three months discharged and returned to the United States.

On my return to Stonemont I was greeted by my grandfather with an extraordinary demonstration of feeling. In addition to the Purple Heart I had been awarded an Air Medal with four Oak Leaf Clusters, which transported him. This is a decoration which was awarded regularly and almost automatically, after the completion of a certain number of combat hours, and involved no conspicuous valor of any kind—an explanation which my grandfather knowingly rejected. He had the medal framed and hung beside his coat-of-arms above the sofa, and on Palm Sunday, which occurred very shortly after my return, he brought home from church a frond of palm leaf and hung it across the top of the frame; it is still draped there, dry and brown. My grandmother was very quiet, with that luminous, speechless joy of old people that borders upon tears, and she seemed, in her age, to have become more beautiful than I remembered her. She used to come into the parlor in the evenings when I was reading the newspaper and sit beside me on the sofa, taking my hand and pressing it silently between her own while she gazed at me with a look of inexpressible happiness. On the first night of my return, sitting beside me in this fashion, she said softly, "Oh, Sonny, you don't know how I've prayed. You don't know how often I've sat in this room and prayed that God would return you to us."

"Yes, Grandma. I could tell. I always felt as if you were real close to me."

"God has been very good to us in our old age."

"Yes, ma'am."

I smiled at her and, leaning toward her, touched her soft silver hair lightly with my lips. In the pale and radiant sweetness of her presence a flood of images from my youth poured over me, so pure and lovely that they seemed never to have been darkened by the veil of time that had fallen over them: blowing curtains, moonlight on village roofs, wistaria blossoms, the hot golden breath of horses. Oh, my grandmother, your life was a long gentle act of duty and mercy, and I thank you for it. How greatly it weighs in the scales against the darker things I have recorded here!

One evening, shortly after my return, when we were sitting after dinner on the front porch, my grandfather broached again, for the first time since my return, the subject of my future.

"Perhaps you remember, Sonny, that we had a long talk about your education just before you went in the army; and I want you to know that I'm as good as my word. Now, the fall term will be starting in a few months—time flies, you know—and I don't think it's too soon to start thinking about getting you enrolled, Lad."

"I don't think I'll go, Grandpa," I said.

"You don't think you'll go?"

"No, sir. I don't feel as if I've earned it."

I was stricken with remorse, even while the words were forming in my mouth, but I could not restrain myself from speaking them. He sat fondling his pipe bowl with his large hairy fingers in a startled, unmistakably hurt way, and said slowly, with the barest suggestion of a tremble in his voice—a sound which made a pain in my heart: "Why, it wasn't a question of earning it, Lad. I'm sure you realize that."

"Well, I just mean that I don't think I'm the type of person who could profit from it enough to make it worthwhile. If I wanted to go to college now, I could use the G.I. Bill, anyway—for a couple of years."

We sat for a couple of minutes without speaking, and then he asked softly and humbly, "Well, but this G.I. Bill, Sonny—it wouldn't see you all the way through, would it? And then I'm sure that you'd get only a very limited allowance outside of your tuition; you'd still need a lot of help, Lad. And I'd be proud to give it to you."

"Well, anyway, it's kind of late for that now," I said. "I'm twenty-two already, and I'm kind of anxious to start working at something."

"Oh. Yes. I see." After a moment he added gently, "What kind of work did you have in mind, Sonny?"

I had nothing in mind; my vision of the quiet neighborhood bookstore had vanished with Eric into the Philippine Sea, and nothing had replaced it. But on an inspiration of the moment— or was it, after all, entirely of that moment?—I said suddenly, "Well, I've been thinking about Poplar Lodge. Maybe I could get some kind of a job over there, where I could help those people, somehow. Mother always wanted me to do something like that."

"I don't have any idea, Lad; but if that's what you want to do, I think it would be a very fine thing. It's an honorable kind of work, and I think it would have made your mother happy, as you say. But I don't know how much of a future you would find in it without a college education behind you."

"Well, I don't really care about making a lot of money, or being a great success or anything, Grandpa. I just want some kind of a job where I can make enough money to live on, and maybe do something to help people who aren't as fortunate as we are."

"Yes. I had hoped that maybe medicine or law would interest you. Those are fine fields for a young man these days. But of course I wish you great success and happiness in whatever you decide to do; and I want you to know that I'm willing to help you in any way that I can, Lad. It would be an interesting thing to try for a while, anyway."

"Yes, sir. Thank you very much," I said. "I think that's what I'd like to do."

$\mathcal{I}$ COME NOW to what is properly, as I have said, the beginning of this story—the part of it which concerns Poplar Lodge and which will be, if I have the strength and ability to set it down, a history of that strange transfiguration of the world and of my heart which began when I first entered its grounds and whose spell, in so transcribing it, I hope to break forever. For although it is finished now, I do not know if, having heard such music, one is ever wholly free from it again. Is it unregenerate of me to make such an admission, even now? I hope not; I hope I have become secure enough in honesty to confess that whatever else it may be that has driven me to set it down at all, it is partly this, at least; and if I were to undertake the task with any less candor it would be useless to begin.

A few days after this dialogue with my grandfather I walked, for the first time in my life, up the stone path from the sidewalk toward the huge screened porch behind its pale purple bower of rose-of-Sharon blossoms. It was strange, after so many years of distant, awed speculation about those grounds, to be entering them; and I had a certain mild sense of trespass—even of desecration—as of one who, by the requirements and privileges of his maturity, is brought at last, a little reluctantly, to invade one of the myths of his childhood. It was a bright warm morning in late April, the early sunlight so hot that the grass was already dry, although it was only eight o'clock, and I saw no one about except a middle-aged man in a soft tweed jacket who was reading a book on one of the stone benches near the driveway. He lifted his head as I approached, and when I said good morning to him he smiled shyly, returning his eyes hurriedly to the pages of his book. The driveway divided in front of the Lodge, one section turning in a loop in front of the main building and the other continuing on past it to the group of cottages beyond. I went up the wide wooden steps and, opening the screen door, entered the long, veranda-like front porch.

I do not know exactly what I expected it to resemble, but I believe I had a pair of rather vague alternate conceptions—either of clinical white-tiled corridors, or of a paneled, deeply carpeted, severely formal look—and it may be that the great contrast between either of these and its actual appearance was responsible for the strange and lasting impression it made on me. It was furnished in the manner of an old-fashioned country hotel, with wicker rocking chairs and settees and a row of ancient cast-iron radiators along the wall. Behind the screens the porch was fitted from floor to ceiling with movable glass shutters of the kind called "jalousies"—now much more common, but at that time the first that I had ever seen—so that it could be used, even throughout the winter, as a kind of greenhouse—a facility which had been exercised with exuberant results, for the whole porch was a veritable jungle of potted plants, their leaves, fronds, trailing vines and blossoms stirring gently in the mild breeze that blew through the screens. There were rubber trees in wooden tubs; enormous *Monstera* plants with deeply lobate, darkly glittering leaves; tiers of begonias of every variety, some with sinister-looking, dark-red, hairy foliage and tiny delicate pom-poms of salmon-colored blossom; hanging moss baskets from which long trailers of Wandering Jew drooped stilly; harlequin plants with splashed and speckled leaves of pink and white; brown orchids, their blossoms shuddering in the green gloom; the scarlet maws of tuberous begonias; and a latticed panel of climbing philodendrons, worked with wonderful accidental patterns of coiled vine and tremblingly suspended heart-shaped shields, each with its tip turned downward, like a heraldic tapestry of luminous and translucent green.

Although the porch faced north, the light seemed to reach and penetrate it (in that curiously oblique manner in which the Lodge was always illumined from without) and, stained and muted by the leaves, filled the whole veranda with an aqueous, pale-green radiance. I can think of nothing it resembled so much as the silent sun deck of an ancient liner, sunken in cool green water and filled with gently waving sea grasses, through which pale rays of light fell downward from the surface. It did not seem extraordinary to suppose that I would see in a moment, flickering through the dense, dim atmosphere, a school of dainty, coral-colored fishes, coming to nibble at my lips and eyeballs and my bleached and wrinkled finger tips; or a great golden carp, gliding between my arm and body with inquisitive, graceful languor, plump and cool and slippery, coated with burnished slime. I filled the vacant wicker chairs with imaginary, drowned passengers who would sit forever, staring out across the railings of the glassed-in deck while the little coral fishes nibbled the flesh from their faces, their chairs rocking gently in the current until their skulls fell off into their laps. They had watched me as a boy, walking past with my grandfather and delivering groceries to the far houses on summer afternoons. One of them, a slender girl with floating yellow hair, smiled with frayed lips to see me standing at the back of a grocery truck and staring in, astonished, from the street.

I stood for several moments, entirely bemused by this atmosphere and somehow loath to interrupt it. It was as if the myth which, a few moments before, I had felt a certain rue at having to intrude upon and dispel, rather than submitting to any such subversion on my part, had begun, on the contrary, to absorb me into it, as many of the fallen cultures of antiquity—a subject of constant fascination to me in my school days—had seduced and assimilated their invaders.

The main building itself, as I saw when I had entered it through the large double doors which opened onto the veranda, although much more formal and institutional in appearance, was pervaded with this same strangely oppressive atmosphere—an atmosphere not of dilapidation (for to say this would not be justified by the cleanliness and order with which it was maintained) but of decline—a sad, silent air of debility, which was evoked, I think, by the fact that the building had been erected not as an asylum but as a home. Everywhere was dignified and tragic evidence of its former purpose: hand-wrought brass hardware, antique doorknobs and key plates of fine Limoges china in pastel-colored floral designs—now chipped and crazed with age—lintels and wainscoting of hand-carved oak, marble-paneled mantels, the fluting of their decorative columns crusted and blunted with countless layers of shiny-surfaced, "practical" paint, and a magnificent plaster ceiling with dentiled molding and, at its center, a huge circular frieze of flying cherubs, massed about the vacant base of a deracinated chandelier. There was a melancholy obsolescence about this elegance, and a painful incongruity between the quiet graceful life it had been built to house and the madness which, with disturbing facility, it had been converted to contain. The ground floor had been given over entirely to administrative quarters, and the huge old high-ceilinged rooms divided into small offices, consulting rooms, a medical library and a lounge, furnished with chintz-covered chairs and an upholstered sofa. In this room a young nurse in a blue-and-white uniform sat holding a paper cup of coffee in one hand and leafing through a magazine. When I paused in the doorway she looked up pleasantly and asked if she could help me.

"Yes, I wanted to apply for a job. I wonder if you could tell me who to see."

"Oh. Miss Crowe is in charge of personnel. Her office is just at the end of the hall, on the right."

"Thank you."

I found the office open and Miss Crowe, a middle-aged nurse in an all-white uniform, with gray hair and glasses, sitting behind a desk which bore her name on a brass plaque. She looked up and smiled at me as I entered. I said, "Good morning," rather stiffly, in a sudden spasm of self-consciousness, and added abruptly that I wished to apply for a job.

"I see. What sort of work did you want to do? Is it a professional position?"

"Well, no, I'm not qualified for any kind of professional work. I thought there might be some kind of a job as an attendant, or something of that kind."

"Yes. Well, I'm in charge of the nursing staff—which includes the floor attendants—and I'm afraid there isn't anything at all right now. But I think there might be something in Occupational Therapy. That's Miss Brice's department, if you'd like to inquire."

"Yes, I would."

"Well, her office is outside. It's the first little cottage on the right as you go down the drive. It's a tiny little place—I don't think you can miss it."

"Thank you very much."

"I'm not sure she's in right now, but she ought to be soon."

"Thank you."

"Not at all."

I went back out of the building, past the spectral passengers staring out from their sunken, exotic porch, and walked toward the tiny cottage to which she had directed me. As I approached it I saw a young woman in a white blouse and woolen skirt, clutching against her hip a stack of books and a large Manila folder, coming toward it also along the asphalt drive from the rear of the grounds. She stopped in front of the door and, supporting the pile of books with her lifted thigh, began searching awkwardly through her pocketbook, apparently for a key.

"Can I help you?" I asked.

"Oh. Yes, thank you. If you could hold these books for a minute it would be a great help."

I took them from her, and while she found her key and unlocked the cottage door I said, "I'm looking for Miss Brice. Miss Crowe said there might be a job available in the Occupational Therapy department."

93

"Yes, that's me. Would you like to come in and talk about it?"

"Yes. Thank you."

Her office, in contrast to the main building and to the plain clapboard exterior of the cottage which it entirely occupied, was furnished and decorated in a very modern style, with steel-and-leather sling seats, a blond-oak desk and sectional bookcase and a large Gauguin print on the wall. I set her books on the desk, and she asked me to sit, which I did, obliquely facing her, in one of the sling seats, having time, while she arranged some papers and made a call on the white telephone, to observe her manner and appearance. She was very little older than I, a fact which, combined with her easy, intelligent and incisive air of authority, I found oddly disconcerting; for young, poised, well-educated professional women of this type—as her telephone conversation revealed her to be—were unknown to me and made me feel uncomfortably provincial. But there was about her a quality of sincerity and sympathy—of genuine, personal, more than professional interest in one—which was very reassuring; and after talking to her for a very few minutes, I felt entirely at ease. Perhaps I should set down our interview in some detail, for it will tell a good deal not only about Bea—as I shall call her now—but about the Lodge as well, more briefly than would otherwise be possible.

When she had replaced the receiver and sighed cheerfully in the manner of one who is used to, and pretends a genial regret for, responsibilities which actually are dear to him, she smiled at me and said, "Well, we could either begin with you telling me all about yourself, or me telling you all about us. Which would you rather do?"

"I'd better tell you about myself," I said. "Then you may not have to bother with the rest of it."

"All right."

"There isn't really very much to tell. I'm twenty-two years old and just got out of the army. I've never had a job before, except part-time work—you know, like mowing lawns and delivering groceries—and I've never been to college. I went into the army right after I got out of high school. I've lived here in Stonemont all my life, and I've always been kind of curious about this place; so I thought it might be interesting to work here."

"Do you mean a permanent job, or just summer work of some kind?"

"No, I mean a permanent job."

"Because if you just got out of the army you'll have the G.I. Bill, won't you? Don't you want to go to college now?"

"No." After a pause in which she seemed to anticipate some further explanation I added, "I'm not really very ambitious. Or maybe I'm too restless, or something. I've never been able to think very far ahead, I guess. But I feel as if I want to go to work right away. I want to learn something about life from experience, not just from books." I stared for a few moments at the Gauguin print on the wall, silently considering how I might better express the reasons for my application. She did not interrupt, and in a moment I went on. "My grandfather owns the Dangerford Tavern here in town. I could go to work for him—I think he really wants me to—but I don't want to. I want to do some kind of work that would be a direct help to people. I suppose that's the only real ambition I have. That's really why I decided to come here."

"But don't you feel that you could help people just as well— much better, even, in more important ways, like medicine or science—if you were better educated, better equipped to help them?"

"Yes, I suppose so. But those are pretty big things for me to try; I'm not sure at all that I could do them well. And anyway, they take too long. I don't think I could wait that long. I might die, or something, before I ever finished getting ready—before I even got to work. And then I'd never get it done. I just want to do some simple thing that I feel pretty sure about, while I can."

"It doesn't sound as if you trust the future very much," she said.

"Maybe not. I don't ever think about it very much. I don't particularly like to."

She folded over the corner of a sheet of paper, creasing it thoroughly into a small triangle with her finger tip, as if considering a further question on this subject, which in a moment she appeared to abandon, however, for a more practical one.

"Are you good at sports?"

"A few of them. I play individual sports pretty well—like tennis and swimming. And I'm a good rider. That's the thing I can do best. I guess that's the only thing I can do really well." She smiled at this confession in a way that made me like her very much.

"Do you have any hobbies?"

"Yes. Well, I used to have, before the war; I used to collect folk-music records and make model airplanes."

"Oh, that would be useful, because we do a lot of crafts, you know—weaving and woodwork and that kind of thing. Are you a good dancer?"

"No. I can't dance at all."

"Really? Do you mean you never have, or you can't?"

"I can't. I've tried to learn, but I just can't get anywhere. I don't think I'll ever be able to dance."

"Oh." She stared at me thoughtfully for a moment, as if summarizing these things in her mind, and then leaned forward across her desk, spreading her fingers on her cheeks casually, while she told me about the Lodge.

"This is a private hospital," she said. "You may know that, but many people don't. That means it's very different from state institutions, both in the type and number of patients and the kind of treatment they're given. We have only thirty-five patients here; they're mostly young people, between sixteen and forty, and all schizophrenics. They are all considered curable, and each one of them has an analyst working with him. That's the only kind of treatment given at the Lodge, and it's very expensive. These people are all from very wealthy families who pay several thousand dollars a month to keep them here. That means they have superior backgrounds—economically superior, anyway—private schools, travel, and so on. Most of them are also of superior intelligence, and many of them were people of considerable distinction in the outside world." She paused for a moment and asked, "Do you know anything about mental illness?"

"Not very much, no."

"Well, schizophrenia is one of the most common and difficult kinds of illness to treat. There is a popular conception that it means 'split personality,' and that all schizophrenics are clear-cut cases of a Jekyll-and-Hyde personality; but that isn't true at all. Schizophrenia is much more complicated than that. People with this disease can have just about every manifestation of mental abnormality there is—there are catatonics, paranoics, hypomanics, and so on. They have the most complex and bewildering syndromes—mixtures of associated symptoms—in the world, which makes their treatment very difficult. The patients here are in all different states of disturbance and deterioration; some of them have been rigid and speechless for months, some of them talk nothing but garbled nonsense and can't feed, clothe or bathe themselves. Others seem to be such assured, vigorous, intelligent people that you wonder what on earth they're doing here. They seem much saner than we do, sometimes. But they're not stable; they move through manic cycles of behavior, and sooner or later they break down. They may be discussing Kant or Shaw with you one afternoon, in the most profound and witty way in the world, and the next morning be rolling and screaming on the floor, completely out of contact."

She paused to examine the effect of this upon me—it was one of genuine fascination—and then went on: "There are different theories about the causes of schizophrenia and the most effective way to treat it. Some people feel that it's an organic disease—that is, that there's something actually physically or chemically wrong with the structure of the brain—and that it can be treated like any other physical illness. Other doctors believe that it's a functional ailment—that there's no actual physical damage or deficiency—but that the mind has become deranged functionally, through acute emotional problems, tensions, conflicts and so on. We tend toward the last interpretation, here; and also we only use classical therapy—that is, analysis. This is so expensive, and usually so prolonged, that most state institutions can't afford it. They do a great deal with shock—electrical or insulin shock—and with drugs and surgery. But we don't feel that those methods are as thorough or permanent. May I ask what you know about psychoanalysis?"

"Almost nothing," I said.

"Well, it means curing by analyzing. Talking with the patient, encouraging him to talk through free association, leading him to discover and examine the causes of his illness. Going back to the old conflicts and tensions, and exploring them until he begins to gain insight into them. This takes years sometimes and requires enormous skill and experience on the part of the analyst. You can see how limited it is, too, because the patient must be in contact before you can communicate with him effectively, and schizophrenics very often aren't. Now, what do you think about all this?"

"It sounds very interesting," I said.

"Really?"

"Yes."

"All right, let me tell you about my department. A very important part of the treatment is to keep the patient engaged in normal and interesting activities; it keeps them in touch with reality, gives them recreation and physical exercise and creative expression. So occupational therapy is a most important part of it. It includes all kinds of things: crafts, like rug-weaving, leatherwork and so on, gardening, sports, music, social activities—we have a tea dance once a week, which is why I asked if you could dance—occasional automobile trips, hiking, bird-watching, picnicking—anything that falls outside of actual clinical treatment.

Which means that we actually spend a great deal more time with the patients than the doctors do. All of these activities are voluntary, but we encourage patients to participate in as many of them as they can without becoming confused or anxious. Naturally, some of them are in better shape to do these things than others and require much less attention and supervision; and individual patients will vary from day to day in their interest and ability to concentrate. Some patients have "privileges"—which means that they can walk about the grounds or engage in activities unattended—but most of them must be accompanied and supervised by an assigned attendant who is personally responsible for them any time they are outside their actual quarters. This means that we have to maintain a fairly large staff, although the nurses help out a great deal. We usually have three or four students here on rotation, from colleges like Antioch, and others—people who are majoring in O.T. and have to do some practical training as part of their course—but I still have to keep a basic permanent staff of at least six, if I can; and right now I only have five.

"The work, as you can see, is difficult, nerve-wracking and sometimes dangerous. It requires a great deal of intelligence, patience, skill at manual crafts, personal authority and integrity, and—oh, heavens, all sorts of things. The ideal O.T. worker has never been born yet. But most of all it requires sympathy, I think—a real interest in these people. Workers who come here just out of curiosity, or on a temporary basis, are never really successful, because they can't endure the abuse they get from the patients, the constant tension, the occasional violence and the—well, the unpleasantness of working in a mental hospital. Because there *is* something unpleasant about spending most of your life with people who are willful, slovenly, abusive, violent and sometimes physically repulsive. Now—" she leaned back in her chair and smiled, brushing her hair with a frank and feminine gesture—"do you still feel the same about working here?"

"Yes."

"You do?"

"Yes, I'm more interested than ever, as a matter of fact."

She laughed. "All right. Then come and have a look around, and I'll show you some of the things we've been talking about."

For the next hour, while we toured the grounds and buildings of the Lodge, there grew in me a strong and positive sense of joy—a feeling of identity and of metier, so long anticipated and so often despaired of that, in being recognized at last, it created in me an almost festive feeling, a kind of jubilation which, although it resembled other, transient, sensations of the kind which I had had before—on winning the tournament, on leaving for the war— I was able to distinguish from these less durable experiences by the more profound, more tranquil thing which accompanied, or perhaps, indeed, produced it: a stilling and quieting, a glowing process of composure, like the formation of a crystal in my spirit. I took a great pleasure and pride in everything—in the grounds themselves, with their gracious landscaping, the great-leaved oaks and poplars casting pearl shadow on the walks, the espaliered apples against the rose-brick walls, the tennis courts and playing fields, with long morning shadows on the velvet grass, the craft shop with its fresh, clean-scented lumber, its great tan-colored rolls of cowhide, bundles of raffia and sheaths of bright, lithe, virgin wicker—as well as the attendants whom we passed sometimes, strolling with patients about the grounds or conducting games or classes, whom I felt to be people of extraordinary sympathy and intelligence and with whom I felt an immediate and profound fraternity. Since my employment here seemed now, so far as Bea was concerned, to be foregone and to depend only upon my own inclination, I was able to presume, without fear of disappointment, my accession to them and to take in them the mystic, proud delight which a devoted novice feels in the paraphernalia of his profession.

We passed a tall, dark-eyed boy with the sallow, gaunt, ascetic face of a Talmudic scholar, standing under a sycamore tree and touching gently with long sensitive fingers the ragged mottled bark, peering closely and wistfully, as if it awakened in him some bewildering memory. He murmured, "Good morning, Miss Brice," turning to stare at us with humble, haunted eyes; and I felt a sudden passionate yet strangely selfish impulse to bless his misfortune, because it ended mine.

"He was a great language scholar," Bea said. "He knew Arabic, Sanskrit and Persian before he was sixteen. He can quote the Upanishads for an hour without pausing. He's only twenty-two now."

In the shop—the converted barn and loft which I had seen sometimes from the street—she introduced me to the foreman, a handsome Scandinavian-looking young man named Lindquist, under whose charge ten or twelve patients, some with personal attendants, were working with quiet absorption. He took me, with a most engaging enthusiasm, around the whole shop, demonstrating its machinery—electric drills, potter's wheels, looms and kilns—and showing me the tools and materials of all the arts and crafts that were practiced there.

"It's a good shop," he said. "We've got good equipment and material, but we need more room, as you can see. I want to have the kilns put downstairs; they're too heavy for these old floors, anyway. There are lots of things that need to be done, but they get a great deal of pleasure out of it as it is, and we've had some wonderful results."

I watched a fierce-eyed man with a stubble of red beard molding a clay vase on the potter's wheel. He had blunt, strong hands with which he shaped firmly and surely the moist, spinning clay, his feet plying the treadle, humming to himself.

"Are you a new patient?" he asked, raising his eyes briefly.

"No. I may be going to work here. I'm just visiting."

"Ah. Do you read Dostoevski?"

"I've read *Crime and Punishment* and *The Brothers Karamazov.*"

"Have you?" he asked intensely, stilling his feet on the treadle and looking up at me. "Do you believe it? That if there is no God, there can be no such thing as virtue?"

"I don't know," I said. "But it seems to me that if there is no God, then virtue is even more remarkable."

"Because it's voluntary, you mean?"

"Yes, and because it's its own reward. If you don't expect any reward in heaven, and probably not on earth, either, then the only reason for practicing virtue is out of respect and sympathy for your fellow men. And that seems more virtuous to me than simply obeying a commandment."

"An idealist!" he cried. "This is delightful! I hope you will come to work here. You have a philosophic mind. We shall be great friends!"

"I hope so," I said.

"You made a great hit with Mr. Palakis," Bea said when we had left the shop. "It was exactly the right way to speak to him. We put a great emphasis on that here—not talking down to patients, not indulging or coddling them. The more you can persuade them into mature and responsible conversations and relationships—as long as you don't demand too much from them—the better it is. You did that very well."

I had spoken, as a matter of fact, entirely without calculation and was somewhat surprised by the spontaneity of my own reply; but I was nevertheless much pleased by the success of this first contact with a patient.

"It's very hard at first," she went on, "not to be self-conscious or patronizing, and this is a feeling that many workers never get over. I think you have to have a certain talent for dealing with these people, and I don't know that it can ever be learned. Of course that doesn't mean that you can enter into perfectly normal and enthusiastic relationships with them—thinking that you can is one of the chief pitfalls of this kind of work. So many of the patients are intellectually equal or superior to us that we sort of automatically assume they are emotionally equal as well; but that isn't true, of course, or they wouldn't be here. And we have to remind ourselves of it constantly.

"We try to maintain a level of perfect candor with them in everything. If we didn't, it would create an oppressive atmosphere for them—a feeling that they were being manipulated or persecuted, that things were being concealed from them, that there was duplicity on our part—an atmosphere that would only nourish the paranoid feelings that most of them have already. But, as I say, this doesn't mean that we can enter into wholehearted relationships. There has to be a certain amount of professional reserve, the worker has to keep himself emotionally detached and intact. Which can be more difficult than it sounds, offhand, because some of these people have very subtle, very powerful personalities."

She paused to nod toward a middle aged man with stiff gray hair, hoeing furiously in a small kitchen garden at the end of the narrow lane down which we had walked behind the shop. "That's Mr. Levitz," she said, smiling. "He is one of my favorite patients. He supplies us with fresh corn and lettuce all summer and writes epic poetry on brown paper bags. He's very kind and dignified and will tell you that the only way to keep really healthy is to drink a glassful of human blood every morning."

I was perhaps a bit disconcerted by the traditional gentle wryness of her tone in referring to these eccentricities of a "crazy" person, but it was belied by the sympathy and experience out of which it was spoken and was, as I came to learn, a common manner of workers at the Lodge—a kind of mild, unmalicious, professional license against oversolemnity. As if to distinguish this attitude from the one of patronization against which she had just enjoined me, she smiled and said, "On the other hand, you mustn't ever lose your sense of humor. You probably need it more here than anywhere in the world."

The grounds of the Lodge, I saw as Bea escorted me about them, were far more extensive than I had ever realized in looking in at the old mansion from the street. Behind it they ran on to include several acres of the fields of the surrounding countryside, a huge old farmhouse in which several of the resident doctors lived, a dormitory for nurses and attendants, and, in the near distance, half a mile beyond the slope of an interceding hill, a large modern brick building, which she called Hillcrest.

"That's where our old people stay," she said. "We have a few senile patients here who only receive custodial care. It's very different from the Lodge. Also, the clinic and hospital are over there, where Lodge patients are taken when they're ill. Do you see the water beyond?"

"Yes."

"That's the pond. It has a dock and a rowboat. Patients with ground privileges can swim and go boating there, as long as there's an attendant on duty. We own that old barn on the other side of it, too. The fields are planted every year with market crops. Patients who want to can work in them, and they're paid a percentage of the profits for their work. We had a wonderful yield of wheat last year, which they raised and harvested almost entirely by themselves. I want to just show you Field House now, and then we can have some lunch."

This was an old brick cottage on the main grounds, a few hundred feet to the rear of the mansion and lying adjacent to the tennis courts and playing greens. It had a large screened porch, furnished with more of the wicker furniture and a ping-pong table, and a huge old-fashioned sunlit living room with a grand piano in one corner, overstuffed furniture, glass-paned bookcases lined with leather-bound classics, a phonograph and a record library. There was a kitchen, as well, on the ground floor, and the upper story had been divided into separate rooms to accommodate seven patients. The door of one of these was open, and, glancing into it, I saw an unmade bed, its sheets trailing on the floor, and a bedside table littered with fragments of a broken mirror, an empty paper cup and scattered pencils, coins and wads of crumpled foil. Above the bed was a print of Delacroix's "Hamlet," which had been disfigured by a bold encirclement, in red ink, of the prince's head.

"This is Warren Evshevsky's room," Bea said. "The boy we saw outside just now." She frowned at the disorder and closed the door gently. "He isn't doing awfully well lately; it's that business with Lilith Arthur." She stood brooding privately for a moment, her hand on the doorknob, and then said more matter-of-factly, "Field House is a sort of weaning place. When patients have had ground privileges for a while and have been able to manage them responsibly, they're transferred over here from the main building. They live here entirely without supervision, as if they were in a small guest home. There's an attendant on duty in the kitchen, but he is there really only in case of emergency. The patients look after themselves, cook simple meals if they like, and do their own housekeeping. They play chess and bridge together, read, organize parties, listen to music, and gradually adjust themselves to a community life. It's a difficult period for them; very often they aren't up to it and have to be returned to the main lodge. But if they do well here for a few months, then they're given town privileges, which means that they can take a room in Stonemont, even do part-time work occasionally, and report to the Lodge only for treatment and conferences. For some of them it's the last stage before final rehabilitation; they spend less and less time here, become gradually independent, and finally ask to be discharged. Field House is really the first big step in their social recovery, and it's very exciting to see them transferred over here— they're always so proud and happy, and rather frightened at the same time. It gives us a feeling of real personal triumph when someone we're particularly interested in is moved over here; and it's always a very sad day if they have to be moved back again."

We had left Field House and were approaching the main lodge from the rear. Looking up at it, I saw for the first time that the entire back of the building had been fitted with a three-tiered structure of concrete porches, each entirely enclosed by the heavy diagonal steel wire which barred all of the Lodge windows, set one upon another, like a stack of cages. On the first of these, a floor above the ground, a grinning dark-haired girl in a torn yellow dress stood clutching the wire with curled fingers and calling down to us in a foolish mechanical voice, as if reciting by rote a list of memorized civilities, "Hi, Miss Brice. Are you going to have lunch now? It's a nice day, isn't it, Miss Brice? I hope you have a nice lunch, Miss Brice. You have a very nice-looking friend. It certainly is a nice day, isn't it?"

"It's a lovely day," Bea said, smiling up at her. "How are you today, Miss Glassman?" She unlocked a large metal door at the rear of the building which opened directly into a self-operated elevator, and as we entered it the endless mild torrent of inanities still floated down from the girl above. We rode the elevator down one level to the basement and walked along a tiled corridor to the staff dining room, a bright and noisy cafeteria, full of the pleasant clatter of steel cutlery and thick commercial china and the cheerful garrulous chatter of the diners, who, after the tension of their work, appeared to relieve themselves with a particularly informal, even boisterous, behavior at luncheon. We sat apart at a small table and Bea smiled at me over a salad of cottage cheese. I felt quite inexplicably happy.

"I don't think I'll take you up to the floors today," she said. "I have a pretty busy afternoon, and I think you've had quite a session for one day already. What do you think of it?"

"I think it's extremely interesting. I'd like to work here very much."

"Really? You don't feel there's anything . . . depressing or frightening about it?"

"No. It appeals to me very much. As a matter of fact, it seems like the only thing I've ever really wanted to do."

"Well, think about it this evening. Then, if you like, you can come back in the morning and I'll take you up on the floors."

"What do you think about me?" I asked after a moment. "Do you think I could do the work all right?"

"Yes. I think you might make a very good O.T. I'd like you to start, if you feel quite sure about it."

"I do. Very sure."

"All right. Then I'll expect you in the morning. The O.T. staff meets at eight-thirty every morning in the craft shop, and we make up a schedule for the day. I'll assign you to one of the other workers tomorrow, and you can accompany him for a week or so, until you get to know your way. Can you plan to spend the whole day tomorrow?"

"Yes."

"Then we'll talk about it in the evening. We meet again every night at five o'clock to go over the whole day and make out reports."

"All right, fine." I lifted my glass of water and could not help smiling into it.

"You seem quite pleased," Bea said.

"Yes. It means a good deal to me. I'm very anxious to do well at it."

"Yes, I can see that," she said.

I left the Lodge full of a strangely agitated and yet pacific feeling which I find it impossible to remember accurately, much less to describe. For how is one to describe that wholesome sense of merriment and gravity uniquely merged which is fulfillment? Perhaps as the sudden illumination and warming of cold, sealed cellars of the spirit by the delightful opening of doors. I clutched a handful of leaves from a privet hedge as I passed and lifted them to my nostrils, blowing them from my hand in a little glittering shower of green. The streets and houses of the village where I had been born seemed to possess, as I felt myself to possess, a new dimension. The town seemed more beautiful to me, for I was to serve it and to see it whole. I was to participate, at last, in one of its mysteries.

I believe my grandfather was disappointed at my news, although he pretended not to be, and offered me, by way of congratulation, a small glass of apple brandy. My grandmother smiled and said softly when I kissed her temple before I went upstairs to bed, "Your poor mother would be very happy, Sonny."

"I know she would, Grandma," I said.

*J* BEGAN keeping a journal on the first day that I went to work at Poplar Lodge. I do not know what prompted me to do this, unless it was a simple manifestation of pride—the desire to record this deed, this achievement, to which I had so long aspired. It was fortunate that I did, however, for from this point on my story can be fortified by the daily transcription of its events, fresh and exact in circumstance and feeling, whereas it might otherwise easily have been distorted by the imperfections of my memory and by the subtle temptation (which I have been aware of already, in recounting it this far) to modify its details ever so slightly, ever so ingeniously, with ever such an air of innocence, to my own advantage. But I cannot doubt the innocence of my journal. Much of it, indeed, is so painfully candid that I am almost unwilling to set it down here; yet, to preserve the sincerity with which I am determined to tell this story, and to restore those portions of it which have been lost or deformed by the curious processes of my memory, I shall copy down here whatever passages I feel to be significant. It is a large old-fashioned ledger bound in green cloth, which I bought at the stationer's on my way home from the Lodge after my first full day of work. I sat up after my grandparents had gone to bed with the lamp on at my table, the windows open and pale moths bumping softly against the screens in the spring darkness, writing carefully, in my neat, overdelicate handwriting, this first entry:

My first day of work at the Lodge. I woke up at six o'clock with excitement and went down to the kitchen. It is pleasant to be up in a house while the others are still sleeping. I wonder what it is that makes certain moments so splendid and permanent? I think I shall always remember that half hour, sitting in the quiet kitchen, smoking a cigarette and drinking a cup of coffee, smiling to myself with happiness. I don't think I have ever been so happy since before my mother died.

We met at eight-thirty in the craft shop, and Bea introduced me to the staff. They are all very pleasant (one possible exception here), and I am sure I shall like them. There are five permanent workers and four students from Antioch. I liked best Greta Pearlman, who is in charge of Recreation, a stocky, dark-haired woman of about thirty-five with a plain, humorous face; Carl Lindquist, the shop attendant, whom I met yesterday; and Iola and Robert Clayfield, a newly married couple who are attending Antioch and training together. Bob is studying on the G.I. Bill, and is about my age, or perhaps a year or two older. I will write about the rest of them as I get to know them better.

The staff is divided into two categories: Recreation and Shop. The Shop workers instruct patients in crafts, and the Recreation group take them walking, supervise them at athletics, etc. I am in the latter group, although I hope I shall be able to learn the shop procedures too, as I am sure I would enjoy it greatly. I love lumber, leather, raffia, clay and everything that you can work with your hands.

At the morning meetings Bea outlines a schedule for the day. Attendants are assigned to certain floors, and try to divide their time as fairly as possible among the unprivileged patients on their floor. It was easy to guess, from the degree of enthusiasm with which assignments were accepted, which floors are the most popular. Fourth Floor is the least so. It is for very disturbed female patients who have to be watched closely, kept from using dangerous tools, and to have their poor concentration and coordination constantly stimulated and corrected. Some of them, apparently, have particularly formidable reputations—one woman, whom they call "The Duchess," seems to be held especially in dread. I hope I will be spared her company for a while.

Third Floor is for disturbed male patients, who, strangely enough, seem to provoke less apprehension than the women. Second Floor is divided into both male and female quarters for patients in relatively good contact. Many of these have ground privileges and do not need to be attended. Field House inmates can come and go at will, without supervision.

Bea has assigned me to Bob Clayfield. I am to accompany him everywhere for a week, observing the way he deals with patients, learning Lodge rules and procedures, and becoming generally orientated to the hospital. At the end of that time, or perhaps of an additional week, I will be issued a set of keys and allowed to escort patients on my own. I must confess this prospect seems none too distant at the moment, for after visiting the floors with Bea this morning I have developed a set of nervous misgivings as to my own capabilities, although she assured me that this is always an unsettling experience to new attendants.

It would have been less harrowing, I think, if we had begun on the second floor and worked our way up through the progressive levels of disorder; but Bea took me directly to the fourth floor. I was prepared to be shocked, or repelled perhaps, and was fiercely determined to survive my first impressions, however forbidding they might be, so important has it become to me to succeed at this work. But the sight of so much tormented, derelict humanity, crowded together in such oppressive, desolate conditions—however necessary—without comfort, privacy or a single grace to dignify their lives, is overwhelmingly sad.

The floor is divided by a wide corridor running down its center, from which the patients' rooms, five on each side, open off. These rooms have no doors and are completely unfurnished except for a wooden bed and a locked wardrobe. Each has a single uncurtained window, barred with steel wire. At the end of the hall are the heavy metal doors of two isolation rooms, each with a small observation window at its top. Immediately beside the elevator door there is a small cubicle which serves as office for the floor attendants, furnished with a desk, a drug cabinet, a steel sink and a small gas burner. On either side of it are the grilled metal doors of two bathrooms. The south end of the corridor opens onto the wire-barred concrete porch with which each floor is fitted.

Sitting on their heels, crouching or wandering about these bleak surroundings were eight or ten women patients, most of them quite young and many of them barefooted, with unkempt hair and torn, stained clothing. One girl ran softly on her toes in little darting steps, humming to herself and picking daintily at a rip in her dress. Another, with tangled black hair, leaned against the wall, beating it hopelessly, spasmodically with her palm while she sobbed with despair. A young woman whose face I could not see sat on the floor staring down into her lap, her forehead resting on her knees, completely motionless for the whole time we were there. A stout, sly-looking woman of thirty with a flushed and haughty face spit at us and smiled sardonically. From within the rooms came the sounds of quiet moaning, excited chatter or sudden hysterical laughter. The whole floor was permeated with a faint sour smell of sweat and urine, like that of a locker room. Spaced here and there along the walls of the corridor were white-coated attendants, watchful and impassive. They lifted their hands sometimes to disengage gently the fingers of patients who wandered close to them and clutched at their clothing, peering and giggling.

Bea introduced me to the nurse in charge, a strong, sober-looking woman in her forties with a broad freckled face, who sat on a tall stool in the tiny office, brewing a pot of tea. I can't remember her name, but I remember Bea telling me that she has been at the Lodge for six years and is one of the finest psychiatric nurses in the country.

I was silent as we went down in the elevator to the next floor, and Bea said only, "It's rather shocking, isn't it, the first time you see it?"

"Yes," I said and asked her suddenly a question which, although it was quite spontaneous and sincere, must have sounded very strange: "Why do you work here?"

She did not seem to be aware—as I was almost instantly—of the foolishness and possible impertinence of the question, but smiled and nodded as if it were not only relevant and logical but anticipated.

"That's something that all of us who work here have to ask ourselves," she said. "And we're better off if we answer it as honestly and thoroughly as we can. I hope you will, too." Although impressed by this answer, I could not help being aware of its obliquity.

The third floor, although it was very much like the fourth with the exception that these were male patients, I found less depressing. Perhaps this is because I was better prepared for what I would see there, but I don't think this is the entire reason. It seems to me that insanity is much less disturbing—I am not sure, here, of the exact word that I want to use—less sinister, perhaps, in a man than in a woman. It may be that violence is more compatible with a masculine nature, or that derangement is manifested in less subtle, less elaborate ways in men. There was something eerie, something witchlike and profound about those women above that I cannot forget and which I did not feel about the men. I had the impression that the strangeness, the faint alarm they made me feel, was invoked not by the loss of their powers but by their *added* powers. Perhaps this has something to do with my attitude toward women, which has never been very real. [The line which follows has been blacked out vigorously with ink, but I remember it imperishably: *I kept thinking about Mother.*]

I believe that Bea's intentions in taking me to the fourth floor first may have been calculated, for on leaving the relative order and normality of the second, which we visited last, I had regained my composure to a passable extent. Here the rooms were furnished in a perfectly orthodox manner, simply but cheerfully, with curtained windows, vanity stands, chintz-covered chairs and all the ordinary appurtenances of a woman's boudoir. There was a common room, as well, with an old upright piano, a writing desk, bridge tables, playing boards and racks of tattered magazines. The patients were neatly dressed and groomed and exhibited at least a social degree of self-control. Several of them asked me intelligent and courteous questions and expressed their pleasure at meeting me.

When we stepped out of the building into the bright morning sunlight I felt exhausted. Bea made us a cup of powdered coffee in her office, and we chatted for a while. I was not very attentive, and I think she must have sensed this, for her conversation was very general and untechnical, as if her purpose was not to equip me with any more information for the moment but to study my reactions to the morning. She said that she would see me again after the evening O.T. meeting.

I spent the afternoon with Bob, working, to my great relief, with second-floor patients. I found this so absorbing that my apprehensions of the morning disappeared very shortly into my fascination with the work. Our first patient was a Miss Behrendt, a slender, intense, darkly pretty girl of about twenty-two, with a sullen manner and enormous energy. She asked to be taken walking, and we accompanied her at her own ferocious pace up the back road past Doctors' House (the big old farm building where many of the resident doctors live), Crowfields, and the pond. She strode with her fists in the pockets of her poplin jacket, her chin held very high with a look of contempt for us and our obvious difficulty in keeping abreast of her. Beyond the pond the road turns to the left, continuing on out of the hospital grounds and joining the state highway which runs adjacent to them; she made directly for it. When we were within a few yards of the road Bob stopped and said, "We'll have to go back now, Miss Behrendt."

"Why?" she asked indignantly.

"I'm sorry, but you're not allowed out of the grounds."

"I went to the movies in Stonemont just two nights ago."

"You had town privileges then, but they've been revoked since."

She stared at him for a moment, her face growing pale with rage, and advanced one foot slowly in front of her. Her socks and shoelaces were plastered with little green "beggar lice" pods from the weeds that grew along the roads.

"There are burs in my shoelaces," she said. "Take them out for me, please."

"We're your attendants, not your servants, Miss Behrendt," Bob said easily.

"*Take them out immediately.*"

"This isn't a very good way of getting your privileges restored."

"What do you mean by that?"

"I mean that I'll have to report your behavior, and if it doesn't improve you stand a very poor chance of getting your privileges back very soon."

"Are you trying to bribe me?"

"No."

"I'm going to report that you attempted to bribe me."

"Just as you like. Now let's go back to the Lodge."

She stood staring at him, her nostrils whitening with tension, and said shrilly, "This is outrageous. Outrageous!"

"Are you ready to go now?" Bob said.

She turned swiftly and walked back, at an even faster pace than we had come, toward the Lodge. When we had returned her to the floor, Bob took me into the office. The charge nurse here is Miss Jackson, a younger woman than most of the charge nurses, with red hair and a droll and melancholy face.

"How was Behrendt?" she asked.

"Pretty nasty," Bob said.

"She's been getting high for the last couple of days. You'd better write it up."

"Yes."

She handed him a report form, which he explained to me as he filled it in, writing the patient's name, the date and the time of the contact. Below, he wrote a brief summary of her activities and behavior: *Patient asked permission to go walking. Surly and uncommunicative. Attempted to leave hospital grounds by entering state highway. When detained became hostile and defiant. Threatened to report being bribed. No physical violence.*

He signed the report, *Robert Clayfield, O.T.,* and returned it to the nurse.

"We make these reports after every contact," he said. "They're very useful to the doctors. They can be pretty brief, but they ought to include anything unusual that happens."

"I see."

"What else can we do for you?" he asked Miss Jackson.

"I'd like to get Meaghan out, if I can. She hasn't been out of the building for days. See what you can do with her."

"All right."

We knocked at Mrs. Meaghan's door and were admitted by a cool, cultured voice, slightly European in quality. Mrs. Meaghan sat by her window reading a paper-bound French novel which she lowered into her lap, her forefinger dividing the leaves, and smiled at us formally. She is a slight, fastidious, Latin-looking woman in her middle thirties, with very fine features, a mass of black, severely styled hair and a constant controlled expression of pain. She said it was "very kind of us to call" but could not be persuaded to leave the building, as she was sure she would be done harm to. "I have many enemies," she explained to me gently.

"I'm sure you'd find it was perfectly safe," Bob said. "In any case, we'd be more than capable of protecting you."

"It is very kind of you. Perhaps another day. I would enjoy playing cards for a while, though, if you have the time."

"Yes, of course," Bob said. "Shall we go in the common room?"

"Yes, perhaps we would be more comfortable."

We sat in the common room and embarked upon a game of

five-hundred rummy, Mrs. Meaghan manipulating the cards with a graceful shrewdness that reminded me of a countess playing baccarat. It was now about three o'clock in the afternoon and the room was illumined with a soft golden glow from the afternoon sunlight, which fell halfway across the carpet and our table, casting a rime of radiance on motes of dust and strands of hair. The room was full of warm silence, broken only by the occasional creak of our wicker chairs or a murmured comment on the play, and a sense of peace, strangely innocent and nostalgic, like that one experiences in looking at old faded photographs in a family album—of people in straw hats, huge mustaches and ankle-length skirts, gathered about an ancient automobile and smiling into the sunlight of a long-forgotten afternoon—a timeless peace, undarkened by any future or anxiety. We had played for perhaps ten minutes when, stealing tranquilly into the still, archaic climate of the room, as if to furnish it appropriately with music from another time and world, came one of the loveliest sounds I have ever heard: a fragile, plaintive fluting of woodwind notes, ruefully, tenderly unreeling the melody of a folk tune, "The Ash Grove." I lifted my head to listen, enchanted by the sound.

"What is it?" I asked.

"It's Miss Arthur," Bob said. "It's a little flute she plays that she made herself. It's very pretty, isn't it?"

"She plays quite magically," Mrs. Meaghan said. She turned her head toward the open door, suspending the game for a moment while she listened. I could judge the extent to which she was moved by the fact that she laid down her cards, exposed, upon the table. In a moment, her eyes darkening, she turned to Bob and said, "I understand that you have limited her playing to certain hours. I think that's monstrous."

"*I* haven't," Bob said. "It was a staff decision. Some of the patients complained, I believe."

"Monstrous."

We resumed the game, rather perfunctorily, and I was scarcely conscious of the play for the next several minutes, listening to the

shower of clear cool notes in the still room, stretched out sometimes in a liquid tremolo, like the quivering of a drop of water
detaching itself from the tip of a leaf, or sprinkled in bright
arpeggios, as if shaken from wet branches by the sudden spring-
ing of a squirrel. She played another English ballad, "Sweet
William," and then a song that I had never heard, of indescribable
beauty. It had much of the quality of a folk tune—the poignant
air of melancholy and the same delicate progression of notes—
but something far more intense, as well: a kind of barbarous
innocence, like that of the most savage Scottish ballads, but
strangely notated and unfamiliar in its quality, as if the music
had been spun out of some unknown culture, long since forgotten
or not yet evolved. It was, as Mrs. Meaghan said, a magic sound.
As great an interest as I have in folk music, and as familiar as I am
with much of it, I have never heard a melody like this, and find
myself extremely eager to meet the performer of it.

Our last contact of the day was with Warren Evshevsky, a tall
scholarly-looking boy whom I met yesterday with Bea. Although
he has ground privileges, being lodged in Field House, he asked
us to play ping-pong with him, and as the rest of the second-floor
patients seemed to have been provided for, Bob agreed. There is
something very attractive about Warren. He is slow and solemn
in speech and movement, and there is a curious shyness and
indirection about the quality of his thought, as if he feared to
consider anything too categorically. He has long and very beautiful hands, the nails of which are bitten so deeply that I could
see tiny clots of dried blood flecking the pink, exposed quicks.
He is very conscious of this, and keeps his hands hidden as much
as possible, having even developed a Chinese-like habit of walking with the tips of his fingers interlocked, to conceal them. He
murmurs to himself almost constantly. Although Bea told me
yesterday that he had been a linguistic prodigy, he seems deliberately to avoid all intellectual subjects, and pointedly evaded
the early remarks about language with which I had hoped to appeal to his interests. He seems to be obsessed with physical illness;

he paused every few minutes as we played to take off or put on again a light woolen jacket that he had brought with him, explaining shyly that he felt either "a little chilly" or a "bit warm."

The evening O.T. meeting was very interesting. The day's activities were discussed briefly but comprehensively, with each worker giving a résumé of his contacts, elaborating on any unusual behavior or attitude, and offering his opinions as to the progress or decline of his patients, while Bea questioned us and took occasional notes. She asked me to wait after the meeting and we had a bottle of soda together from the dispensing machine inside the shop. She asked how I had got on, and I gave her my reactions as frankly as I could. These, in spite of my general enthusiasm and interest, included the confession that I felt some qualms at the prospect of working alone with patients.

"I would be surprised if you didn't," she said. "Even workers who are training for a career in O.T. feel that way in the beginning. After a week or two we'll know much better what your permanent reactions will be."

She is a delightful person; not really pretty, but attractive because of her warmth and intelligence. She has soft short brown hair, which she frequently lifts her hand to stroke in a pleasant feminine gesture, not of vanity but of concentration, frowning sometimes while she does so; and gray eyes of slightly different shades of color, which gives her round, rather old-fashioned-looking face a strangely disorganized appearance. I feel that we shall get on very well. She asked if I had formed any preferences among the patients I had worked with, and I said that I had found Warren Evshevsky the most interesting and sympathetic of the few that I had met and Miss Behrendt perhaps the least so.

"Yes, Warren is a very nice person," she said. "Everyone is fond of him. He's made a great deal of progress since he's been here, but for the last few months he's been in a terrible state. He's fallen in love with one of the women patients. That happens sometimes, of course, and it's always very difficult."

I asked how such a situation was handled.

"Well, if one of them is indifferent, it isn't so bad. But if they share the feeling, then it's much more difficult. We have to chaperone them, of course, if they're together; but if one or both of them have ground privileges, that isn't always possible. Usually it means that one of them has to have his privileges limited in order to prevent clandestine meetings. It isn't fair, but it's the best we can do. It's awkward, all around. I'm particularly anxious about Warren because he's such a sensitive soul and, when he's depressed, strongly suicidal; and he seems to have it awfully bad. I've seen him stand under her window for hours, listening to her play her flute. She plays a little wooden flute that she made."

"Oh, I heard her this afternoon," I said. "She plays beautifully."

"Yes. She's a fascinating girl—one of the most interesting patients we have, and the most difficult. None of us can do anything with her."

"Does she feel the same way about him?" I asked.

"No, not at all. I'm afraid it's going to be very hard on him. She's not the kind of person it would be much fun to be in love with."

She locked up the shop and we strolled across the grounds in the warm spring evening.

"Are you going into town?" I asked.

"No, I live here on the grounds, in the dormitory. I only go into Stonemont to the movies once in a while, and about every three months I go into Washington on a real binge and get tighter than a drumhead." She smiled at me in a professionally intimate way—as if already I shared with her a deep enough mutual feeling about this work to appreciate the feigned irony of her remark—which delighted me. I think it's fortunate for Bea that she is such a dedicated person, or she would be very lonely; or perhaps it is her loneliness that has made her so. I feel there is a great deal I can learn from her. From everyone here.

I am going to get into bed now and read for a while. I am reading *The Red and the Black*, which I think is a very powerful book; but I do not have much hope for Julien.

Grandma woke up just now, and I heard her call out in confusion, "Oh, Sonny, are you hurt? Have they wounded you?" I went down the hall and opened the door of her room very quietly and tiptoed in to their bed. She was asleep again, lying with her beautiful old work-worn hands curled up into fists with fear, and I could see the moonlight glinting on the gold band of her wedding ring. I kissed her on the cheek and whispered, "I'm all right now, Grandma," and she murmured, "Thank the Lord."

¶ FRI., APRIL 17:

This morning we had Case Histories. These are read to us in the lecture room by Dr. Lavrier, who is a sort of liaison officer between the professional and O.T. staffs. He is a remarkable man—not older than thirty-five, I would guess—whose appearance does not correspond at all with my idea of a psychiatrist's, as he wears a checkered sports jacket, a pink shirt and a spotted bow tie. He also has an aluminum-stemmed pipe of very complicated design, which looks like a piece of laboratory apparatus and around which he has developed a whole repertoire of manual mannerisms. This very dapper style of dress has been adopted, I think, as concealment for a painful sensitivity which gives his boyish face a strained and rather sorrowful look and invades his voice sometimes in the form of a nervous tremolo. It is an appearance which seems very much at odds with the precision and grasp of his thought, the swiftness and insight with which he understands and replies to inexpertly worded queries, and the expression of essential seriousness—even of severity—of his eyes.

The lectures—one of which is delivered to us every week—are to familiarize the therapy staff with the personal and medical histories of the patients they work with, and are fascinating in themselves. This morning's history I found particularly interesting, as the subject of it was Mrs. Meaghan, whom I met yesterday. She was the child of an American mining engineer living abroad, and was sent, from the ages of ten to sixteen, to a

Catholic boarding school in Belgium. Here she developed a homosexual relationship with a classmate, an English girl of her own age, an affair which went on for nearly two years. When it was finally discovered, both girls were sent home in disgrace, and Mrs. Meaghan spent the next several years under the very closely confined and troubled surveillance of her parents, who apparently were shocked and embittered by the affair. She became more and more subdued and eccentric, and at twenty-four was married, more or less at her parents' instigation and in what seems to have been a combined experimental, punitive and precautionary measure, to an English tutor, an ineffectual and complaisant man of thirty-seven who had been engaged to complete her education. The marriage was tacitly subsidized by her parents, and for the next three years the couple lived a retiring life in Berne. Here she renewed her association with the English girl, who had in some way discovered her whereabouts and begun corresponding with her. When the English girl moved, finally, to Berne and took an apartment in their immediate neighborhood, Mrs. Meaghan began very rapidly to deteriorate and had finally to be hospitalized. She does not believe that she has ever been married, although strangely enough she consents to being addressed as "Mrs. Meaghan." She has also developed "paranoid fantasies" about the Catholic Church, believes that it is conspiring to exterminate her, and has a terrible fear of anyone in clerical clothing. Neither will she recognize her parents or her relationship to them, insisting that she was a Belgian foundling whom they adopted. Her great obsession now is to locate her "true" parents, and to this end she engages in endless correspondence with European orphanages and welfare societies, which she keeps filed carefully in a large cardboard carton in her room. Her illness is also marked by frequent and periodic depression, during which she will not feed or clothe herself. She has an institutional history of three previous hospitals—two European and one American— and is considered to have made considerable progress, particularly within the last eight months of her stay here.

After the reading of this report—which was much more detailed than the brief summary I have given here—there was a discussion period, in which Dr. Lavrier commented freely, interpreted events and behavior of the history in psychiatric terms, and directed us as to the most useful and effective means of dealing with the patient.

"I think the best general course to follow," he said, "is a kind of liberal realism. I wouldn't tolerate her fantasies—even at the cost of losing companionship or contact with her—and certainly would never indulge them; but there's no need to be aggressive about it. I think it's best to make a consistent, calm distinction between fantasy and reality, without being argumentative about it, or getting her worked up. I wouldn't insist on activities for her, but continue to offer them daily, with a little mild persuasion. I'd like particularly to get her to one of the tea dances, although I understand she won't go near them. I hope you'll keep working on that."

He seemed to regard her case as a classical one—and therefore a particularly instructive one for us—in that it offered a "fairly simple pattern of withdrawal from reality." By this he meant, as he explained, that her delusions of persecution by the Church were a fairly straightforward dramatization and exaggeration of the feelings of guilt and the fear of punishment created by her expulsion from the convent school where she had studied; and the rejection of her parents an equally apparent reaction to the shame and outrage with which they had received the news of her behavior and the vindictive manner in which they had subsequently treated her. The delusional system of this patient, Dr. Lavrier explained, is so closely related to its cause that it is unusually easy to study the process of evasion by which she has escaped from an intolerable reality—the delusion being, in her case, simply an extension and hyperbole of the reality: "The Church punished me once, so it is determined to punish me still, even more severely; my parents virtually disowned me, so I will acknowledge being disowned by them; I will not recognize them."

There is a simplicity about this, a kind of insanely innocent logic, which I find oddly appealing and which increases my sympathy for these people greatly.

Bea introduced me to Dr. Lavrier after the discussion, and he asked me—it had apparently been prearranged between them—to stay for a few minutes. Our conversation, although it was conducted in a very informal way, was in fact, I suspect, an interview and part of a regular Lodge procedure to insure that their employees are of an acceptable standard of character and intelligence.

"Bea tells me you've made a good start," he said.

"I hope so. I haven't really had a chance to make many mistakes yet. I guess I'll make my share of them when I do."

"Well, we all do," Dr. Lavrier said. "But you feel reasonably confident about the work?"

"Yes. And very excited about it."

"Good. I don't know if Bea told you, but I'm a sort of counselor for the O.T. staff. Any problem you have of relationships with patients that seems to require a medical interpretation—something you can't work out with Bea—I'll be happy to help you with. And of course anything else that comes up that you might want to talk about—your own orientation, project ideas, anything at all. Perhaps you'd like to do some reading in the field."

"Yes, I would very much," I said. "I was going to ask Bea for some titles."

"Well, she can give you a better list than I can, on O.T. itself. For general background in psychiatry and mental illness, here are a couple of good standard surveys." He wrote the titles on his desk pad while he spoke. "And of course you can't do better than to read the masters: Freud, Jung, Adler. You may find this pretty steep going, but you can dip around in them until it takes a firm hold somewhere."

"Thank you very much."

"We don't have a strictly scholastic attitude here, although most of the doctors have been educated and analyzed in the Freudian tradition. But I think it's a good thing—particularly for a novice—to be aware of all the influences and attitudes that have gone into modern psychiatry. We have lectures once a week—besides case histories—which you'll find useful, too. A different staff doctor speaks every Monday morning from nine till ten. You ought to try and attend those pretty regularly."

"Yes, I will. I'm looking forward to them."

Our conversation came to a sudden halt—not an end, as I understood, for it was obvious that he had more to say—during which, while he studied frowningly and with unnecessary attention the list of titles he had written, corrected a perhaps imaginary error in his spelling and restored with elaborate care his fountain pen to his breast pocket, I sensed that he was suffering from the embarrassment of being required, by the responsibilities of his position, to make a succinct official estimate of my character; and being a man of natural diffidence and delicacy, he found it distasteful, I was aware, to do so under the pretense of a private relationship. I could not help wondering if this kind of fastidiousness was not a liability to a man whose very profession was the investigation of personality by means of expertly stimulated and sustained conversation; but then, I suppose that the interviewing of applicants represents a very incidental part of his duties and that the relationships of employer to employee and of analyst to patient are not, at any rate, comparable, the latter being so much more profound that a man might, by the very nature of the superior sensibility which makes him an artist at it, find himself handicapped at the former.

It is really astonishing how quickly certain personalities can become attuned to one another and how swiftly a sympathy can be established between them. I found myself so sensitive to Dr. Lavrier's position as my reluctant interlocutor and so anxious to relieve his embarrassment that I myself began casting about for topics which he might find productive and which I might introduce, with apparent innocence, for the purpose of my own improvisation upon them. On the wall behind his desk there was a group of three original oil paintings, framed in "antiqued" oak. Although I know nothing about art, these were remarkable enough to attract my unfeigned interest. They were abstractions, very vividly and boldly executed, the paint applied so thickly that it seemed to have been plastered to the canvas with a knife blade, and crusted here and there with bits of extraneous material— splinters of colored glass, wisps of straw and coarse grains of sand—which were incorporated with dazzling ingenuity into the fierce and somber improvisations in line, texture and color that the paintings appeared to represent. They gave me the feeling of bitter excitement with which I remember certain incidents of the war.

"Those are the work of a patient," Dr. Lavrier said, noting my attention to them, "an engineer who was here about two years ago. A remarkable man. Do you find them interesting?"

"Yes. I don't know why, but they remind me of a lot of modern poetry: a kind of explosive quality."

"Yes, they have. Schizophrenic art is fascinating. And astonishingly like what we call 'modern art' in many respects. Modern poetry, in particular, as you say, has many devices that resemble the aberrations of a certain type of schizophrenia which we call hypomania: the fragmentation, the same intense symbology, the neologisms, the compulsive internal rhyme and word association. It's quite amazing."

"Is the significance of that as obvious as it seems?" I asked.

Dr. Lavrier smiled and tossed his head in a gesture of pleased amusement. "That's something I'm really not allowed to speculate on—professionally, at any rate," he said. "I must leave that to the sociologists, or the critics. I don't think there's any doubt, though, that the world has been greatly influenced by the work of some extraordinary schizophrenic minds: Savonarola, Hitler, Van Gogh, Kafka—the Lord knows how many. The schizophrenic is not always easy to identify, even today. Particularly the very gifted paranoid type, with a highly organized delusional system and great intelligence and energy. They are very persuasive people, and there's no doubt that in times past they've been extremely active and influential members of society. They still are."

I asked how, if they were so effective in the world, it could be justified in calling them insane.

"Well, insanity is a matter of degree, of course: the degree of appropriateness of the delusion. And in marginal cases it's a very delicate thing to decide. How are we to regard Blake's visions? Or St. Teresa's? Or the testimony of St. John of the Cross? As madness or revelation? I suppose there are many modern psychiatrists who wouldn't hesitate to call them hallucinations, but they've comforted and inspired millions of people." He had all the while been manipulating his curious pipe, and now he tapped his teeth thoughtfully with the stem. "Mad people have a strange history," he said. "They've been savagely abused in many societies and treated with reverence in others. I suppose the fact is that we've never been quite sure about them. We're not yet. But we know a good deal more today than ever before; particularly in the last five or six years, the strides that have been taken are enormous. It's a very exciting thing to be alive at a time of so many critical developments in a science."

"Is it really a science?" I asked.

"I'm very pleased that you ask," he answered, smiling. "I much prefer to think of it as an art, myself; but I'm never sure of being forgiven for the idea."

I think he is a very likable man, for whom I felt a strong and immediate affinity.

This afternoon I worked with second-floor male patients, whose quarters are divided by a central partition from the female section of the floor. As Bob was away on a field trip, I accompanied Charles Mandel, who is the single member of the staff I have met so far that I do not like. He is a short, muscular, wiry-haired young man with a constant rather bitter expression on his face. His attitude to the patients seems abrupt and impatient, and to me it was unpleasantly officious. He made, for my benefit, a great show of his experience and authority, offering much gratuitous and rather condescending instruction and emphasizing his seniority by reminding me, at least three times, that he has been here for over eighteen months and was "in line" to succeed Greta as head of Recreation.

We worked with three patients, only one of whom I had not met before. This was a boy named Howard Thurmond, who cannot be older than sixteen and seems to be in a much poorer condition than the other second-floor patients. He talks and giggles incessantly, making extravagant comic gestures with his hands and peering with a look of owlish merriment from behind his thick-lensed glasses. He had been reading a book called *Zotz!*, which apparently concerns a character who has the preposterous ability to kill people by pointing his forefinger at them and shouting this nonsense syllable, a faculty which so delighted Howard that he attempted to duplicate it all the while we were with him, exterminating every nurse, attendant and patient who came our way. His constant manic good spirits, which I found infectious at first, became unbearably tedious in a very short while.

Our second patient was Mr. Palakis, a middle-aged man with whom I talked briefly in the shop about Dostoevski, the first day that I was here. Today he seemed anxious and depressed, mumbled a good deal and, when I attempted to resume our discussion, shook his head wearily and murmured something about, "Noisy . . . fatuous . . . useless." He has a habit of stopping suddenly while walking, lifting his clenched fist and staring at it sorrowfully in thought.

"These 'great' books," he said a moment later, ironically isolating the word, "make a lot of noise—oh, thundering great rhapsodies, they are—and for a while, while one is reading them, they succeed. They drown it out, you know: that terrible sound. One actually believes, for a moment, that it is possible to snare divinity in a web of rhetoric. But does it really matter that somewhere, sometime, a man has written a book? Does it change our condition? Even if one's attitude is changed, is his condition any different? I ask you quite humbly."

I said I was not sure of his meaning.

"That sound is always there," he said, "when the other noises stop; no matter how beautiful they've been—fiddle strings, iambs, the feet of dancers—when they stop, one hears it still. Listen." He lifted his hands, laying them on my and Mandel's arms, holding his head in an attitude of attention. "Do you hear it?"

"No."

"Listen."

I did, indeed, hear something then—perhaps the wind in the leaves, or the rummaging of a sparrow—as I confessed.

"Do you know what it is?" he said.

"The wind in the leaves, I think."

"No, it is the sound of teeth," he said. "Teeth, crunching through bone and muscle. It never stops. In my room it is particularly bad. I think there are rats in the walls. Last night it was fearful."

This is apparently a chronic auditory hallucination of his—one from which it must be dreadful to suffer. We walked for about forty minutes, and in a little while he seemed to have regained his spirits somewhat, launching into a long discussion of Dostoevski's minor . characters, particularly Lise, in *The Brothers Karamazov*, which was very perceptive and vigorous.

Our final patient, as yesterday, was Warren Evshevsky, who is now on Second Floor. I was surprised and disappointed to find that he had been returned there last night from Field House in a state of severe depression—not long, apparently, after our contact with him. He seemed to be suffering both humiliation and loss of confidence at this relapse, and was far less animated than yesterday. I was gratified and touched, however, to see that he greeted me with obvious if subdued pleasure, and was encouraged by his request for us to take him walking. He asked if he might go as far as the pond, but as we turned into the open stretch of road that leads across the farmland he caught sight of a group of women patients playing croquet on the green behind Field House, and he asked if he might watch them for a while instead. Mandel agreed, and we sat for perhaps half an hour in garden chairs on the flagstone terrace that overlooks the green, exchanging occasional random observations while we watched the women playing in the sunlight. With their unbound hair and light summer dresses and the mannered attitudes of the game, they had a pretty, old-fashioned look of pastoral charm, like the figures in an eighteenth-century landscape. I realized that Warren was hoping to find Miss Arthur, and although I have never seen her I was sure, from his air of disappointed melancholy, that she was not among them. He seemed content to remain, however, and sat with his elbows on the arms of his chair, his slender hands folded together with the finger tips clenched inside his palms, staring out with a brooding look of combined pleasure and affliction at the white limbs of the players, bare and bright in the sunlight, and the flashing of their hands and the soft confusion of their hair.

"It would be nice," he said once, "if we could have an outdoor concert sometime. I think many of the patients play."

Mandel objected that it would be impossible to transport a piano.

"Yes," Warren said. "Perhaps some chamber music, though. There are some lovely ensembles of Mozart's; one with a flute, which I think would be particularly appropriate."

I supported him animatedly, somewhat indignant at seeing this faint flicker of enthusiasm crushed so arbitrarily, and feeling that Mandel's objection was very poorly calculated to improve his state of despondency.

"I'll mention it to Bea this evening," I said.

"Will you really? I think it would make a very pleasant afternoon. Perhaps we could substitute it for one of the tea dances sometime during the summer."

"I don't see why it couldn't be managed," I said. "If we can find enough musicians."

"I'd be very happy to help," he said. "I play a violin, you know. Not well, of course, but adequately, I think."

A little later, as we walked back to the main building, he asked my nationality, and when I replied that I was of English derivation he said, "Oh, the English are the most beautiful of all the races. Will you marry an English girl? I mean a girl of English descent?"

"I have no idea," I said, and could not help smiling. "Right now it doesn't seem very likely that I'll ever marry anyone."

"Are you opposed to marriage?"

"No, not at all. But just now there isn't anyone I'm interested in marrying; and even if there were, I don't make nearly enough money to support a family."

It seemed perfectly natural to make such a remark at the time, but it now seems an unduly personal thing to have said. I think this was an indiscretion which I must guard against in the future. As we went up in the elevator to return him to his floor he asked, twisting his clenched hand nervously, "Would you think that I was Jewish?" I was about to reply that I hadn't really thought about it at all, when I remembered Bea's injunction always to be perfectly candid with the patients; so I said instead, "Yes, I imagined that you were."

"Yes, many people think so," he said, nodding with a kind of vigorous disillusionment. "But I am Polish. My grandfather was a priest."

I mentioned his plan for a concert at the evening O.T. meeting. I think Mandel must have resented this degree of initiative on my part, for he certainly did his best to discourage it, contending that patients who were interested in music would much prefer to use the record collection in Field House, where they can enjoy both privacy and their own choice of selections, that there was always the threat of bad weather on any prearranged date and the possibility of inattention or misconduct on the part of the

audience, which would be severely embarrassing to the performers and might well end in chaos.

Greta met these objections by saying that it need not be a
matter of compulsory attendance and that, as only those who
were genuinely interested in music would be present, one should
be able to anticipate good order on their part. Bob supported the
suggestion by adding that, in case of bad weather, the concert
could always be postponed or moved into Field House lounge.
Mandel, however, insisted that patients with a particular interest
in music were all the more likely to be critical of an inexpert
performance and to express their displeasure with proportionate
vehemence. Other objections were that there was no one on the
O.T. staff sufficiently trained in music to rehearse and direct
such a project competently, the amount of time it would take to
prepare, and difficulty of making up a program for the limited
number of performers who could expect to be recruited.

I was disappointed but at the same time, I think, persuaded to
a more realistic view of the matter by Bea's opinion that it might,
considering the capriciousness of the patients and their char-
acteristic lack of ability to sustain interest or effort in anything,
prove too ambitious an undertaking.

"It would take several weeks of concentrated rehearsal to bring
a program up to concert level," she said, "even acknowledging that
we don't expect a professional performance; and with all the ups
and downs they go through, I don't know if we ought to demand
such an effort of them. If it were done at all, I think it ought to
be done in a very leisurely way: an occasional 'musical afternoon'
together, without the pressure of a schedule or any fixed date for
the performance. Then, perhaps, after they had practiced a piece
together for a number of sessions, ask if they would like to invite
some of the other patients to hear them play. I think the anxiety
and discipline of a formal concert would be too strenuous for
them."

She suggested that we postpone our decision and take it up,
after everyone's further consideration, at a later meeting. She

asked me to wait again while she locked up the shop and said, smiling, "I hope you don't have any hard feelings about my stepping on your idea."

"No, of course not. You convinced me that it was a pretty foolish one."

"It isn't foolish at all. I'm delighted you brought it up. I had the feeling that you really cared about it."

"Yes, I did. I feel as if I'd like to do something for Warren."

"I know," she said. "And I'm sure that you will. It's a pity he had to be sent back to Second, but I was expecting it."

"Yes."

We were walking across the lawn toward the cafeteria and she stopped to pick up one of the fallen blossoms from the poplars, plucking the petals off it while she spoke.

"You see, we have to consider these things very thoroughly, because it's so easy to make a disastrous mistake. I'm sure that Warren's real idea is to make some kind of a permanent arrangement by which he can enjoy Lilith's company; I think he hopes to persuade her to participate—his suggesting the flute concerto is a pretty good clue. After all, it's pretty enterprising of him; but I'm not so sure that such a sustained exposure to Lilith would be good for him. Especially considering the shape he's in right now. I want to talk to Dr. Lavrier about it first, anyway. By the way, what did you think of him—Dr. Lavrier, I mean?"

"I liked him very much. And I enjoyed his lecture tremendously."

"Good. I think you made quite an impression on him," she said. "He thinks you'll get along very well here; and so do I."

It is impossible to describe how pleased I was by these words.

This evening, on my way home from the Lodge, I met Laura. I had stopped at the library to take out some of the books that Dr. Lavrier had listed for me, and was glancing through one of them as I walked back up toward Frederick Avenue. When I looked up, at the corner, she was standing in front of me with a bag full of groceries, waiting for the light. My first impulse was to glance hastily away, but as she was looking directly at me from a distance of not more than five feet, this was impossible and would have been, at any rate—as I realized immediately—a childish thing to do. The realization did nothing, however, to improve the spontaneity of my conversation, for I stood smiling dumbly, leaving it to Laura to speak first.

"Hello, Vincent. How are you?" she said, with what seemed to be a certain amount of confusion.

"Hello. My goodness. I didn't expect to see you, Laura."

"I know. I thought you were going to walk right off the curb, you were so wrapped up in that book."

She looked a little older and thinner, but also prettier than she used to be, and for the first time that I can ever remember she seemed a little embarrassed. She said she had heard that I was back and was very pleased about it.

"Someone said that you'd been wounded, Vincent. I hope it wasn't anything serious."

"No, it wasn't too serious," I said.

"Oh, that's good. You certainly look well."

"Thank you," I said. "You do too, Laura. I guess marriage must agree with you."

"Well, I suppose it does."

"How is your husband?"

"He's very well, thank you. He's working with the Electric Power Company right now. He's hoping to be made office manager next fall."

"Oh, that's fine," I said.

"What are you doing, Vincent? Are you going to college?"

"No, I'm working over at Poplar Lodge."

"At the asylum?"

"Yes. Well, it's not really an asylum; it's a private mental hospital. I'm in the Occupational Therapy department."

"Really? Do you like it?"

"Yes, I like it very much," I said. "I think it's turned out to be just the thing I've always wanted to do."

"Oh, that's fine. I'm sure you'll do very well, if you feel that way about it."

We lapsed into a strained silence, and it seemed as if the light would never change. I finally thought of asking how her mother was.

"She's pretty well, but she's aging, you know. Especially since Father died."

"Yes, I guess she must be. Well, I hope you'll say hello to her for me."

"I will. We want you to come and visit us sometime, Vincent. I'd like you to meet Norman."

"Yes, I certainly will, sometime," I said. "It's very nice to have seen you, Laura."

"It's nice to have seen you too, Vincent."

The light had changed, finally, and I turned away, as if starting down Diamond Avenue, and then looked back for a moment to watch her cross the street. I remember Howie Elliot telling me once that girls walk differently after they have lost their virginity, and I could not help watching to see if I could distinguish any such difference in the way Laura walked. I could not, and I'm sure it's just a schoolboy's tale, anyway; but I wish I hadn't done it. It's one of those small, insignificant weaknesses that for some reason you can never quite get out of your mind and that rankle you for years.

I HAVE PRAISED the candor of my journal and its usefulness in sustaining the veracity of this narrative, but having come to what is one of the most important single events of my story I find myself, on this occasion at least, betrayed by both its brevity and obliquity. The day of my first meeting with Lilith is recorded in this singularly short and ambiguous entry:

¶ *THURS., APRIL* 23:
When I heard Miss Arthur playing the flute the other day I *felt* there was something familiar about that music. I don't mean about the tune itself—I had never heard it before—but about the *quality* of the music—as if by listening to it I had come in contact with something I had known or seen somewhere, however briefly, the way an odor or a scrap of conversation or the exact look of a landscape will suddenly remind you of something you can't quite identify but which you are sure you have experienced before. This looks absurd when I write it down on paper, and it probably isn't very important, anyway; but I think it's rather interesting and exciting just the same, because after meeting her today I'm *sure* she's the girl. I must have acted pretty strangely: I think I stared at her for a full ten seconds while I was trying to remember, but she said nothing. Was it because she recognized me, too? I'm almost sure of it! There was that look in her eyes when she turned around from the window—but I suppose I could have imagined that, as well, because it was four years ago and she saw me only for an instant. But then there was that remark she made about "breaking things." A very faint allusion, perhaps, but possible.

And it *is* possible; because Bea told me earlier that she had been at the Lodge before—about four years ago! There was something intensely familiar, too, about the way she ran and danced. If only I had heard her laugh, I could be positive, I think; but she would not laugh all the while we were with her.

Should not have helped her to pick away those grass blades. Something not right about that, but what could I do? Remember Miss Behrendt making a similar request about burs in shoelaces, but how differently it was made! Tone of insolent command made it possible to refuse. But this was very different. What should I have said? "No, you'd better do it yourself"? Bob didn't seem to feel there was anything unusual about it, though.

I can't get down to this journal tonight. I think I'll leave some blank space and fill it in later, when I feel more like it. Want to remember these:

The rain. Inscription on wall in her language. Spinning wheel. My story about Shelley—did not laugh. Running barefoot on the lawn. (Was she barefoot before? One thing I can't remember. Feel less sure all the time that I ever saw her at all that day.) Dull meeting afterward. Bea cranky.

I must remember to buy a can of white enamel for my bed. It must be years since it was painted, because it's turning brown and is all chipped off around the bottoms of the legs where the carpet sweeper has bumped into it. I hate sordid-looking beds.

Rain has stopped. Must get out and walk. Perhaps tomorrow I will make Lilith laugh.

This entry is followed by two blank pages which, my intentions notwithstanding, have never been filled in; and because of the importance of the day it is an omission which I feel I must amend in some detail. Fortunately, my delinquency as a journalist does not matter greatly here, as the events of that morning are fixed indelibly in my mind.

It was raining when I woke up—a very fine, cool rain that misted the kitchen windows and gave to objects outside, as I sat having coffee, a misshapen and somewhat mournful appearance. I remember particularly the look of an old small-wheeled sidewalk bicycle that had belonged to me when I was ten or twelve and which, in clearing out the storage shed at the back of the yard a few evenings before, I had left leaning against the cherry tree. It stood, dripping and ruined, under the dark tree, its handlebars warped mournfully by the wet pane, its saddle frayed and rotting and its wheels drawn out into the writhing oblates that one sees in fun-house mirrors, a deformed and derelict memento of my childhood. I remember that it made me feel quite sad. I walked to work through the rain, and as I never wear a hat my hair was soaked by the time I arrived at the Lodge. I sat rubbing it with brown-paper towels from the staff lavatory when Bea came up the outside steps into the shop.

"You ought to wear a hat," she said.

"Yes, I guess I should."

"You look very gloomy. Don't you like the rain?"

"No, not since the war."

"Because of flying in it?"

"Yes. The first thing we used to do when we woke up was to look at the sky; and when it's raining now in the mornings I still feel sort of uneasy. About the only thing we used to pray for with real conviction was good weather."

"We do, here, too," Bea said. "Rainy days are hell, because they've all got to be kept indoors. The shop and floors are crowded and everyone's in a nasty temper." She stood her umbrella in the sink and, according to her daily custom, put a percolator on the little gas burner and measured several spoons of coffee into it; every morning, while the day's schedule was discussed, we sprawled in the big leather armchairs and drank it out of paper cups. "It's funny how rain affects many of these people," she said, standing at the window when she had finished preparing the coffee and looking out at the wet grounds. "They're so indifferent to external things, you wouldn't expect it. The third and fourth floors are particularly restless on a day like this. I was going to

137

send you up there this morning, but I think you'd better go to Second, instead. Bob's going to work with Lilith Arthur this morning. You haven't met her, have you?"

"No. The one with the flute?"

"Yes, I was telling you about her the other day. She's a fascinating girl. She has one of the most perfectly constructed delusional systems of any patient on record here—or anywhere, I imagine. Usually a schizophrenic's 'other world' is fragmentary, illogical and never very stable; but hers is astonishingly methodical and complete. She doesn't just escape into a jumble of disorderly hallucinations; she's constructed an entire universe for herself, with its own history, its own cosmology, its own laws and art, even its own language." She nodded at my murmur of surprise and went on. "She's literally invented a language of her own—a very good one, too, I understand, although I haven't studied it— which she speaks and writes in most of the time. She's even composed a literature in it for her private world—two or three novels, poems, stories, and a whole tradition of folk music, which she plays on her flute."

"That must have been what I heard her playing the other day," I said. "It was the strangest music I've ever heard."

"Yes, it is strange. She's made up a tonal system of her own, with quarter notes, something like the Oriental scale, I think. She makes her own clothes, too—even the cloth for some of them, on a loom in her room—paints remarkable pictures with vegetable colors which she extracts by hand, cooks when she's allowed to— anything but meat, which she won't touch—and practices a kind of private religion-magic. However mad it may sound, this is a tremendous creative achievement, and a wonderfully orderly and scientific one, which makes most of our own seem pretty trivial. I wonder sometimes if she shouldn't just be allowed to enjoy it."

"I don't understand why anyone with an intellect like that can't learn to get along in the world," I said.

"No, it's hard to. But it seems to me sometimes as if that weren't the question—not that she *can't*, but almost as if she refuses to."

Bea poured out the coffee for us and carried her cup to the window sill, where she stood stirring it thoughtfully. In a moment she appeared to complete her thought, saying, "Out of pride, or anger."

"Why?" I asked. "What makes her proud, or angry?"

"Well, there are one or two clues, but she resists analysis so strongly and effectively that it's pretty hard to explore them. I suppose the main one is that she had an older brother who was killed in an accident—a fall of some kind; but whether there's any real connection between that and Lilith's illness is difficult to determine. It happened about three years before she was hospitalized, and there doesn't seem to have been any deleterious effect at the time. She had a normal reaction of grief, which she got over, apparently, in a reasonable amount of time. But outside of that, there aren't any particularly critical incidents, or any long chain of predisposing circumstances, such as you often find.

"She comes from a cultured, upper-class family who gave her everything in the world—including love, as far as we can discover. They seem to be stable and rational people who are devoted to Lilith and have raised her in a most generous and affectionate way. She was sent to a private school in Vermont, where she was a brilliant scholar and formed quite normal and apparently happy relationships, both with her classmates and teachers. She had already distinguished herself in several fields—mathematics, philosophy and music—by the time she was fifteen. Then, after her second year at college, she simply began to withdraw. There doesn't seem to be any immediate reason for it, at all. She just stopped going to classes, stopped seeing her friends, became negligent and contemptuous and, finally, completely dissociated. Apparently she must have expressed some pretty defiant or unorthodox viewpoints, because she was finally expelled from college, and I remember that the phrase 'unsuitable influence' was used. But just what that means—whether there was any overt misconduct on her part—is pretty hard to find out, because small, exclusive schools maintain a professional discretion about those things, particularly when there isn't any tangible evidence; and I'm sure Lilith is too subtle, and somehow too dignified, to expose herself to ordinary mortal policework, anyway." Bea lifted her coffee cup, sipped at it for a moment and then smiled at me. "I'm a little in awe of her, as you can probably see. Most of the patients have pretty obvious frailties, which sooner or later you discover; but she seems completely invulnerable, somehow. I don't like to go near her. I really dislike her very much."

She paused and frowned into her cup as if somewhat disconcerted by the failure of her objectivity, but in a moment she went on to give me, very briefly, a summary of Miss Arthur's medical history. I was surprised to learn that she had been here before— about four years ago, when she was only eighteen—treated for ten months and then discharged, at her parents' wish and with the divided consent of the staff, as having achieved a "cosmetic cure." This is to say that although she was known not to be permanently and entirely well, it was believed that she could behave responsibly in most social situations and that a gradual reintroduction to outside life, with perhaps a limited degree of professional activity of some kind, might be the best possible therapy for her at the time. She was returned to her home, did part-time work at a public library and went on privately with her studies; but after a time she began to fall back into the same pattern of withdrawal and deep fantasy, and eighteen months ago had been sent back by her parents to the Lodge.

While we talked other members of the staff arrived, and during the meeting that followed their arrival there were brief periods of sunlight between the morning showers, which made the wet panes of the windows sparkle brilliantly. When I walked across to the main building with Bob there were pools of water in the gray gravel of the walks and many earthworms, dead and bleached pale, lying about on the wet ground. I have always hated this phenomenon after a rain; it is like offal from a flooded sewer.

The showers were still too frequent and heavy for outdoor activity, and I felt the restlessness of which Bea had spoken among the second-floor patients, who were gathered sullenly in the lounge or stood staring out through the wire netting of the screened porch. Miss Arthur did not answer when we knocked at her door. After waiting for a moment Bob knocked at it more sharply, and when there was still no reply he turned the handle and went into her room. I did not see Lilith immediately, as she was standing at the window directly in front of him, and in the moment of automatic orientation which one's eyes make on entering an unknown room I had time to take a swift inventory of its furnishings. These were extraordinary, as I have already indicated: a spinning wheel with a spindle of ragged flax, a small monk's desk with a sloping top on which lay a sheet of manuscript text with a half-completed illumination, a clutter of paintboxes, jars and brushes, and on the wall above her bed, painted in huge black letters, a line of text in her invented language: HIARA PIRLU RESH KAVAWN. There was a scent in the room, too, which I cannot describe—not a perfume, for no other woman I have ever known has used it—but which was always about her and which I can recall now, as delicate and heady as ever, as I write this: a freshness, moist, cool and faintly bitter, like crushed verbena leaves. These impressions were made in a single instant; as Bob moved aside to allow me entrance my eyes went quickly beyond him to Lilith's figure, where she stood beside the window, following with her finger tip the trickle of a water drop down the wet pane. Although her back was toward us, there was something so startlingly evocative in the posture of her body and in her soft, loose hair, fired into frosty radiance by the sunlight through the wet glass, that I felt the sudden stilling of my breath and body.

"I did not ask you to visit me," she said.

"I know; but I thought you might like to meet Mr. Bruce," Bob said. 'He's very interested in your music."

She turned to face me slowly, and as my recognition—if it was such—grew complete I stared at her, as I have written in my journal, for a full ten seconds, studying with a strange, welling delight the features that I had remembered with astonishing fidelity from one moment of a summer four years past: the pale, fragile face that had peered at me with shy mockery from the parted willows, the dark violet eyes and somewhat savage tenderness of mouth and the lovely hands whose movements had altered the rhythm of my imagination for years. Her eyes seemed to widen for an instant with a look which for some reason I was eager to interpret also as recognition, but after a moment she lowered them and, looking at the floor, said softly, "Does it disturb you?"

"What?"

"My music?"

"No; I think it's beautiful. I heard you the other afternoon, when I was in the common room."

"They only let me play for an hour a day. Do you think that's fair?"

"We have to consider the comfort of all the patients, Miss Arthur," Bob said ingratiatingly. "Most of them enjoy it, I know; but to those who don't appreciate art, we must be merciful."

She smiled and leaned back against the sill, lifting her hand and parting a strand of her long hair. Looking up at me from her lowered eyes, she asked, "Are you the new O.T.?"

"Yes."

"And have you come to instruct me in mercy also, Mr. Bruce?"

"I hope not," I said, composing myself determinedly. "I don't trust anyone who teaches virtue. Do you know Shelley's story about that?"

"No."

"He had a schoolmaster who used to instruct his class in the Beatitudes by saying, 'Now, boys, be merciful; or I shall flog you until you are.'"

I hoped fervently that she would laugh—I could not fail to recognize that cool, sweet spray of merriment—and found myself leaning tensely forward in anticipation. I think she very nearly did; but sensing my eagerness for her to do so, she suppressed it and confined herself, with some restraint and out of an imponderable perversity, to a swift appreciative smile.

"Oh, yes; that's how they teach mercy, isn't it?" she said. And after a moment, with a note of grave approval which delighted me: "I'm glad you liked my flute."

"Yes, very much. It has a beautiful tone. Bob says you made it yourself."

"No, that isn't true. It was given me by the Elders as my Wisdom Gift. It's a very old one. Would you like to see it?"

"Yes, very much."

She left the window in a rapid gentle movement and, opening a drawer of her desk, took out a little bamboo flute and handed it to me. It was a double block flute, something like a recorder, with two tubes, for separate fingering with each hand, bound together with little bands of brass and decorated with a design in red lacquer. The holes and mouthpiece were carved with great skill and precision, and the whole instrument was an example of exquisite craftsmanship. She stood watching as I turned it over in my hands.

"Do you play?"

"No. I wish I did. It's a beautiful instrument. What does it mean—a wisdom gift?"

"It is given for our first deed of understanding, the first thing we do, or say, or in some way express, that shows the beginning of wisdom."

"Like a coming-of-age present," I said.

"Yes; but it has nothing to do with age. Some people receive it when they're five or six, and some never do."

I was about to say that it was a charming custom—which indeed it struck me as being—when it occurred to me that it might be a very poor policy to encourage her fantasies by applauding them, however appealing they might seem. Not having dealt before with so persuasive or highly organized a delusion in a patient, I felt suddenly very uncertain as to what degree of acceptance or resistance I should offer it and was consequently grateful for Bob's comment that he could not understand why she preferred to believe the flute had been given to her. "I would be very proud of having made it myself," he said.

She took the flute from me without replying and laid it back in the drawer, looking down at it for a moment and smiling as she touched the slender lacquered tubes with her finger tip.

"Can you remember the first wise thing you ever did, Mr. Bruce?" she asked.

"No. I'm afraid it has yet to occur."

"Good. Then perhaps I shall have the opportunity of witnessing it." She looked at me gaily as she said this, and I smiled at her.

"I hope you won't have to stay here that long," I said. "I'm afraid it may be some time yet."

She sat down on the bed and laced her fingers, dropping her hands into her blue skirt and looking down at her bare feet, her head a little inclined. The window had darkened suddenly and the room was gray.

"I'd like to offer you some tea," she said, "but I only have one cup and saucer. Or do you drink tea in the morning?"

"Not ordinarily," Bob said, "but it sounds like a very good idea. I'll see if I can get some cups from the office."

"Thank you."

He went out into the hall and I stood silently for a moment, looking down at the sheet of decorated manuscript on her desk.

"What is this?" I asked.

"It's a very old copy of the Data—a section of the Gospels— which I have been permitted to illuminate because I have a certain skill with my hands."

"It's beautiful work," I said.

"Thank you." She sat motionless, watching me gently. "Won't you sit down, Mr. Bruce?"

"Thank you." I sat down in the chair facing her, meeting with some difficulty the level studiousness of her eyes.

"Why did you come here?" she asked in a moment.

"Well, I had to have a job."

"Of course; but you could have gone to work in a butcher shop."

"No. I've been working in a butcher shop for the last three years. I wanted to do something that would . . . help."

"Not just for adventure?"

"I don't think so. I'm not much of an adventurer."

"Oh, I think you are," she said.

"Why?"

"Will you think I'm rude? You will."

"No."

"Well, adventurous people always look rather ill at ease. They are shy, you know—not bold at all, as people believe. They go stumbling about the world, being scolded, breaking things, always looking for a place where they will feel they belong. They have that crooked look."

"That crooked look?"

"Yes. Of not matching anything. Other people are sort of smoothed-down looking, you know; they get worn away by life until they fit it. But really adventurous people never do—they're full of points and angles that stick out everywhere. They have that crooked look. That . . . terrible uniqueness."

The quality of her voice changed as she spoke this last phrase, as if the effort of discovering and pronouncing it had suddenly solemnized her thought. She sat watching my hands for a moment in reverie.

"Their hands, for example, don't seem to fit anything in the world; not a plow handle, or a keyboard, or a sword. Nothing that we know." She made a slight oppressed movement of her head. "And when they are dead they lie so empty, as if they had never held the thing they yearned for. Never, in all their life. As if they begged to hold it—even for an instant—even in death."

I had taken, I must confess, an immodest pleasure in her obvious, if indirect, attention to myself and in what I was pleased to consider the cunning of her reference to my "breaking things"; but seeing suddenly the austerity of her eyes, I felt myself—I am aware of the absurdity of the word—betrayed; betrayed and inexplicably repelled by her aspect. Still staring at my hands, she turned her own over in her lap, curling the fingers upward slightly in a strengthless, groping attitude, to illustrate the image she had spoken.

"A golden apple, or a scroll of fire. Or the breast of some impossible girl that they could never touch."

I folded my hands involuntarily in a quaint, fastidious way, as if to dissociate them from any such desire, asking, "Have you known many such adventurers?"

She lifted her face to me wearily. "No, there are not many."

I remember feeling a distinct sense of relief at Bob's re-entry into the room and at the cheerful clink of china which accompanied it.

She served us tea, boiling the water on a small hot plate which she kept in her closet and handing the cups to us with a sedate formality that seemed half parody and half genuine demureness. There were alternate sunlight and shadow on the windowpane which made her hair flame and then wane suddenly, like a blown fire.

Once I looked up from my teacup to see her smiling at me.

"Do you think I am successful as a chatelaine, Mr. Bruce?" she asked.

I said I was not sure what the word meant.

"The mistress of a great estate. I like to pretend that I am, sometimes, with many handsome, earnest knights to serve me. Is that what you call a delusion, Mr. Clayfield?"

"Not if you can distinguish it as such," Bob said.

"Oh, I can," she said. "You all help me to make the distinction constantly, by so generously refusing to be chivalrous."

"I don't call that fair." Bob said. "Aren't we always the soul of courtesy?"

"And yet you wouldn't let me have tin snips in my room to cut the brass for my . . . for my metalwork."

"Tin snips are also very useful for cutting the wire from windows."

She smiled and lifted her chin reproachfully, murmuring, "*Honi soit qui mal y pense*. I wish you would make that the motto of this house."

"What is yours?" I asked, raising my eyes to the printed words on the wall above her bed.

"Oh, mine is very different. Only your mottoes are about evil. Ours are always about joy." She did not offer to explain it literally, however, but turned her eyes to the window and sat staring at the wet pane. In a moment she set down her teacup and asked, "May I go for a walk?"

"It's raining," Bob said.

"Only a little, now and then. And if it starts to rain heavily I promise to come in right away." Bob stared at her with a droll look of severity. "I'll be very good," she murmured.

"All right. But I'll make you remember that promise if you aren't."

"You really are very good to me!" she cried, jumping up delightedly. "I'm sorry I said such hateful things about you. Will you forgive me?"

As we went down in the elevator she stood beside me, staring at the round leather insignia which I had not yet cut from the breast of the old flight jacket I was wearing: a snarling black cat imposed upon the scarlet numeral 13.

"What does it mean?" she asked, touching it with her finger tip.

"It's my squadron insignia, from the war."

She ran her finger over the brightly painted surface of the leather disk and asked placidly, "Have you been in a war?"

"Yes, I just got back from one."

"And are you a hero?"

"No."

"No, I thought not. It doesn't fit you properly."

Bob had no sooner opened the elevator door than she bounded out of it with the fresh, wild gaiety of an uncaged animal and began to run joyfully about the wet grass of the lawn.

"Oh, it's wonderful!" she called to us. "Come and see. Take off your shoes and run. It feels so wonderful!"

Bob shook his head and smiled. We stood watching her with our hands in our pockets, feeling faintly self-conscious at the somewhat ignominious contrast between her exuberant beauty and our own air of rather uneasily preserved authority. Yet it was delightful to watch her running and pirouetting under the rainy trees, her yellow hair splashing and her blue skirt billowing about her bare legs, vaulting over the stone benches and leaping high into the air sometimes to catch the lower branches of the willows and shake down a shower of raindrops from the wet leaves. She would brush them out of her hair and eyes, laughing with pleasure and shivering with their coldness on her bare arms. When it began to rain again—as it did very soon—she came quite obediently, panting from her run, and stood beside us on the steps of Field House under the shelter of the eaves.

The lawn had been mowed the evening before, and there were many little blades of wet grass stuck to her feet and ankles. She crouched down to remove them, her chin resting on her knee and her hair falling in damp strands across her face as she plucked the grass blades singly from her skin.

"Oh, there are hundreds!" she said impatiently. "I'm covered with them. Mr. Bruce, won't you help me?"

It seemed so innocent and natural an appeal that one could not refuse without appearing unpleasantly officious or prudish, or without producing a delicately complicated set of reactions which would have been far more provocative, I felt, than a good-natured, spontaneous compliance. Yet, as I knelt down to help her I could not help feeling a faint throe of misgiving as to the entire propriety of my doing so; and I was troubled that evening, as my journal indicates, by the memory of the panting girl with her damp skirts and ragged shining hair, smiling softly as I knelt before her to pick the bright-green blades of wet grass from her white feet.

O<small>N THE DAY</small> after I met Lilith for the first time a field trip had been organized to Great Falls. These day-long excursions were a monthly feature of the O.T. department and much anticipated by the patients. They automatically included all second-floor and Field House patients who wished to attend, and any from the third and fourth floors who were considered to be in a responsible enough condition. This generally made up a group of from ten to fifteen people, who, under the supervision of three or four members of the O.T. staff, were driven in the Lodge limousines to such neighboring points of interest as Sugar Loaf, the Sky-line Drive, or the monuments and memorials of Washington.

These trips were scheduled only tentatively, as, being outdoor projects, they depended for their success on the weather; but as the showers of the previous day had cleared away completely, Bea decided, at the morning meeting, that the trip should take place. Mandel, Wren Thomas—one of the Antioch students—and Bob Clayfield were assigned as escorts, and I was very greatly pleased that Bea asked me to accompany them. It was, on this occasion, a small group of only eight patients, with most of whom I was already acquainted: Warren Evshevsky; Howard Thurmond, the giggling second-floor patient; Sonia Behrendt; Mr. Palakis, the Dostoevski enthusiast; and Lilith Arthur. Those whom I knew only briefly were Daniel Hagan, a scowling middle-aged Irishman from Field House, and two girls from Second Floor. Bea gave us instructions about accidents, insubordination and so forth, and cautioned us especially about keeping Warren and Lilith under surveillance.

"It must be done tactfully, of course," she said, "but firmly and frankly, nevertheless. Warren, of course, will consider it a heaven-sent opportunity, so you'll have to be careful that he doesn't annoy her. Vincent, you can make that your special province, if you like; you get along with him very well. Lilith almost never signs for these trips, and Dr. Lavrier is delighted that she has. We want to encourage her to take more of them, so try to keep her from getting upset. We've made special sandwiches for her—no meat or eggs—and I think you ought to let her take her flute, or prisms, or anything else she might want to bring along. I just hope she doesn't back out before you get her in the car; that's what usually happens."

Bea's fears were justified; when we knocked at Lilith's door there was no answer. Bob knocked again and asked if she was ready.

"Oh, it's you," she said. "Come in."

She was sitting in her window seat playing with a pair of crystal prisms, which, as we talked, she would hold in the sunlight to cast miniature rainbows, sometimes upon the white flesh of her forearm, sometimes upon the sill or through a square of pale-blue silk that she held draped across her fingers, peering all the while with soft fascination at the livid, glowing bars of color of the projected spectrums and varying the effects she produced in many imaginative and often startling ways. She would let the rays of chromatically divided light fall on a mirror, and from there reflect them to the wall or ceiling where they would form quivering, vivid, many-colored patches of illumination; or sometimes fit the prisms together, their bases opposed, so that the light would enter through one apex and, after being broken into its band of bitter primary hues and then recomposed—re-fused, as it were—in its passage through the crystal, emerge from the other as white light again, its purity and integrity restored.

"We're waiting for you, Miss Arthur," Bob said. She breathed on one of the prisms and polished it gently on her sleeve, her eyes declined.

"I'm sorry, I don't think I can go."

"Why can't you go?" he asked.

"They told me not to."

"Who told you?"

"My people." She turned her face toward us with a look of genuine regret. "I wanted to go very much. But they came last night and told me that it would be unwise. I mustn't disobey them."

"But you signed to go," Bob said.

"Yes. That was why they came."

We stood staring at her for a moment in silence, baffled by her unseen counselors. She closed her eyes and turned the prism slowly, casting the light upon her lids, where it lay in tremulous, beautiful disintegration. "It doesn't matter very much, does it?" she asked.

"It doesn't matter to us," Bob said. "But I think it would do you a lot of good. You haven't had a trip for months."

"I know. And I wanted to see the falls. Are they very high?"

"Yes. It's a beautiful sight."

"It must be lovely." She opened her eyes slightly, still holding the prism to cast the light upon her face, and murmured from behind her mask of luminous motley, "Are you going, then, Mr. Bruce?"

"Yes."

"Oh, I'm sorry. I would have liked to talk to you again. But I mustn't disobey them. You have no idea how they torment me when I do."

"Why did they say it was unwise?" Bob asked.

"Because I would have to eat meat."

"No; we've made you a special lunch."

"You're very kind."

"So you see, you have nothing to fear. You can bring your paints, if you like, and do a picture. You needn't speak to a soul if you don't feel like it."

She lifted her head with an expression of grateful appeal.

"Really? You wouldn't mind? I can't stand it when they babble and cluster around me. Especially in the cars. I can't breathe."

"You can sit by a window, if you like," Bob said. "It isn't a long drive, anyway."

She set the prisms down on the window sill and began to tie the blue silk scarf about her throat, saying with an air of gentle reproach, as if to indict us for having persuaded her, "I'll come, then. I'll be punished, but I will."

Bob and Mandel drove the two limousines, while Wren and I, sitting on the back seat of either car, kept order among the patients. As it was a fine warm morning, and they were full of the cheerful excitement of the outing, this was not difficult. Lilith sat directly in front of me beside Bob, turned away to face out of the open window so that, from the rear seat, I could see her plainly, clasping her flying, snapping hair to her head with her spread fingers, her eyes narrowed and her lips a little parted, drinking the wind with a ravenous, intoxicated look.

Great Falls is a beautiful and awesome place, only a few miles from Stonemont, where the waters of the Potomac, thundering down from the sheer granite shelves of the Piedmont Plateau, run roaring and foaming over a mile-long race of deep, boulder-strewn rapids. The banks are very high at this point, rising over a thousand yards above the boiling channels below, and half a mile across this vast stone cauldron one can see the green, heavily forested slopes of the Virginia shore. There are observation platforms cut out of the rocky cliffs, railed with iron pipe and furnished with coin-operated telescopes; but what is more enjoyable is to lie flat on the great gray boulders in the sunlight, staring up into the blue sky and listening to the endless thunder of the falls below, or to roam among the willow and laurel thickets of the many narrow islands which have been sliced off from the mainland and isolated by a network of vagrant torrents, threading off from the main body of the river. Here one can search for herons or blackberries, or plunge one's wrist into the icy water of the inshore channels to bring up, cold and dripping in one's clenched fingers, a round, bright, perfectly polished pebble that has spun chortling for centuries in one of the worn potholes of the shore. Although a beautiful and unusual place, it was one that would require, because of its many natural hazards, exceptional vigilance from we attendants, and I was filled with determination to justify Bea's confidence in sending me along as escort.

To reach the falls one must cross the old Chesapeake & Ohio Canal, which runs parallel with the Potomac as far as Cumberland. Although its former purpose as a freight canal has been long outmoded by the railroads, the locks are still maintained, and many of the tollhouses—fine old buildings made of native granite—have been restored. At Great Falls there is a splendid one that has been made into a museum and luncheon pavilion; here we parked the limousines and unpacked our provisions. Lilith had brought her paints in a wooden box, a drawing pad and a portable easel with collapsible legs. As I was removing them from the trunk, Warren, who as a matter of discretion had been placed in the other car, approached us and asked in a voice of hesitant reverence if he might carry the equipment for her. As the question was addressed to Lilith, and obviously constituted a grave and courteous overture on his part, I felt that in spite of my authority it was not my province to answer and that she should be allowed to indicate for herself whether or not she desired his company. But Lilith, after gazing at him for a moment, turned to me with a winsome air of submissiveness and said, "Why, I don't know. May he, Mr. Bruce?"

"Yes, of course," I said. "Can you manage the easel and box both, Warren? I'll take one of the lunch baskets, if you can."

"Oh, yes, easily."

He accepted the burdens happily, and, joining the group, we crossed the small bridge that spans the canal and followed a well-worn footpath through the thickets beyond toward the river. The small islands along the riverbank are joined by a series of wooden foot bridges built over the rushing torrents which divide them. We crossed these cautiously, pausing sometimes to lean on the sleeve-worn handrails and stare down at the swift, glassy turbulence of the water below. I thought several times that Warren would speak to her, but his initiative appeared to have been exhausted by his offer to carry her baggage, and he seemed content to stand shyly, following the direction of her eyes with his own and then returning them unobtrusively to her face, as if simply to share some common object of vision with her made him mysteriously happy. Once she set down her paintbox and, catching her hair in two strands with her hands, leaned over the railing and spit into the stream. The white patch of her spittle slid down swiftly over the glittering surface, dissolving as it did so, and disappeared beneath the planks of the bridge. Warren laughed softly with a strangely primitive sound of delight which I found quite unpleasant.

. I remember Dr. Lavrier reminding me once, in a conversation about Lilith which I shall record presently, that the word "rapture" in the English of Shakespeare's day meant "madness," and adding, in the gently evocative manner which I came so greatly to admire, "I think all of us here are concerned with rapture in some way—I told you once that I liked to consider psychoanalysis as an art rather than a science—and when a man devotes himself to studying the nature of rapture he may find himself dispossessed, as it were. Categories dissolve, values and verities reverse themselves, things he reaches out to touch for comfort or guidance startle, and sometimes sicken, him with their unfamiliarity. It is a thing we are all aware of in this profession."

I am always reminded of his statement when I think of Lilith's face as, stepping out of the willow thicket through which we had followed the path toward the river, she stood on the granite bluffs above the water and looked out at the mighty tumult of the falls; for if ever I saw rapture in a human face, or felt in myself the beginnings of such troubled contemplation of it, it was at that moment. Her eyes widened with gathering joy and then fixed in a look of idle brilliance, as if she were held in some bitterly beautiful dream, while her features fell softly into an almost weary expression of ecstasy which seemed to me, remembering suddenly my mother's face as she lay dead in the winter sunlight of her bedroom, to represent the total opposite of that look of consummate composure. There was a rough wind blowing off the falls; it flattened her skirt against her thighs and scattered her hair across her face, tangling strands of it about her lips and eyes. She raked it away with her finger tips and stood clutching the box of paints against her breast, staring out at the massive sheets of water thundering down from the great shelves of the falls and murmuring to herself in the strange sharp syllables of her own tongue. She turned toward me in a moment and said softly, her voice distorted by the roaring of the rapids, "Don't you think that water is the most beautiful of all things, and demands a sacrifice?"

"It is beautiful," I said. "But I don't understand why it should demand a sacrifice."

"Oh, I do," said Warren, who stood beside me clutching Lilith's paraphernalia in a comically conscientious way, his eyes shining with happiness at this opportunity to express a concord with the creature that he loved. "I think all beautiful things do. I remember going to the cathedral once at Eastertime with my sister when I was only twelve years old. They sang the 'Mass in G Minor' by Vaughan Williams, and it was so beautiful that I cried. I was wearing a new blazer with brass buttons on it; they had the arms of my school engraved on them, and I loved them very much. So I cut them off with my penknife and put them in the tray. I had a dollar in my pocket that my mother had given me for the offering; but that would not have been a sacrifice, you see. So I cut the buttons off my jacket. There were four down the front and three on each sleeve." This was the longest and most fervent speech that I had ever heard him make.

Lilith listened, smiling, and said, "Mr. Evshevsky understands, you see. Haven't you ever had such a feeling, Mr. Bruce?"

"No. I can't remember it, if I have. The only thing that makes me feel as if I ought to make a sacrifice of some kind is misery."

She dropped her eyes as I said this and fondled the latch of her paintbox for a moment, saying quietly, "How ugly, how brutal. I would not like to be served in that way. I would like people to love me and make sacrifices to me because I was beautiful, not as a tribute to my wretchedness."

"Yes, that's what I mean!" Warren said excitedly. "That's what I felt in the cathedral. That God wants to be served in that way, too—not because of the miserable symbols of His power, but because He is beautiful."

Lilith raised her eyes to his in a long thoughtful glance and turned back to the falls, lifting her head to breathe deeply the gusty air with its fresh smell of mist. The rest of the group had assembled to our left along the wide mound of rock on which we stood—an advantageous place for our picnic, as it was a large level area with a fine view of the falls, and yet lay back ten or fifteen yards from the steep and dangerous edge of the bank cliffs. I saw that Bob had reached the same conclusion, for he called to me, "I think this is a good place to eat, Vince. Let's unpack the baskets."

"All right."

"I have Miss Arthur's here, if you want to come for it."

"Oh, let me get it," Warren said. "I would be glad to."

He set down his burdens and went quickly in his awkward shambling stride across the rocks to fetch it for her, returning in a moment with the waxed-paper parcel of sandwiches held carefully in his fine hands, grinning with satisfaction. Lilith took it from him silently. While Warren and I unpacked the hamper I had carried from the limousine, she sat down on the smooth warm face of the boulder, clasping her knees and bowing her neck in the sunlight. It was a most perfunctory luncheon; Warren bolted his food with abstracted voracity, watching Lilith constantly in his innocent and ardent way and speaking, at every opportunity, with a nervous elation and at a length I had never known in him. Lilith ate idly, her eyes almost constantly upon the falls, breaking her sandwiches into pieces with her finger tips and then nibbling and abandoning them one by one. She half turned toward him once, keeping her eyes upon the blown foam of the rapids, and asked, "Do you think power is beautiful, Mr. Evshevsky?"

"Oh, yes, yes," he answered eagerly. "And it is made beautiful by the things on which it is inscribed. I think that when there is a power abroad we must submit to it; it is a kind of natural obedience. How would we know that lightning is magnificent if we didn't see it split the rocks and blast the trees? It is the rock's destiny to be split, and the tree's destiny to be blasted, because that is the only way the magnificence of the lightning can be revealed. We must submit to God's power, too, because it's the only way that He can be revealed. Don't you feel that? That it's our destiny to reveal His nature by yielding to it with our own?" He lifted and clasped his long hands excitedly as he spoke, bending his head forward in a yearning and zealous way, as if borne toward her by the torrent of his thought. "Surely you felt that when you said the river was beautiful."

"No."

"You didn't? But then why does it seem beautiful to you?"

"I didn't say that. I said the water was beautiful, not the river. The water is beautiful because it makes rainbows in the mist above the falls, the way my prisms do. And because it is all broken into crystal spray above the boulders, like chandeliers. And because there are drowned queens floating in it with their lungs full of silver." She stood up impatiently, shaking her head like a dog emerging from water, and spread her fingers in the sunlight. "I want to paint," she said. "May I, Mr. Bruce?"

"Yes, of course. I'll set up the easel for you."

"Not here. It will blow over in the wind, and I can't see where the cascade breaks, down there. Can you bring it a little closer for me?"

"I don't know," I said. "I'll see what Mr. Clayfield says."

I walked across the boulder to where Bob, Mandel and Wren sat with the other patients amid a litter of waxed paper, sandwiches and Thermos bottles.

"Miss Arthur wants to go down a little further, to paint," I said. "She says it's too windy here, and she can't see well. Is it all right?"

"I guess so," Bob said. "There are only eight of them; and if we're responsible for two each it ought to work out. How are they getting along?"

"Very well, I think. Warren is full of very frank admiration, but he seems to be well behaved, and I think she's rather enjoying him."

"Good. As long as he doesn't get on her nerves I'd let them stay together."

I think it was partly Lilith's pleasure—how warm, artless and genuine it always seemed on such occasions!—at Bob's agreement that made me less cautious than I should have been; for this, together with the staff's eagerness to encourage her participation in more such outings, made me particularly anxious to insure her enjoyment of the trip, and more liberal than I should have been, perhaps, in judging the suitability of the site she chose to paint from. This was on a high flat shelf of rock in the lee of a great boulder which shielded her easel from the wind, and selected, apparently, out of her passion for privacy and originality, as it stood far back from any of the footpaths that wound among the bracken. We had to forge our way to it through a thicket of chokecherry which scratched our wrists and ankles and ripped a large triangular tear in Lilith's skirt, through which the white flesh of her thigh flashed rhythmically as she walked. She stopped sometimes to break clusters of purple pokeweed berries from the tall, soft-stemmed bushes that grew among the thicket, or to pluck up handfuls of young grass, or strip the bright scarlet berries from another flowering plant, which I did not know.

"What are they for?" Warren asked.

"To paint with."

"Really? You really paint with them?"

"Oh, yes. They make lovely colors."

She stuffed them into the pocket of her skirt and climbed with swift, lithe movements up the shelf of rock that she had led us to. When she had gained the top of it she lifted her bent arm to her forehead, staring across the chasm into the sun.

"Oh, this is a lovely spot!" she said. "Can we stay here?"

I saw with some misgiving that less than ten yards in front of us the bank dropped steeply to the river in an almost vertical slope, strewn with shattered boulders, slate and the rotting trunks of fallen pines; but as a concession to her enthusiasm I did not protest. Warren set up her easel with many ostentatious manipulations of its bolts and braces and, while she began to sketch, stretched out on the rock a little behind her to watch, beaming with obvious delight at the privilege. I sat beside him and smoked a cigarette, falling into a state of luxurious somnolence from the sunlight, the droning of bees in the wildflowers, the rumble of the falls and the occasional casual murmur of their conversation.

It was astonishing to watch with what skill Lilith used the natural colors of the berries and herbs that she had gathered. She crushed the grass blades on the stone and rubbed the moist, frayed fibers on her paper to make cloudy masses of vegetation in many different tones. The stamens of the wild flags she used like pencils, touching their tufts of pollen to her painting and then brushing it with her finger tip to produce points of scattered yellow, brilliant as buttercups.

"It's wonderful!" Warren said. "I had no idea you could paint like that—simply with grasses and things of that kind."

"Yes. They fade, of course; but there are no such colors while they last."

"But don't you need many more? How can you paint with so few?"

"I have others here, in my box, that I've made—permanent colors. This red is cochineal, the black is simply charcoal, the ocher is clay from the garden at Crowfields. And here's a white

I made out of limestone; I slaked it myself and pulverized it in a mortar." He murmured with admiration while she burst one of the pokeberries with her finger tips and drew a streak of vivid violet across the paper.

"I should like to be able to paint," he said, "or to do anything of that kind. I have always had a great love of the arts; when I look at a painting or listen to music, I'm very moved. I understand them, but I can't do them myself."

He watched, frowning with fascination, while Lilith's fingers flashed about the easel. "How do you begin?" he asked. "I can never understand how you begin. When I pick up a violin or a paintbrush I suddenly feel exhausted and embarrassed. What is it that you do?"

"I do nothing," Lilith said. "My hand moves, and I follow it."

"Ah, that's it!" Warren said. "The hand moves! Mine doesn't move, of course. Or if it does, it moves only in the direction of the salted almonds. I always have a bowl of them beside me when I work; it is a great mistake. I sat all one afternoon last week, trying to write a poem, and could do nothing but nibble salted nuts. The more I tried to concentrate the more of them I ate. It's what always happens. I can't trust my hands, you see."

"I think that is where you fail," Lilith said. "You must learn to trust them, if you want them to lead you to things you love."

"Do you think they will? Perhaps it is only that I love salted almonds. What a terrible thought—to be a gourmet by nature! A taster and sampler of things. Still, it may be true, I'm afraid. I have a scholar's mind, you know, not an artist's. It's a very different faculty."

"But you have the gift of tongues. That's a great gift."

"Oh, it's nothing, compared to yours. I've studied them, yes; I know their grammar. But you've invented one of your own. That is the greatest gift."

"I did not invent it," Lilith said, turning toward him with a fiercely solemn look. "It was taught to me. I learned it, just as you do."

"How?" Warren said. "Who have you learned it from? Do you mean it's a spoken language?"

"Yes. It is spoken by my people."

"Really? And you actually hear them, then? You hear them speaking it? I would love to hear it, too. I'm fascinated by languages. Do you think they would speak to me?"

She watched him studiously for a moment, seeming to search his face for signs of mockery; but there was nothing to be seen in it but guileless eagerness.

"Perhaps," she said. "But it's very difficult to learn to hear them. It was many years before they would reveal themselves to me."

"I'm sure I could learn it," Warren said. "I learn very quickly, you know. I learned to speak Hungarian in less than a month. Perhaps you would teach me." He clasped his knees in his hands, leaning forward with excitement.

"No, I wouldn't be allowed to teach you, unless it was approved. It's a language that very few are permitted to speak."

"But what would I have to do?" he asked. "I'm sure I could persuade them."

She lifted her brush and clenched the tip of it lightly between her teeth, staring softly at the ground. "You would have to demonstrate great courage," she said. "And a great capacity—for joy."

"But I have!" he cried. "There are so many things that I take joy in. I have a very exuberant nature. Perhaps you haven't noticed it. But I'm not very brave. I admit I'm not very brave. I'm afraid of all sorts of things—cuts and bruises, sudden changes of temperature, for example. I catch cold very easily, you know. I have never been physically very strong."

Lilith burst into a peal of laughter and turned back to her painting. "You are a fraud!" she said. "You talk about submitting to holy powers, but you're terrified of little bruises or of catching cold. I think you're as devoted to misery as Mr. Bruce is. And you boast of your capacity for joy!"

"But I have it!" Warren cried. "You don't understand me. I have!"

"Eat these, then."

She turned suddenly, plunging her hand into her pocket and flinging a handful of the scarlet berries toward him. They bounced and rolled on the gray rock, settling in the crevices, where they lay glittering like little beads. I lunged forward involuntarily in the beginning of a gesture to clutch his hand if he should reach for them, but I saw there was no need. He stared at the red berries with a sudden look of fright, drawing his hand inward against his breast and recoiling from them humbly.

"Oh, no. They would make me sick. They may be poisonous."

"Perhaps," Lilith said. "But perhaps they have a thrilling, exotic flavor, like nothing you have ever tasted."

She took another handful of the berries from her pocket and, dropping her head back, tossed them into her mouth. Before I could reach her to prevent it she had swallowed them and drawn her wrist across her lips to wipe away the scarlet stain.

"They're delicious. Clean and bitter, like anise. You see how foolish you are."

I had leapt to my feet—much too late, as I say, to interfere—and stood frowning at her with chagrin.

"Have I made you angry, Mr. Bruce?" she asked softly.

"It was very foolish. They may be poisonous, as he says."

"They won't hurt me if they are."

"I hope not. If you do any more foolish things like that I'll have to take you back."

"Are you worried about me, then?"

"Of course," I said. "I'm responsible for you."

"Yes. Then I'll be very good. I promise not to get sick. I wouldn't want to embarrass you." She held her hand out toward me, her palm glittering with scarlet juice from the crushed berries. "Would you like to taste it, too?"

"No, thank you."

"You see, you are both alike. You're concerned about your

health. But I have tasted a flavor of this world that you will never know."

"Yes, but I'm afraid of things like that," Warren said. He sat with his head drooped, staring rather shamefully at the ground. "Poison, and things of that kind. I've read about it in books—how you die in agony. I believe you draw your knees up against your chest and resume the fetal posture. It's really dreadful."

He rose and prowled restlessly about the rock, examining the boulder wall with his long fingers, which he poked in a sorrowful and abstracted way into the dust and rubble of its crevices, turning sometimes to look at Lilith. We were both suffering, I believe, from the same curious sense of defeat at her hands, and went without speaking for several minutes, each silently considering his own inadequacy. In a moment he turned, chuckling in his noisy childish way, and called excitedly, "Look what I've found! A mantis! Look how huge it is!"

It was indeed an enormous insect, with a plump brilliant-green body the size of a large cigar, and great flat forelegs which it held lifted and bent in an attitude of savage piety. It had fallen from the foliage above and stood with calm and monstrous dignity on a ledge of the boulder, turning its small head in a deliberate way from side to side while it regarded us with a look of fearful intelligence in its bulging eyes.

"How beautiful he is!" Lilith said. "And how wise he looks!" She had come to stand beside Warren at the boulder, and the three of us, our shoulders touching, peered with fascination at the little monster.

"I wonder what he's praying for?" I said.

"For victims." Lilith laughed as the mantis revolved its head slowly, seeming to survey each of us in turn. "I wonder which of us he will choose?"

"It's an ugly thing," Warren said suddenly. He picked up a long flat blade of shale which lay broken in a rift of the rock and lifted it to strike the insect.

"Oh, no, don't kill him!" Lilith cried. "No, no!" She clutched at Warren's hand as it descended, but insufficiently to deflect the blow; the mantis lay crushed and quivering against the gray rock. "What a terrible thing to do! He was beautiful!"

"I didn't know it really mattered to you," Warren mumbled. He raised his hand and stared at the long ragged scratch her nails had made across the back of it. "You scratched me."

"Let me see," Lilith said.

He turned his hand toward her and she stared at it somberly for a moment.

"Why, you have beautiful hands," she said in a quaintly reflective way, as if she had never before observed them.

Warren blushed and closed his fingers quickly. "I bite my nails," he murmured, and then, with a terrible effort of will which one could read in the tension and deepening color of his face, he straightened his fingers slowly, as if to exhibit his disgrace, and asked softly, "Do you really think that if I learned to trust them, as you say, they would find me things I loved?"

"Yes, I know they would."

Knowing the painful shyness and formality of his nature, I was more than ever aware of the intensity of the impulse which made him raise his hand in a slow, trembling gesture of agonized determination and take very gently between his fingers a strand of her soft bright hair. She did not withdraw, or look at him directly, but bowed her head slightly in a delicately feigned unawareness, suffering his touch.

"Then I will try to learn to," he murmured. He withdrew his hand and stood watching her averted face with a composed radiance of expression that was quite moving to see. Lilith turned suddenly and walked back to her easel, dipping her hand into her pocket and taking out more of her wild berries. She worked swiftly for a moment, making broad violet strokes across the top of her paper, and then said suddenly, "I need some water to wash it out; I've gotten it too dark. May I get some?"

"Where?" I asked.

"There's a pool in the rocks back there, where we climbed up."

She pointed down the shelf of rock and I saw the water shining among the branches of an elder bush. It was scarcely ten yards away, a little below us and easily in sight of the boulder on which we stood. When I hesitated for a moment, she said, "It will only take me a minute." I am not sure, although I had much time and occasion to consider it in the days that followed, just what prompted my unfortunate reply to her request; surely even with the few yards' advantage she would have had if she had tried to run away I could easily have overtaken her, and she would, at any rate, have been able to make very little headway through the dense thicket. Yet Bea had told me that she had tried previously to escape, and the possibility remained that she might do so again and might, however futile the attempt, have injured herself stumbling about the rocks and through the bracken. I think my reasoning was that it was better to keep her in front of me, with the only possible avenue of escape—the thicket behind the rock—barred by myself. It was also the forthrightness of the request which made me suspect that if she intended to deceive me in any way, it was in order to separate herself from Warren and me by getting the water herself. It was the first time I had had to trust my own initiative with patients and was not yet fully familiar with the involutions of their cunning. (I say "cunning," although I am not yet sure, and perhaps never will be, if it was such.) I am not really sure, in my threadbare and guilty memory of the event, what my reasoning was; but I soon had shocking evidence of its error.

"Let me get it for you," I said with assumed casualness.

"That's very kind of you."

"Do you have a cup or something in your box?"

"No. You can just soak my scarf in it, if you will. That's all I need." She untied the pale silk scarf from her throat and tossed it to me lightly. It fell across my fingers like breath.

"It will get all stained," I said.

"Oh, that doesn't matter."

I tucked it into the pocket of my shirt and clambered down the boulder, picking my way to the pool among the rocks. I parted the elder branches and knelt above the water, holding her scarf beneath the surface to saturate it.

"Oh, I've dropped my brush, Mr. Evshevsky," I heard Lilith say. "Will you get it for me?"

"Yes, I will."

I did not look up immediately, as there seemed nothing extraordinary either in the question or in his reply to it. But a moment later the considerable pause before he had answered, and the exact intonation of his voice when finally he had—thrilled and a little harsh with fright—echoed darkly in my mind, like the black image one sees a moment after staring into the sun. I raised my head swiftly, feeling a cold glitter of fear run throughout my body. Warren had disappeared from sight, and Lilith, her hands lifted and laid lightly against her breast, stood at the very edge of the boulder, where it fell away to the river, staring down raptly into the chasm.

I was wearing leather-soled shoes which slipped on the smooth rock face, making my panicky, overhasty effort to scale the boulder a floundering, hideously comic and interminable burlesque. It seemed to me an age of excruciating length before I managed to reach the top of it and run to where Lilith stood at its edge; and when I did I was so convinced that Warren was dead and swept away in the waters below that I was almost more shocked than I would have been if this were true to see him halfway down the slope, clinging desperately to stony outcroppings of rock and lying almost flat against the sheer face of the cliff as he worked his way with terrified determination downward.

"Stay still," I shouted. "Don't go any farther."

He turned his face up slowly, clutching the stones to preserve his balance, and called weakly, "But I haven't got it yet."

"Don't be a fool. It doesn't matter. Don't move from where you are. I'll come down and help you back."

He turned his head to look downward again and called out

in a moment, "I think perhaps I'd better. I can't see it any more, anyway. I think it may have fallen on down."

I took off my shoes and socks to gain better traction on the stone and, dropping my legs over the edge of the boulder, began what is surely the most terrifying adventure of my life. I have always been afraid of great heights and was in a constant sickening state of fear as I lowered myself down the face of the cliff, sliding in mounds of loose shale, clutching at roots and stony projections in the bank, pausing sometimes to look down, trembling, at Warren's slight figure, superimposed with pitiful fragility against the thundering mass of water far below. Yet when I reached him he seemed to be as bewilderedly repentant as afraid, lowering his head and murmuring, "I'm sorry. I hope I haven't caused you too much trouble. I didn't realize it was quite so difficult."

As I had no rope, or any other equipment, there was perhaps little practical advantage in my presence; but I think it was of psychological assistance to him, for he seemed greatly reassured to see me and climbed with surprising confidence, following the route I picked for our ascent with the unperturbed obedience of a child who has unquestioning faith in the ability of its parent to deliver it from any peril; and I was able, from time to time, to offer him the more tangible assistance of reaching down, when I had gained the relative security of a boulder or a firm foothold above, and helping him toward it. I had to fight constantly against the horrible dizziness which threatened all the while to send me reeling outward from the face of the cliff to which we clung; and for this reason, and out of an extraordinary sense of pride as well, I did not dare look upward to the top of it. I did not know if Lilith was still standing there or not, or whether, if she was, she might not roll a boulder down upon us at any moment. And yet, all the while I was climbing, I felt a profound conviction of her presence there; I was sure that she was standing above us at the edge of the cliff, as I had left her—her hands still lifted and laid against her breast in an oddly devout attitude, staring down at us with her deep, enchanted gaze—and experienced a peculiar satisfaction, so strong and so nearly embarrassing in its incongruity that I was, as I say, too proud (and too dizzy!) to confirm it.

It was only when I had reached the top of the cliff and was grappling for a handhold to haul myself up onto it that I allowed myself to look at her. She was standing, just as I had imagined and just as I had left her, with her bare feet touching the very edge of the rock, enthralled. She did not smile or speak.

When I had helped Warren up onto the boulder, we both collapsed and sat panting, with our backs against a stone. I was full of an idle, thoughtless feeling of vacancy which always follows great physical or emotional excitement on my part, and had neither the will nor inclination to reprimand Lilith nor to try to determine exactly what it was that she had done. She came and sat in front of us on the rock, spreading her torn skirt daintily.

"How brave you are," she said gently. "It was beautiful to watch."

"I'm sorry I couldn't get your brush," Warren said. "I think it must have fallen further down. I couldn't see it anywhere."

"It doesn't matter. I can make another one easily."

"Then why in God's name did you ask him to get it?" I said with sudden anger, which I think was as much irritation at Warren's simplicity as at the outrageousness of her remark.

"I'm sorry. It was thoughtless of me. But he didn't have to, of course."

"Oh, no, it was my fault entirely," Warren said. "She didn't realize how dangerous it was. I shouldn't have gone down."

Lilith dropped her head and stared at her white hands thoughtfully, twining her fingers together in her lap. In a moment she said, "I believe we were both rather foolish. I hope Mr. Bruce won't report us too severely, because if he does I'm afraid it will prejudice our chances of taking any more trips with him."

I believe this remark was the most disturbing thing she said or did in the entire day. It seemed to me, the more I thought about it, to be a very clear invitation to conceal or adjust the details of our misadventure in my report—not only to disguise my own inadequacy, but to reduce the possibility of any interpretation by the staff of malice or dangerous mischief on her part, and to offer me, by way of incentive, the preserved prospect of future outings in her company. What a presumptuous and insidious suggestion! Yet even more disturbing was the fact that, being able to make so sensitive an analysis of its significance, I could not have been entirely invulnerable to it. I was perhaps so anxious to acquit myself of any such indictment, and Lilith of any such design, that I began to dwell determinedly instead on what must after all have been her entirely uncalculating and natural enough desire to escape the suspicions of the staff and any possible penalty for her behavior; and also upon the unfortunate—if fascinating—ambiguity about everything she said or did, which made it possible to interpret this as a darkly hinted offer of collusion.

Still, I could not permanently or entirely evade the implications of her remark; all the while we were driving home I had the unhappy opportunity of considering my utter failure at this first assignment and the possible consequences of a full and conscientious report of it to Bea. I *might*—how terrible and total a humiliation!—be dismissed from the staff; or I might, if retained on a probationary basis, have my responsibilities greatly limited— perhaps even to the point of not being entrusted alone with patients again. I would, at any rate, suffer an inevitable loss of respect and trust on the part of Bea and other members of the staff, have undermined my own confidence and crippled my effectiveness at the only thing in which I had ever taken pride and wished to do well. (All this could be avoided or reduced, if I invented some less culpable account, in which, of course, she would support me!)

To Bob, whose guarded inquiries about the condition of our clothing—torn and soiled from the climb—and our general state of fatigue invited it, I was able to postpone a full explanation of the event by means of an exaggerated air of circumspection in the presence of the other patients; but with every mile of the drive toward the Lodge I was more miserably aware of the imminent necessity of producing one for Bea and of the malicious alternative which Lilith's words had suggested to me. She seemed exquisitely unaware of the distress she had caused me, leaning her head on the open sill with a soft smile and letting her golden hair stream out beside us in the wind, like a pennon of frayed and glittering silk.

When we reached the Lodge she had become contrite, replying to my directions in a modest, obedient tone and following me silently along the hall while I carried the paintbox and easel to her room. As I unfolded and set it up in its accustomed corner she unrolled the sheet of work that she had done and spread it out on her desk top, holding it flat with her finger tips.

"You haven't said anything about my picture," she murmured.

"I don't want to. However good it may be, it isn't worth what it cost."

"What is that?"

"Very nearly Warren's life, and very likely my job."

"Oh, I hope not." She looked up at me with a long grievous gaze which failed slightly before my sustained ironic silence. "Really I do, Mr. Bruce."

"It's difficult to believe you're so concerned about me," I said.

She lowered her head sedately. "I think you can do a great deal of good here," she said hesitantly but clearly. "I think the patients . . . trust you. It would be so foolish if you—if you were to leave."

Her anxiety for me to remain seemed so honest and touching that I found it difficult to resist being moved by it and was somewhat startled by the harshness of my own words when, after a considerable pause, I asked, "Why do I have the impression that you're trying to bribe me, Miss Arthur?"

"To bribe you?"

"Yes."

"I have no idea."

She raised her eyes with a look of astonishment and injury that made me feel immediately callous and absurd. How could I suspect her of wishing only to conceal her own behavior? After all, she was not responsible for it, and any penalty she might incur would be only a temporary and relatively minor one—further postponement of her privileges, perhaps—in which she seemed to take little interest anyway. Surely her real concern was for me to stay. She sensed in me, as she had confessed, a sympathetic personality, one whom she trusted and who she felt could help her greatly. How grossly I had misinterpreted her humble appeal to me to forgive her irresponsibility, to remain and help to cure her of it! Yet some devil of doubt made me persist in my sudden determination to expose her.

"How could you 'drop' your paintbrush ten yards in front of you, over the edge of a cliff?" I demanded.

"I was flipping it—like this—in my fingers, to shake the color out. I always do that." Her hurt and startled look gathered slowly into anger as we spoke. "You are very stern."

"Yes, I am. You've made me fail at something I cared very much about."

"Perhaps it was your own incompetence that made you fail."

"It was. But you've reminded me of it."

"And you hate being reminded of it, don't you?"

"Yes, I do. Why did you ask Warren to get the brush?"

"Because he is a fool."

"Then why did you let him . . . touch your hair that way?"

"Because I am mad."

She turned abruptly toward the window, leaving me suddenly aghast at the unreasonable and undignified way in which I had questioned her. Far from being a calm, professional effort to help an emotionally unstable person to solve her difficulties, it had developed suddenly into a heated, vulgar quarrel, leaving me with this fresh and added sense of failure to carry to my interview with Bea. She would say nothing more, standing with her back to me beside the window and refusing to answer either my murmured apology or, as I stood with my hand on the door, my conciliatory goodbye.

$J$ KNOCKED at the door of Bea's cottage in a state of total despondency. She must have been anticipating my arrival, for she asked me immediately to come in and greeted me with a look of prepared cheerfulness, sitting on the edge of her desk as I entered.

"Well, have you got them all back safely?"

"They're all back safely," I said, "but with very little thanks to me."

She watched me for a moment and smiled. "You'd better sit down and have a drink. I have a bottle of Scotch here that I keep especially for stricken therapists."

"Thank you." I sat down wearily and watched her pour the whiskey into glasses on her desk.

"I talked to Bob, and he said you looked pretty miserable on the way back, but hadn't had much chance to talk about it." She set a glass on the edge of the desk in front of me and lifted her own. I nodded to her and drank, feeling with the scalding benison of the whiskey in my throat, a sudden bitter recall of nights of drinking under a steaming tarpaulin in the jungles of New Guinea.

"So you had a pretty rugged time," Bea said.

"I think I violated, categorically, every piece of advice you've given me: improper vigilance, gullibility, permitting myself to be persuaded against my judgment, failure of objectivity, and even quarreling with a patient."

"Well, you're thorough, anyway. How did all this happen?"

I gave her laboriously, pausing to recall details with painful precision, a description of the entire day's events, just as I have recorded it here. Only once or twice did she interrupt, at particularly critical or ambiguous points, to question me more closely. When I had finished she sat in serious silence for a moment before she answered, "Now tell me, Vincent, how do you feel about it?"

"I think, frankly, that I've made a mistake in coming here. It seems pretty obvious to me that I'm not suited for this work. I just don't have the temperament for it."

"Do you mean you want to quit? That you've had enough?"

"No, it isn't that; I'd like very much to succeed at it, but I don't think I can."

"Are you resigning, then?"

"I don't really know," I said. "I think perhaps I'm hoping you'll ask me to."

"I see. Now let's go back and take every one of these 'failures' of yours as they occurred, right in order. What was first?"

"Well . . . letting her choose a place herself to paint from, I suppose."

"You had Bob's authority for that. You asked his permission, quite properly, and it was entirely in keeping with our policy of 'babying' her a little—to get her out more often—that he agreed to it. Then what?"

"I don't know—letting her collect those weeds and things."

"I would have done just the same—I have, as a matter of fact. It's a harmless enough thing, and she probably couldn't have done her painting without them."

"But it wasn't harmless; she ate some of them," I said.

"No one could have prevented that. She could snatch a handful of berries and eat them any time she's out walking, before anyone could interfere. What else did you do?"

"I approved a dangerous place for her to paint."

Bea nodded. "Yes, it was relatively dangerous. But there are always many things to consider in making such a decision. Is she in general a violent or suicidal patient? No. Is it dangerous enough to warrant earning her hostility by refusing? That's doubtful. Is it worth permitting her to stay there as a demonstration of your confidence in her? What is her general condition at the time? Is she cheerful, responsible, obedient, or sullen, depressed, antagonistic? Can you offset any danger there may be by being particularly alert? All these things considered, I think I would have let her stay there, too."

"But I *didn't* offset its danger," I said. "She lured me away, and then coaxed Warren down that cliff. She was so *damned* cheerful and obedient that she fooled me."

"Are you sure she lured you away? Do you think it was a premeditated ruse?"

"No. I'm not sure of anything she does."

"But you think she intended to kill Warren?"

"I don't know."

"If she wanted to kill him, why do you suppose she didn't simply push him off the edge when he started down?"

"I don't know. Perhaps she didn't want to be directly responsible. I don't think Lilith would actually strike the blow herself—it would be too crude. But if he had been killed this other way, there would have been a kind of poetry about it—if you see what I mean—that I think would appeal to her." I looked out of the window, recalling her rapt gaze as she had stared at Warren down the cliff. "I had the feeling she was testing him," I said. "That she was demanding a 'demonstration of courage' from him, as she called it. Maybe she was fascinated by his fear; she knows he's rather timid. Or perhaps she accepted it as an act of worship from him, the only kind that's possible to them in their situation. I don't know what it was. But whatever it was, she succeeded at it. She was too clever for me."

"Yes, that's true," Bea said. "Well, you've learned something there; she's very clever. And it's something you can never really appreciate until you've had experience of it." She paused for a moment, reconsidering the circumstances. "I think the wisest thing would have been to let Warren go for the water. It's curious he didn't offer to. Still, there was a lot of logic in your reasoning, too. You see, it wasn't a gross mistake—one of wanton negligence or stupidity. You thought about it, but you thought wrong; you were simply outwitted—if that's what it really amounted to. And there's no disgrace in being outwitted by a lot of these people. I can tell you very truthfully that I made many worse mistakes than that when I first started here."

"Did you really?" I asked, looking up at her with considerable gratitude, not only for this confession but for the charity with which she had considered all my actions.

"Oh, yes. And I do still. As a matter of fact, of all the mistakes made today, I think mine was probably the worst, in sending you out on what was a very difficult assignment, when you are relatively so inexperienced. Still, we never know what's going to happen; I thought it would be good training for you. And there's no such thing as living without taking chances." She shrugged and shook her head humorously. "Now what was this quarreling you mentioned?"

"Yes. That was almost the worst thing I did. I don't know why. I was angry and disappointed in myself, I suppose. I felt that she had made me fail deliberately, that she'd wanted to humiliate me for some reason, and succeeded; so I wanted to get even with her, I suppose. It was a stupid, childish thing to do. Instead of being objective—calm and sympathetic, as I should have been—I started accusing her. Trying to make her confess the wrongness of her actions. Trying to make her confess that she's insane is what it amounts to. But you almost forget she's a patient, she's so clever."

"Yes, that's the most difficult thing of all, as I think I warned you once. Because they're intellectually equal or superior, we assume they're emotionally equal, as well. But the reason they're here, of course, is because they're not; and it's awfully hard to remember sometimes, particularly when you've been here as short a while as you have. It's certainly no reason to feel that you're a total failure, Vincent."

It was useless, I felt—not without a curious sense of relief—to convey to Bea the exact and troubling nuances of emotion I had experienced during my angry exchange with Lilith in her room; and she had so generously and effectively rationalized my failings that I felt it would be almost an indication of ingratitude to protest them any further. At any rate, in the cheerful, tolerant atmosphere of her presence they had begun to dwindle in gravity and number until I was almost ready to accept her own charitable estimate of them.

But we never totally deceive ourselves. The danger to which my patients had been subjected by my negligence, and the shock that I had suffered at it, were too recent and severe to be dismissed with such convenience; but perhaps even more significant was my sudden awareness of the jeopardy in which my fallibility had placed not only my charges but, in some obscure, darkly alarming way, myself. If I should fail at my newly discovered metier, it would not be, I felt, for lack of diligence, intelligence or simple skill, but for some far more profound imperfection, whose nature and whose consequences I was unwilling to explore. I finished my drink and set the glass before me on the desk, staring in silence at the pale oily film of fluid which withdrew slowly from its rim.

"You seem to think that you've failed utterly," Bea said. "But it seems to me a little early to decide that. I don't really think you've given it a fair trial yet."

"I'm afraid I might, though," I said. "And to be a failure at this kind of work is so much more serious than in some other job. If you make a mess of bricklaying or shopkeeping it doesn't really matter much—there's no particular danger to anyone. But in this kind of work a mistake can be mortal, both to people you're responsible for and to yourself."

Bea lifted her hand to brush her short hair thoughtfully, turning her head to stare out of the window.

"Do you mean that you're afraid?" she asked. I was relieved that she had said it.

"Yes, I suppose I am."

"But I think a person is often afraid when he's doing something that matters deeply to him. With other things it doesn't matter so much. There should be joy and enthusiasm in your work, of course; but when you have a real sense of vocation about a thing, I think there's often a certain amount of . . . awe as well." She stroked her hair restlessly. "I'm often afraid," she said. "And I don't just mean of falling off cliffs, or being belted by the Duchess." She smiled at me modestly and, seeming to sense the humility with which I was forced to disengage my eyes from hers, went on with great kindliness, "Vincent, do you feel that perhaps I'll think differently about you now? That I've lost a certain amount of confidence in you?"

"I think it would be impossible for you not to have," I said.

"Yes." She rose and walked behind her desk, unlocking a drawer and leaning over it while she spoke. "Do you remember me telling you that we never issue a set of keys to a worker until we've decided that he's fully capable?"

"Yes."

"Well, I'd like you to have these now, if you want to stay and use them." She took a set of keys from the drawer as she said this and laid them on the desk in front of me.

I have had much reason to bless Bea's kindness and understanding since the morning when I first met her, but never more than at that moment. I felt absurdly close to tears as I took the keys up and weighed them in my hand.

"They're very heavy," I said softly.

"Take them home and think about it," she said. "And if you still feel any doubts about it in the morning, you can give them back."

"I don't think I will," I said.

"Good. You know, Vincent, I would really have had less respect for you if you hadn't felt so deeply about this."

"I think you must be kind of a wise woman," I said.

"I'm wise enough to know when I have a really good worker on my staff."

So it was that Bea preserved for me—for the time, at any rate—my peace of mind and my profession. I hope the irony of its outcome is no discredit to her act of faith, yet if I had not been persuaded by her tolerance and trust to stay on at the Lodge, none of what I have still to record would have occurred, and I would be now—what? I have no idea. Picking fruit, perhaps, as an itinerant laborer, or faring in reeking merchantmen to island after island of disappointment. They are not glorious alternatives, but how willingly would I have exchanged them for the estate to which I was brought by pursuing one of the glories of this world!

*J*HE STATE of mind which Bea's demonstration of confidence produced in me was immediate and profound. I went about my work for the next several days with fresh resolution and a vigorous, determined self-assurance that is reflected in my journal:

¶ *THURS., APRIL* 30:

Sense of pride like nothing I have known before at using my own keys and escorting patients by myself; a kind of smiling solemnity, like a girl returning from her First Communion. I am getting used to their great weight and feel quite naked when I take them off. Bea is a really wonderful person; she must have realized how much I needed her to make a gesture of that kind, and what it meant to me.

Third Floor this morning, Second in afternoon. Behrendt, Glassman, Duchess before lunch; Palakis, Warren, Hagan, after. Did not see Lilith at all, and enjoyed, in a mildly perverse way, the suspense she must be enduring about my report to Bea.

Behrendt was her usual scornful, silent self. Asked to play tennis, and beat me, 6–0, 6–2. Snarled at all my errors and called me a duffer. I was no match for her. She used to play for a Long Island club and was once Middle Atlantic Junior Champion. I can't begin to make contact with her, and don't know quite what line to follow, as she seems to despise all scholarly and introspective types. I am going to make a determined effort to learn to dance, as this seems to be her greatest interest; she attends every tea dance and listens avidly for hours to all the pop albums in Field House, tapping her feet, fondling her hair and giggling all the while. Strange girl. She is a real challenge, and one which I am determined to meet.

In spite of all reason and resolution, was terribly embarrassed this morning by Glassman's sudden public urge to urinate. What can you do in a situation like that? Couldn't stop the poor girl, who was obviously in a desperate condition, and yet it's impossible to look dignified, impassive, or even properly patient—and you certainly can't pretend to be unaware—when a young lady is squatting at your feet with her skirt hitched up, relieving herself in the middle of the path. Some aspects of this business that I suspect one never gets adjusted to. There seems little hope with her, outside of custodial attention. Absolutely no contact, and never any remission in her idiotic, parrot-like good nature. Feeling of abuse here, more terrible than with any of them.

Duchess is frightening—as I was warned—but very droll and engaging if flattered and unless crossed. Great temptation to take the easy way with her. When I called for her she kept me waiting pointedly while she made many little briskly elegant adjustments to her rumpled, soiled, utterly unimprovable dress, and then announced with a wonderful patrician graciousness, "I am ready now, young man." When she stepped out of the elevator she took a deep breath of the fresh morning air and said, "I think we will speak in French today. It is just the day for French." Carried on an uninterrupted discourse in this language all the way to Crowfields, seeming to become aware of my modest silence only about halfway back, when she stopped to make what I gathered to be a demand for comment of some sort on my part. So I said, "*Madame, je vous adore,*" which kept her chuckling all the way back to Field House. I beat her twice consecutively at ping-pong, producing a sudden, terrifying, narrow-eyed silence, which was relieved a little by my observation that she was "way off form." Would hate to have to cross her, but I suppose the day must come. She looks as strong as a bull. Bob says when she really runs amuck it takes four men to handle her. I like her tremendously, in spite of being frightened to death of her, and feel there is much I can accomplish here.

Had lunch with Bob and Kit, and could not help feeling annoyed when Mandel joined our table. Much ostentatious inquiry about how I was getting along and far too solemn congratulations about having been issued keys. The Old Pro. He is one of those people who promote their self-esteem not by honest constructive achievements of their own, however modest they may be, but by criticizing and destroying the achievements of others. It has sometimes occurred to me that this is the only absolute form of evil there is. Too harsh a judgment, perhaps; but there is certainly something wrong with that boy. I would hate to be in debt to him.

Palakis seems to be "getting high." Marched me feverishly to the pond and told me in a hectic, garrulous state of humor that he has decided to further complicate the academic turmoil by launching his own theory of Shakespeare: Not only was Shakespeare somebody else, but there were *two* Shakespeares, *both* of whom were somebody else. A certain amount of sardonic justice in his argument. The "Idiot" Shakespeare—the darling of the "fatuous orthodoxy"—the "shallow, sentimental, jingoistic apologist"—was an Inns-of-Court blade and homosexual, probably a castoff friend of Greene's; the "great" Shakespeare—the "anguished Titan" of *Coriolanus, Titus Andronicus, Lear* and *Timon*—was an oppressed nobleman—"probably Sir Walter Raleigh"—whose work, after his death, was discovered by the "Idiot," confiscated, badly and superficially amended, and published under his own nom de plume. All this he told me with wild, ironic delight, ending his peroration, however, with a sudden note of sincerity as he regarded his clenched fist somberly and murmured, "It is impossible for the man who wrote 'Once more into the breach' to have also written Titus' 'If there were reason for these ills'; and monstrous that the world should accept only half his vision, and dismiss or apologize for what was the greater half of it." I said I did not know the world was guilty of such discrimination, and he replied, "Oh, yes. *The Tempest,* for example, is almost universally put forward as his supreme philosophic achievement and the consummation of his thought— when actually *Timon* much better expresses his mature vision. Yet how often do we see that play performed, or responsibly interpreted? Or *Pericles?* Or *Titus?* There has been a centuries-long conspiracy to deprecate them. It is absurd, undignified!" He became so fiercely indignant that I tried to change the conversation or somehow amend his dangerous mood; but had little luck until we met the terrapin, which delighted him. He picked it up, touched and examined it from every angle, chuckling at its look of torpid hauteur and calling it a "wonderful, primordial truth-bearer." He asked if he might keep it, but when I suggested that it might be more humane to let it go, he agreed with unexpected enthusiasm: "Yes! Let it go and spread its ancient, lumbering truth about the world! Perhaps they will believe him; they do not believe that other old tortoise." A little later, when we had almost reached the Lodge, he asked suddenly, "But they eat them, don't they? Isn't there a famous regional delicacy?"

I said yes, there was: Terrapin Maryland.

"They eat everything!" he said. "Lord, how disgusting! How debased!"

There is a terrible excruciated quality about this man which makes it unbearable to be in his presence long.

Saw Warren briefly when I returned Palakis to his floor. Was not scheduled to escort him, but agreed to take him walking for a quarter of an hour, as Hagan, my next patient, was still in hydrotherapy. He was in a great state of exhilaration, and scarcely inside the elevator before releasing a torrent of questions about Lilith: "Have you seen her? Is she well? Has she asked about me?" Did not know quite how to deal with this, but decided, in spite of my sympathy for him, to adopt a severely formal tone.

"Do you mean Miss Arthur?"

"Yes, yes. Has she asked about me? Did she say anything about last week?"

"I haven't seen her at all."

"You haven't? Oh, that's disappointing. I hoped you would have some news of her. I haven't seen her, either, or heard her playing, even. You don't suppose she's ill?"

"I don't believe so," I said; and after a pause in which he began to pick at his ragged nails with a haggard and abstracted look, I added, "Anyway, I think you ought to realize that it would be highly irregular for me to act as a go-between."

"Oh. Yes. I understand, of course. I beg your pardon. I hope you aren't offended."

"No. But I do want you to know that we're expressly instructed not to be involved in any—any such affair." (God, what a monster! I can hear myself saying it. Why, in heaven's name?)

"I'm sorry. I understand it's improper for me to . . . to ask you. But I thought you would understand my being anxious."

Sudden remorse made me lean too far the other way, I suppose. Put my hand on his shoulder in most inappropriate way and said, "Yes, I can understand it, Warren. I'll let her know you asked about her."

"Will you really? That's very kind of you. I really don't want to embarrass you, Mr. Bruce. But you see, it means a great deal to me."

"Yes, I know." He lifted his clasped hands and blew upon them nervously, although it was very warm.

"I suppose you think it's rather foolish—rather absurd—this attachment of mine," he murmured, keeping his eyes declined.

"No, I don't think there's anything foolish about love."

"You don't? Not even under such . . . grotesque conditions? I know that many people do. Mr. Palakis, for example, makes fun of me all the time."

"I don't think he's a very happy man," I said.

"No. Still, it's very possible to think of it as . . . a rather foolish thing. She is so proud, you know, such a delicate creature. And yet she allowed me to touch her hair for a moment. You saw that she allowed me?"

"Yes, I saw," I said uncomfortably.

He stood chafing his hands, staring with bleak intensity at the ground. "You see, I really have nothing else to live for," he murmured.

There was something shameful about this sudden nudity of spirit, or perhaps about my realization of the truth of what he said—he really *has* nothing else to live for. And I resented, I think, his exemption from the normal responsibility of restraining so intimate and intense a revelation which dignity demands. I didn't *want* to know about his wretched, total worship of this girl, and even though I had had much visual evidence of it already, I regretted having it declared to me in so unequivocal a way. Had to make a conscious effort to repress my sudden feeling of dislike by reminding myself that you can hardly hold a man who is mentally ill responsible for lack of taste. This, because of our natural affinity, is a very delicate relationship, which will require great tact and discipline on my part.

Hagan is a small, fierce, restless Irishman with an atmosphere of violence about him which is very discouraging. Watched the badminton for a while with his hands in pockets, scowling and snorting softly to himself. Don't think I can ever hope to get on well with this one, but must wait and see. Very little conversation, outside of simple requests for matches, the time, etc., and occasional muttered obscenities.

No evening O.T. meeting, as Bea was busy at a staff conference. Did not go directly home, but walked up to Hillcrest and stood for a while by the fence, looking down with a pleasant sense of domain. There were swallows flying over the pond in the dusk, apparently hunting for insects; they circled swiftly very close above the surface, their wing tips sometimes touching it so delicately that the glaze was barely broken. Lovely birds, like purple shadows over the dark silver water. The Lodge seemed very quiet and tranquil when I walked back through the grounds. There was a smell of sweetgrass in the evening air, and I could hear the sound of Lilith's flute, wandering softly, like a fume of smoke, among the mulberry trees. I glanced up at her window as I walked beneath it down the drive and could see her pale face and slender fluttering fingers, shadowed by the netting, where she sat playing at the open sill. She did not speak to me.

¶ *FRI., MAY 1:*
Training lecture this morning from Dr. Newman, a dark, stocky, soiled-looking man of middle age with a hairless glittering skull and a New England accent. His subject was "Selective Inattention"—a fascinating device by which the mentally ill—and sometimes normal people, as well, apparently—fail to hear or observe things that would be painful, inconvenient or too strongly challenging to them. Ordinarily this is an "eliminative" process, some other more compatible piece of contemporaneous information being selected for attention in preference to the disagreeable one, and the mind concentrating on it to the exclusion of the other. The unawareness, however, is genuine, the faculty of "editing out" of one's consciousness the distressing stimulus—whether it be a remark, a sight, a situation or a fact—being so mysteriously

effective that one is quite literally oblivious of it. The principle, of course—the evasion of an oppressive reality—is exactly the same as that of delusion, except that in this case the alternative is provided from among competitive fragments of reality rather than by the subject's imagination. It differs from the normal social maneuver of *pretending* not to have heard, for example, a critical or incriminating remark—either to avoid embarrassment or to give oneself more time in which to frame an adequate reply —in that, in the latter case, perception is not impaired; the reality is observed and consciously adjusted to, always with a careful and often elaborate disguise of any possible incongruity in one's behavior. But in the other, there is no conscious adjustment to reality and no concern for the plausibility of one's disbelief in it; although the fact is registered by the senses, the mind blankly refuses to recognize it, "plunging its head into the sand—or rather into a pile of alternate distractions—like an ostrich," as Dr. Newman put it. It is a kind of instantaneous amnesia.

What is astonishing to me is the familiarity, in less acute forms, of all these aberrations. We constantly practice them, in degrees which are still deliberate and controlled, as everyday stratagems of life—to protect our pride or vanity, or to satisfy our impossible or impractical desires. The pleasant afternoon daydream is not very far removed from the fantasy or delusion; the expediently overlooked insult is only a step from hysterical deafness, and the comfortable conclusion that our teacher grades us poorly because she is "down on us" is a very close cousin to the paranoid persecution complex. But in psychopathic people, as Dr. Newman pointed out, these devices have become involuntary and extreme—perhaps because these people have more need of them than we, and practice them more intensely. They have lost control of them, and in doing so they often, ironically enough, suffer more than they profit by them, through the horrors of hallucination and delusion. There is something truly terrible in this—the idea of a wretched mind outwitted by its own virtuosity—as if, in so skillfully and passionately evading its oppressions, it had failed in some human obligation,

185

had broken some natural covenant of suffering and been made to suffer even more.

Had what I consider a great success today with a third-floor patient named Sutton. He is a catatonic—a tall, stooped, sallow boy of about twenty-three who has not spoken a single word in the eight months he has been here. He is frozen into a tense, round-shouldered, standing position, his clenched fists plunged into his pockets and his thin face turned downward with a look of bitter apathy. He has to be tube-fed, but can, if pushed gently forward off balance, be gotten into an unpleasantly mechanical kind of motion, like one of those tin wind-up soldiers; after which he has to be stopped by pressing a hand against his chest. Took him down in the elevator for a walk and started him off in the direction of Hillcrest, following along at his side in a cheerfully subjective mood, as he is utterly passive and demands nothing from one in caution, conversation or attention, other than an occasional minor adjustment of his machinery.

I don't know what gave me the idea, but as we were passing Field House it suddenly occurred to me that it would be an interesting experiment to take him into the lounge and have him listen to some music. I got him into a chair and put on the Brahms Second Piano Concerto. He sat silently, staring at the floor with his usual immobility of face and body as the music thundered, ebbed and poured around him. Although I watched him carefully for about ten minutes, it was impossible to distinguish any reaction whatever, or even, indeed, to tell if he were listening to it. About halfway through the second movement I decided that the experiment was not going to be a very productive one and gave up my vigil, idly picking a volume off the bookshelf beside me and thumbing through it while I listened to the remainder of the concerto. It was a copy of Joyce's collected works, and fell open to a play called *Exiles*, which I had never read before. This proved to be such a brilliant and exciting piece of writing that I became completely absorbed in it, and had read almost through the first act before I was aware that the music had stopped. I

glanced up at Richard, who sat in the same rigid attitude of senseless preoccupation.

As there was no particular urgency to return I began—out of
my enthusiasm for the play, and perhaps a half-conscious inspiration to transpose the experiment into a literary form—to read it
aloud to him. It contains a scene between two friends, one of
whom, whose name is Richard and who is a fairly candid projection of Joyce himself, has just returned from several years of self-
exile to Dublin, the city of his youth, where he is being offered
assistance in securing a suitable position by the other, whose
name is Robert. This man—a companion of the hero's youth—
has arranged for his friend at eight-thirty on the following evening an interview which will almost certainly secure for him the
post he so desperately needs, and urgently advises Richard to be
punctual in keeping it. The irony of this benevolence has been
developed in the previous scene, in which we have seen him
also arranging a tryst with Richard's wife at the very same hour
as the interview, in the course of which he will be making a
spirited effort to seduce her. Richard's darkly beautiful insight
into this piece of treachery is contained in muted speeches of
wonderful intensity and complexity, which, in my excitement,
I read with considerable effect. I was about halfway through the
scene when my excitement was immeasurably increased from
quite another source—a series of guttural, animal-like grunts
from Richard Sutton. Raising my eyes swiftly from the page, I
saw that he had taken his clenched fists from his pockets, pushed
himself up out of the chair by the pressure of his elbows on its
arms, and sat leaning toward me in an attitude of rigid, trembling
attention, his eyes and features filled with fierce animation while
he made quivering, spastic efforts to speak. It was a truly thrilling—if somewhat startling—thing to see, being the first effort
at communication of any kind that I have ever known him to
make; or, for that matter, the first evidence I have seen that it is
possible in any way to establish contact with him.

"Do you want me to go on?" I asked.

There was an unmistakably positive quality about his grunted, eager sounds and the convulsive jerking of his head. I lifted the book again and continued, for another speech or two, to read the scene; but the sounds and spasmodic movements that he made grew so violent that I stopped and set the book down, afraid that he would become too severely agitated. I had another inspiration then.

"Would you like to read with me?" I asked.

Again there was the fierce mumbled expression of assent. I moved my chair next to his and held out the book to him. His hands unclenched gradually in an agonized, arthritic way, and, lifting them slowly, he clutched the edges of the book, taking it tensely into his lap, and in a clear, perfectly articulate voice, and with great intelligence and feeling, began reading the part of Richard. I cannot express how astonished, delighted and profoundly moved I was.

We read through the whole scene and went on to the next, a particularly difficult one between Richard and his wife, in which she reveals Robert's deception to him, and he, from a strangely involuted motive whose investigation becomes the point of the whole play, permits her to keep the assignation if she wishes. Although my sudden switch of characterization to Richard's wife was so disastrously comic that it would have unsettled the most dedicated professional actor, it did not seem at all to disturb the vitality and authority of Richard's reading. It is hard to say that it was an *interpretation* of the part (in the sense of being an impersonation of some character other than his own), because, knowing so little about his original personality, it was impossible to tell in what respects it differs from the character which emerged out of the lines he was reading; but it was certainly a highly sensitive and appropriate reading which he maintained with absolute consistency, and which, in transforming him suddenly before my eyes from a rigid, mute automaton, sunken in depths of unfathomable apathy, into a volatile, gifted, highly articulate young novelist, was truly bewildering, and gave me a feeling very near to awe.

It was only when we had finished the scene and come to the beginning of the next act, in which Richard does not appear, that his transfiguration ended, as abruptly as it had begun. He searched the page of text, apparently to discover the identity of the speakers, and, seeing that Richard was absent from the scene, dropped his head suddenly, the animation fading from his eyes and features, and slumped back into the chair, as remote, inert and impassive as before. When I asked if he would not like to read Robert in the scene that followed, he made no sign of response whatever, sitting with his head sunken down upon his chest, apparently totally unaware of the open book which he still held clutched in his hands. I thought for a moment of going on to further scenes of Richard's, but decided, from his previous evidence of agitation, that he had had enough for one such session, and that, as an experiment, it had already provided more than enough material for consideration.

My report of this event caused a considerable stir among the staff and won me the congratulations of Bea, Dr. Lavrier and Dr. Newman, who is Sutton's analyst—which I must admit has kept me in a glow of satisfaction all day! What a strange thing it was! I shall never forget my sensations on hearing that first perfectly spoken line of dialogue come from Richard's lips. I suppose it's impossible to know just what it was that caused him to react as he did—whether the simple coincidence of his name being the same as the protagonist's, or the opportunity for him to escape entirely out of his own problems and personality into a totally foreign life and set of circumstances; or, on the contrary, a strong similarity in the situation to something which has occurred in his own life (I am inclined to believe it was this, remembering the bitter look of absorption with which he followed Joyce's profound and beautifully evoked ironies of the scene of Robert's treachery). At any rate, it is not only a fascinating development in itself, but will—as Dr. Newman himself agreed—provide many useful and exciting clues for his analyst to pursue.

What a sense of achievement it has given me! Something I sorely needed after my disastrous day with Lilith. I realize, of course, that it was largely accidental—but then, so was penicillin and many other scientific discoveries, which were nevertheless, as Dr. Lavrier reminded me (I am going to write his words down here, I am so proud of them!), "born out of the intelligence and patience of the investigator, and what is probably the greatest natural gift there is—the ability to improvise and capitalize on any interesting accidents that occur along the way."

I feel that all of these experiences, however discouraging or inscrutable they may seem at the time, are deepening my insights, strengthening my sensitivity to these people's needs and natures and making me gradually into a really effective member of a profession I am beginning to love. I wonder if I have begun to learn for the first time what it means to be ambitious!

Going to make an earnest beginning this weekend on the psychology books I took out. Have done little but dabble in them so far. Think I will begin Jung's *Modern Man in Search of a Soul*, which seems, from glancing through it, to be a tremendously exciting book. I have not yet finished *The Red and the Black*, and have been so absorbed in my work for the past few days that I have had little time to go on with it. I feel somewhat ashamed of having left Julien so long in prison, but perhaps it is a kindness. There is no possible place for him to end but at the guillotine; and I don't feel very much inclined, just now, to tread the gallows with him.

¶ *MON., MAY 4:*

Received my first pay check this evening! We get paid every two weeks, and I earn $55 a week—110 wonderful, well-earned dollars. (Actually only about $85, by the time social security, income tax, etc., are taken out.) Never felt this way about my army pay, which I could never help thinking of as conscience money of some sort, and was always a little ashamed of accepting. Gave fifty dollars to Grandma as soon as I got home. She said, "Oh, my . . . why, Vincent, Sonny . . ." and stood in the middle of the kitchen floor with misty eyes, looking desolate with emotion. Felt as I did when I was eleven and gave her a little imitation amethyst brooch for Christmas. Then I ruined this, and the pleasure of being paid, and the whole evening, by the ugly scene with Grandpa after dinner. Went out to water the porch geraniums and was sitting on the front steps afterward when he came out to talk to me.

"Your grandma tells me you've given her fifty dollars, Sonny," he said.

"Yes, sir. I get fifty dollars a week, and I feel as if I ought to pay at least twenty-five into the house," I said.

"That's very generous, Lad."

"Well, I'm twenty-three years old now, and I ought to be helping with expenses by this time. If I was working in Washington or somewhere, I'd have to pay that much for my board and room, at least."

"Why, I know, Lad; but you're not working away from home. Don't think I don't appreciate what you've done, but as we can get along all right without it, I think you ought to be putting that money away. You might change your mind about going to college someday, for example, and you'd find it would come in very useful."

There must be some terrible weakness or vindictiveness in me that I'm afraid I will never learn to overcome: why did I suddenly dredge up out of my memory a remark of his that was made four years ago and quote it back to him in such a heartless way? "Yes, sir, but I think I ought to. We all have debts to pay, every step of the way." That is *not* why I gave her the money—at least not entirely, not consciously, as honestly as I can determine. How terrible it is when two people who love each other have each irreparably wounded the other, so that they know they can never be truly reconciled!

191

In spite of this unhappy conclusion, had an interesting and productive day at the Lodge. Worked with Behrendt, Palakis, Meaghan, Thurmond and Hagan. Palakis is deteriorating rapidly, and will probably be back on Third Floor by tomorrow. Spoke rapidly and wildly and was seldom in contact, scattering chessmen across the floor at one point and crying out (apparently referring to his king), "It is useless, useless, to defend him! He is doomed already! Doomed by the guilt of his Manipulator!"

Curious incident with Mrs. Meaghan. When I brought in Behrendt from playing tennis—another inglorious defeat for me! —Lilith was playing her flute, and she (Mrs. Meaghan) was standing at the open door of her own room, staring sightlessly into the corridor and listening with that same look of thrilled attention which I suddenly remembered her exhibiting on the first day that I met her, when Bob and I were playing cards with her in the lounge, and the sound of Lilith's instrument had drifted into the room.

When I offered her my company for an hour she raised her finger to her lips and said with savage impatience, "Ssh! Be still!" After the music had stopped, and it had become apparent from the length of the pause that followed that it was not to be resumed, she turned her eyes toward me, still dark with anger, and said fiercely in her elegant European voice, "How stupid of you. How very cruel. It was so beautiful."

"I'm sorry," I said. "I didn't realize you were listening."

She stared at me for a moment, her look of anger changing slowly to her more habitual one of cool formality, and murmured, "Of course. I beg your pardon."

When I repeated my invitation, she accepted it, surprisingly enough, asking me into her room in a rather abstracted way and sitting silently for some time while she stared into the branches of the poplar tree outside her window and tapped with her finger tips the rim of a blue bowl full of floating anemone blossoms which stood beside her on the table. After several minutes she turned to me and said, "I hope you understand. It is just that these are very unusual moments which, in spite of their rarity, are constantly being interfered with—out of policy, indifference, expedience, or some equally callous 'practical' reason. It is extraordinary that beauty can exist at all, when there is so much determined opposition to it. Do you like music?"

I said that my understanding of it was limited to rather primitive forms.

"It is nothing to be ashamed of. Folk music is infinitely preferable, I think, to many of the so-called 'masters.' How eternally the world is deluded by bombast! Wagner, Brahms, Tchaikovsky—I would exchange them all for one Mass of Palestrina's, or this tune which we have just heard."

"It was certainly beautiful," I said.

"Do you think so?"

"Yes. It has some of the loveliest phrases I've ever heard."

"Yes. I've always felt that communication required true simplicity and delicacy, rather than volume or virtuosity. Don't you agree?" While she spoke she parted the anemone blossoms gently and dipped the tips of her fingers into the water. There was something in her voice and manner that I found faintly annoying and which added to my reluctance to support an opinion which seemed so arbitrarily exquisite and not entirely candid.

"Still, I suppose it could be considered a good thing that there are many different kinds of music, since there are so many different tastes," I said.

"Perhaps you are right. Perhaps we are fortunate that there is such a vast audience of vulgarians for the commonplace, and that it is only we few to whom the great ones wish to speak." She lifted one of the blossoms and fondled its stem for a moment, smiling thoughtfully. "When I was a little girl I used to go in the summertime to a lake in Austria, and there were water lilies growing along the bank. I used to lie there in the sun and pluck them up. Their stems are coated with a kind of brown slime that you can strip off in your fingers. There is no more delicious sensation in the world." She lifted her hand to her mouth and very

193

delicately touched the tip of her tongue to her fingers. "It is a taste you never forget: cool and dark, like olives."

There was an unaccountable pause, and I asked with sudden discomfort, "Would you like to play cards?"

"No, thank you."

"We have time for a game of Five Hundred, if you like."

She turned her eyes toward me slowly and smiled. "I'm sure you think of yourself as a very persuasive young man, but I am really not inclined."

"As 'persuasive'?" I said.

"I could not help noticing that when you went on your motor trip the other day you succeeded in persuading Miss Arthur to accompany you—which is really quite remarkable, considering that she hasn't been on such a trip in months. But I think you will find me a match for you."

"Well, I won't insist, if you don't want to. I thought you might enjoy it," I said.

"Thank you." She drew a handkerchief out of her sleeve and clasped her wet fingers in it, inclining her head a little to watch. "You seem to be a very nice young man. Do you write poetry?"

"No, I don't."

"May I ask why you are working here?"

"There doesn't seem to be anything else I can do," I said. "And I enjoy it."

"Really? I don't think I would enjoy it at all. Are you married?"

"No."

"I should think it would be a most depressing kind of work—entertaining eccentric spinsters, pushing witless girls about."

"That isn't quite the way I think of it," I said.

"Of course it isn't. I'm sure you are very *serieux*. You have that strangely anxious look about you of men of principle. You remind me, if you will forgive the comparison, of a priest."

"I don't think I deserve it," I said.

"It is less flattering than you believe." She finished drying her fingers and spread them out like the spines of a fan, studying them gently. "Principles will bear examining, you know. That is something the young are always too proud, and too busy trying to practice them, to discover. There was a young nun, for example, who used to be very kind to me when I was a girl. My parents were killed in the war, and I was sent to a Catholic orphanage. I was very lonely and miserable at first, and I often used to cry all night. This nun would come into the dormitory and sit beside my bed, sometimes until two o'clock in the morning, to comfort me. But curiously enough, it seemed to cause her considerable distress. I remember once, when she took me into her arms and held my head against her breast, that she was weeping. I thought at the time that it was a religious emotion—charity, or simply pity for a lonely child—as indeed it would have been accepted by anyone who witnessed it. But not long after this she asked to be released from her vows, and left the orphanage. Do you know what it was that troubled her?" She paused, creating a deliberate and skillful suspense, to which I found myself extremely vulnerable.

"No."

"She wanted a child. It was an instinct whose strength she had never fully realized until she held a lonely little girl in her arms, and which she then had desperately misinterpreted as piety for as long as she was able. But she could not continue to deceive herself."

"How do you know this?" I asked.

"Because I met her many years later, in civil life, at a little mountain village in Austria. She was happily married and had three children, to whom she was joyfully dedicated. We had tea together one afternoon in Zell-am-Zee, watching them swimming in the lake in front of us."

"But surely it was *because* of her principles that she was able to make the break," I said.

"Exactly. Because of her *examined* principles. There are forms

195

of activity which are incompatible with certain temperaments—
they are too exalted, perhaps, too disciplined, or too full of
temptations for one's nature. And the person of real integrity will
be honest enough to relinquish them, rather than making a
mockery of his whole life, or deforming his nature by attempting
to extend it too far. It is worth remembering."

She tucked her handkerchief into her sleeve and, while I
stared at her with a vague and confused sense of dismay, began
musingly to rearrange the anemone blossoms in the blue bowl.
Our conversation ended with mumbled inanities on my part and
an air of courteous detachment on hers.

What a disturbing woman she is—both for the devilish insight which she appears to have into my own misgivings and
the cruelly sophisticated way in which she is able to express it.
I had an impression of profound and finely controlled hostility—
even of threat—from her, and am afraid that in any conflict she
may choose to ordain between us I will find her more than "a
match for me," as she put it.

I had intended to stop in and speak to Lilith for a moment, as
it is several days since I have seen her, but I felt so strangely de-
bilitated by what Mrs. Meaghan had said, and was so preoccupied
with sorting out its implications, that I decided not to. I must
do so tomorrow, however, or she will feel that I am deliberately
avoiding her; must make some effort to show that I don't bear
her any childish ill-will for her behavior on the picnic, and try to
repair the bad impression I must have made on her with my own.
Also, I have not yet given her Warren's message, which I promised
to do. Every time I see him in the second-floor common room, or
pass him out walking, he gives me a long anxious look of inquiry,
which is beginning to get quite irritating. I think I have made
a mistake in allowing myself to accept the role of confidant—
even to the extent that I have—and will have to guard against this
indiscretion in the future. (It seems to me I have made this
resolution before!)

I am going to find it difficult to be conscientious about keeping this journal regularly, with Jung to look forward to every evening. I have read myself to sleep with it the last two nights—and what a wonderful and illuminating experience it has been! Can't remember being so delighted and rewarded by a book since Eric introduced me to *A Passage to India*. Find I can't read more than ten or a dozen pages at a time, however, as this is enormously profound and complex writing. What an original and brilliant man he is! And how unfalteringly honest—when not inspired—in his opinions! I intend to copy down every evening a passage that has been particularly significant for me, and make it a sort of text for the day. How much I will have learned in a year's time, if I keep this resolution! Yesterday, for example, in his essay on "The Problems of Modern Psychotherapy," I found these lines:

> *How can I be substantial if I fail to cast a shadow? I must have a dark side also if I am to be whole . . . psychology has profited greatly from Freud's pioneer work; it has learned that human nature has also a black side, and that not man alone possesses this side, but his works, his institutions, and his convictions as well. Even our purest and holiest beliefs can be traced to the crudest origins. . . . It is painful—there is no denying it—to interpret radiant things from the shadow-side, and thus in a measure reduce them to their origins in dreary filth. But it seems to me to be an imperfection in things of beauty, and a weakness in man, if an explanation from the shadow-side has a destructive effect. The horror which we feel for Freudian interpretations is entirely due to our own barbaric or childish naïveté, which believes that there can be heights without corresponding depths, and which blinds us to the really "final" truth that, when carried to the extreme, opposites meet.*

Can't explain my excitement on reading this passage. It seems to me that in every line of it there is more honor, hope and pride than in anything I have ever heard from my sweetheart, my minister, my neighbors, or my officers. Maybe if I had had a father he would have told me such things. But it doesn't seem very likely, from the way they talk about him.

*A*T THE O.T. meeting the next morning Bea asked if I had seen Lilith lately.

"Not since the picnic," I said. "I've been meaning to stop in every day, but something always seems to come up."

"Well, I wish you would. She may be brooding about it. See if you can get her outside for a while; but if she won't go, spend half an hour or so with her in her room, anyway. She gets herself locked in there for weeks, sometimes, and we don't want that to happen again."

"I haven't been quite certain of what attitude to take about the picnic," I said.

"I'm sure it will occur to you on the way up." She smiled and clapped her hands together in a facetiously pedagogical way, as if she were quoting from a text: "Frankness, and perfect self-possession, if such a combination is possible. It's never wise to put on a great show of magnanimity—because our feelings *are* involved, we *do* get honestly annoyed or alarmed sometimes—but on the other hand we don't want any recriminations; that's never the way to help, or to heal. I must have said all this before, but I know it helps to hear it again, sometimes."

"Yes, it does."

I do not think I had realized, until I was obliged by Bea's assignment to put an end to it, that my delay in seeing Lilith again was a deliberate, if scarcely conscious, postponement on my part; but I could not any longer remain unaware of the apprehension that had produced it when I found myself muttering, as I walked toward the Lodge, imaginary lines of opening conversation, in order to practice the attitude of equanimity which Bea had recommended to me. It did not prepare me, however, for the enchanting vagary which met my eyes when I entered Lilith's room. I found her seated at her loom in front of a half-completed tapestry, her head held close against the warp in what must have been an extraordinarily uncomfortable position, smiling dreamily while she wove into the fabric her own long yellow hair. I stood staring at her for a moment with unwilling delight at the grotesque charm of the sight, until she turned her head toward me painfully, bound, as she was, to the loom.

"It will be very unusual cloth," I said.

"Yes. Do you think it's beautiful?"

"Very. But it seems too much of a sacrifice. What are you going to do? Cut it off?"

"Yes. There are some scissors there on the table. Will you hand them to me?"

"No."

"You won't?"

"Part of my duty is to protect you; and I wouldn't be observing it if I allowed a desecration like that."

"You are not so stern today," she said.

"I was angry the last time I saw you, because I had failed at my duty."

"And now you are more determined than ever to succeed?"

"Yes."

"But you can't make me ruin my tapestry; that would be too cruel. It was to be a present for you—a throw for your bed. I made it especially for you."

"Why?"

"To make you dream." I stood smiling at her, thinking what

little avail it was to "prepare" oneself for an interview with such a creature. "What will you do, then? Leave me chained here by my hair until I starve?"

In spite of my determined composure, her words created in my mind a weird and unpleasantly compelling image: a heap of silver bones fallen beside a moldering loom in a silent sunny room, and, hanging by its shining hair from the dusty, unfinished tapestry, a skull, to which her shriveled features had shrunken in a blind, eternal mask of pain.

"No, I won't do that," I murmured. I went to the table and found her scissors among a litter of paintbrushes and jars of powdered pigments.

"What are you going to do?" she asked.

"I'm going to cut the threads and set you free."

"Oh, that will be very difficult."

She turned her face toward me and watched solemnly as I knelt beside her chair and cut the warp threads one by one, prying the strands of her hair from between them.

"You are very gentle," she said.

"I don't want to hurt you."

She gathered her freed hair in her hands and shook out the braided strands, looking ruefully at the clipped threads hanging in the loom.

"Do you know how long I worked on it?" she said.

"No."

"All morning. For hours."

"Then it's time you got outside for a while. Come and take a walk with me."

"I can't go outside today. There were crows in the poplar trees this morning."

"And what does that signify?" I asked.

"They were sent by my people to warn me. But we can go down and sit on the veranda, if you like. It's very pleasant there."

"All right."

She followed beside me silently, barefoot, along the corridor and downstairs in the elevator to the ground floor, where, while I sat watching her from one of the wicker armchairs, she wandered quietly among the greenery, pausing sometimes to touch leaves with her finger tips and set them tremblingly astir, or to purse her lips and blow gently at the petals of begonia blossoms.

"Is it all right for me to go on trips again?"

"Yes, I think it would be good for you."

"I thought perhaps they wouldn't let me, after the picnic."

"No one said anything about it," I said.

"And you haven't lost your job."

"No. They're very kind, wise people here."

"I'm very glad. You said that you might; and I would have been very sorry if you had left."

"Well, I haven't," I said. "So nothing bad has come of it at all; and the next time you can go along with an easy conscience."

"Oh, no," she said. "They punished me for going."

"They punished you?"

"Yes. I told you they would, for disobeying them."

"What did they do to you?" I asked.

"They wept. It's how they always punish me; they come and kneel at my bed and make it shudder with their sobbing. Does that seem like a mild punishment to you? If it does, you have never heard anyone that you love weeping."

"No, it doesn't," I said. "I've heard my mother crying."

"Have you?" She turned toward me with a look of tenderness that I could never have imagined in her face. "Why is she un-happy?"

"She isn't, now," I said. "I hope she isn't, anyway."

She stood silently for a moment and then came and sat beside me, holding in her hand a little spiral of vine that she had plucked. Outside the veranda I heard Howard Thurmond shout-ing, "Zotz, zotz, zotz!" and shrieking with laughter. I saw him through the screen, running across the lawn toward the drive and stopping to fling horse chestnuts at Mandel, who ran after him, his arms lifted to protect his face. "Die!" Howard shouted. "Zotz, zotz, zotz! You're dead! You stink! You're rotting!"

Lilith raised her hand and held it in front of my eyes to block my sight. "Don't listen to them," she said. "Give me your hand." When I hesitated she lifted my hand from the arm of the chair and, separating my third finger, slipped the spiral of vine over it, like an old-fashioned serpent ring. I turned it idly between my thumb and finger tip, and said in a moment, "Tell me something, truthfully, will you?"

"Yes."

"It was you who laughed at me, wasn't it—that day I broke the eggs?"

"Yes. If you want to believe it was."

"I knew it was, the minute I saw you. Why didn't you say anything?"

"I didn't think it needed to be spoken about," she said. "When two people recognize each other, nothing needs to be said." She dropped her head, resting her chin on her shoulder, and stared out at the lawn. Howard and Mandel had disappeared, and under the willows I could see mist rising from the wet grass. We did not speak for some time, and I became aware of a growing sense of tranquillity as I sat in the soft green light of the veranda turning Lilith's vine ring on my finger and looking out beyond the end of the grounds to where townspeople passed occasionally in the street. A woman pushing a baby carriage, whose wobbling wheel caused her to pause sometimes and examine it with ineffectual anxiety, made a slow, halting progress toward Diamond Avenue. How far away they seemed—and how droll their dilemmas—separated from us by the shadows of the poplars and the panes of sunlight that fell between the trees! I must have smiled—perhaps I even made a murmur of amusement—for Lilith turned to look at me and asked, "What is her name?"

"I don't know. Mrs. Carmichael, I think."

"Don't you know her?"

"Not very well. I see her in the grocery store sometimes."

"Why did you smile, then?"

"I don't know. It just seemed sort of . . . amusing, somehow."

She turned her head to watch Mrs. Carmichael disappearing slowly among the shadows of the elms.

"Are they nice people?" she asked. "What is it like, living in this town?"

"I don't really know," I said. "I was born here and I've been here all my life; but I don't really feel as if I've lived here, somehow. They have a way of making you feel alone, and ashamed."

She listened with her eyes lowered, closing them slowly with a look of soft intensity as she asked, "Why are you ashamed, Vincent?"

"My father was a strange man," I said. "He was cruel, and selfish, I suppose; he wanted to be free. And my mother was . . . different from most of the women in this town; I think she was more generous. And they've never forgiven me for it."

"Oh, I know," Lilith murmured. "That is the great prize they offer, isn't it? Their forgiveness." She raised her head and leaned a little forward, whispering with a look of mischievous woe to the retreating figure in the street, "Mrs. Carmichael, forgive me, please. I am barefoot. I have yellow hair. And look at my arms, Mrs. Carmichael; see how soft and white they are. Forgive me for them. Forgive me because I am beautiful, and full of joy, and because I have visions." She broke into glittering laughter, stretching her throat sweetly and shaking her tangled hair. As much to compose myself as for any reason, I said, "That isn't really fair."

"No, I'm not fair," she said. "It's a long while since I tried to be. But you are, still, aren't you? So terribly fair." She regarded me gently for a moment. "And your poor mother, Vincent? Did they kill her?"

"I don't know," I muttered, truly distressed by her question. "They helped, perhaps, although I would hate to think so. They made her feel very bad; none of them ever came to see her, and they would hardly speak to her in the street. And she felt things very deeply. But I don't think it was that so much as—"

"As your father?"

"Yes."

"Your wicked, wandering father." She smiled slowly in a way that caused me suddenly to be profoundly shocked at the willingness of my confidences and at the way I had exposed myself, in making them, to both her irony and her disturbing sympathy. (For I had spoken with a sense of release—at expressing to someone feelings I had kept so long concealed—that was as surprising as it was profound.)

"Do you hate him, Vincent?"

"I don't know him," I said, "and I would have no right to condemn him if I did."

My sudden defensive diffidence must have made its way into my tone of voice, for she appeared to accept this as a rebuke, dropping her eyes and turning her head away from me.

"Are your people any different?" I asked her gently, in a rather conciliatory way, to lessen the severity of my last remark.

"Oh, yes. They are generous and gentle."

"There are such people here," I said.

"Yes, there are a few; you are one, Vincent. But my people are wise as well." She moved her hand toward me quickly in a gesture of contrition. "I didn't mean to offend you."

"I have no illusions about my wisdom," I said.

"But I think you have more than most. You have had moments of vision, Vincent, which I can see in your eyes; they are more like the eyes of my people than any others I have seen. And you have a way of walking, and of using your body, that reminds me of my people. When you were climbing the cliff the other day I saw how much you resembled them."

"You actually see them, then?" I asked, somewhat unwillingly gratified by this distinction. "Their bodies and faces? What are they like?"

She watched me for a moment, as if examining the impulse

that had made me question her. "They are tall and fair—do you think my hair is beautiful? It is growing more like theirs, but still it has nothing of their beauty. In my next Degree it will become more beautiful." She paused to catch a strand of her hair and spread it in her fingers, smiling while she studied the separate golden filaments. "Do you see how coarse it is? It makes a sound like sand when you rub it in your fingers; theirs is finer than silk, and soundless."

"They must be very beautiful," I said.

"Oh, yes. They are too beautiful to describe. Their eyes are so clean, like diamonds, and their breath and bodies smell as sweet as cinnamon. They are not stuffed with filth, because they do not eat, as we do; they are nourished by light. Only sometimes, for joy, they touch their lips with nectar or cold spring water. They speak the purest language in the world, which they have taught me very early, because I am talented—it isn't generally allowed until much later. And when they pass one another they do not turn their eyes away and pass in silence; they hold their hands out to one another and clasp each other's fingers for a moment, without shame. There is no shame."

"But there is sorrow?" I asked. "You say they weep for you."

"Only for me. Only when they fear that I will not be faithful, that I will slip away." She raised her eyes slowly to the lawn, staring wanly for a moment. "They are afraid that I may . . . return. That I will find something . . . desirable again."

"Something that you love?"

"Yes."

"Don't they believe in love, then?" I asked her softly.

"It is all that they believe in," she said. "But they love nobly— for joy—as they are teaching me to love. Not out of pity, or necessity, or guilt. As only children love, in your world." The wind stirred, and she watched the leaping shadows of the elms along the distant street. "But perhaps there is still such love here. In this town, even. Can you tell me?"

I watched the far houses for a moment with their porch swings and rocking chairs, thinking of the evenings I had spent on them with Laura.

"No, I can't tell you if there is."

We sat in silence while an old gray horse went past in the street, pulling a creaking wagon full of split oak firewood. A farmer in faded overalls, sitting on the wagon seat, lashed its haunches while it struggled between the shafts, its lips foaming and working convulsively about the bit.

"Poor beast," Lilith said. "They shouldn't be made to work; they are too beautiful."

"Do you like horses?" I asked.

"Oh, yes, more than anything! Do you?"

"Yes. You must see one of the tournaments, then, before the summer's over. There's some wonderful riding."

"A tournament!" She turned toward me swiftly with an expression of delight. "Do they really have them? With lances and armor? Oh, I'd love to see one!"

"Well, not with armor," I said. "We don't try to knock each other off the horses any more. Only to spear targets."

"Do you ride in them, then?"

"I used to, before the war. I had a little mare of my own once."

"How wonderful!" she said. "Will you take me to one, Vincent? Do you think they'll let me go?"

"I think they'd be delighted that you want to," I said. "I'll let you know when the next one is held, and we'll ask."

"Oh, please! And will you ride in it? You must! I want to see you ride."

"I don't have a horse now," I said. "And I can't very well, anyway, if I'm going to look after you." She frowned wistfully. "What about your people?" I said. "Won't they punish you for going?"

"Oh, not now," she said. "They can't, now."

When I returned her to her room she stood just inside the door, her head hanging, looking down at her white feet.

"I almost forgot to tell you," I said. "Mr. Evshevsky sent you his regards." She raised her head and, after watching me for a moment with an amused and quizzical look, laughed softly. "He said he hadn't seen you for several days and was afraid you might be ill. He asked about your health."

"Tell him I am incurable."

I could not help smiling at this. "I refuse to believe it," I said. "You will see."

When I turned to go she touched my sleeve and said, "You won't be so long in coming to see me again, will you? That wasn't kind."

"Well, I have lots of other patients to see," I said. "I can't get up every day; but I'll see that someone does, if you want company. I'm glad to hear that you do." She did not reply, looking somberly into my eyes for a moment before turning away toward the window.

I have not said a great deal here about my own sensations during this interview, perhaps because I am still too uncertain of what they must have been, at this stage of my acquaintance with Lilith, to set them down; but there is a long passage in my journal—I shall not quote it entirely—which will indicate the state of mind in which, that evening, I sat down to record them.

¶ *TUES., MAY 5:*

. . . a suggestion of understanding—even of intimacy—which I cannot deny is unsettling, even though I have seen her behave in much the same way to Warren, and understand that it is part of her sickness. When we were sitting on the veranda, for example, and she slipped the tendril of vine onto my finger, I had a sense of peace which, even while I was experiencing it, I felt the strangeness of. A feeling of—what? Imperfect content, sorrowful content—which is absurd to say. Is peace an imperfect or sorrowful thing? I can't believe it, and don't understand it. I have tried to think of something to compare this feeling to; but I have had only one other experience which is even faintly comparable, and it is equally odd:

When I was on leave in Sydney and shopping with the fifty

pounds that I had saved to buy a Christmas present for Grandma; and I met the American deserter in civilian clothes in the milk bar at Bondi. He looked hunted, and begged me for money to get out of Australia; he said that he could bribe a freighter captain to smuggle him into San Francisco. He was afraid to turn himself in, he said, and couldn't, anyway; because he had thrown his uniform away, and would have been shot if he were caught without it. I believed him, and gave him the money— I don't know why—so that I had nothing left to buy a present for Grandma with. It left me with a feeling that was a little like this: peace, of a kind, but imperfect peace; peace that is half grief. (I have made too much of this. How confused it all is!)

And yet, in spite of the confusion that she makes me feel, and the obscurity of what she says, I feel that I understand her— almost perfectly, sometimes—and burn with ambition to help her, to perform some miracle cure that will astonish everyone. When I listen to her speak there are moments when I feel as if I knew exactly what it is that she needs, and can show her how to find it; that only I can heal her.

But why on earth did I say those things to her about my parents? They were far too intimate, far too intense. I had the feeling suddenly that our roles had become entirely reversed— that I was the patient and she the therapist. Perhaps it was that curious sense of fraternity that she made me feel; of understand-ing—even anticipating—my feelings, and sharing and supporting me in them. Much of what she says—her ironic litany to Mrs. Carmichael, for example—I seem to recognize, to have felt my-self, and for some reason to rejoice at hearing her express. This is perhaps the most alarming thing about it all.

She does alarm me, I must confess, after my experience at Great Falls. When I think of taking her alone to the tournament (as I promised to do!) I have a rather chilly feeling of anxiety. Perhaps it was not wise to offer to, without Bea's advice. (But I'm sure she will approve, and Dr. Lavrier as well.) Still, it may go very well; and at any rate it would be quite unnatural, as Bea says, not to feel some nervousness at such an early stage of my career. Particularly when I have made such an impressive contact with a patient whom the rest of the staff finds so difficult, and have the opportunity to perform a really valuable and individual piece of work. It is the delicacy and originality of the opportunity that makes it so disturbing, I suppose.

¶ *Later* (2:00 A.M.):
Have been reading more of Jung, and have found this passage, which I must set down, however cheerlessly. It seems to me to illuminate not only my feelings about Lilith, but also—very greatly—the conversation which I had yesterday with Mrs. Meaghan. While I could not find within myself the full relevance of her words, I seem to have found it here in Jung; and reading them back, now (from yesterday's entry), in the light of this remarkable comment, how much more profound, how bitterly penetrating, they have become!

> *The man who uses modern psychology to look behind the scenes not only of his patients' lives but more especially of his own—and the modern psychotherapist must do this if he is not to be merely an unconscious fraud—will admit that to accept himself in all his wretchedness is the hardest of tasks, and one which it is almost impossible to fulfil. The very thought can make us livid with fear. We therefore do not hesitate, but lightheartedly choose the complicated course of remaining in ignorance about ourselves while busying ourselves with other people and their troubles and sins. This activity lends us an air of virtue, and we thus deceive ourselves and those around us. In this way, thank God, we can escape from ourselves. There are countless people who can do this with impunity, but not everyone can, and these few break down on the road to Damascus. . . .*

And then, a few lines later, these most disturbing words of all:

*How can I help these persons if I am myself a fugitive?*

I know I won't be able to get to sleep immediately, because these words are clamoring in my mind; so I think I'll go out and take a walk before I go to bed. There is a really savage moon above the cherry tree. I may walk down to the Lodge. I've always wanted to see what it looks like in the moonlight.

𝓗ERE ARE FRAGMENTS from my journal for the next several days:

¶ *FRI., MAY 8:*
. . . Not much time tonight, because it is quite late. Just come in from specialing Mrs. Johnson and Susan Turner. ["Specialing" was a kind of extracurricular escort service, outside of regular working hours (i.e., on Saturdays, Sundays, or weekday evenings), which was paid for privately by the patients concerned, rather than by the Lodge. It generally meant no more than accompanying them to the movies in Stonemont, although occasionally on a more elaborate excursion into Washington for a theater performance or concert; and was not very strenuous, as they had to have "special privileges" in order to make such trips and were therefore in a fairly reliable condition.] Interesting to see them outside the hospital surroundings in a normal civil environment. Both second-floor patients with whom I have not had much contact so far, and found them very quiet and agreeable. Saw a Randolph Scott western, which they watched with

evident glee, and stopped afterward for a soda at Wingate's. Among patients in better condition there is a kind of naïveté when they are outside, which is probably a result of their confinement and is very appealing. Felt like an indulgent uncle taking his two favorite nieces out on a special occasion. After eleven when I got them back to the Lodge. Mrs. Daniels, the second-floor night nurse, gave me a cup of coffee, and we smoked and chatted for half an hour. Very nice, housewifely type from South Dakota.

Floors are strange at night. So quiet, and with the bright white light in the corridors. Big electric clock with second hand sweeping soundlessly. Attendants prowling, opening doors sometimes and peering in. Darkness, breathing, occasional whimpering or soft sobs. Last night's linen spread out in the hydro rooms, being examined for semen, blood or excrement. Their poor mad nighttime secrets pried into. Gives you a feeling of rage sometimes: "Oh, leave them alone! Leave their wretched dreams alone!"

When I came down in the elevator remembered that I had used a tire pump this afternoon, and went back to see if I had locked the bicycle shed. Wonderful warm summer night, with locusts singing in the trees and the poplar leaves stirring softly. There was someone there behind the shed, lying in the dark grass. Could see them faintly through the hedge, and hear their whispering. Mandel and a girl. I stood there listening for a minute until I heard him whisper, "No, leave them on." Could not go then until I had discovered her identity. Waited, listening and peering with rabid curiosity through the hedge until I caught a glimpse of her clothing in the moonlight—blue-striped uniform with white collar and apron: one of the student nurses. Do not understand why I was so shocked and disturbed by this. Ugly feeling in the mind. I can't stand that boy.

Then, when I came back down the drive, saw someone standing under Lilith's window in the moonlight. Warren, looking enormously tall and sallow, with dark hollows in his eye pits and huge luminous hands. He was moved from Second Floor to Field House this morning.

"Is anything the matter?" I asked him.

"No, no. I'm just not very sleepy. He raised his eyes rather feverishly. "She sits at her window sometimes at night. I've seen her. I think she sits there all night sometimes."

"Well, not tonight," I said. "You'd better go to bed."

"Yes. Did you know that I was in Field House now? They moved me this morning."

"I know. Congratulations. I hope you'll stay."

"Oh, I will. I know I will. Until I move out for good, that is. I feel so much better. So much surer of everything. I think I'm beginning to make some real progress."

"It's good to hear that, Warren."

"Thank you. I'll be outside by this time next year, I'm sure of it. Even working, perhaps. I feel as if I *could* work again; my mind is so much steadier. I may even be married—you can't tell. What would you think of that?"

"I'd be delighted to hear it."

"Yes. That's very kind of you." He raised his head again to her window and lifted his long hands, glowing in the moonlight, to bite pieces of flesh from the tips of his fingers, spitting them out with an unpleasant soft plosive sound.

"You'd better go to bed now, Warren."

"I will, yes." He turned his face down suddenly, looking at me out of the black hollows of his eyes. "Have you given her my message? That I asked about her?"

"Yes."

"What did she say?"

"She said to thank you. She isn't ill. She's been very busy on a piece of tapestry she's making."

"Oh, thank you! That was very good of you. You've no idea how pleased I am to hear it! Good night, Mr. Bruce."

"Good night."

He turned and walked off under the shadow of the poplars, chuckling and muttering to himself.

Should not have lied to him, but the poor devil needed it. What else could I do? I'm glad he wasn't there last night. . . .

¶ *MON., MAY 11:*

. . . Stopped by this afternoon to speak to Lilith for a moment. She did not answer my tap, but as her door was slightly ajar I pushed it open and looked into her room. She was standing in front of the window, her body latticed by pale gray diamonds of shadow from the wire netting and patched with blazing rags of sunlight, like a slender, smiling Harlequin, holding her breasts and dreaming. I closed the door gently, without speaking to her.

Terrible scene with Mr. Palakis. He is on Third Floor again, and in a dreadful hunted state of fear. After much persuasion I got him downstairs, but as we came out of the elevator he looked down at that slowly rotating ventilation fan in the basement window. A clatter of cutlery and kitchenware and the smell of cooking meat blew out from between its blades. He stared down at it with a look of horror, his face turning pale.

"What is down there?" he asked.

"The kitchen."

"Yes." He raised his head and stared at me, asking in a terrified voice, "That's where you're taking me, isn't it?"

"No. I thought we'd walk down to the pond."

"Oh, that's very clever; but I know what they're going to do."

"What do you mean?"

"They're going to eat me! That's what they want, isn't it? That's what they do with all of us." He thrust his face forward suddenly, peering into my eyes with a stealthy, cunning look. "What's happened to Waters and Archmore?"

"Why, they've been discharged," I said. "They went home last month."

"Oh, yes, that's a very satisfactory answer! Do you think I

213

don't know what's happened to them? Do you think I don't know what it is that you give us to eat? You keep us locked in here until you eat us, one by one!"

"That's nonsense, Mr. Palakis," I said.

He backed away from me suddenly, striking out with his hand. "You want to take me down there and kill me. Hack my body into pieces and cook it, and then sit there munching it at those long white tables. Monsters! Eaters of the earth!"

He turned and began to run wildly across the lawn toward Crowfields. I caught up to him at the edge of the plowed soil and we struggled for several minutes, stumbling in the furrows. He is very strong, in spite of his size, and I couldn't have held him very long if Mandel had not run down the shop stairs to help me. One of the few times I've ever been pleased to see him. Bob and Brewster, one of the floor attendants, came to our aid in a few minutes, and the four of us carried him back to the Lodge, shrieking and stammering, his face scarlet and his lips covered with spittle. We dragged him into an isolation room and stripped him of everything but his underwear. He became suddenly inert, slumping onto the padded floor, where he lay moaning and breathing heavily, like a wounded animal. Have been in an unpleasant state of agitation ever since. My hand is still trembling as I write this. . . .

¶ *THURS., MAY 14:*

Took Lilith walking this morning to the pond. It was quite early and there was still dew on the grass and mist above the water. She sat on the bank with her skirt touseled about her, gathering tulip blossoms that fell down from the poplars. They were all blown and broken; she smoothed the orange petals with her fingers, making them like candle flames. On the opposite shore there was a blue heron hunting for frogs, wading very slowly with delicate stealth, lifting its spoked feet clear of the surface with every step and turning its head sideways to peer among the rushes, its cockade trembling. There was sometimes the soft plash

214

of the falling blossoms on the water. It was delightful to lean against one of the poplars, watching her.

"May I wade?" she asked.

"Yes, if you promise not to drown." She swung her shining head to look at me. "I would hate to have to go in after you," I said immediately. And then, while I looked at her, another of those vivid, startling images that come into my mind when I am with her: myself walking up through the rushes with her body in my arms, her wet frock clinging to her slender body, her drenched hair hanging in ragged, dripping strands, her drowned eyes open, their violet washed pale as opals.

"What's the matter?" she asked.

"Nothing. Are you going in?"

"Yes. Will you come?"

"No. When my feet get cold I'm miserable all day."

She stood up in the grass and gathered her skirt in her hands, stepping out cautiously into the placid water that glittered in the morning light. There were two Liliths, joined at their calves: one fallen, tremulous girl with rippling breasts looking up from her silver underworld, mocking every move my Lilith made. They watched each other merrily and tenderly.

"Look at her," Lilith said. "She wants to be like me. Oh, she is lovely!" She leaned down swiftly and kissed the floating face, which shattered at the touch of her lips, then stood watching with astonished, rueful eyes.

"My kisses kill her. She is like all of them; it destroys them to be loved."

"Is it cold?" I asked, although I did not wish to speak.

"Oh, it's sweet. You must come, Vincent."

"No."

She moved out farther into the pond, clutching her skirt in her hands, the cool water devouring the white columns of her legs, wading in mercury to her thighs. In a moment she had almost disappeared into a bank of milky mist that hung above the water. Only her head and shoulders faded forth from it into the nebulous light above the lake which made her hair glow with a soft, tarnished brilliance. She stood silently, sunken in pale mist, staring out across the water; and I had for a moment the bewildering conviction that she would truly vanish.

"Lilith, come back!" I called, my voice hollow over the lake in the quiet morning air. It echoed three times from the far shore. She turned and came toward me through a patch of water lilies by the shore, the great green leaves and floating lavender blossoms slipping along her wet thighs as she parted them. She stopped and lifted one, glowing in her hand like palely tinted paraffin, the long tubular stem dripping silver.

"Isn't it beautiful?"

"Yes."

"I must take one to Yvonne."

She lifted it higher and, leaning down to the water, bit the stem through with her teeth, her head turned sideways and her hair floating, smiling at me as she did so.

"They're bitter." She waded to the bank and held her hand out to me. "Help me."

Cold, fragile hands, like a frozen sparrow I picked up once when I was a boy. I pulled her up onto the bank and she stood with her wet hair clinging to her throat, lifting the pale flower to her nostrils.

"Do you mean Mrs. Meaghan?" I asked.

"Yes."

"Why do you take her flowers?"

"Because she loves them, and she is afraid to go out by herself to get them." She watched me for a moment, her eyes becoming still. "Do you mind?"

"No, of course not."

"You called me 'Lilith.' "

"It seems a little odd to go on being so formal."

"Yes."

"You're all wet," I said. "We must go back and get you dry, or you'll catch cold."

"I never catch cold," she said. "But we'll go, because I want to take my flower back before it withers."

We walked back silently to the Lodge, a curious tension between us, almost a bitterness.

I felt listless all the rest of the day, impatient and disinterested in my work. Kept thinking about the pond and wanting to return there. Had the feeling that I had forgotten something that I must return for. Even went through my pockets to see if I could discover what was "missing."

It is not possible any longer to consider this a general and "normal" anxiety about my work. It may be partly this; but I recognize, too, my involvement with this girl. She "persuades" me, in some unaccountable way, although she is never openly disobedient or defiant. I can never seem to understand what it is that she persuades me to, although I am aware that in spite of my determination my handling of her is never successfully objective, and I know that I cannot be effective here until I learn to correct this. She makes me see things with her eyes, as it were—there are those "visions," for example, which she seems to evoke. They are not really visions, of course, but ideas about her—conceptions—which are so spontaneous and intense that I almost seem to see them.

I must speak to Dr. Lavrier about it. I feel that these things need to be discussed with him, because it is impossible to get them into a report. When I brought her back this afternoon, for example, I had only the time and space to write: *"Accompanied patient to pond at her suggestion. Agreeable and composed. Went wading, gathered flowers, and talked in lighthearted, happy way. Habitual carelessness about appearance. Asked if she could go out again tomorrow. 9:00–10:00 A.M."* Yet how little does this express what actually occurred, or what I felt to have occurred, beyond the actual events. How totally misleading or inadequate language can be if used in too precise, too categorical a way! I'm sure that much of this can be illuminated if I speak to him in person. After all, what I feel disturbed about may be some very common occupational thing that he can give me immediate insight into. I will try to make an appointment with him tomorrow. . . .

$\mathcal{A}$T THE NEXT morning's meeting I said to Bea, "I took Lilith down to the pond yesterday. She seemed in very good spirits."

"Good, Vincent. Keep her stirring if you can."

"She wants to go to one of the tournaments they have around the county. I told her I'd ask about it."

"Why, that's wonderful," Bea said. "But she'll have to have special permission to go outside the grounds, and I don't have the authority for that. You'll have to ask Dr. Lavrier about it."

"Yes, I wanted to. I wonder when I can see him?"

"This morning, if you like. He has staff conferences from eleven to twelve. Shall I ring him?"

"Yes, I wish you would."

I took Doris Glassman to Field House for a game of ping-pong in the early morning, enjoying in a vagrant, thoughtless way the incessant clattering rhythm of the celluloid ball and the swift mechanical adjustments my bent arm made from side to side, to meet it with the paddle. She kept up her endless senseless civilities while we played: "You're a very good player, Mr. Bruce. Oh, that was very good. I guess you must be winning, aren't you, Mr. Bruce? You certainly play well, Mr. Bruce." Once, when she stooped to retrieve the ball, she held it for a moment in her fingers, seeming to lose her orientation completely while she stared at it.

"What kind of an egg is this, Mr. Bruce?" she asked.

"A linnet egg," I said. "A silver songbird will hatch out of it if you hold it to your throat."

"Will it really, Mr. Bruce? I will, then. That would be very exciting." She lifted the ball to her throat and clasped it there with her hand, smiling at me foolishly. I had not said this out of mockery or impatience with the poor girl—I don't really know why I said it—but watching her stand there at the end of the table, holding the ball against her throat with foolish, patient delight, I felt suddenly alarmed and ashamed. She must have sensed this in some unexpectedly acute manner, for she removed the ball and laid it on the table, her smile widening with a look of apallingly sensitive and humble understanding, and said, "I guess you must have been fooling me, Mr. Bruce."

"Yes, I was," I said gently. "I'm sorry."

"That's all right, Mr. Bruce. I like to joke myself. I like people with a sense of humor. You certainly seem to be a very nice young man, Mr. Bruce."

"I'm afraid I'm not, Doris," I said.

When I had returned her to her floor I felt compelled, out of some nameless uncertainty, to visit Lilith for a moment before my interview with Dr. Lavrier. She was bent above her desk, working with painful concentration on her illuminations. I stood above her and pointed to a line of the ornate Gothic script.

"What does that say?" I asked her.

"This is one of the very oldest of the Data," she said. "Which is a sort of Gospel. It was given by a scribe from Lamoru, after his Recapitulation."

"What does that mean?"

"After many years the Elders are required, for a period, to renounce. They must abjure joy, and resume the old gods, and relive their mortality. It is a kind of imposed anguish, which greatens the joy of those who are wise enough to bear it, and to understand. The line says, 'Although I was grown too great for them, I found that my old sins fitted me like the folded garments of childhood, if one should remove them from an attic hamper. And in this was my astonishment and delight. For how should we trust God if He did not allow us to possess what He had, in love, relieved us of?' "

I tried for a moment to understand it, but I suppose I must have been too preoccupied, for it seemed to shimmer just beyond the reach of reason.

"It seems that your sages have the same passion for obscurity as ours," I said.

"You must remember that he was writing out of darkness. He was suffering. These are the Dark Gospels."

She laid a sheet of tissue across her work and stood up, stretching her hands above her head, her fingers twined together, while she arched her back.

"I don't want to work any more. Will you take me walking?"

"I can't just now," I said. "I have an interview with Dr. Lavrier in a few minutes."

She dropped her laced hands to the back of her head, clasping her neck with them, and looked out at me somberly from between her pointing elbows.

"He is my analyst."

"I know."

"What are you going to talk to him about? Me?"

"I suppose we will, among other things."

"What will you say about me? Will you tell him how wicked I am?"

"Since he is your analyst, I suppose he knows already."

"But I think he likes to be reassured, from other sources. He is such a simple man, but very kind. I talk to him for hours about my childhood, inventing all sorts of things to please him."

"Do you think he believes them?"

"He will believe anything about me, except that I am happy. He thinks, for some reason, that I should be as miserable as he is, and works devotedly to make me so." She wandered to the window and, raising her hands to the level of her face, clutched the wire netting with her curled fingers. It gave her a lithe, ferocious appearance, like a cat poised to pounce. "It is all he exists for," she said. "Inventions and confessions. He thinks he sees truth in them. Don't you see that he's such a fool, Vincent?"

"No. I think he's a very intelligent and sympathetic man. I like him very much."

"And do you want him to have the same opinion of you?"

"I'd like him to, yes."

"Then you must produce some of your own for him. It will please him."

"Some of my own what?"

"Confessions."

While I tried to think of a reply she stood clinging to the netting and staring down upon the prone and vulnerable world, a lovely, jailed predator. Becoming suddenly conscious of the inappropriate length of the silence, I said rather harshly, "What should I confess to him?"

She half turned toward me, laughing. "Why, Vincent, how should I know? If you have nothing that you believe in to confess, invent something for him, as I do."

"What good would that do?" I asked.

"None at all. Except that you would both feel rather pleased. You would feel that you had done the right thing, and be quite proud about it, I suppose." She turned to face me fully, sitting on the sill and leaning back against the wire netting, her eyes becoming somber. "There is no telling what he will prescribe—a long trip, or a change of jobs, perhaps. But no matter what it is, I can tell you from my own experience that it will not cure what possesses you."

With my resolution very little improved by this exchange, I knocked a few minutes later at the door of Dr. Lavrier's office. I saw that Bea had informed him of the subject of my interview, for he had Lilith's clinical records spread out on his desk, along with a sheaf of therapists' reports, among which I recognized several in my own handwriting.

"Bea says you want to talk about Lilith," he said. "She wants to go to some event outside, is that it?"

"Yes. A tournament. There's one at Kingston next week, and I promised her I'd ask about it."

"Did you suggest it yourself?" he asked.

"We were talking about horses the other day, and she said she liked them. When I mentioned the tournaments she said right away that she'd love to go to one. She seemed quite excited about it."

"I see." He began sorting out the stack of reports that I had made on Lilith, glancing through them rapidly while he spoke to me. "You've had extraordinary success with her. I'm pleased to see it. I don't see any mention of hostility here anywhere. Doesn't she ever express any?"

"That's why I wanted to talk to you," I said. "Those reports aren't always very accurate. That is, they're factual, but they don't express what actually happens: the atmosphere of the relationship, if you know what I mean."

"Yes. And you feel that the atmosphere of your relationship is different from what these reports indicate? Are you disturbed about it?"

"Yes, a little."

"Why?"

"Well, it's hard—when you're faced with the direct question—to explain it. But I feel as if she's set up an atmosphere of confidence between us, in some way. I've had the feeling once or twice, for example, that she might have been offering to bribe me."

"For what reason?"

"I don't really know. It seems a little bit silly, now that I actually say it. But I've had the impression that she wanted me to conceal her conduct—not only her conduct, but everything that occurs between us. I don't know whether it's out of a desire for privacy, or a fear of having her behavior interpreted in some way that she doesn't want, or perhaps a fear of being penalized, or what. It's as if she were testing me, in a way—testing my loyalty to her, or something of that sort."

"Well, if she wants to bribe you, there must be something that she offers as a bribe," Dr. Lavrier said. He watched me steadily and kindly. "Let me put it quite candidly: do you ever feel that she's trying to seduce you? It isn't unknown, you know, for patients to seduce personnel—or vice versa, I'm ashamed to say. No matter how confused they may be mentally, there's no suspension of their physiological needs; on the contrary, they're often accelerated. They build up some powerful physical tensions, you know, being isolated as they are. Aside from which, many of them have heightened erotic feelings anyway."

"No, it isn't really that simple," I said. "And yet I suppose you could call it that, although I'm not sure what it is she's offering me. Not just her body, but far more than that; her mind, perhaps—her spirit. I don't know." I stared out of the window, frowning, while I groped for a means of expressing myself. "Does it sound absurd to say this: a kind of glory that she owns, and intimates that she will share with me?"

"No, that doesn't sound absurd." Dr. Lavrier dropped his eyes again to the reports and straightened their edges with his finger tips. "Do you ever feel inclined to accept?" he asked.

"Yes. I don't know what it is, but I do, sometimes." I returned my eyes to his and began to speak more rapidly, having found a point of departure for my thoughts. "You see, I don't really think she's unhappy," I said. "I suppose many of them are, but not Lilith. She has a kind of . . . rapture about her which is very compelling. Do you know what I mean? A kind of rapture that perhaps I'm jealous of."

"Yes, I do," he said, nodding at me and smiling. "It's a good word. In Shakespeare's time, you know, it meant madness—as the words 'ecstasy' and 'innocence' often did. I think all of us here are concerned with rapture in some way—I told you once that I liked to consider psychoanalysis as an art rather than a science—and when a man devotes himself to studying the nature of rapture he may find himself dispossessed, as it were. Categories dissolve, values and verities reverse themselves, things he reaches out to touch for comfort or guidance startle, and sometimes sicken, him with their unfamiliarity. It is a thing we are all aware of in this profession." He picked up his pipe from the desk and stared at it for a moment. "She talks to you about her delusions, then?"

"Yes, quite often. They're very detailed, as you know, and often quite beautiful. She described her people to me the other day, and I must say they seemed much more appealing than any I have ever met." He laughed and rapped the bowl of his pipe into his palm with a pleasant hollow sound. "And yet I detest them," I said in a moment, with surprising intensity. "There's really something hideous about their perfection. I think I hate things that rob people of their sorrow; it's as if they were robbed of their humanity."

"Still, humanity couldn't very well exist without its illusions," he said. "Our fear of truth is as much a part of us as our love of it, I think." He began to fill his pipe, sprinkling dark tobacco into the bowl from a bright-yellow can. "Has it ever occurred to you that half of human institutions are elaborate artistic disguises or compensations for brutal realities? I don't think we should be too severe with Lilith for her own private ones. Perhaps what we resent about them *is* their privacy, and their originality—the fact that she refuses to share our own common delusions, rejecting them as being equally as ignoble as the reality they evade—and has invented fresh ones for herself, sometimes more orderly, more dignified and more beautiful than our own. We cherish our illusions so fondly that we can't help resenting the implication that they're foolish, archaic or corrupt. No one is innocent of illusions, of course; it would be inhuman not to have them. It is only too great a degree of individuality that we distrust. Our image of the insane seems to alternate between the prophet and the renegade, and neither is a very reassuring one. It makes, on the one hand, for a kind of uneasy reverence, and on the other for contempt, or envy—as you said yourself just now. I think this helps to explain the ambivalence with which they have been regarded for centuries, the mixture of reverence and scorn we've always felt for them. Which you appear to feel. You find a 'kind of glory' about her, and yet you 'detest' her fantasies and find them 'hideous.' I don't think this is an unusual attitude at all—quite an orthodox one, as a matter of fact."

"Yes, I see that much more clearly when you explain it like this."

"But it still disturbs you?"

"Well, I don't feel that I'm sufficiently objective about her," I said. "I wouldn't mind a certain amount of confusion in my attitude—"

"If it were not so intense?"

"Perhaps that's it, yes."

"Well, if it's any comfort to you, I often feel much the same way, as her analyst. And not about Lilith only. So many of these people have such extraordinary minds, such extraordinary sensibilities. Too extraordinary, I think sometimes. It may be a romantic conception, but I often compare them to fine crystal which has been shattered by the shock of some intolerable revelation." He tore a match from a paper folder and struck it, staring for a moment at the flame. "I often have the feeling when I talk with them that they have seen too much, with too fine an instrument; that they have been close to some extreme—to something absolute—and been blasted by it. That they have been destroyed, one might say, by their own excellence—by the exercise of their highest, most godly faculty. It gives one a very great respect for them. One thinks of them as the honorable wounded in man's mortal struggle to understand. Regarded in this way, they are the heroes of the universe—its finest product and its noblest casualty."

The match having burned down to his fingers, he shook it violently into an ash tray and blew on his scalded finger tips—a misfortune which appeared to dissipate the "romantic" quality of his thought, as he had called it. He said in a moment, flapping his burned hand and smiling in a deprecatory way, "It isn't a very scientific theory, of course, because schizophrenia is far from being an exclusive affliction of superior minds. As a matter of fact it has been induced in dogs and spiders as well as men. A most unsettling fact."

"In spiders?" I said, astonished.

"Yes. By introducing into their bodies a substance from the blood of human schizophrenics. Their mating and hunting habits are affected very strangely, and they weave weird and totally uncharacteristic patterns with their webs. The webs of most spider species are as distinctive and invariable as their coloring, but 'mad' ones spin out fantastic, asymmetrical and rather nightmarish designs. I find that extremely interesting."

"Yes, it is," I said, finding it oddly horrible as well. Spiders of the most stable variety had little attraction for me; and the thought of an insane one, clinging to its firmament of frail, aberrant gossamer and peering out with little jeweled, demented eyes, was startlingly repulsive.

"Is it possible to consider it infectious, then?"

"Oh, not in an ordinary way," he said. "It can be artificially induced, apparently; and there is some evidence that prolonged contact with disturbed and influential personalities is predisposing—just as exposure to any disorderly environment may be— but not in the strict medical sense of the word." He struck another match and lit his pipe, blowing out dense pale clouds of fragrant smoke which he studied musingly. "Lilith is very difficult to analyze," he said in a moment, "because she lies so expertly. A lie, of course, if it is recognized as such, can sometimes be examined more productively than a direct confession. But in Lilith's case it is seldom possible to know what is fantasy and what is fact. She has a most astonishing capacity for invention. Has she ever spoken to you about her family?"

"No."

"She had a brother who was killed accidentally, you know. She's never mentioned him, I suppose?"

"No, she never talks about anything personal; and I've never questioned her."

"No; well, I wouldn't. That's apt to be disastrous. But if she should, voluntarily, don't fail to let me know about it."

"No, I won't."

"Good. Now, about the tournament. I'm very much in favor of it, so long as you don't feel any exceptional anxiety. I don't think she'd go with anyone else; and I'd like very much to know how she behaves. It would be the first time she's been off the grounds alone since she was readmitted."

"All right. I think she'll be delighted to hear that she can go."

"I suppose Bea has told you that she's made two previous attempts to escape?"

"Yes," I said. "I can't understand that. She seems so happy here. Things irritate her, of course, and I know she takes a high ironic view of most of us; but she's so absorbed in her work, and has her own little world so well contained up there in her room, that I can't imagine her wanting to run away."

Dr. Lavrier picked up his pipe again and after a long reflective pause he said, "Mr. Bruce, in matters of human psychology—and particularly abnormal psychology—you must learn never to accept appearances."

"I'm learning very rapidly to distrust them," I said.

"Good. She is always quite obedient with you, I gather?"

"Yes."

"I see. As to your objectivity in dealing with her, I wouldn't be too worried about it; I'm sure it will improve. Would you like to see her walk out of here some day into a happy, useful, creative and courageous life?"

"Yes, very much," I said, stirred in a great and sudden manner by the prospect.

"So would I," Dr. Lavrier said. "For anyone who admired her

it would be worth every effort that could be made towards realizing it. Psychotherapy is a long and often exhausting process; but when we consider what it can and has achieved, it more than justifies the patience with which we must pursue it."

"Yes, I'm sure of that," I said, and added after a moment's thought, "Do you think it's really possible, in Lilith's case? She speaks of herself, you know, as being 'incurable.' I don't really think she wants to be well."

"It's very difficult to say. She was eighteen when she was first hospitalized, and she's now twenty-three. It isn't, frankly, a very favorable picture. If there were to have been a permanent spontaneous remission it should have occurred before this. A pernicious, well-entrenched delusional system in an otherwise intact personality is a pretty insidious indication, particularly when it has persisted for more than three years; the classical development is towards a total disintegration of personality, or a permanent paranoid state. Still, you never can tell. She's been doing very well lately. I'm particularly pleased with the influence you seem to have had on her. I think she's holding her own, and possibly even making a little progress. We must wait and see." He swung his body in the chair, staring out of the window and squinting into the sunlight. "I don't know if I've helped to clear things up very much," he said. "We must both go away and think about it. But if you have any misgivings, don't hesitate to come and see me."

"I won't. I think it's been a great help," I said. "Thank you for taking so much time."

"Not at all. These things are important; they deserve all the time we can give them."

I felt greatly reassured by this interview and more than ever attracted to Dr. Lavrier.


¶ *THURS., MAY* 21:
For the last few days I have been enjoying—I was about to say "suffering from"—a kind of heightened sensitivity. All my per-

ceptions seem finer and more penetrating, and not only my actual physical perceptions, but that instantaneous interpretation of the thing perceived which is so large a part of the total act of perception. It is something like the experience of going outdoors after a rain and seeing the world anew, freshly and vividly. All the stones are washed clean, the leaves glitter, even the air has a bright and almost bitter clarity; and with this there comes a quite original and exciting sense of the significance of things. Yesterday, for example, when I stepped out of the elevator, I saw that someone—one of the nurses, apparently, hurrying from the Lodge to Field House with a tray of medicines—had dropped a bottle of some vivid purple fluid (gentian violet, I suppose) which had broken on the paving and spread out in a gorgeous, darkly glittering pool, through which the splinters of stained glass stuck up like shattered peaks of tinted ice in a silent, wine-dark sea. And while I stood staring down at it I experienced Odysseys of emotion; how many delectable images flashed through my mind in those few seconds! The faces and bodies of Sirens, splashed by purple foam, their hair and white limbs streaming with indigo, their eyes stained darkly as stained stones in the cold violet depths from which they had emerged. One with her mouth smashed against the rocks in the surf, moaning and turning her face toward me to be kissed, her lips burst like grapes. And beaches of glinting amethyst sand where their blue bones rolled forever in the lapse of lovely water. I must have crouched there for several minutes in a kind of trance, until Kit came up the drive toward me with a patient, at which intrusion I began to scrape together the splinters of glass in a hasty pretense of busyness.

I find that I can stare into the petals of a flower for ten or fifteen minutes at a time without exhausting its attraction, feeling, on the contrary, a gathering intensity of pleasure which approaches exaltation. The fuchsias on the front veranda are particularly fascinating. They have a vividness of tone which seems to oscillate, to awaken all kinds of thrilling vibrations in the senses, drawing one deeper and deeper into the profundities of color until the universe seems composed exclusively of it; there are no other stimuli, no other modes of being, no reality but color. God, grief, mortality, eternity, all these become shades or aspects of glowing fuchsia. It is a really extraordinary and delightful experience, for which I cannot account; but it has given me an understanding of the pleasure Lilith must derive from the light-games she plays with her prisms.

I have a wonderful tactile sensitivity, too, which unfortunately is not always enjoyable. Wind on my lips can cause an almost unbearable tingling sensation of pleasure; the touch of cork or rubber is often oddly repulsive. And certain sounds have become excruciating; I was filling a Thermos jug the other day and as I screwed the cork into the neck to tighten it the faint dull squealing sound it made against the glass sent a sudden agonized electric shudder through my nerves, such as the sound of chalk shrieking on a blackboard used to give me. When I was walking home last night there was a workman shoveling rubble from the sidewalk, and the sound of the steel shovel scraping on the concrete made me very nearly scream with pain. My hearing seems to be much more acute, as well, and to be astonishingly increased in its power to orientate sounds spatially. For example, I was able the other day to isolate and follow to its source in the grass under the kitchen window the singing of a single cricket—something I have never before been able to do, although I often used to try when I was a child.

My sense of smell is most affected. Odors intoxicate me, even many of which I have never before been aware. The scent of certain flowers, particularly—those with an astringent, herblike bitter scent, such as geraniums, dahlias and verbena—gives me a sense of delicate and rather sinister excitement which often puts me into a state of nervous exhilaration before I am aware of the cause of it; and that of sweet, heavy "tropical" flowers—gardenias, magnolias and honeysuckle—is virtually overpowering. I went walking the other evening before I went to bed and passed a group of high-school students coming home from a dance at Langley. One of the girls was wearing gardenias in her hair, and as she went by on the sidewalk the scent of those white blossoms in the warm night air made me very nearly reel with a sudden wave of hopeless, yearning tenderness. Now where did that sudden wave of emotion come from—to leave me trembling with loneliness in the street as their voices faded away under the dark elms?

I can smell the wind, now, too. I know when it is blowing from the west—however gently—because it always brings that dark, humiliating smell of Niggertown: clay, soaked hard and sour in soapy water; grease and cheap cologne. It makes me wince. But tonight it is blowing from the north, and I can smell the orchards: fruit-tree gum, and Hales and Elbertas ripening in the warm wind. I wonder if those girls who used to pick the peaches are still sitting in the branches, singing ballads in the moonlight? I would like to go up there and lie in the grass under those dark trees among the fallen fruit—brown and overripe, with a sweet, moist, slippery softness that you can plunge your thumbs into until they touch the stone. I wonder if one of them would come to me? How lovely that would be: with the heavy boughs above us raining their faint mist of resin through the dark, and her pale naked body beside me, stained and scented with the slippery, rotting peaches.

¶ *MON. MAY 27:*

I have not been asked to escort Lilith again for a whole week now. Yet every morning at the O.T. meetings Bea has asked one of the others—Kit, Mandel or Bob—to invite her out; and twice Lilith has agreed to accompany them. Bea seems very pleased about this, but has not offered to discuss it with me. I have managed to pretend an appropriate degree of satisfaction when the contacts were discussed, and an indifference to the fact that it was someone other than myself who made them; but I cannot help wondering what it means. Have they decided that it is unwise for me to see her any more? Perhaps my talk with Dr. Lavrier was more revealing than I was aware, or than he let me know. I have gone over and over it in my mind, lying in bed sometimes at night and murmuring our conversation to myself as accurately as I can remember it, out of a restless dissatisfaction—sometimes with what I said, and sometimes with what I imagine I must have left unsaid. Can it have disclosed to him some buried fear, some potential weakness or element of incompetence in myself that I myself am scarcely aware of, and which he feels would prejudice any further relationship with Lilith? I am satisfied that I tried to express to him my feelings toward her as candidly and completely as I could, and if I was not entirely successful it was only for the reason that I was honestly not certain of what my feelings were. It was after all the purpose of my interview to try to clarify them to a comfortable and practical extent—which I am sure he understood, and in which, for a time at least, I felt I had succeeded. But every day I feel those insights fading, and become less certain of my actual attitudes.

It's three days now since I have even seen her. I stopped by on Friday to speak to her for a moment, but she was out with Mandel somewhere, and although I watched for her around the grounds I couldn't see her anywhere. I suppose they went down to the lake again.

I'm sure that Bea and Dr. Lavrier have discussed my relationship with Lilith between them, but I am for some reason very unwilling to question her about it. Still, it doesn't seem reasonable that they would behave in such a surreptitious way. Candor seems to be the cornerstone of Bea's gospel, and if she can extend it to her patients it doesn't seem very consistent or honorable for her to refuse it to me. If she doesn't offer some explanation soon I'll have to ask for one. I feel an increasing confusion and anxiety about it all.

$\mathcal{T}$ HE ANXIETY expressed in this last extract from my journal was relieved on the following day when Bea asked me if I would take Lilith on the "experimental trip" which Dr. Lavrier had suggested.

"She seems to be becoming much more sociable," she said. "Which is something we are all pleased with. Dr. Lavrier says she is offering less resistance in analysis, as well. He's very anxious to start getting her abroad again, but thinks it should be done in stages. Why don't you take her bicycling for an hour or so, out on those back roads towards Frederick?"

I said I would be happy to, and added, with a carefully suppressed elation, that as I knew the roads well from having ridden there so often as a boy, I would have the advantage of a close familiarity with the countryside in the event of an attempt to escape on Lilith's part. Bea seemed quite pleased with my foresight. How foolish my apprehensions had been! How perfectly natural it was for a general test of Lilith's growing sociability to have been made! I felt quite merry when I presented myself to her, a frame of mind which she seemed to find amusing.

"You seem very happy, Vincent. Is it because you've had such a long holiday from me?"

"Oh, no; that was unavoidable," I said. "You don't seem to have lacked company, anyway."

"No; I thought it would be more discreet."

"More discreet?"

"If I were not too exclusive in my choice of escorts." It was impossible to know if she was mocking me.

"How would you like to go bicycling?" I asked. "It's a lovely morning."

She stared at me somberly for several moments before she answered, "Do you think they would approve?"

"Of course they'd approve. As a matter of fact, Bea suggested herself that I ask you."

"Oh, did she?" She was sitting at the sill with the glass prisms lying on her palm, glittering in the sunlight. She lifted one and, spreading her fingers, ran the tips of them through the rainbow of colors that it threw upon the sill. It made a hectic effect: the livid flickering of her finger tips down through the spectrum and into light again. "All right, then, if you like." She paused for a moment and then added, "You haven't told me what you said to Dr. Lavrier."

"No, I don't intend to," I said. She turned to face me swiftly with an expression of contempt that was truly unnerving. "Do you think I should?" She did not answer. "Did you think I would?"

She turned away from me and began to adjust the prisms in her palm. "I see that he has filled you with courage. He must have reassured you greatly."

"Do you want to go out?" I asked again rather bluntly.

"Yes." She set the prisms carefully together on the sill and stood up, smiling at me.

"Don't you think you ought to put your shoes on? Won't the pedals hurt your feet?"

"No."

"I thought we'd cycle out along the Frederick road. There's not much traffic and it's pretty country."

"If you like. Did they really ask you to take me?"

"Yes. Doesn't that please you?"

"Yes."

She said nothing else all the while we were going down in the elevator and walking across the grounds to the bicycle shed. While I was unlocking it and taking out a pair of bicycles Warren came toward us from Field House, walking hastily across the shadowed lawn.

"Good morning, Miss Arthur," he said, smiling at her in an abject way that made me cringe. Lilith said nothing, standing with her head bowed. "I'm making something for you. In the shop. They told me your birthday was next week, and I wanted to give you something. I wonder if I ought to tell you. Still, I think it's going to be quite nice. I've been working on it for some time now. It should be finished in a day or two." She would still not raise her head or speak to him. He stood clutching his hands together with distress. "Are you going bicycling?" he asked. "It's a lovely morning for it. Would you mind if I came with you?"

"I'm afraid that isn't possible, Warren," I said.

"It isn't? Oh, that's disappointing. Perhaps after you come back Miss Arthur would like to come to Field House and hear some music. There are some new recordings of Chopin that are very good."

I had brought with me a canteen of water and a parcel of watercress sandwiches which I placed in the leather pouch beneath my saddle, giving her a moment to reply; but she stood as silently as ever all the while. When I had finished buckling it I said, "I don't think we'd better arrange that for today. Perhaps later in the week."

"Oh, I hope so. I'd be happy to play them for you any time. I'm staying there now, you know—in Field House. I'm getting much better. I'm planning to write very soon about a job."

"I'm glad to hear that," I said. "Goodbye for now, Warren."

"Goodbye. Goodbye, Miss Arthur."

He stood looking after us with writhing hands as we walked down the drive with the bicycles. At the entrance to the grounds we mounted them, and Lilith sat obediently in the saddle, bracing herself with one bare foot against the curb.

"Which way are we going?" she asked.

"Straight down the street, out of town. I'll follow you."

She pedaled slowly down the quiet street under the great elms, her hair flashing in the alternate patches of sunlight that fell between the leaves. It was less than a mile to the edge of town; the rows of houses on either side of the street ended suddenly, and the soft hills of the countryside, many of them green with late crops of barley, opened out before us. There were no longer elms along the road, nor shadow; we rode in morning sunlight along the narrow country road into which Montgomery Avenue extends. It sloped gently upward into the hills north of the town, so that we were obliged to pedal quite slowly up the incline. Lilith stopped after a while and stood with one foot on the ground, turning in her saddle to wait for me.

"Can't you ride beside me?" she said as I came abreast of her. "It makes me very uncomfortable to have you there behind me, and I don't think it's very courteous."

"All right. I didn't think you were particularly anxious for my company."

"I wouldn't have come if I weren't."

We pedaled on, side by side, in silence, between the swollen hedges of honeysuckle. Below us there were sheep grazing in many of the valleys along the shallow creeks, and their bleating reached us sometimes very thinly through the hot bright silence, a mournful and contemptuous sound. I could hear also the soft snarling of bees among the honeysuckle, and all the while the sweet heavy odor of the coral-colored blossoms fumed about us. Lilith lifted her hand once, swerving in the road, and wiped the damp hair from her forehead.

"Are you hot?" I asked.

"Yes."

"It's shady a little farther along. There are lanes of cedars along the road."

"Can we stop there?"

"Yes."

We pedaled for another few minutes until we reached the row of trees, feeling their cool bath of shadow fall upon us. There was a "crazy fence" of weather-darkened cedar rails along the road, against which we leaned our bicycles. Lilith climbed up onto it and unknotted the blue silk scarf she wore about her throat, clutching the rail with one hand while she did so.

"Are you tired?" I asked.

"No. I'm never tired. I'm only hot. Can I have some of the water?"

I unscrewed the cap of the canteen and handed it to her. She tilted her head back, her throat stretched and rippling as she drank. When she had finished she pressed the cool aluminum of the flask against her cheek, cringing a little from its coldness, and gazed off at the distant hills. On many of their slopes there were outcroppings of blunt, gray, rain-smoothed rock, and above these, where the soil was no longer workable, dark-green wooded patches of maple and gum.

There was a disturbing familiarity about the slope of the hill in front of us; the disposition of the few silver maples that ran down in diminishing numbers from its crest, the arrangement of the visible boulders among them, and the shining course of the creek in the narrow valley below were all part of a pattern that oppressed me in a vague and fugitive way, like the sudden re-membering, at midday, of a dream. I had stood looking down at it for several minutes before I realized, with a faint, cool rebirth of the dread which had accompanied it, that it was here I had had the accident with my mare. I wondered while I looked down at the landscape if it were entirely by coincidence that I had chosen this spot to stop and rest, or if those mysterious subliminal powers of selection with which I was becoming increasingly familiar from my reading and lectures could have been responsible for it. I could hardly believe in this latter possibility, for I could think of nothing to be gained by bringing her to a place that held such painful memories for me.

"I'm glad you brought me," Lilith said. "It's a lovely spot."

"Yes. I used to ride all through these hills when I was a boy."

She turned toward me, smiling. "On quests, Vincent? Are there dragons in the woods, or evil sorcerers?"

"I think there may be," I said.

"Really? Oh, I want to see them!" She slipped down from the rails and stood with the fence between us, laying her hand on mine. "Come and show me."

"No, I think we'd better stay up here."

"I'll go alone, then."

Before I could make a move to seize her she had fled down the slope of the hill, her hair splashing about her shoulders and her skirt flying. As it was evident that I could easily overtake her and that the woods were far too sparse for her to hide in, her flight was obviously more a demonstration of caprice, or perhaps a test of wills between us, than a serious attempt at escape; and I was for this reason very leisurely in my pursuit of her. I vaulted the fence and walked down the hill behind her—it seemed to display much more authority than running—being careful nevertheless to keep the distance between us a reasonably limited one. She had entered the thin patch of woodland in a moment and ran through its gray shadow like a dryad, looking back at me over her shoulder and laughing merrily. The slope of the hill dropped steeply here, and I had only just increased the pace of my pursuit to a mild trot, to prevent her from disappearing from my sight below the fall of land, when I saw her stop, lifting her hands to clasp her throat lightly and staring down at the ground. As I approached I saw that she stood amongst a litter of huge bleached bones, scattered for yards among the stones and dead leaves of the forest floor, the work of vultures, rain and frost. They had lost all design, except for half of the broken rib cage, which lay with its pale curved staves standing upright, like a ruined harp. Beside it, half buried in a mound of rotting leaves, lay the shattered skull, its splintered bone washed clean and dry as chalk. It gave me an inconsolable feeling to look at them, being my only monument upon the earth. A little yellow butterfly was fluttering among them.

"Oh, look!" Lilith said with soft amazement. "Is it a dragon?"

"No, it's a horse. It was killed with a rock—you see how the skull is crushed? With that rock there."

"How do you know?" Lilith said.

"Because I killed it."

She raised her eyes to me slowly, still clutching her throat in an attitude of startled languor.

"She got hurt," I said. "She was suffering terribly. And I didn't have any gun. I had to do it."

She lowered her eyes to the strewn bones, extending her hand in a timid, covetous gesture toward them.

"May I have one?"

It was an odd, unpleasant question, which made it sound as if I held over these bleached remains some disturbing proprietorship —one which I was eager to disclaim.

"They're not mine. What do you mean? Why do you want one?"

"As a gift from you. My earthly birthday is next week. Don't you want to give me something?"

She stooped down quickly, startling away the yellow butterfly, and lifted the broken skull from the moist black leaf-mold in which it was sunken, holding it gently before her and peering into the dark splintered hollow where the rock had crushed it. I felt a wave of disgust.

"Put it down," I said. "It's a dirty thing. I can't see why you want a thing like that."

"I do. I want to keep it. Let me, Vincent."

"Well, keep it, then, if you want. But it's no gift from me." I felt intolerably oppressed by the silence of the forest and by the place. "Let's go out of here. Let's go down there in the sun."

"Yes."

She followed me through the trees to the edge of the forest, cradling the skull in the bend of her arm, gazing down at it with a strange look of sentiment and touching it solicitously with her fingers, like a young mother with a child. We walked out of the shadow of the trees to a cluster of boulders that stood in the open pastureland above the creek. I leaned against one of the larger of them and Lilith sank down onto the grass at my feet, watching my hand with soft absorption while I stroked the surface of the rock. In a moment she reached up and touched the back of it gently and hesitantly with her finger tips.

"You killed an animal with them," she said. "I mean an intelligent animal."

"Oh, I've killed much more intelligent animals than that," I said, withdrawing it quickly.

"What do you mean, Vincent?"

"I've killed men with them, too."

"You've killed men?" she whispered. "*Why?*"

"Well, that's the business of soldiers. It seems to be the only thing I've ever done in my life with any consistent success." I became distressed by the unyielding length of her gaze and asked rather roughly, "What did you do with the canteen? Did you leave it?"

"Yes, I'm sorry. Shall I get it for you?"

"No, it doesn't matter."

I sat down in the grass a little apart from her with my back against the boulder and watched the sweeping flight of a meadowlark along the creek below us. It flung out a volley of bright, bronzelike notes across the field, to which Lilith turned her head attentively. When the sound had ceased she said, "You must love them very much."

"Who?"

"Your people, and your God. To kill for them, and then to go on loving them after you have killed. They must have been very good to you to deserve such love."

"I thought all gods and all nations demanded sacrifices," I said.

"Oh, no." She dropped her head so that her hair flooded her lap. "I would never ask that of a lover. I would only ask his joy." The sudden gravity of atmosphere which her words created gave me a faint, breathless feeling of alarm, and I found myself saying, with a callow and somewhat desperate attempt at virtuosity, "But you aren't a goddess, or a nation."

She allowed me, in a pause of perfectly calculated length, to consider my own words, murmuring in a moment, with reproving modesty, "No, I'm only a wild girl with dirty hair whom you keep locked in your attic."

"I try to get you out of it as often as I can," I said. "You're the one who seems to prefer it. I want you to run free."

"Do you, Vincent?" She raised her head to look at the hills across the valley, raking the hair from her eyes and smiling into the distance. "Where shall I go? To Samarkand? Or Knossos, or Trebizond? No; I know a city where I can wait for you. Shall I, Vincent? You will find me by the fountain in the city square, in the shadow of a white tower with an iron bell in it, all streaked with linnet lime, that creaks faintly in the wind from Persia."

"How will I know you?" I asked in a low, hesitant voice, unable to resist the fanciful pleasure of this game.

"I will carry a bowl of limes, and wear a silver veil; and my feet will be the slimmest in the city."

I dropped my eyes to where they rested in the grass, acknowledging this mutely.

"Yes; I will recognize you by them," I said.

She turned her head toward me.

"When may I go?"

"Soon. When you're well."

"When I am well that city will disappear."

"Then you'll find another one. A better one, that won't disappear."

She shook her head gently, looking into my eyes. "But I will disappear, too. You must remember that."

"What do you mean?" I asked harshly.

"I don't think either of us would recognize the other, then. That would be a poor reward for your patience, Vincent."

I sat staring at the ground for some time, and said at last, "Well, I'm used to unrewarded patience."

"But you weren't made for it. You had to learn it, back there in that town—of which you have never been a citizen."

I plucked a grass blade and crumpled it in my fingers, unable to deny what she had said, but filled with a stubborn and indignant sense of loyalty by her words.

"Nevertheless it's my town, and they're my people," I said. "No matter how imperfect they may be, or how imperfectly I may love them. They're the only ones I have."

"What have you to do with them?" Lilith said. "You don't belong to those people. Your mother was a wanton and your father a rogue. They're not your people, Vincent. I know who you are. I knew you even before you told me."

I clenched my hands suddenly, bowing my head in anger and humiliation.

"You have no right to say that . . . about my parents," I said in a bitter whisper.

"I didn't say it because I despise them, Vincent. I think if I had known them I would have loved them best of all, as you did." When I did not reply she added softly, "Or do you really love them? Perhaps you are ashamed of them, too."

I raised my eyes to her slowly, feeling afflicted by a sudden ugly spasm of self-distrust, a sudden nausea of spirit, from her question; then, almost immediately afterward, I was nearly exalted by a profound and perfectly recognizable hatred for her. It gave me a clarity of mind and a vitality that for once, in my relationship with her, made me feel entirely independent and articulate.

"It's possible to be ashamed of someone and still to love them," I said fiercely. "I'm ashamed of the people in that town because of the way they treated my mother and me; but I love them, too, because they suffer, just like me. That's why I understand them and belong to them. I'm ashamed of my grandfather because of something he did once, something mean, something far beneath him. He tried to bribe me to join the army; he offered me a college education if I would enlist. He didn't want me to be drafted. I had to be one of the first people in our town to enlist, because that was the only way it would help to restore the family honor. I guess it would have been more effective if I'd gotten my head blown off. But I love him very much, because I know he's ashamed of it, too, and because he suffers for having done it. He couldn't help doing it. His pride was hurt once—very greatly—by my father, and he can't help trying to mend it, even when it means wounding people that he loves. So then I had to hurt him, too, in return—to show how much he had hurt me. I said something cruel and vindictive to him, and he knows that I suffer because of that, too. And even though we know we can't ever repair it, that we can't ever start again, we still go on loving each other— even more than before, I think. Because I think that's what human love is—everything but children's love, anyway—loving the wounds we give each other, and that we can't help giving each other; you can't stay alive if you don't hurt people. But what do you know about that? You don't know anything about it, and don't care anything about it. You've forgotten how hard it is to love them."

I stared at her hotly, expecting—and, for once, almost welcoming—her anger and irony; but again she was not to be predicted. I saw that there were tears in her eyes, and she bent down quickly, pressing her lips with a sudden startling tenderness against my forearm and murmuring, "Do you have to wound me, too, to love me, Vincent?"

It may hardly be believable that never until that moment had I understood fully and consciously the meaning of my feelings toward Lilith. If I had been subconsciously aware of it—as I must have been—I had, in my desperation, so totally and effectively forbidden myself to acknowledge it that I experienced now a virginal feeling of bewilderment, and somehow of bereavement, at the sudden realization of how hopelessly and entirely I was in love with her. Perhaps I had had, in fact, some insight into the true significance of my growing confusion and anxiety, and had deliberately obscured it to myself with all sorts of complex and apparently conscientious interpretations, for even the most conspicuously intimate or romantic of our exchanges I had been able to accept as a kind of game, a graceful, somewhat frivolous, but useful, concession to her nature and condition, by which it had been more possible to approach and understand her and to gain her confidence. This may seem like the grossest kind of self-deception and utterly incongruous to anyone who reads this manuscript, but it must be remembered that I have written this account of our meetings and dialogues (all but the extracts from my journal) in the light of later understanding, which makes it almost impossible to reproduce the innocence, or ignorance, with which I played my part in them.

But however subtle and determined the method I had used to preserve my self-respect, to disguise from myself the nature of such untenable emotions, I could not sustain it any longer. I felt the lover's glorious and overwhelming impulse to declare himself; I wanted to take her in my arms and whisper, "I love you, Lilith," in hushed, endless, exquisite confessions. It was only by an excruciating effort of will—surely the grandest of my life—that I was able to compromise this impulse by saying merely, with a tremulously imperfect effort to control my voice, "I'm sorry. I didn't mean to be unjust to you, Lilith. I know you've suffered, too. Much more than most of us, I think."

She must have sensed the passion in my voice and contented herself with this as an evidence of triumph; for she did not pursue the question I had ignored, but sat with her head bowed and her face hidden while I stared at the cool bright curve of her head with ravaged eyes.

In a moment she stretched her hands out to the skull which lay beside her in the grass and began to caress it while she spoke to me: "I know why you suffer, Vincent. You have the cruelest of all talents, a gift which always estranges. How terrible it is that there are so few opportunities to exercise it in your world, and so many to exercise a talent for destroying." She plunged her fingers into the broken sockets of the skull, clutching it so tightly that her knuckles whitened and there was a sudden scarlet seam of blood across the bone from her pierced skin. "Do you think I don't know how you suffer? Oh, I do. I know how terrible it is to love and not be able to confess your love. It is enough to drive one mad." She turned toward me, her face transformed by a look of unearthly compassion, her voice falling to a tormenting whisper as she said, "Oh, tell me now. Please. I can't bear it any longer."

And again she made me feel unworthy in my loyalty; again she made me despise my own courage; for I said the words in my heart—oh, many times!—"I love you, Lilith"; but still I would not speak them.

"You've hurt yourself," I murmured.

She lifted her bleeding hand and slung it in my face, scattering drops of blood across my cheek and lips. I raised my hand involuntarily to wipe them, but suspended the gesture humbly, bowing my head before her anger. She stood up quickly and stared down at me, her eyes dark with fury.

"Oh, you're a fool!" she said shrilly. "It's very true—you *are* one of these people. Yes, you must stay here in this town, because you belong here. Ignorant country lout!"

She turned and began to climb swiftly up the slope, either forgetting or abandoning the skull in her anger—as I was very relieved to see. But when we reached the fence where we had left the bicycles she turned and looked back down the hill.

"I must go back and get it," she said.

"Oh, leave it there. It's an ugly thing."

"No. I want to keep it. It's little enough you've given me."

So I was obliged to return with her to the cluster of boulders where she had left the skull, and once more up the slope to the bicycles. We were both panting when we reached the top of the hill for the second time, and stood leaning against the cedar fence to regain our breath.

"There's blood on your mouth," Lilith said. I took my handkerchief out and rather self-consciously wiped my lips with it. "Do you feel cleaner now?" I did not reply. "Are you afraid I have infected you?" She laughed softly and bent down to wrap the

245

skull in the hem of her skirt, where she tied it with her scarf. It swung between her thighs all the while we were riding home, and I remembered once seeing a country girl walking home from the fair with melons tied up in her skirt in much the same manner.

When we returned to her room she untied it and set it on a pile of her manuscripts, raising her eyes to me modestly. She had become quite demure.

"Must you keep it?" I asked again.

"I would like to very much."

"And you refused Warren's gift."

"It was no such gift as this."

"No; it was a better one. He made it, out of love."

"But you destroyed this, out of love. It is more valuable." She lifted her cut hand and looked at it idly.

"Does it hurt?" I asked.

"Not any more."

"I'll ask the nurse to come and look at it."

"No, don't, please."

"I'll have to report it. We have to report all injuries."

She raised her eyes to me gently. "All of them, Vincent?"

While she looked at me with mild, steadfast reproach I allowed myself, for the first time since I had known her, fully to examine and define the beauty of her face. How delicate the modeling of her lips and nostrils; how firm and lovely the swell of bone above her violet eyes; how slender and exquisitely arched the glistening crescents of her brows! I longed to touch and claim each feature with my finger tips, and felt again desperately near to declaring this desire.

"Lilith," I said in a hushed, constricted voice.

"Yes."

"I've never in my life done anything worth while. I wish . . . you would help me to do one thing well."

"Do you think you can do it well without me?" she asked.

When I did not reply she turned away with gentle impatience, her hair swinging across her shoulders with a demoralizing grace, and stood in silence for a long time, gazing out of the window into the sunlight. I did not trust myself to break the pause. She said quietly at last, "I thought I knew what your passion was, Vincent. I thought you wanted to make something beautiful. And yet you talk about nothing but honor. It's a word that poets and lovers seldom use."

"I think it's too late for me to make anything beautiful," I said. "All I can hope to be now is honorable."

"Then if you want to help me, go away," she said. "I cannot be saved by honor."

I left her room in a state of feverish agitation, thanking God that the charge nurse was busy with a restless patient, and the floor office vacant, as I let myself in and with trembling hands wrote, destroyed and wrote again a report that was neither honorable nor beautiful: *Special duty. Took patient bicycling four or five miles into country. Obedient, cooperative and in good contact throughout. Conversation general and cheerful, with less fantasy material. Seemed very observant and responsive to everything we saw, landscape, wildlife, etc. Found skull of an animal beside the road and asked to be allowed to keep it, which I granted. Cut her hand slightly, probably requiring minor treatment. Seems considerably improved. 9:30–11:15 A.M. V. Bruce, O.T.*

I left the report on the nurse's desk so that she could not fail to see it and went out into the hall, feeling a strange sense of haste, as if I were pursued. While I waited impatiently for the elevator to arrive I glanced down the hall and saw Mrs. Meaghan standing in the corridor, looking into the open door of Lilith's room. She turned toward me and smiled wryly.

I spent the rest of the day in a state of nervous apprehension at the necessity of facing Bea at the evening O.T. meeting, a condition which intensified as the hour of that necessity approached until it was very nearly one of hysteria. What would I say to her? I tried for a time, while carrying out my duties with other patients in a most abstracted way, to prepare an account for her—it must be thoroughly ambiguous and must, while omitting all that was compromising, contain no actual untruths, no actual inventions or distortions; it was to be only a delaying action which would give me time to think and which, like my written report, would be consistent either with greater subterfuge or subsequent confession. This was a brief, harassed and fragmentary effort, which I abandoned in a sudden enervating wave of shame. This is not to say that I decided to tell Bea all that had happened, including the revelation of my true feelings for Lilith; for I had in fact decided nothing, leaving my behavior ultimately—not so much through resolution as through the lack of it—entirely to the disposition of the moment. Whether it would be governed by candor or deceit—whether I would break forth with a confession of all that I had said and felt, or whether I would sustain the noncommittal cunning of my report—I could not say until I was actually face to face with Bea, and I had not the stamina to determine.

As it developed, it was a decision that I was temporarily to be spared, for Bea was once again busy at a staff conference, and our meeting was postponed. My relief at this reprieve was not so great as may be imagined; it left me with a feeling of dismay at having gained what I had so short a while ago been conspiring to secure: time to think. I almost wished that I had forfeited this privilege, and the night of lonely and tormented questioning which it would incur, by the spontaneous confession I had half anticipated making.

As I walked down the hospital drive toward the street I looked up at Lilith's window, feeling sure that she would be waiting there to see me pass; and I was not mistaken. Neither of us spoke, and I did not dare to pause, for I heard the chattering of a group of nurses in the drive behind me; but I felt that there was almost more exchanged between us in that brief passing glance than in all that we had said that morning.

$\mathcal{M}$y journal for the next several days is voluminous and agonized. It is, in its harrowed ruminations, neither literature nor very effective fact, and I can see no need to include it here in its entirety. But as these few days are perhaps the most crucial of my entire story, I think that one or two abbreviated extracts are necessary and sufficient to illustrate the state of mind into which I was plunged by this crisis in my relationship with Lilith.

### ¶ TUES., MAY 26:

. . . That I am in love with her I cannot deny, and would not wish to (I am surely not responsible for that); but I haven't yet, thank God, betrayed my trust by expressing it to her. Perhaps that report I wrote can be excused on the basis of confusion, astonishment or panic—at any rate an O.T. report is not the place for the full, complex and conscientious statement which I shall have to make. I will explain this to Dr. Lavrier tomorrow when I see him. There is nothing for me to do but resign. No doubt whatever about this. I have tried for hours to think of some other solution, but there is none which is even remotely practical or which I would trust myself to attempt.

How long have I loved her? From the very morning I met her, I think, when Bob took me to her room for the first time; no, before that: from the moment I first looked into her eyes, four years ago, that summer afternoon when she was standing behind the willows on the lawn. Or even earlier—forever, it seems to me. How have I remained unaware of it for so long? I can't believe that I am so obtuse by nature; yet to believe the only possible alternative—

that I am so consummately cunning as to have deceived myself completely—is hardly more comforting. It is more likely, however, for reading back through these pages I seem to find them riddled with equivocation. But there is no point in accusing myself this way. There is still time, thank heaven, to make an end of it without disgracing my profession.

It is reassuring to know that Dr. Lavrier is a man of such great understanding. Perhaps he will be able to recommend me to some other hospital. I would like very much to go on with this work; and I am sure he will appreciate my sincerity and be willing to help me. But could I do that? Could I go away from this town, where she is? Well, I will have to, of course. Unless I go to work for Grandpa in the tavern, or find something else to do around Stonemont. What a foolish thought that is! It would be agony to stay here, knowing she is there, inside the Lodge, and not being able to see her. But then, of course, she may soon be well enough to be allowed into town alone—many of the patients are. Perhaps I could meet her there sometimes. What an insidious thought! Why leave the Lodge at all, if that were my intention! And what would I have to offer her, then, anyway? What would she have to do with a garage attendant or a busboy, which is all I could hope to be if I stayed here in Stonemont. If she really loves me, of course, it would make no difference at all. But *does* she really love me? God, if I only knew the answer to that question, I think I could make any sacrifice, I could wait forever for her— if waiting were any use.

A heavy wind has come up and the cherry tree is creaking like ship's rigging. I have just opened my window and found the sill littered with little black twigs. I don't know what time it is now; around three o'clock, I think. I've been lying on my back for hours, trying to sleep, but it's impossible. It has taken me half the night to work up the honesty and courage to ask the question that Lilith answered with such sure anticipation this morning (she has more of both than I): *I think neither of us would recognize the other, then.* Why do I love this girl? Is it because she is—the way

she is? Mad, inspired, enchanted, whatever she is? What will
she be like when she is well? *Will* I recognize her, then; or will
she recognize me?

I have been trying to visualize this restored, this "normal"
Lilith (Lilith does not seem to be her name): pretty (not wildly
beautiful); carefully, expensively dressed; modest and agreeable,
but rather formal in her manner (I have always felt this, somewhere, buried and despised within her); intellectual, industrious,
anxious to resume her studies, to take up a career; interested only
in the companionship of young men of her own social class and
education; gracious, however—oh, very understanding, very appreciative! I have even managed to conjure up an image of her
speaking: she is leaving the hospital, surrounded by expensive
luggage, pausing at the open door of a glittering limousine in
which her mother, smilingly adjusting a mink stole, waits for her.
She turns toward me and offers me her gloved hand—"Thank you
so much for everything you've done for me, Mr. Bruce. I hope you
will forgive some of my more outrageous eccentricities. I never
meant to embarrass you." Oh, my Lilith, what has happened to
your ragged skirt, your bare white feet, your flying yellow hair,
the flashing, tender cruelty of your eyes? And to all the shining
villages of your mind, and the tall, fair, sandaled folk who lived in
them, and their songs and instruments and gospels? And what
will happen to me, alone in this bleak vale of sanity, haunted
forever by your face and the sound of your running feet?

I clench my eyes shut and demand an answer of myself: Do
I *want* her to be well? What is "well" for her? She was never
happy in this world—my world (when did it ever claim me as a
son?). She does not want to return to it; I am sure of that. I have
heard her say so. *She does not want to be well.*

I must have fallen asleep a while ago, for I woke up with a
shutter banging, sitting at the open window with the rain lashing
at me coldly. My head and shoulders were drenched, and there
was a pool of water on the floor around me. I have mopped
it up with a towel, and am sitting now watching the storm out-

side the window, which rattles softly in the sill. Sometimes in the flashes of lightning I can see the hard silhouettes of the housetops across the street and the black, plunging trees. Just now a wet leaf blew against the pane and stuck there, a little cherry leaf with delicate shark's-tooth edges, fragile victim of the storm.

Are you watching, too, Lilith—your white face suddenly flooded with light, your throat wet with rain and your fingers clutching the crossed bars? Oh, my dear, I love you. I have loved you forever, and I will love you always. God help me to relinquish you!

¶ *WED., MAY 27:*
I am astonished at myself. I have powers of deception I never dreamed of. What a masterpiece of quiet bravura my interview with Dr. Lavrier turned out to be! And I did not even arrange it—which is probably the reason for that wonderfully calm bold confidence that I felt; for if I had not met him by chance like that, walking in the drive, I'm sure I would never have been able to carry it off the way I did. If I had had to wait through the whole morning for an interview with him, for a specified and inevitable hour, I would have been demoralized by the strain. ("Demoralized" seems hardly the appropriate word!) But meeting and walking along together as we did, quite accidentally and casually—it seemed so easy, so perfectly spontaneous, so inspired, even!

He lives at Doctors' House, and was just coming to work up the driveway as I started up the shop steps.

"Good morning," he said.

"Oh, good morning." (Genuine surprise, a moment of panic, of the desire to flee, a rather startled smile, then, as we began to speak, a gathering feeling of resolution, of confidence in my own powers of dissimulation and of joy in exercising them that was really quite delightful—like an actor's, I suppose, before a royal audience.)

"That was some storm we had last night. Did you see any of it?"

"Yes, a shutter broke loose around three o'clock and woke me up. I never saw it rain so hard."

"There's a tree down in the pond. One of the poplars."

"Really? I was going to take a group down for a swim this afternoon, but I guess I'd better call it off."

"Yes, the water's full of rubbish. By the way, did you get Lilith out yesterday?"

"Yes. It went very well, I think. I've never seen her better."

"Good. Have you got a minute? Walk down to the Lodge with me."

I fell in beside him and we walked slowly under the dripping trees.

"Behaved herself, did she?" he asked.

"Very well. I left the report on the floor."

"Yes, I haven't had a chance to look at them yet. How do you feel about yourself? Any more secure?"

"Oh, I think so. Maybe it was all imagination, I don't know. Or beginner's nerves, or something. I felt perfectly comfortable with her yesterday. I think I just needed to talk it over a little; I'm so afraid of making a mistake, you know."

"Well, it's a good thing to feel that way. But it's perfectly natural. I don't think you've got anything to worry about. She still wants to go to the tournament?"

"She seems to, yes."

"Good. I think we'll let her, then. I'm quite pleased with her, on the whole. She's been out several times this last week or two, with different O.T.s, and they all give good reports. Are you still getting a lot of fantasy?"

"No, not so much yesterday. I mentioned that in my report."

"No personal talk of any kind?"

"No."

"Well, keep in touch with me. Thanks very much. I think you're doing a good job with her, Vincent."

I watched him walk up the veranda steps, a quiet, modest, devoted man, my mentor, my patron! And all the while I was talking to him, in spite of my terrible excitement, my swiftly, corruptly functioning intelligence—a sense of ease, of perfect exterior calm, of effortless improvisation; even a kind of craftsman's pride in my skillfully constructed imposture. I know that if I stop to think of what I am doing, if I for a moment relinquish the excitement or momentum of my course, I will collapse with shame. But I feel within myself a ferocious energy, a faint incessant furor which is like a fuel; it gives me a vitality I have never had before. I long to do some heroic thing—climb mountains, charge and shatter phalanxes with my sword, produce in an instant epics out of my swarming mind. Indeed if it were not for the quaintness of the phrase, I could call myself possessed.

I did not see Lilith all day. What a monstrous effort of will it took to prevent myself from stopping, even for a moment, at her door! Perhaps it was a subtle form of self-chastisement for my dishonesty this morning. I must not stay away too long, however, or there is no telling what she will do. And yet I must not seem too eager to escort her; that could create a fatal suspicion. We must await our hour, Lilith. (How quickly I am learning the art of discretion!) But there is a tournament a week away—I saw it advertised this evening on a poster in Wingate's window! Can I wait so long to have you to myself again? Perhaps we can invent some other way. Truly, I am beginning to understand the uses of intelligence!

§ THURS., MAY 28:
. . . It is sickening, sickening. When I read back through these last few pages I am horrified. Can I have written these words? I can't recognize my own personality in them.

What has happened to all that splendid energy? I have been so hopelessly weary all day; weary with shame, I suppose. I feel weak with fatigue, bruised, abased—as if I had been trampled by horses. I have even dreamed about them. When was it I saw them so clearly—last night? No, the night before. Black stallions with swollen necks, great rolling eyes, bared teeth and livid gums, charging over me, their hoofs lifted, falling, lifting again, now stained and splashed with gore from my shattered head; and far off, on a plain behind them, one lone white horse with a mane as pure as snow, galloping off into the distance, his saddle empty.

It is not too late to put an end to it. Tomorrow I shall tell Dr. Lavrier everything and give him my resignation. Thank God I shall be able to sleep tonight.

¶ *FRI., MAY 29:*

. . . I was prepared for anything, I think, except her tears. But when I came into her room she was weeping, sitting on the floor beside her loom, her forehead pressed against the wall, her face and shoulders shrouded by her yellow hair, which trembled softly while she sobbed. I knelt beside her, helpless, burning with wild tenderness. "Lilith, Lilith, what is it? Why are you sad?"

"Oh, Vincent," she said. "I'm afraid they will leave me. They have threatened never to come back again. Oh, my beautiful people! What will I do if they leave me alone?"

The door was open; there were attendants passing in the hall. I did not dare to lay my hand on her head. I could only say in a soft, demented whisper, "Don't cry. Don't cry, Lilith. I'm here. I'm here, if you want me."

After several minutes she stifled her sobbing and asked if I would read to her.

"Yes. What shall I read?"

"I don't know. There's nothing here that you can read. Do you know some poetry?"

"No."

"Then speak to me. Anything. Invent it, if you like."

So I began to speak to her. A great long, fantastic speech that it seemed to me I had always yearned to make. Rambling, passionate nonsense. What on earth did I say? I can't remember all of it: "Once, when I was a boy, I tried to fly. I fell down, stunned, from the porch banisters; and just in front of me in the grass, where I was lying, there were two little green lizards making love. Their bodies were joined together, utterly motionless except for their breathing, which was perfectly in unison. I thought for a moment that I was dead, and that this was my first glimpse of heaven: a place where green monsters lay locked together in eternal, motionless ecstasy. A terrible vision of Paradise; so terrible that I thought immediately, No, it isn't heaven; it's hell, of course. But I was dazed, you see, not really thinking well; so that I could not be sure which of them it was, or if there was any difference between them. A moment later, when I had recovered my senses a bit, I thought, Oh, it's only earth. I am not dead. But I was neither very convinced nor very reassured; I don't think I have ever been, because I am still haunted by those spellbound monsters. I have always wanted to tell that to someone.

"And also about my mother's grave: I went there one day and planted an azalea, one of those beautiful pale salmon-colored ones. But while I was planting it the gardener came—he had been working in another corner of the cemetery—and made me dig it up. 'No, you can't plant it here,' he said. 'Nothing must be planted in the cemetery.' 'Oh. Why?' I asked. 'Because of the mowing. How do you expect me to mow the grass if there are bushes planted everywhere?' It was something I had never thought about before, but he was right, of course. I suppose they have to mow it. But it gave me a terrible feeling about dead people: that even after they're dead they're not really free, they haven't really escaped. There are still all kinds of rules that they have to abide by; they have to be mowed regularly, and made to look tidy. And there are those awful tidy words that they put on their headstones—I hate them. I should think when you're dead, at least, you shouldn't be expected to be neat any more. My mother was never very neat. She always had yellow ribbons hanging down all over her; she could never keep them tied. And when she was alive there were always little gold-colored hairpins lying around, all over the house. It's awful to think of them making her lie there like that, so neatly, forever . . ."

I went on and on, for five or ten minutes, I think, sitting beside her on the floor, saying any kind of nonsense that came into my mind. And I was supposed to be comforting her—my God! It must be the strangest declaration of love that was ever made. But the odd thing is that I think she understood me, because she listened so attentively, so appreciatively, as if I were saying the most eloquent piece of poetry ever written. And when I had finished she laid her head against my knee, closing her eyes and smiling softly. She had stopped crying.

¶ *MON., JUNE 1:*
. . . That inscription on the wall above her bed will drive me mad. What in God's name can it mean? IIIANA PIRIII RESH KAVAWN. I lie and whisper it to myself for hours, seeing the great black letters in my mind. Sometimes there is a gathering sense of revelation, a hectic intensification, as of growing insight, and I feel that in a moment its meaning will burst open in my mind like a great white flower of light, an exploding star; and then I shall know the answer! But it never finishes; always it fades with a ghostly waning grace, like the moon on a cloudy night, and I am left rigid with terrible suspense. What must I do to learn it? She will not tell me—no matter how I threaten or cajole her. This morning I asked her again, and she said, "I can't tell you, Vincent; please don't ask me any more. Do you want me to be punished? They would punish me dreadfully." Looking at me with those great plaintive eyes. Some day I will take her hand and twist and bend her fingers—even if she screams with pain—until she tells me. She has as much as promised me, and by Heaven I mean to know. Arrogant, tormenting creature!

¶ *TUES., JUNE 2:*
. . . I could not help being amused by Bea this morning. I am sure she was trying to outwit me: "I'm worried about Warren; do you think you could persuade her at least to be civil to him?" Now how on earth did she expect me to react to that? Certainly

not with such polished self-possession! "I'll try, if you like. Perhaps I could get her to the tea dance this week, and have her dance with him." Oh, I have far too much at stake to be deceived by that sort of trumpery! It's disturbing, however, to think that they may be aware of what I feel. They are very perceptive people, and it would be easy for me to betray myself. I must be extremely cautious. . . .

Tomorrow I am to take her to the tournament at Kingston! I am blazing, feverish with excitement. I have walked back and forth from the window to my desk twenty times, clenching my hands, pressing my knuckles against my mouth, smiling with delight at the surprise I have in store for her! Yesterday evening when I was coming home I met Howie Elliot in front of the drugstore, his arm in a cast. He is about my age, and used to ride sometimes at the county fair before the war. We chatted for a few minutes, and I asked if he was going to the tournament tomorrow.

"I'm going," he said, "but I can't do no more than watch, now. I was going to ride till I broke this damn thing rabbit hunting last week. You going to ride?"

"No, I haven't got a horse any more," I said.

"Well, hell, ride mine! He's all trained and ready to go. I got him entered, anyway."

"Do you mean it?"

"Sure! I'm going to take him over, anyway. You can just ride for me. I'd like to see him win. He's a real nice little stallion— five years old and real sweet to run."

"By gosh, I'd like to!" I said. "But I haven't ridden since before the war. I'm probably rusty as an old nail."

"Hell, you won't have no trouble. Take a crack at it, anyway. I'd like for somebody to run him. I'll bring you a lance and all."

"All right, I will!" I said. "I'd really like to. Thanks a million, Howie."

"That's the idea. I'll meet you up there about eleven, then. It don't start till noon."

So I am going to ride for her, after all! There must have been Providence in such an opportunity—there's really no other way to explain it! I can't believe my good fortune. It gives me a feeling of pride which is quite unlike anything I've ever felt before—but of apprehension, too. I'm so out of practice that I'm afraid I'll perform disgracefully in front of her, which is too terrible to think about. I don't expect to win, of course, but if I could come in at least third or fourth, and win a ribbon for her—even a yellow one—it would be the most wonderful day of my life, I think! O Lord, help me win a ribbon for my love!

*T*HE DAY of the tournament was an exceptionally beautiful one—one of those early summer days on which the quality of light gives to all objects a pale incandescence. The morning air was so fresh and sweet that I left the bathroom window open while I shaved so that the cool delicious breeze might blow across my naked shoulders. In spite of my haste and my impatience for the day's events to begin I felt impelled to study my face in the mirror with unusual attention and curiosity while I shaved, almost as one studies the face of a stranger on whom a known felicity is about to descend, feeling that odd combination of envy and respect which such a distinction commands.

What an odd-looking young man! I thought with a delightfully artificial naïveté. His nose is too large, his lashes are too long. And yet how I wish I were him! His face has a look of importance about it. He will do something of consequence today! And I remember a pathetic look of mortified surprise that came into my eyes at the sudden devastating intimation of my own vanity—

vanity of a dimension I had never before suspected in myself. I set my razor down with a little clink on the side of the enamel basin and stood with my eyes closed for a moment in desolate awareness of the things a man may do in the hunger to distinguish himself before his fellows, or before God. But when I had had my coffee in the silent kitchen and stepped out into the moist cool stir of morning I felt myself reclaimed by the passions of the day, and all the way down the street to Poplar Lodge I gathered invisible reins in my clenched hand and hoisted a heavy lance beneath my armpit, sighting and leveling it adroitly while with my knees I steadied my galloping, ghostly steed.

As it was known that I would be "specialing" most of the day, I was excused from the morning meeting to make preparations for our trip. I fueled the staff limousine at our private gasoline pump and went down to the kitchen to order a special luncheon for Lilith: honey and watercress sandwiches, a Thermos of milk, and tangerines, all of which I knew she liked especially. I began to be very afraid that she would decide, at the last minute, not to go; but when I arrived at the door of her room I found her not only prepared but as nearly eager to go as I had ever seen her. She was barefoot, however.

"You're going out into the world today," I said. "And you must dress as the world demands."

"Won't you take me if I don't?"

"No."

"But I haven't worn shoes in so long. They'll hurt my feet."

"You must get used to suffering again."

"Oh, you're going to be sententious! I won't go at all, if you're going to be like that. I thought you wanted me to be happy, and I find you only want to make me suffer. You should be ashamed."

She made me feel altogether ridiculous with these words, and I watched in penitent silence while she searched in her closet, where, after much rummaging about, she discovered a pair of little black ballet slippers, which she stooped to slip onto her feet.

"There. You see what sacrifices I make for you? Will they think I am respectable now?"

"I believe so. As you say, they are very easily deceived."

She laughed and lifted her head toward me in an intimate and affectionate way that made my heart beat quickly. We descended in the elevator in a kind of silent gaiety, shyly and excitedly avoiding each other's eyes. She seemed not to have considered how we should get to the tournament, and the sight of the limousine made her eyes sparkle with amused surprise. She entered it silently and demurely, smiling while I started the car and drove it slowly down the curve of the drive. When we had entered the street and driven for a few hundred yards along it she said, "I had no idea you could drive a car. How did you learn?"

"I learned in the army," I said.

"Really? You don't look at all as if you could drive. I wanted to see you riding a horse, and here you are driving this huge machine instead. It makes me feel as if you had been deceiving me somehow."

"I'm sorry, but I don't know any other way to get there. It's much too far to bicycle." I turned to smile at her. "I haven't been deceiving you, anyway. It's just a sort of incidental skill that I've picked up."

"I know. One must be very skillful to live in your world; and I hadn't thought of you at all as a skillful person. I'm terrified of them."

"Not of me?" I said.

"I don't know. I don't really know anything about you, Vincent. Sometimes I have the feeling that you may do me harm."

This exchange made a brief hiatus in our happy intimacy. I glanced at her and saw that she sat with a huddled and forlorn look in the corner of the limousine. To get to Kingston, where the tournament was to be held, it was necessary to go through Stonemont and take the north road out of town. As we passed the county courthouse a flag on the tall white pole above the portico was ranting in the blue air, snapping and snarling as if delivering an hysterical manifesto. Lilith watched it with a subdued look of fear.

"Have you been downtown before?" I asked.

"No, not for months. Maybe it's years; I can't remember."

"It isn't much of a town," I said somewhat apologetically, for the streets seemed suddenly to have been humbled by her presence.

"But I want to see it. It's what you want me to come back to, isn't it? I know it must be wonderful."

As we entered the commercial section of the street she sat up attentively, looking out at the shop windows with restored interest. While we paused at the traffic light—Stonemont's single one, an ancient ornamental device, suspended on cables over the center of the principal intersection—she peered with innocent curiosity into the window of Wingate's Pharmacy, on the opposite curb. Under her scrutiny I became aware for the first time, really, of the ignobility of its contents. There were boxes and bottles of depilatories, mouth washes, cosmetics, perfumes, deodorants, razors, rubber syringes, aspirin, sleeping tablets, cigarettes, and even canned beer—a whole museum of devices, I realized with a kind of personal mortification, for producing illusions of the least glorious sort—for making the human mind less sensitive, less prone to its perceptions, less original; and the human body less restless, less beastlike in appearance, less repugnant in odor, and sterile. Beside these wares there was also a glittering pyramidal display, in brightly bound paper covers, of the New Testament, the Baghavad Gita and a savagely illustrated novel entitled *Dead Virgins Don't Sing*. In one corner of the window there was a two-color printed poster advertising a double feature at the local cinema: *The Voice of the Turtle* and *The Fiend from Outer Space*.

Lilith turned to smile at me gently. "It *is* wonderful," she said, "but do you really want me to exchange my loom and my flute for these wonders?"

I could produce no more than an embarrassed murmur in reply, and felt greatly relieved when the light had changed and I could turn the corner and proceed down the upper length of Main Street. At the end of it stood the music shop into whose window I had so often stared with fascination as a child. I slowed the car instinctively to peer in through the dusty glass at the ancient dulcimer which lay there in the sunlight. (This was an invariable and rather anxious habit of mine, for I dreaded the day when mysteriously, apocalyptically, it would be gone and put forever beyond my reach.) Lilith's eyes lit softly at the sight of the old wine-colored instrument.

"Oh, how lovely," she said. "What is it doing here? A dulcimer!"

"I don't know. It's been there as long as I can remember."

"What a nice old shop. I'd like to go in there; is it closed?"

"Yes, I think it must have gone out of business long ago; it's never been open as long as I can remember. But the dulcimer has always been there. I always wanted to play it, when I was a boy. I used to think that I'd buy it some day and learn to."

"Why didn't you, ever?"

"I don't know—it seemed like kind of a silly thing to do. People said it was, anyway."

"What people?"

"Well, a girl I used to know."

She turned toward me curiously. "A girl? Was she your sweetheart?"

"I guess so. I used to think she was."

"What happened to her, Vincent?"

"Well, she married somebody else, while I was away."

"Oh." She turned back to watch the old shop front lingeringly as we drove beyond it, asking in a moment, "Would you still like to play it, Vincent?"

"Oh, I don't think I could, now," I said. "And I don't know if I really want to any more. I have a feeling it would disappear, anyway—crumble away or something—if I touched it."

She looked at me softly—again with that scarifying look of tenderness—and laid her hand gently on the back of my own, where it rested on the wheel.

"You would have played it beautifully," she said.

We had driven on beyond the last commercial buildings of the street, and as we entered the open highway Lilith turned to look back for a moment at the diminishing brick and timber façades of the town with the tall portico of the courthouse rising above them. "You have such an angry flag," she said. She dropped her head, spreading her fingers on the gray upholstery of the automobile seat and falling into thoughtful silence.

It took us an hour to drive to Kingston, a tiny hill town in the shadow of Sugar Loaf. It is one of the loveliest towns in central Maryland, a Revolutionary village with a green, an ancient stone well with a shingled roof, and a main street lined with narrow sagging houses of weathered clapboard. There were beautiful black cockerels with scarlet combs strutting in the sunlight, and the whole town was full of the scent of roses and wild jasmine. Lilith leaned from the open window, her face as radiant, almost, as the sunlight itself, with happiness.

"Oh, Vincent, it *is* beautiful!" she said. "I think you have found me an enchanted village!"

I was more than in accord with this opinion, for on looking into the window of the music shop, we seemed to have left behind us, figuratively as well as in fact, all the ugly merchandise and prosaism of the town; and the morning with its roses, its strutting burnished cockerels and its soft sunlight on the fieldstone of the old cellars seemed indeed to have become a song.

The tournament was to be held in a grove of gray oaks beyond a wooden church at the outskirts of the village. We drove toward it slowly under the clumsily lettered muslin banners that hung above the street, blowing our horn in festive warning to the crowds who drifted with us toward the grounds. Although it was only eleven o'clock, there were already many of them, and the Methodist congregation who were patrons of the event were busily setting up refreshment booths, barbecue pits, ring tosses and horseshoe pitches. An old man with an official's badge pinned to his faded blue work shirt directed our parking on a square of green lawn in front of the church, and we left the car to saunter about the grounds.

I had experienced, as we left the hospital, a somewhat fugitive feeling, a sense of guilty abdication, which, in spite of my excitement at the adventure, had made me uneasy and unable to appreciate entirely even the air of "enchantment" of the village; but as we strolled about under the old oaks, cool in our summer clothes, among the stir and shouting of the crowd, I felt this anxiety fade away into the warm fragrant air, and became aware of a growing easy delight, a sense of long-desired escape and of private intimacy, like that of eloping lovers, which all the while made me smile to myself with achievement and, even more, with anticipation—for I had still my great surprise to announce to her! There were men carrying long wooden trestle tables up from the basement of the church and setting them in rows under the shade of the trees; already a horseshoe pit had been established, and from far away under the oaks came the ringing clang of metal and the sudden bursts of applausive laughter of onlookers; an electrician in white overalls, clinging to the branches of a giant oak and cheerfully rejecting the suggestions of grinning farmhands underneath, was stringing up a loudspeaker system above the picnic tables. All these preparations Lilith watched in happy silence, looking into my face sometimes to smile as she walked beside me. I did not speak either, for I was so acutely aware of every move she made, and often, when her summer dress or her loose hair brushed against me, so tremblingly sensitive to her presence that I hardly trusted my voice. She stood laughing to watch two small boys staggering with a zinc washtub full of chunks of ice and floating dark-green watermelons. When she called to them they set it down and came shyly to stand in front of her with downcast faces.

Lilith knelt to look into their eyes. "It must be very heavy," she said.

"Yes, ma'am, it's right heavy," the older of the boys said.

"And you've splashed your trousers with water. It must feel lovely and cool."

"Yes, ma'am, it does, because that's real hot work."

"Hit's real hot work," the smaller boy said.

Lilith smiled at him. "How much are your watermelons?" she asked.

"Twenty-five cents," the older boy said. "The big ones is twenty-five cents."

"And how much is the ice?"

"We're not sellin' the ice, ma'am."

"Oh. I think I'd rather have a piece of ice. Do you think you could let me have just a tiny piece?"

"Yes, ma'am." They walked soberly ahead of her to the tub and he lifted a dripping kitchen knife from the water.

"I want to chop it," Lilith said. I had a moment of anxiety as he handed the knife to her, but she crouched down beside the tub and hacked at the floating ice with innocent absorption, the pale-blue splinters flashing in the sunlight. She dipped her hand into the tub and picked out a lump of ice, holding it in her palm like a cold sparkling jewel.

"It's like a diamond," Lilith said.

"Yes, ma'am."

She lifted her hand and took the ice into her mouth from the flat of her palm.

"She swallit a diman," the small one said.

"Hit'd cut her all up inside, if it was," the older boy said. "She'd bleed. Dimans ah hard." He watched, fascinated, while Lilith bit the lump of ice, shuddering as she swallowed the cold chips. Her teeth made a sharp ferocious sound. "You bitin' it, ain't you?" he said.

"Yes. I ate the diamond. Do you want to see my blood?"

"Yes, ma'am."

"Touch my lips." He reached out shyly and laid his finger tips on them. "Now look."

"Hit ain't none," he said, withdrawing and examining his hand. "I known you was foolin'."

"Oh, there is, but you can't see it, because it's clear, like water."

"She got white blood," the small one said.

"Yes. What color is yours?"

"Mine's red," the older boy said. "I get cut a lot."

"No, it's blue," Lilith said. She raised her hand and touched the fine blue vein that ran down his throat. "Hot and blue." He stood with a quality of somber obedience under her touch. "I can't pay you for the diamond," she said in a moment. "I have no money. Shall I give you a kiss instead?"

"Yes, ma'am."

She leaned forward slowly and pressed her lips against the shallow hollow of his temple. As she did so she murmured something which made him drop his head.

"We'll have to hurry if you want to see the horses in the paddock," I said. "They'll be running soon."

"Yes, Vincent."

She stood up and smiled down at them. "Goodbye. And thank you; it was delicious."

"How come she to kiss you, Jerome?" the smaller boy asked.

"Hush. Because," the older one said. He added softly in a moment, "She had real cold lips."

He stood watching us, bemused, as we walked away. Lilith turned to wave to them.

"How sweet they are!"

"Do you like children?" I asked.

"Yes. They're so alive, so aware. And so wise!"

"Would you like to have some of your own?" I said, watching her. Her face changed utterly at this question. All the animation faded from it instantly, leaving her with a still, austere expression, almost frightening in its suddenness and severity. She lowered her eyes, saying, "No," in a dull, tense voice that was very foreign to her; and I was forbidden by her demeanor to pursue the topic.

We had come to a clearing in the oaks where the list was being roped off with long yellow coils of new hemp cord. Inside the boundaries there were men on stepladders decorating the arches from which the rings were to be hung, wrapping the wooden poles with red and blue crepe-paper bunting.

"What are they doing here?" Lilith asked.

"This is the course," I said. "They hang metal rings from the arches, and you have to gallop under and pierce them with a lance."

"It must be very difficult. How big are they?"

"Like this." I made a ring in the air with my curled fingers. "But they look even smaller when you're trying to take them at full gallop."

"And were you very good at it?"

"I used to be," I said. "I won the Junior Championship one year at the county fair."

"Did you really, Vincent? Oh, I wish I could see you! I'd give anything if you would ride for me!"

I turned to smile at her, leaning with assumed casualness against the trunk of the oak beneath which we were standing.

"What would you give?" I asked.

"Oh, anything. I have so little. My flute, my loom, my prisms."

"Your happiness?" I asked.

Her eyes darkened instantly with a look of solemn intensity. "I can't barter and trade with that," she said. "That I must give freely, or it has no value."

I looked into her eyes in a long-sustained gaze of growing gravity, feeling within myself the ebbing of will and pride in a strangely craven and ecstatic process of submission for which it seemed that I had yearned all my life. I do not think I have a more abject or exalted memory from all my days with Lilith than this: myself taking her fingers in my hands and bowing my head before her in an attitude of obeisance to kiss them lightly and ceremoniously, murmuring, "I'll ride for you, Lilith, if you want me to."

"Oh, my love," she whispered. She left her hands in mine for a moment, standing motionless with joy, and then loosened one gently to lay it on my shoulder in a quaint courtly gesture.

"There, I have knighted you," she said. "And you must wear my colors in the tournament." She unwound the blue silk scarf from her throat and tied it about my forearm, which I held out obediently, watching her eyes. They had become marvelously gay. "Now you are my champion."

"How shall I ride?" I asked. "As the Knight of Poplar Lodge?"

"Yes, that sounds splendid. And it *is* my domain, isn't it? Are you glad to ride for me?"

"Yes." I lifted my arm and fingered the pale silken tassel. "It's a beautiful banner. I hope I can do it credit."

"Oh, you will," she said. "But it doesn't matter if you don't win a prize, because I've won enough today."

"Well, I'll try," I said. "But you mustn't expect too much; I haven't ridden for years."

She laughed suddenly with delight. "How did you arrange it, Vincent? You told me you didn't have a horse!"

"I don't. But I had a wonderful stroke of luck. Come down to the paddock and we'll look at our horse. I haven't even seen him myself, yet."

We walked down among the gathering crowd, past a hastily erected wooden platform where the heralds were to sit with their trumpets and trombones, to a railed paddock in a wooded hollow below the course. Here there were horses being saddled and curried, their fine hides gleaming in the dappled sunlight among the trees. They lifted their hoofs sometimes, stamping, tossing their heads and blowing long nervous whinnies in the warm silence of the summer afternoon. The air was full of their odor— a heroic smell which I have always loved—warm, salty and golden, like sunlight on blood. Lilith stood at the paddock rails to watch them, clutching her yellow hair close about her face like a coif and smiling with delight at their beauty.

"How lovely they are! Which is yours, Vincent?"

"There, I think."

I pointed to where my friend Howie Elliot crouched at the feet of a great bronze-colored stallion, polishing its hoofs with an oiled rag. He hooted to it softly sometimes when it dipped its head and shifted its feet impatiently, arching its huge burnished neck.

"Oh, he's the most beautiful of all!" Lilith cried, clasping her hands together. "What a wonderful horse we have!"

"Yes, he is." I felt a mingled sense of pride and apprehension and the privilege and responsibility of riding so wonderful an animal. I called to Howie, who raised his head and waved to me.

"Hey, Vince! I thought you was lost! Come on over and have a look at him."

We climbed through the railings and walked to where the stallion was tethered under a large oak. Howie stood up as we approached, lifting his plaster-encased arm and grinning regretfully.

"Can't do much good with this thing," he said, "but he don't look too bad, does he?"

"He's the most beautiful one of all," Lilith said. "He shines like gold."

"This is Miss Scott, Howie," I said, introducing her by the conventional pseudonym for protecting the identity of patients. "Howie Elliot."

"How-do, ma'am. Vince never told me he was goin' to bring you. He's a sly devil. I reckon you'll bring him all the luck he needs."

"I don't think he'll need any, with a horse like this," Lilith said. She reached out to lay her hand on the stallion's muzzle. The animal shivered and whinnied under her touch, nuzzling her breast with its great gaping nostrils and leaving a smear of moisture on her blouse. She laughed and hugged its huge sleek snout against her.

"Howie's letting me ride him because he broke his arm," I said.

"That's very kind of you," Lilith said. "And I have to thank you, too, because I've never seen a tournament before."

"Aw, it's a favor to me," Howie said. He stood looking puzzled and abashed by her careless loveliness. "You come from Stonemont, ma'am?"

"No, I'm only visiting here."

"I didn't remember seein' you before."

"No."

"Can I take him for a little run in the woods here, Howie?" I asked. "I'd like to get the feel of him a little before I ride."

"Yeah, I was goin' to tell you to do that. You better take the lance, too. I got it right over yonder by the tree."

"Oh, let me get it!" Lilith cried. She ran to where the long oaken shaft stood propped against a branch and lowered it slowly, running her hands along the polished wood, touching the steel ferrule and cord-bound haft with wonder. "I've never seen one," she said, looking up at us with a delighted smile. "I didn't know they were even made any more. How heavy it is!"

"Yeah, it's too heavy for you, ma'am," Howie said. He relieved her of it laughingly and, when I had mounted the stallion, handed it up to me.

"Now, let me tell you a little bit about him," he said. "His name's Prince, an' he likes to hear it now an' then. I got him so's I can turn him with my knees: just a little nudge'll get him back in line, but if he's goin' way off, bang him good an' hard a couple of licks. He's got a good flat run when he's gallopin' all out; if he starts slowin' up just yell his name a couple of times. He's used to that. He knows about them arches, an' you won't have no trouble. Let him have lots of rein, though; he's got a real soft mouth. Just handle him with the knees, is best."

"All right. Thanks, Howie."

I swung the stallion out of the paddock and settled the lance under my arm. It was one of those profoundly remembered acts which bring back with them a bewildering wave of perfectly preserved emotions, giving one for an instant the ghostly sensation of having slipped in time. How many summer Sunday afternoons were recaptured by that set of simple movements! Not the afternoons themselves, that is, but my response to them. The tug of the lance under my armpit, the heft of it along my forearm, the clasp of thighs about the horse's barrel, the creak of leather, the fume of horse flesh re-created, in an instant of tumultuous waking wonder, the boy's spirit which had inhabited me on those afternoons and seemed to make run fresh in me some eternal vein of valor which I had never thought to tap again.

I rode the stallion down through the oak woods to a stretch of open meadowland, testing his reactions to the physical commands of my knees, feeling his sensitivity to the bit and adjusting myself to the rhythms of his body, aware, as I did so, of his own examinations of my capacities as a horseman; each of us subtly assessing the skill, strength and courage of the other as we established that mysterious covenant between mount and rider which is one of the great delights of horsemanship. At the edge of the woods I urged him from a trot into a thrilling headlong gallop, holding the lance level and sighting along it while I watched with hypnotic pleasure the solid world ahead of us, sundered by his speed, loosen and pour past in a stream of riven, helter-skelter things. Horses' hoofs have always broken the world apart for me—and time, as well, I think—providing me with a wild entry into what seems to be (when I try to imagine it at all) the heart of reality: a splendid panoramic flux, the taste of wind, and the blown scent of a thousand forfeited flowers.

After a few minutes I reined the stallion in, calling his name to settle him, and came cantering back through the oaks to where Lilith and Howie stood waiting at the paddock rails.

"Vincent, you ride beautifully," Lilith said. I felt my heart glow with pride as she lifted her face to me, her eyes brilliant with admiration.

"How do you like him?" Howie asked, grinning.

"He's a real beauty, Howie."

"Yeah, you looked real good up there. You'll do real good." He nodded and stroked the stallion's muzzle, speaking to it with rough affection. "You-all git along all right, don't you? Big old Prince."

"You'd better go find a place along the ropes," I said to Lilith. "It'll be getting crowded soon, and you won't be able to see."

"Yes." She stretched her hand up to me and I reached down to feel the cool momentary clasp of her fingers.

As she walked away among the crowd of gathering spectators I had, in spite of my conviction of her great and genuine interest in the event, a moment of anxious realization that if she wished to escape she would have an excellent opportunity of doing so, among the throngs and confusion of the tournament grounds; but I was reassured to find that from my position in the saddle I could see along the whole length of the list, whose roped boundaries stretched down to the paddock area, and that, with moderate vigilance, I would be able to keep her in sight throughout the tournament. I watched her move up through the crowd—how easy it was to identify her by her wild golden hair—to the upper end of the course, finding a place beside the ropes, where a pair of awed farmers parted to admit her.

"You got a real pretty girl there," Howie said. "By golly, I never seen one just like that in my life. That her scarf you got on your arm?"

"Yes."

He grinned and nodded. "How you want to ride? I got to make out a entry card with your name on it."

"As the Knight of Poplar Lodge," I said. "Is that all right with you? It's where I work."

"Yeah, sure. I'm down as owner an' trainer; that's all I care about. I'll take it on up there, 'cause they're gittin ready to start."

"Thanks, Howie."

He walked away toward the judges' stand with the entry slip, and I used the interim to make myself more familiar to the stallion, leaning forward to pat his neck and speaking to him softly. The other riders had mounted, and with the hushed stir of readiness in the paddock the horses had become nervous, snorting and sidling tensely. There were twelve entries, most of them trim, long-legged hunters of the type that Maryland breeders favor, as well as several placid-looking work horses, nondescript in appearance, but, I knew from experience, well trained and cunning in this type of contest. The riders for the most part were serious-faced country boys in faded jeans and calico shirts, although there was a sprinkling among them of "Hunt Club types"—breeders and gentleman farmers—in gleaming boots and jodhpurs. All of them had a charming and challenging air of earnestness which I greatly respected; the tournament was a small affair—not one of the major county contests—but they nevertheless took part in it with a quiet determination which gave to such events, in spite of their invariable outward air of improvisation, a kind of intensity and dignity to which I was extremely sensitive. I looked about at my fellow riders with admiration.

In a moment Howie returned and stood waiting to hand me up the lance, which I had set down after my trial gallop. There was a delay of several minutes, due to a crisis of some kind that had arisen in the judges' stand, calling forth all the parliamentary instincts of two ladies in straw hats and printed cotton frocks who scurried about with documents clutched to their bosoms, consulting faintly embarrassed, vaguely nodding officials with judges' badges pinned to their suspender straps. When this had been resolved the musicians in the bandstand opposite, after much confused exchanging of sheet music, adjusting of stands and scraping of folding chairs, raised their brass instruments and broke into a blaring rendition of "The Star-Spangled Banner." It was followed by a tremendous cheer from the crowd, who added to their appreciation several chicken bones and empty popcorn boxes, flung in jocular tribute toward the bandstand. I raised my eyes to where Lilith stood watching at the upper end of the course. She lifted her hand to me and then carried it to her lips, touching them lightly with her finger tips in the token of a kiss. As she did so a sudden hellish wail broke forth above the tournament grounds— a rising, anguished, demonic howl, increasing in pitch by bitter quivering octaves until it had faded across the threshold of audible intensity. The hush which followed it was broken by a series of ugly regurgitative sounds, and then a mechanized and chucklingly apologetic voice, introducing the order of events over the loudspeakers. I felt the stallion shudder and start at the sound, and I leaned forward to comfort him, grinning somewhat foolishly at Howie, for I, too, had been shaken.

The judges and sponsors were introduced by microphone, the procedure of tournament announced, and then the Roll of Knights —interrupted by a cheer from the crowd after each champion's name—called grandly. I could not repress a smile of pride on seeing Lilith clasp her hands together excitedly when my own was called. There were to be ten charges by each competitor, with the Tournament Prize going to whichever knight won the greatest number of charges. Victory in an individual charge was determined both by accuracy and speed, a tie in the number of taken rings being resolved by the time of the charge. As there were only three arches on the course, and a considerable number of riders might be expected to take all three rings successfully, this made speed a vital factor. I was to ride eighth, a position which seemed very favorable to me, for I considered it a psychological disadvantage to ride early and have to compete with the as yet unknown achievements of my rivals.

When the formalities had been concluded there was a trumpet flourish from the herald in the bandstand, and the first challenger —the Knight of Darnestown—was announced. He was a boy of not much more than eighteen, mounted on a slender black mare who stood dancing prettily by the starting flag. She had a look of enormous, disciplined speed, which was not misleading, for she broke swiftly, in perfect control, at the starting gun. I watched her flash past the stands under the banners and balloons to the wonderful triple throbbing of her hoofs, her head thrust forward avidly, her haunches glittering like black satin in the sunlight. Her knight rode standing in the stirrups, his body poised in an attitude of fastidious and earnest action, both elbows up, his shoulders tensely rounded, the long shaft of his lance piercing the sunlight in a precise level projection, thrilling in its accuracy. He took the first ring cleanly, without the smallest perceptible adjustment of his weapon; I saw the ring slip onto the tip of his lance and skitter for an inch or two along the shaft. The second he took with equal skill; and although I was too far away to see the details of his try at the third arch, I could tell by the burst of applause from the spectators that he had captured that as well. I felt like cheering, myself, for it had been a beautiful performance.

"He's going to be hard to beat," I said to Howie.

"Boy, you know it!"

The knight had reined in his mount and came cantering back down the list, grinning with pleasure. As he passed the judges' stand the result of his charge was announced over the loudspeakers: "Three rings, with a time of 11.6 seconds."

Howie had taken out a small pocket pad and pencil and was keeping a record of the results.

"That's real good time, too. They usually start off a lot slower than that."

"Yes. I'm going to have to push to beat that."

"Well, old Prince can do it; I've done better time than that with him. Hell, you ain't lost yet."

The Knight of Three Forks had now entered the list, a young man of about my own age, mounted on a big-chested sorrel gelding. It was an ugly horse, which proved to be as uncontrollable as it was unattractive; it balked and bridled at the starting flag, and broke away broadside at the gun. I could see that the knight was having difficulty managing it, because he was very busy with his left hand. The sorrel carried him so far out of line at the first arch that he had to lower his lance; at the second he was working too hard with his heels and reins to make a good approach, and knocked the ring off its clip into the dust. He managed to take the final ring, as I could tell from the scattered handclapping at the far end of the course, but in a time of over fifteen seconds, which was far short of the first challenger's. He rode back to the paddock gloomily, cursing his mount.

"Nothin' to worry about there, anyway," Howie said.

"Not this time."

As the tournament progressed I looked up often to where Lilith stood at the far end of the list. She had not moved, and was obviously entranced by the event. Sometimes, after a particularly skillful charge, she would laugh and clap her hands with pleasure; and I felt—with a rather shamed and startled sensation, for it was the first time in my life I had recognized the feeling in my-self—a painful stab of jealousy. I awaited my turn in the list with growing excitement and with growing trepidation as well; for I had a terrible fear of being proven unworthy.

The initial charge by the Knight of Darnestown had proved to be even more remarkable than we had thought, for it was not matched by the time I entered the list. Three other knights, in-cluding the last who rode before me, had taken all three rings, but in poorer times; and with only four riders left to follow it seemed almost certainly to be this first performance which I must better if I hoped to win the charge.

As the seventh knight reined in and rode back down the list I turned the big stallion's head toward the paddock gate, my heart pounding wildly and a brave commotion warming my whole body.

"Now take it real easy," Howie said. "If you don't win this'n they's lots more to go."

"I want to win this one," I said. I did, indeed, for I had no hope whatever of taking the Tournament Prize, and to win the initial charge seemed to me almost equally desirable. This was Lilith's first experience of a tournament, and I felt that what happened on the opening joust would make as great an impression on her as the whole succeeding course of the day's events. If I could come off gloriously in it, I would have had enough of triumph, no matter what followed. I reached down to take the lance from him, and when I felt its limber, cleanly balanced and heroic weight, a feeling of composure came over me like a benediction. I rode out of the railed enclosure to the starting flag and turned the stallion to face up the list, while the Knight of Washington Grove, who had preceded me, trotted back toward the paddock, shaking his head at me and grinning as he went past. I stared up between the roped boundaries, making many instant observations—the height of the arches, the lighting on the rings, the deep hoof prints where dark soil showed through the scattered tanbark of the course—to where Lilith stood at the end of the list. I saw that she had raised her finger tips to her cheeks and waited breathlessly. There was a brazen flourish from the herald's stand, and my name rolled forth with monstrous portent from the loudspeakers: "The Knight of Poplar Lodge." I waited the exactly accurate fraction of time, loosening my rein and racking the stallion's sides with my knees at the very instant that the starting gun went off. He bolted forward like a loosed arrow, gaining his full stride almost instantly, his forequarters plunging and his bronze mane raving like flames before my face. I had not realized his full quality before; the list awakened a spirit of competition in him that was truly thrilling, and I could feel the exultation of his great body as he carried me up the course under the fluttering crepe-paper bunting with the wind like warm surf in my face and the blue silk of Lilith's scarf streaming from my arm. He took the delicate directions of my knees with wonderful intelligence, making our approach slightly to the left of the arch's center as I wished, for my style of jousting

278

was to ride with a very high elbow, leaning my head far to the side and sighting my lance like a rifle.

The body has an astonishing kind of kinetic memory which seems to be quite apart from any intellectual faculty. It can, after years of disuse, recall and perfectly execute a very complex pattern of physical behavior which the mind has long forgotten, as if the memory were buried in the muscles themselves, and preserved there. I was fascinated to behold my own body now demonstrating this remarkable ability, making instant calculations and adjustments of its own with perfect authority and a kind of joyful renaissance of faculty, which made me almost more a witness than a principal to the event. Every factor of horsemanship that I had learned in the tournaments of my boyhood was redeemed through this magical bodily intelligence: the stance of foot in stirrup, the angle of knee to thigh, the slant of back, the slope of shoulder, and all the many delicate degrees of tension in the muscles required to preserve them.

I watched the tiny cord-bound circle of the jousting ring swell slowly in diameter as the steel tip of my lance bore in upon it; it was a white dot, then an embroidered eyelet, then the loop of a window-shade cord, then, as the bar of shadow from the arch darkened the gleam of my lance tip for an instant, a mouth, open and pale-lipped with horror. I lunged my shoulder forward with a triumphant ferocity which astonished me, shattering the skull of some royal phantom foe and ending his ancient lineage forever. I could not lose; I was inspired. Burning with my own invincibility, I thundered down the list on my incomparable charger, taking the second ring, and then the third, with equal magnificence. As I swept beneath the final arch I lifted my lance, with the three captured rings encircling it, in a salute to Lilith, whose bright hair blazed by me like a torch.

I reined the stallion in and turned him about slowly, loitering back down the list with arrogant indolence amid the cheering of the crowd and seeking out Lilith's eyes with my own. As I came abreast of her my time was announced over the loudspeakers: "Three rings, with a time of nine seconds." It was the best charge made so far; I had bettered the Knight of Darnestown's time by more than two seconds. There was a second great round of applause and a waving of straw hats and handkerchiefs; then my heart halted for an instant with delight as Lilith slipped beneath the boundary ropes and ran out into the list beside me, her blue skirt rustling about her legs and her hair flying. At this demonstration there was an even greater burst of cheering, whistling, and a ribald flurry of handfuls of flung popcorn. She ran to the stallion's side and reached up to take my rein hand in her own, her eyes glittering with triumph.

"Oh, Vincent, you were beautiful!" she whispered. I looked down, drunken with pride, into her flushed face—never had it been more beautiful—reading in her eyes the acknowledgment of myself as her lord and suffering the possession of her white hand as she ran laughing down the list beside me through showers of white popcorn and pleated paper fans. At the paddock gate she kissed my fingers and fled back into the crowd, while I rode burning with triumph into the enclosure.

Howie took the lance from me, chuckling with delight. "You got this'n for sure!" he said. "They ain't anybody goin' to beat that!"

I knew that it was true; and indeed my performance seemed to have demoralized the remaining riders, for only one of them took all three rings, and he in a time far inferior to my own. As he finished his charge one of the page girls ran down from the judges' stand to the paddock and asked if I had a banner to run up.

"Give her the scarf," Howie said. I did so, untying and dropping it down to her; and after a particularly elaborate flourish from the herald's stand I saw the square of blue silk being hoisted up the pole above the pavilion, billowing out into the breeze with airy lightness, as my victory in the charge was called across the tournament grounds.

I have never known such happiness in my life as I felt at that moment. I have set down its circumstances here in some detail, hoping, by doing so, to recapture it in some poor measure. I have not, of course; here there are only paper ribbons and the ghosts of horses, where in my heart there was the splendor of all chivalry.

I did not win the tournament, but I very nearly did—and all that I desired, as well. On the second charge neither the Knight of Darnestown nor myself placed among the winning three; perhaps we had spent too much in the first. But by the third, both he and the little black mare that he rode had regained their fire and won it easily. I did not ride well again until the fifth charge, when I took second place. This gave me the sudden fantastic hope that I might yet win a ribbon, and brought ambition singing back into my blood. I martialed all my skill and strength, took second again in the sixth, and by an almost brutal act of determination won my second charge of the day in the seventh joust. This was my final victory, but it was enough. When the final scores had been tabulated I heard my name proclaimed again—as winner of the Tournament Red Ribbon—and for the third time on the afternoon saw Lilith's blue scarf ride shimmering against the summer sky, this time just below the black banner of the Knight of Darnestown.

In a blaze of fanfare we paraded past the pavilion, each escorted by a herald in a red hunting jacket, to receive our trophies from the tribune. When the huge red rosette had been pinned to the stallion's bridle I galloped up the list to where Lilith stood watching with shining eyes, and, reaching down my arm, lifted her up onto the stallion behind my saddle. She fastened her arms about my waist and clung to me with frightened exhilaration as we galloped down the list, past the paddock rails and out into the oak woods beyond the tournament grounds.

The forest was golden with the late-afternoon light, and full of birdsong which seemed to fall in jeweled notes from the ballad-laden trees. Veil after veil of sunlight broke before our flight, and the warm air washed our faces in a torrent of delicious odors:

stone, soil, wild blackberries, water and honeysuckle. We leapt over boulders and fallen logs in breathless, weightless, soaring flights, reaching up, once, to shake down a shower of wild persimmons that fell about us like bursting hearts. At the edge of the forest we plunged out into open meadowland, scattering a flock of red-winged blackbirds who rose about us with a great hoarse scuffling sound of wings and broke apart in vivid shards of black and scarlet, like fragments of a shattered urn. I do not know how long we rode like that—with Lilith's arms about me and her golden hair streaming—for it is well known (or often reported, at any rate) how ecstasy deforms the sense of time; but I think it must have been half an hour, at least, for we were far from the tournament grounds when the stallion at last began to tire. I held the reins loosely and let him walk at whatever pace he chose, our bodies rolling gently with the idle rhythm of his own. He followed the bed of a small creek westward through the valley floor, stopping sometimes to nibble a choice tuft of grass or to stand with darkened hoofs in the shallow, shining water and dip his muzzle into the quickly flowing stream. There were sheep grazing in the valley, their shadows lengthening in the declining light; they scarcely lifted their heads to us as we went by. Lilith lay against me lightly, her head resting on my shoulder, murmuring softly in her own tongue. The faint, verbena-like perfume of her hair touched my nostrils intermittently, a delicate, inconstant rumor of some bewildering event.

"What are you saying?" I asked.

"That we are heroes. That it is the most beautiful of all days. That I love you."

"Why do you say that?"

"Because it is true."

The valley ahead of us was wooded, and a fallen stone hut of some kind stood in ruins among the trees.

"What is that?" Lilith asked.

"An old springhouse, I think. There are lots of them in the woods."

"Can we go there?"

"If you like."

I guided the stallion in among the maples and sycamores to the hut. It had been built above the creek, and the crumbled fieldstone of the old walls had fallen into the water and been dispersed for many yards by the spring torrents, forming a stony shallows where the smoothly flowing surface was broken brightly and noisily. It could be seen that the banks overflowed here at every thaw, for all about the ruined springhouse the ground was carpeted with deep grass of brilliant green, and much of the ancient masonry was buried in a clump of rushes, their roots in black cool spongy turf. A frog leapt into them with a single solemn splash as we approached.

"Oh, this is the place!" Lilith whispered. The sound of the words made my heart bolt madly. She reached down to pluck off her black ballet slippers, flinging them away into the rushes, and slid down from the stallion's back, standing ankle-deep in the bright turf. I plucked the red rosette from the bridle and tossed it down to her. She caught it and lifted it to her breast, fondling the trailing satin ribbons smilingly.

"I'm sorry it's only the second prize," I said. "I'd like to have won the blue for you."

"Oh, no, it's just what we deserve," she said. "I don't think we will ever be first in the world's honors, and I wouldn't want us to."

She lifted the ribbon and fastened it into her hair, raising her head to smile at me.

"How beautiful you are," I said, looking down at her.

"You haven't seen."

I swung down out of the saddle and stood before her, trembling. Her eyes shone with the ghostly brilliance of mirage. I moved toward her and she raised her hand quickly, saying, "No, wait. I want to be naked for you."

She unbuttoned her blouse and let it fall from her lowered arms; then, unfastening her skirt, she dropped it to the grass and stepped out of it, standing utterly naked, her body white as lime, exquisitely slender, sovereign in its beauty. She shook her long hair across her shoulders to bare her breasts and lifted her face triumphantly to me.

"Now do you see? Do you see what I've wanted you to know?" She moved toward me with a swift, famished movement, as shameless, glorious and generous, it seemed to me, as light itself. I gathered her body against me, burying my lips in her warm wild hair and murmuring senselessly, "I never knew, I never knew. You are more beautiful than I ever dreamed. I love you, Lilith."

In the cool grass, in the shadow of the ruined wall, with the great stallion grazing peacefully beside us, I had my desire.

As the sun fell, the shadow moved beyond us, and the grotto was filled with soft evening light that warmed our exhausted bodies and cast a bronze luster upon them. We lay caressing each other with serene and unself-conscious privilege while the stallion cropped the deep grass about us idly, glowing in his hide of golden lacquer.

"Will you tell me something now?" I asked.

"Yes."

"What do they mean—the words above your bed?"

"I'll teach you my language, Vincent, so we can talk together in it; and then you can read them for yourself. But I think you know, now."

I took her hand and kissed her cool fingers, murmuring with content.

"Will you teach me your songs, too?"

"Yes. Everything I know."

She raised herself on one elbow to look down upon me, running her hands lightly over the contours of my body, laying her fingers in the hollows of my ribs and stroking the gilded skin.

"How beautiful you are—all smooth and coppery. Everywhere but here—where they wounded you." She touched the ugly, knife-shaped scar very gently with her finger tips. "Does it still hurt?"

"A little. It aches, sometimes."

"I'll make it well." She leaned over me to press her lips softly against the glazed, jagged bluish weal, murmuring in her throat, "Now it will be well. Even the scar will go."

I took her head in my hands, pressing her mouth to my wound, feeling the flood of her warm bright hair across my body, faint with delight.

"You can't be real," I said. "There are no such girls as you. I've dreamed of you all my life, but you're even more than I dreamed of."

"Was your other girl so different? Wouldn't she teach you her songs?"

"I don't think she knew any songs," I said.

"Poor Vincent. She thought your dulcimer was foolish! Did she teach you nothing, then?"

"Yes. She taught me shame. I suppose it was all she had to teach."

She turned to face me tenderly. "Vincent, have you never had a friend?"

"I had one," I said. "But they killed him."

She watched my eyes for a moment and her face softened into a tranquil smile. "Then I'm all the happier, because there is no one to take any of your love from me. I can be everything for you: friend, lover, tutor, everything."

"Yes, you are everything, now," I said. "There is certainly nothing else."

"And am I enough?"

"Much more than enough."

"Truly? If I died tonight, would it have been enough?"

"No, not if you died tonight. You don't know how long I've waited for you. I need much more of you than an hour." I clenched her hair, pressing her with gentle avidity against me. "I'm very hungry."

"Then I will live forever. As long as men like you shall need me."

285

There was mist above the creek and dusk in the trees as we rode back through the silent fields, our bodies drooping in the saddle with exalted fatigue. She sang one of her ballads to me, the strange words fading sweetly in the darkening air.

Do you think that abandoned things, deserted things, are not beautiful? Oh, you have never seen them with such a companion! How beautiful the empty list was in the dusk as we rode back idly into the tournament grounds. There were torn ribbons of paper bunting hanging from the arches, blowing gently in the evening wind, and the trampled tanbark of the course was littered with empty Dixie cups, the cores of apples, crumpled paper fans and scraps of glittering foil. A ruined corsage with a twisted wire stem and withering brown gardenia petals stirred softly in the breeze. Somewhere among the debris, with the blood still seeping from his broken casque, lay the pale knight whom I had slain beneath her banner.

One or two horses stood silently in the paddock. The workman was taking down the swaying wires. A man with a wire basket and a rubbish fork was clearing up the grounds. A pair of lovers sat laughing softly, their heads together, at one of the littered picnic tables. A group of horsemen with a bucket of ice and dripping, copper-colored cans of beer stood in a swaying group, singing, under the dark trees. Howie detached himself from them, greeting us jubilantly and offering us beer; but we were tired, and felt shyly isolated by our love, and impatient for our long ride home together through the twilight.

Lilith sat beside me silently in the limousine, fondling the red rosette at her breast and staring out at the quiet darkening fields. We spoke hardly at all. Only once she stretched out her hand to touch my arm and said quite timidly, "Will you be angry if I tell you something?"

"No."

"Your hands are not quite so nice as I thought they would be. Let me see one—can you drive like that?" She studied my hand for a moment, touching my fingers with her own. "Yes, it's your thumbs. There's something wrong about your thumbs."

"I'll cut them off," I said.

"No." She clasped my hand beneath her chin and laughed softly. "I think they are quite nice enough, after all."

As we turned into the hospital drive she laid her hand on my thigh and asked, "Are you frightened?"

"Not now."

"I'll help you. I'm much stronger than you think, and I'll always help you. Remember."

"Yes."

"Tonight, especially. I think you may need to remember it tonight."

I stopped the car for a moment in the deep evening shade of the poplars and, gathering her body against me, kissed her soft mouth—gently at first, then with growing passion, clenching her hair and bending her against me with tender fury, as if in a mournful and abandoned demonstration of my constancy. Perhaps I wished deliberately to fill myself with fresh desire for her so that I should be burning with it, and impregnable in my resolution, when I returned to lie to her guardians. She leaned back from me, her eyes blazing with delight at my recklessness.

"Oh, Vincent, how splendid you are! How could anyone not be proud to have you for a lover!" She raked the hair from her cheeks with her finger tips and, bending forward to kiss my hands, whispered more soberly in a moment, "But we must be more careful; we mustn't lose our happiness."

"No."

I put the car in gear and continued on up the driveway, carrying her back to the great dark mansion over which she reigned, with its sunken veranda, its glimmering golden fishes and its sea plants waving gently in the long tides of magic that flow forever through the fathoms of its shifting cellars.

𝒥 HAVE SPOKEN of the astonishment I felt at my own powers of deception in concealing from Dr. Lavrier my true relationship with Lilith; but these earlier successes are insignificant compared with my achievements of the weeks that followed the tournament. I raised dissimulation to an art; I learned to reproduce the exact modes of sincerity, innocence and honor with a virtuosity which the most accomplished hypocrite would envy—the earnest, rather halting tone of voice, perfectly combining modesty with zeal; the somewhat anxious expression in the eyes when recalling a piece of inexplicable—and entirely imaginary—behavior on her part; the troubled, rather touching flashes of candor in confessing my own inadequacies; the little groping, inarticulate gestures with which to illustrate the imperfection of my understanding and my passion for instruction; my humble delight at her improvements, my despair at her relapses!

In my attitude toward my other patients I was careful to maintain an appearance of undiminished interest and attention; I even increased it, inventing and executing all sorts of original diversions for them and keeping meticulous records of their progress, to which, with great but modest enthusiasm, and to the delight of my colleagues, I was able instantly to refer. To Warren I was particularly solicitous—a device which was not entirely affected, for, perhaps by some curious kind of inverted penitence, my natural affection for him seemed to increase in ratio with my own felicity. I remember that once, when by mutual consent Lilith and I had decided that it would be expedient for her to appear at one of the Wednesday tea dances and to be conspicuously attentive to him, he took me aside afterward and in a rush of garbled confidence expressed his joy: "Did you see? Did you see how she danced with me! Did you notice her manner?" (I had, indeed: the little alluring glances, the challenging demureness, the subtly feigned esteem by which, with a strange combination of scorn and pity, I had watched him beguiled.) "I think she is really beginning to feel something for me! Is it absurd to talk this way? I really feel it!"

We were walking across the green from Field House in the summer evening. He looked up into the maples, which were rustling in the stir of breeze, his excitement seeming suddenly to be quieted to a deep content by their gentle furor. "How beautiful everything is. Only last night those trees terrified me." He turned toward me, smiling, and laid his hand on my arm. "You arranged it, didn't you? You persuaded her to come?"

"Yes."

"It was very good of you. I am very grateful. Do you know, of all the people here, I feel that you are the one who really cares about us. The one who really understands."

"No, I think you're mistaken about that, Warren."

"No, no; I think you feel with us. With me, at any rate. I hope I will be able to repay you some day." He reached up as if to pluck a leaf, and then withdrew his hand quickly. "Do you know, I was about to destroy that leaf—to kill it, just out of happiness! How careless joy can make us!" He smiled and nodded at the dark branches. "It's strange how well I feel when I am happy. I feel that I can work, organize my life again, have friends and interests, do all sorts of wonderful things." He paused thoughtfully for a moment. "Do you think that . . . insanity could be anything so simple as unhappiness?"

"I don't know. I think perhaps it might be just the opposite."

"I don't understand you. What do you mean?"

"I don't know," I said, feeling somewhat abashed by my own words. "I talk a lot of nonsense. You mustn't trust me."

289

"Oh, but I do," he said, laughing. "Just as I trust this happiness I feel. If I don't trust these, what do I have to trust?"

I wanted to tell him to trust yesterday's trees; but it was too brutal a thing to say. I merely smiled and said gently, "I'm sure you must be right to trust your happiness, Warren."

Flashes of conscience such as this were tolerable because, as I have said, they did not last. As it was with Warren, it was with me: nothing could contradict my happiness. I should like to report that I felt great and constant shame at my duplicity, but I did not. I felt, I suppose, somewhat like an artist who abandons or abuses his family and friends for the sake of his art: like him, whatever shame I felt was momentary, and extinguished by the joy of its rewards—for, like him, I had many.

How many were they, in actual number, these rewards? Not more than twelve or fourteen trysts with her, I suppose, in as many weeks; but they are the few jewels I have strung upon the weak thread of my life. It has broken with their weight; but at each point where they hung, see how splendidly it is raveled:

We drove once to the battlefield at Gettysburg and wandered all morning among the tablets and memorials, chasing each other among the rows of blazing headstones and kissing on the graves. (How clearly I see her, sitting on a cannon which faces out across the quiet sunlit field where Pickett's men were slaughtered, her skirt blowing back across the great spoked wheels, leaning forward to clasp the barrel with her arms and peering with great-eyed fascination into the huge mouth of the old field piece that had destroyed so many brave young men!) Later, hiding in the Devil's Cavern, we joined our bodies on a bed of bluets whose roots were fed by the blood of all the slain rebels whom we lay among. At Sugar Loaf, on a day of northeast wind and driven clouds, at the summit, on the very plateau where I had first met Laura, I scourged her memory among the shuddering laurel. We went once to a concert in Washington, and in the darkened vastness of Constitution Hall, surrounded by the rapt, perfumed and elegant audience, we sat in glorious, secret intimacy, washed by the waves of a music more beautiful than Brahms's. Sometimes, to avoid suspicion, she refused to accompany me, asking for another escort instead, or slighted me conspicuously in sight of other members of the staff; and the pained regret at these contrivances which I read in her eyes would create in both of us a wildly sweet anticipation of our next adventure.

We often took bicycle trips together (physical exercise was good for her, my innocent colleagues agreed!); but our most constant pleasure was simply wandering in the fields to the north and west of Stonemont, reveling in the open privacy of the meadows, forests, creek valleys and the hot blue summer sky. Lilith loved water, and often we swam together, naked, in the clear creeks of the valleys. This is one of my most agonizing images of those days: Lilith, standing at the stream's edge to strip off her skirt and blouse, then running out into the pebbly shallows of the creek, the water splashing about her thighs in showers of sunlit crystal. She would clutch her arms about her body, shivering with cold, and bend down slowly in the icy water, the slender curve of her white back sliding into it until her shoulders were submerged; then leap up suddenly, panting with the shock, her body glittering, the tips of her yellow hair drenched and clinging to her throat and shoulders, shouting to me to join her, splashing the shining water toward me in broken brilliant sprays. When I waded out to her, trembling with delight, her small breasts touched me with their cold points, like tines—an exquisite chill which still runs through my blood. I never felt the slightest physical embarrassment with her. She stripped shame from me like a caul. How sweet it was to lie beside her in the sand of the creek shore, our legs half in the cool running water, speaking softly while the sunlight dried our bodies.

"Where do you live? You never told me."

"Not far from you. Only five or six blocks."

"Will you show me some day? I want to see your house."

"Yes. It's a nice old house. My room is upstairs, under the eaves. I can see the chimney of the Lodge and the tops of the poplars from my window."

"What is it like? Tell me about your room. What do you have in it?"

"Oh, silly things. Mostly things I put up when I was a boy and never bothered to take down: high-school pennants, my diploma in a frame, a picture of my horse, a model airplane I made once—the only one that ever flew. Things like that. And on the dresser there's a picture of my mother when she was sixteen. It's brown and sort of faded, but you can see how beautiful she was. And I have a photograph of my squadron, with all their autographs above their heads."

"Nothing of mine?"

"No. I was going to hang your scarf on the wall, but then I thought my grandmother might ask me about it; and I don't want to have to tell anyone about you."

"Why?"

"I don't know. I just don't."

"You tell Dr. Lavrier about me."

"Yes, I tell Dr. Lavrier."

"Does that make you sad?"

"It makes me ashamed. It's the only thing that does, now. I hate pretending to be innocent and honorable—that seems to me to be the only sinful thing we do."

"You don't think loving me is sinful?"

"No. If I thought it hurt anyone—if I thought it hurt you, or Dr. Lavrier, or myself—it would seem sinful. But I don't. I don't see how it can. I'm not ashamed of loving you; only of having to pretend not to."

"Then you are still not perfectly happy."

"Maybe not. But if I'm unhappy, I want to stay this way forever."

"Can you, Vincent? Do you think you will?"

"I don't know. I suppose not. I suppose if you want a love that will last forever you have to be in love with sorrow."

"You are still speaking with the world's tongue. If you were perfectly happy you wouldn't believe that. I don't think you've learned my motto yet."

"I have. I can say it."

"Say it."

" 'Hiara pirlu resh kavawn.' "

"And what does it mean?"

" 'If you can read this, you will know I love you.' " I laid my hand on her closed eyes, looking up into the sky. "Those are beautiful words. I wish it had been God's motto, when He made the world."

"No, I'm glad it wasn't," she said. "I think if it had been, you would not love me now."

I picked up a handful of the yellow sand and, opening my fingers, studied the tiny white and brown and scarlet grains with a kind of forgotten yearning.

"What does it say?" she whispered, smiling at me.

"Nothing. Nothing that I can read."

"But it is beautiful; we enjoy it."

"No, it wasn't beautiful before I met you. You make it beautiful. You are all the beauty of the world, and all the joy I have in it."

I turned toward her, looking for a moment into her eyes. "How do you manage to be always glad? If I take my joy from you, where do you take yours from?"

"From my people, and my nation. They teach me joy."

"But you invented them," I said, and, when she smiled at me reproachfully, leaned toward her and kissed her eyes. "I think you are a genius."

She clasped my head against her breast and after a moment asked gently, "And if my genius were even greater than you thought, would that dismay you? Would you stop loving me?"

"What do you mean?"

"If you should find that my capacity for joy is . . . boundless, would you love me still?"

"Even more; then my love would be boundless, too."

"Ah, Vincent, you are sweet to me. Now you are speaking as I wish you to."

She began, as she had promised, to teach me her language. This, which knowing my limitations as a scholar I undertook rather frivolously and more to please her than for any other reason, I ended by pursuing fervently, so fascinated did I become by the grace and vigor of the language itself and by the insight which it gave me into the quality of her mind and imagination. I had expected, in keeping with her personality, to find it rather elaborate and capricious, and was astonished by the formality and dignity of the grammar. It is a very strange fact that I have forgotten almost every word of it now and that every day it fades further from my mind, like the rhymes and conundrums of childhood. I can remember only odd phrases, scraps of verse and a few rules of its syntax, although I do recall its quality perfectly—precise, severe, yet swift and dextrous and, in the delicate austerity of its sounds, delightful to speak. Its greatest originality was in vocabulary—particularly its descriptive adjectives—which was far richer than that of English. There were over forty words for colors, almost as many for varieties of odor, and over a hundred for differing degrees and modes of happiness—as if the sensibility which was its source was infinitely finer than that which produced the English tongue, and required a much greater vocabulary to cover the range of its perceptions. There was only one conjugation, and I remember this remarkable fact about her nouns: they were divided into two categories, not of gender, but of darkness and light, each of which was differently declined. Under the declension of Light came such words as noise, thirst, action, man, survival, war, pride, art and life; and under that of Dark were silence, stillness, woman, peace, humility, perfection. This curious division gave to every noun—unlike most modern languages—a moral rather than a sexual quality, and provided fascinating material for speculation as to the basis of her assignment of a word to either category. (I remember, in this respect, that there were two distinct words for beauty, one connoting perfect beauty and one imperfect; the former being relegated to the Dark declension and the latter to the Light.) Throughout the structure of her grammar there was evidence of this same preoccupation with paradox. All words which had an opposite, for example, were composed of the same letters as the antonym, spelled backward (Paral—Light; Larap—Darkness); and a particularly subtle—and rather bewildering—feature was that for certain literary or liturgical purposes a noun might change its declension—that is, be transferred from the Light to the Dark category—thus altering completely the texture and atmosphere of the prose, as if rays of light had been shot suddenly through a shower of rain, producing rainbows of radiantly invoked meaning. Although I never learned—there was not time!—to solve or practice these finer shades of significance, the study of them became a rich and engrossing adventure which gave me, as I proceeded in it, the faint and thrilling conviction that with the final mastery of her tongue there would come a kind of revelation. How fervent, how increasingly certain, this belief became! She would give me a page of text to take home, and I would pore over it for hours, into the middle of the night, by the open window of my room, feeling, with every scrap of progress in my study, that I had come a step closer toward some consummate understanding which lay within its grave and beautiful complexities. I remember with what delight I succeeded in translating the first verse of her Gospels (it is copied down in my journal so that I can reproduce it here, although I have forgotten the original):

*There was Music; and it was entire, eternal, Perfectly Beautiful.*

*But He said: There must be an Instrument, for it is unfitting that there should be Music and no Instrument.*

*Therefore He made an Instrument, one as might produce such music; but it was Imperfectly Beautiful.*

*And I said:* This is profane. How can any Instrument be fitted to Music which is Perfectly Beautiful? *Therefore I swore my Oath, in which is all my Love:* I will unmake this ignoble instrument. In its own music shall this rude harp be consumed, as in a fire.

I took it to her, spelled out tremulously on one of the lined pages of my journal, watching with breathless suspense while she whispered the English words of my rendition. I cannot express how deeply moved I was when she turned toward me, taking my hand and clinging to it silently, her eyes shining.

"Is is correct?" I asked.

"Oh, Vincent, it's beautiful. It is a great gift to understand and to translate· so perfectly. Almost a poet's gift. Do you feel closer to me now?"

"Yes," I said, my heart burning with fantastic pride.

By my intense application I developed very quickly a command of her language which, though somewhat halting, was sufficient to allow simple spoken exchanges between us; and this was a source of exquisite pleasure to me. What a sense of private, inviolable communion it gave us to wander in the sunlight on the hillsides, calling out to each other our discoveries of wildflowers, pretty stones or orioles in the rippling chiaroscuro phrases, dappled with alternate consonant and vowel sounds, like the passage of swallows through an arbor. Why have I forgotten them so soon? I remember only this fragment of a ballad that she often sang— one of the oldest, she said, in her literature:

> *Tomáslar, Tomáslar, Irian?*
> *Iría, bar dolán shalár . . .*
> *True Thomas, True Thomas, do you follow?*
> *I follow, although the way be wild . . .*

I knew many, then, however; and loved to sing with her. She would droop her head, her hanging hair glowing with an incandescent brilliance in the sunlight, gazing sorrowfully at her laced hands while her soft voice wandered by plaintive half tones over the rueful verses.

Once, in the shadow of an oak to which we had run for shelter in a sudden dazzling shower of sunlit rain, she paused, crouching against the gray bole and stretching out her hand to touch my own, her face transformed.

"What is it?" I said.

"Hush! Listen—do you hear it?"

"No, I don't hear anything."

"The music! Can't you hear the music? Oh, listen! It's my people, singing."

I bent my head breathlessly, watching her eyes, which were intensely bright and seemed to plead with me to hear it, too.

"They're singing in your presence! Oh, Vincent, I think they are almost ready to reveal themselves to you!"

I felt a swift cold spray of delight run through my nerves and stood motionless with weird anticipation.

"You don't hear them? They're there—among those boulders— Alman and Roth and Trygg. They're dressed in silver."

"Do you see them?"

"Yes. Not clearly, because there is so much shadow. But they're there."

I moved my head toward the place she indicated with quick involuntary caution; and it was this movement, I think, which wakened me into a state of shocked dismay—this absurdly stealthy, credulous maneuver, seeking with my eyes the imaginary creatures of her fantasy, which I suddenly discovered myself performing. There was a strange willful innocence about it which I found disgusting; and in a wave of startled indignation I said severely, "I don't hear anything. There isn't anything to hear."

"Oh, you will soon, Vincent! I'm sure of it. They would not

sing in your presence if they didn't mean you to hear them."

The quiet confidence with which she said these words—the very modesty of her conviction—increased unpleasantly the obscure alarm by which I had been touched, and it was with difficulty, and no very great success, that I concealed my discomposure from her for the rest of the afternoon. She was not impatient or critical of my mood, however, seeming to interpret it as one of appropriate gravity at so distinguished an advent, and pressing my hand, when we parted in her room, with an unusual, benedictory-like caress.

"You frowned. Didn't you like the way I touched you?"

"Yes."

"You mustn't lie to me."

"I don't know; it seemed . . . possessive."

"And you don't like possessive love?"

"No."

"Why, Vincent?"

"Because . . . my grandfather loves that way."

"I think all love is a possession," she said.

Whatever dismay I felt at this occurrence was overwhelmed—like my guilt, my sense of shame, my every misgiving—by the constant delight of her company, the wild, bewildering joy of her favors, the brilliance of her mind—all things, I was now willing to confess, which I could no longer live without. If I had been inclined to condemn my credulity as wanton or fatuous, I was able to condone it by reminding myself that in a world where most dreams are of money, power or personal glory, it is very easy to forgive—even to prefer—a dream which is of a noble, gentle, imaginary race of men, of song, wisdom and delight; and equally easy to forgive—even to love—the maker of such a dream, a graceful, generous, joyful creature who spoke with so true and original a tongue amid the babel of the world.

So such dark moments of perturbation and self-mistrust were swept aside by golden August afternoons in the fields surrounding Stonemont; by a visit to the county fair which still reigns in my heart with the brazen witchery of carousel music, and from which I have a hundred haunted images:

Lilith, shrieking in my arms, her hair streaming and her eyes wild with horrified delight, as the two of us go hurtling outward from the earth in a spinning, dizzy, sickeningly exalted violation of all its gravities—then, as the machinery slows, leaning forward to grasp the bar of our "Torpedo," shaking her head from side to side and laughing with soft hysterical hilarity; Lilith with her lips stained and her cheeks appliquéd with a fine scarlet web of spun sugar, refusing to wipe it off; and a sudden sticky kiss in a canvas-walled passage between two tents: cloyed, candy-tasting kiss, our lips adhering slightly, magnificent maudlin leaping of my heart; Lilith with an apple, glittering, red, shellacked, Original; Lilith crouching at a spigot to drink, her head turned sideways, her eyes closed, making dulcet noises with her dripping lips; Lilith standing with her arm about the shoulders of a little girl with equally golden hair to watch a puppet show, their faces equally innocent, serene, enchanted, gravely offering each other salted cashews—"Why did he hit her with the stick?" "He is very wicked." "Will he hit her again?" "Oh, I hope not."; Lilith deformed, hideous, with a ravaged, hollowed face and blighted body, staring at me with steadfast mockery from the mirror of a fun-fair; Lilith sleeping sweetly as a child in my arms, in the shadow of the gray oaks above the cemetery, her fingers clasped about the body of a china fairy with blue, inane glass eyes, a shred of pink, diaphanous skirt and a tinseled, star-tipped wand. (A piece of bark falls in her hair; I pick it out cautiously, staring down at her with wounded eyes.) Oh, my love, my lady!

Once, when she had signed for an evening movie trip to Stonemont, we went instead to the orchards north of town, and in among the silent, moon-drenched trees, in the darkness with its fragrant reek of fruit-tree sap, with a dog distantly lamenting our iniquity, and her whole body wet with the juice of rotting peaches, I purged myself of a fantasy that had harrowed me for months.

299

$J$ DO NOT know how long I expected this state of heedless rapture to endure—a week, a month, two months, perhaps; I do not think much longer, for although I never gave it conscious consideration (the states of faith, love, ecstasy and so forth being, by their very nature, immune to any awareness of their finitude) I do remember my persistent, barely conscious preoccupation with time, and the constant obsessive calculations which I made: "There are eight weeks of summer left, there are seven weeks of summer left, there are six weeks of summer left . . ." Still, this may have been more a concern with the future complexity and disjunction of our relationship than with its actual ending, for I realized that when the winter came our outdoor idylls would have to be suspended, there would be many less opportunities and pretexts for escorting her, and that we should have to resort to the difficult and dangerous business of arranging indoor trysts. I suppose if I had thought about it consciously at all, I should have felt that with proper caution and barring the possibility that she might be transferred to another hospital there was no reason why it could not go on forever; certainly I had lost all fear of detection, for I had gained, as I say, a bitter confidence in my own duplicity; and I knew that Lilith would never be discharged. She was resolved to resist all efforts to "rehabilitate" her, and I had come to respect her will as greatly as I later learned to fear it. But, as I say, I never made any such conscious estimations; I lived in a trancelike state of joy, with only faintly—ever more faintly— recurring spasms of shame at my own deceptions, breathing an atmosphere which seemed to blow from some far country where

I had always longed to go, and which is as lost to me now as the shrill scent of her hair and the sovereignty of her beautiful white hands.

Certainly I had never expected it to be so soon transmuted into the torment and the horror which I have to describe now—not by her own hand.

Under the date of the 23rd of August there is written the briefest of all the entries in my journal:

Maybe if I try to write it down here some of the awfulness will go away, because they say that if you

I can remember dropping my pen with a shudder at this point and bending suddenly forward over my desk, grinding my forehead against the warm wood in a helpless, prayerlike throe of anguish. A few lines below—undated, although I think it was written about three days later—is inscribed a fuller testimony of my degradation:

"Nothing exists but joy," she told me once. "Its servants do not exist, because if they are perfect servants they will be consumed by it." Conjuror, whore! Nothing exists but perfidy!

What am I to do? I can see nothing ahead but horror. But I am hopelessly trapped. What will she force me to do next? Will she go on forever, demonstrating this "boundless capacity for joy" of hers? And she expects me to share it! To increase in my devotion to her with every monstrous thing she does. To enjoy these awful things myself, and even help her—willingly—to accomplish them! And the ghastly, the really fearful thing about it is that I may—she may persuade me to! Because the other morning, just for an instant, when I was standing there outside the barn, listening in that terrible way, I felt the faintest stirring of a hideous delight in my heart.

And afterward, when I was half mad with pain and indignation, when I seized her hair and shook her wildly, flinging her against the wall, she confronted me with this vicious piece of sophistry: "If you discovered that your beastly God loved others as greatly as he loved you, would you hate him for it? He shows love for none of you, and you worship him; I show my love for all of you, and you despise me."

I think it has cost me my soul to learn the nature of her madness. It was suddenly so apparent when she said those words; why have I never been aware of it before? She believes—she really believes—that she is divine.

Good God, what can I do? I must somehow force myself to be calm, to think properly. There must be some way to defeat her. But the terrible thing is that she knows—she knows as well as I—that I will not betray her to them; not to protect myself, but because I will do anything to keep her love. For some monstrous reason I want her more now than I ever did before! Whore, monster, oh, beautiful tender child!

*THERE* is a hypnotic quality about terrible things. Whenever I recall the various disasters of my life—killing my horse, my mother's and Eric's deaths, the grenades in the amphitheater— I find myself re-creating their details, one after another, with a trancelike attention and respect, as if I found them strangely beautiful and just. I do not reflect upon them at all, but simply record them, tensely and involuntarily, hypnotized by the strange purity they assume. It is in this way that I recall the details of the morning mentioned above in the extract from my journal: meticulous, remote, fascinating in their known and inexorable progression. I see myself, as if behind a pane of polished glass, shaving at the bathroom mirror, carrying my shoes downstairs so that I will not wake my grandparents, who sleep later and later in their age; making my coffee and drinking it at the porcelain table in the silent kitchen (smiling all the while, staring up at the quavering violet webs of my cigarette smoke which marble the morning air); emerging from the front door with an air of controlled, expectant haste; pausing, as I cross the street, to examine a flattened toad on the pavement (it must have been run over days ago, because it is crisp, dry and leathery, its legs spread out in a perfectly symmetrical, ridiculously romantic attitude, as if attempting to embrace the whole world in some strange, mortal, primitive passion); walking under the cool elms, in spite of myself, with a constantly accelerating pace; pausing impatiently at the traffic light on Diamond Avenue; continuing briskly, smiling, until I stop suddenly—having seen a Negress in a red dress approaching me—cross the street again and continue down the opposite sidewalk with scarcely any adjustment of expression or emotion, the maneuver having become so habitual. (Once, many years ago, I did meet her, coming home from school, and, burning with humiliation, forced myself to look into her eyes, to watch her bitter contemptuous smile, as she approached and passed me. I could not do that again.) I enter the Lodge grounds, plucking the tip from an arbor vitae branch and crumbling it nervously in my fingers as I walk quickly up the drive. At the main building I pause, glance about with assumed indifference, then raise my eyes swiftly to her window. She is there, her gold hair glinting in its snood of shadow from the wire netting, her eyes vivid with anticipation. She purses her mouth to me in a soft, pleated rose of tenderness. My mind wanes wildly with delight. (Today I am to take her walking past the pond!) I go on up the drive, constraining with terrible determination the precious furor of my heart. I mount the shop steps, pausing at the top to look toward her window, then enter with inspired insouciance.

Dr. Lavrier is present to hold one of his occasional seminars with us. We discuss the patients earnestly, attentively, sipping our coffee out of paper cups, sprawling in the red leather armchairs. I give a cunning, extremely eager, diversionary report on Sonia Behrendt. She has expressed, as many of the patients have, an interest in fishing. I suggest stocking the lake with bass and blue-gills for this purpose. The suggestion is a great success. There is much animated discussion, in the course of which I offer to obtain details from the Fish & Wildlife Division. Bea is particularly pleased, smiling her gratification at me. I am asked about Warren. "He is considerably happier lately. I think it's because of the attention he's been getting from Lilith at the tea dances. He's more active, too, and more productive." Dr. Lavrier nods. "That was a good piece of work, getting her to attend them. It's certainly done him good, as well as her. But we mustn't let him build up any false illusions about Lilith's affection for him; that could be disastrous, you know, as well as dishonest and un-dignified. But to enjoy her company and to dance with her occasionally—that seems to me to be perfectly acceptable, as long as he's realistic about it. Try to keep it on that note. How has Lilith seemed this week?" "Well, I think she's continuing to improve a little. I think Bob had her out yesterday, didn't you, Bob? How did she seem to you?" Ah—adroit that was! Attention is shifted. (I have no monopoly on her company.)

Bea listens to the discussion with earnest, intelligent absorption, lightly brushing her brown hair. I move my eyes alternately to all their faces, my mind wandering. They are so intent, devoted. For a moment I am shamed by their sincerity; then I remember her laughter, the dazzling length of her thighs, a way she has of plucking at her eyelashes while she sits musing. She is waiting! Will they never finish their idiotic chatter? My love is waiting!

After the meeting I cross toward the main building with hectic, carefully disciplined excitement, determinedly limiting the length of my strides. My key sticks for a moment in the elevator door. I twist it savagely, in a rage of impatience, swinging back the heavy metal door, which closes with a solemn clangor behind me.

*Lasciate ogni speranza.* I stand for a minute in mild, perpendicular propulsion while the hidden machinery hums infernally. At the second floor I push the steel door open tremblingly; it seems to scald my hand. I stop at the floor office. Miss Donohue is checking the night attendant's reports, holding the sheets in one hand while she lays out towels for the morning baths. She is too harassed to notice that my whole body is flaming softly, like wind-blown coals. "Hello, Vincent. Who do you have this morning?" "I'm taking Lilith out by the pond." "Good. Keep her out for as long as you can, will you? Give us a little peace around here." "I'll try. Are you having trouble?" "Oh God. Carter's gone back up to Fourth; she just bit one of the attendants. God, it's like a madhouse around here this morning. Where are the scissors?" I smile mechanically at her joke, proceed down the corridor with feet of fire.

The door of Lilith's room is ajar; I knock twice lightly in an accustomed, intimate way, and enter, closing it behind me. She springs softly from her window seat, standing with her ankles in a pool of sunlight, and breathes *Hello* to me, her silent lips holding the O position of the final vowel in the same warm rose she offered me from the window. We stand for a moment in marvelous silence, our eyes joined, my heart raving. I say, "Good morning" rather harshly. She does not reply. Her eyes wander for a moment; she seems thoughtful. There are her manuscripts on the desk in front of me; she has been illuminating letters of her Gospels. I touch a great Gothic gold-leafed *A* with my finger tip. "That's beautiful," I say, raising my head. She lifts her hand, twisting a strand of hair between her fingers. "Are you ready?" I ask.

"Yes. Where are we going?"

"To the pond. Isn't that what you wanted to do?"

"Yes. But, Vincent—I want to ask you a favor. A very special one. Will you promise?"

"I suppose so. What is it?"

"No, you have to promise."

"All right. What is it?"

"Can we—can someone else go with us?"

"Someone else go with us?" (A joke of some kind—one of her pranks, whose delightful meaning will be revealed in a moment.)

"Yes. Yvonne. She asked me if she could. I know she wants to very much."

"Yvonne?" (Cold. So cold suddenly. Must wait and see. Certainly not.)

"Yes. Do you mind, just this once? She so seldom gets out."

I refuse to acknowledge the dread that has touched me. I am suddenly sternly matter-of-fact. I must dismiss the whole thing instantly. A brusque manner will help me to believe it does not exist. "If she wants to go out, I'll get an escort for her. Greta can take her; she's on casual duty this morning."

"No, she wants to go with *us*. You see, there's something she wants to talk to me about."

"Why doesn't she talk to you about it here?"

"It's something very personal, and we have no privacy here. You know we're not allowed to close the door when we're visiting."

"Well, if she goes with us, I'll be there. She still won't have any privacy."

"Oh. I thought perhaps you'd let us . . . be alone for a little while." She drops her head, watching patiently her slender, sunlit feet. A monstrous indignation swells suddenly within me. I begin to speak quickly, rather senselessly.

"I don't understand you. What do you expect me to do? I don't want her to go with us. How can we—"

"Oh, Vincent, please. Just this once. She's been such a dear friend to me here, and she's such a sweet person. Won't you do this for her?"

"No. She's no friend of mine. I don't like her at all. I don't like you having her for a friend. I won't do it."

She stands patiently, gazing at her white feet, crouching down in a moment to clasp their warm arches in her hands, her shoulders huddled, her hair blazing. I stare down at her, in spite of my indignation weakened by her beauty.

"I thought you would be kinder to me, Vincent."

"I don't call that a kindness," I say bitterly. She does not reply, and I add less violently in a moment, thinking she has relinquished the request, "You know I couldn't allow you to be alone together, anyway. Neither of you has privileges. It's very strictly forbidden." I am not aware of the absurdity of my protest until I have spoken it. She crouches before me, caressing her feet musingly, and says very gently in a moment, "Yes, there are many forbidden things; but we have done them, Vincent. I wonder what they would do if they knew?"

A wave of incredulity, outrage, pain that scalds my mind and heart like fumes of acid. I say harshly, agonized, "What do you mean?"

"If you don't let her come with us, I'll tell them, Vincent."

It is true, then. Some ancient, lugubrious sage within me nods wearily. I feel my lips and eyes grow pale with fury. Very well, then. Nothing is barred. But I shall win. My voice is strained, softly shrill: "Tell them, if you like. Do you think they'll believe you? I have a reputation here for being very conscientious—a very honest, dedicated worker. And you are a madwoman. Do you think they'll take your word against my own? Tell them."

She looks up at me with a pained, importunate expression, as if she hates to hurt me in this way. "But if someone on the staff were to support my story, were to offer evidence, even, then perhaps they would."

"Someone on the staff? What are you talking about? You don't know these people!"

"Yes, I do. I think perhaps Mr. Mandel could be persuaded to support me."

I stand pale and shocked with anguished disbelief at this piece of treachery. She rises quickly, her face suddenly weary with a compassion which I cannot believe or understand.

"Oh, my dear." She reaches toward me and touches my hand timidly.

"Don't touch me," I say harshly.

"You mustn't suffer, Vincent. Oh, my love, I don't want to make you suffer, believe me. Don't you understand?"

"Yes. I understand. It's monstrous, terrible."

"No, Vincent. It's beautiful. We mustn't deny each other joy—any joy that is possible. We must rejoice at it. We must help each other to be perfect in our capacity for it. Don't you understand that I love you now as much as I ever have, as much as I always shall love you?"

I stare at her in grief, still not able to believe. "Lilith, you wouldn't really tell them?" I whisper hoarsely. "You couldn't do anything so terrible. Don't you know they would dismiss me? That I'd never see you again?"

She watches my eyes pityingly but unwaveringly. "Yes, I suppose they would."

"And doesn't it matter to you? Doesn't it matter that we'd never see each other again?"

"If you aren't strong enough to follow me, if you don't love me enough to follow me—then it will not matter." She takes my hand and bows her head above it, clasping it to her cheek. Her hair spills over my forearm, warm from the sun. She kisses my fingers, murmuring passionately, "Afterwards you will understand, I know. I'll teach you to understand, and to rejoice with me." I stand, weak with revulsion, betrayal. "Now come with me. Come and tell Yvonne she may go with us."

What can I do? There must be something I can do! I follow her numbly to the door. Perhaps on the way I will think of something—while we are walking. I must have time to think. I follow her mechanically down the corridor, my mind apparently paralyzed. We stop outside of Mrs. Meaghan's door, at which I stare wanly for a moment.

"You must knock," Lilith whispers. I look at her desperately.

Her eyes are cool, unyielding, almost lifeless in their purity, like those of the china fairy I won for her with the toss of a rope quoit at the fair. "Knock, Vincent." An attendant prowls stolidly past us down the corridor—small, clipped, knoblike head, big shoulders, arrogant gait; it is Mandel. Lilith looks toward him briefly, then at me, with perfect, implacable eyes. Ah, God! I raise my clenched hand quickly, rap the panel twice. How loud it sounds! The gentle astringent European voice invites me in immediately. I push the door open and stand on the threshold clutching the doorknob, as if unwilling wholly to enter this lair. She is seated at the table by her window, writing letters. The blue bowl is filled this morning with floating purple asters. Her pale-violet stationery has an embossed silver crest at the top which she strokes lightly with her finger tips while she speaks. She raises her head with a mild, ironic look of inquiry.

"Good morning, Mr. Bruce."

"Good morning." My voice is parched with shame and has the slightly unnatural rapidity of hysteria. "Miss Arthur says you have asked to go walking with us."

"Why, I did, yes."

"Would you still like to come?"

"How very kind of you to ask. Are you sure it won't be an inconvenience?"

"No, not at all," I say, with a craven, idiotic pretense of ignorance of the plot, which seems to be the only way I can salvage any semblance of dignity. I stumble on in a pathetic attempt to reinforce the impression. "I'm sure it will do you good."

"So you have been telling me all summer; and at last I am convinced. You see how persuasive you have been?" Foul woman! I stare at her with crippled loathing. She rises, setting her pen down gently on the table. "I wonder if I have time to change my shoes?"

"Yes, of course. I have to report to the office, anyway. You can meet me at the elevator."

"Thank you."

I close the door, swinging past Lilith blindly toward the office. Miss Donohue is still busy with her towels.

"Are you checking out?" she asks, barely glancing at me.

"Yes. I'm taking Meaghan too."

"Meaghan?" She looks up at me with surprise.

"Yes. She asked to go."

"Wonderful. I don't think she's been out in six weeks. How did you do it?" Another minor triumph for me! I cringe at her look of approbation, feigning interest in a syringe that lies on the shelf beside me so that I can turn my face from her.

"She wanted to go. Who's having sedative?"

"Oh, that was Carter's. Did I tell you she blew up?"

"Oh, yes."

"Don't forget to give us a report on Meaghan when you get back. They'll want to see that."

"No, I won't."

They are standing together in casual conversation at the elevator door as I emerge from the office. We descend in burning silence, Mrs. Meaghan, with an air of satirical fastidiousness, arranging the pleats of her light woolen skirt. Outside, in the morning sunlight, she seems for a moment unsure, pausing and turning toward us with a faint look of alarm. I rejoice at her fear, silently and savagely invoking all her nameless devils to beset her. But Lilith, with a swift, fleeting gesture of comfort—of command, perhaps—takes her hand; I see their fingers twine and clench for an instant, then loosen and part convulsively. (How often has she taken my hand in just that way—both in the promise of love and in its consummation! A white knife of pain divides my mind.) A moment later the woman is perfectly assured, walking beside us in dignified composure through the shadows of the poplars that fall across the drive.

"I think it was wise of me to come," she says. "It is a beautiful morning. What are these trees? They are quite lovely."

Lilith waits for a moment for me to reply, but I cannot speak. "They are poplars," she says gently.

"Poplars. I thought poplars were something quite different—a tall slender tree."

"Those are Lombardy poplars, Yvonne."

"Oh, yes. I have never taken much interest in nature. It repels me."

"But you love flowers."

"Oh, yes; I have a passion for flowers. But that is quite different, I think. I believe that flowers transcend nature, in the way that certain persons transcend humanity; and these deserve our admiration." Her voice pauses, pursues its topic with a delicate allusiveness, "They somehow escape their nature by becoming consummate specimens of it. This is a theme of Dergson's. Do you know him?"

They go on with their dreadful spurious sociability. I walk beside them in a state of stark and desperate despair, trying frantically, vainly to invent a solution of some kind before we have gone too far. I watch Field House approach, loom to our left for a moment, slide inexorably past. Then Bea's cottage, then the shop, the bicycle shed, Doctors' House, my mind all the while lurching numbly, spastically, at mad straws of hope: A rock; pick up a rock and crush her skull, like a horse's; say it was an accident; she fell and injured herself; had to be destroyed. The lake; drown her in the lake; luminous, rotting, ragged face, fish-bitten; drenched, death-coated eyes. Drown both of them. Rot there in their warm, foul sea, their peeling fingers and floating hair entwined. O God, deliver me. We are on the open stretch of road that leads to Hillcrest. Beyond is the lake, with the barn behind it at the edge of the oak woods. Very little time. What will she do? How will she say it? What shall I reply? Then suddenly, from the sky, whose aspect I have been too preoccupied to notice, comes what for a moment I misconstrue as divine intervention: a drop of rain upon my wrist. I look up fervently. A great purple-black cloud has drifted across the fields, its edge devouring the disk of sun above us.

"It's going to rain!" I exclaim with wretched exultation. "We'll have to go back. We'll get soaked!"

But this day's gods are in league with her, of course, or she has conjured up the storm herself.

"Oh, no, it's much too far! But we can make the barn, I think."

She is right, of course. The barn is only one third of the distance that we have already come. It has a look of sinister isolation, standing at the edge of the forest; but there is nothing to do but run toward it. We hurry across the field where thistles bend in the gathering wind, along the embanked footpath that circles the darkening water of the lake, raindrops pattering about us in the dust. I am aware of a growing savage resignation. I hardly care, now—I care, that is; but I have almost lost all hope of forestalling it. Even nature has conspired against me. I feel my will to oppose her waning, my mind assuming a kind of desolate composure. What does it matter? It has been a strange enough adventure; let it be even stranger. Perhaps something will be salvaged. She says she loves me still. At least I will not lose her utterly.

We have reached the shelter of the eaves, which overhang broadly. Her white silk blouse is spattered with raindrops which make it stick to her skin. It clings moistly to her breasts, stippled with pink spots, swelling softly with her breath. Only two days ago she bared them to me. I close my eyes.

"We barely made it! Oh, look how hard it's falling now!" She shakes out her moist hair, still panting with exertion. "Are you wet, Yvonne?"

"Only a little. I must confess I found it rather exhilarating."

The woman's eyes are glowing with a fresh, somber excitement. Her face, too, has a feverish flush which makes me realize suddenly and bitterly how handsome she really is. I note with a kind of revolted admiration the delicate modeling of her lips, the sensitive, sorrowful cast of features which many Latin women have. I turn away quickly, looking out at the rain-lashed fields. A pair of ragged crows go hobbling and flapping, their wings lifted, in a hasty comic scuttle into the shelter of the woods.

"Look, the barn is open," Lilith says. I follow her eyes to the great dark door which breathes out its warm dry incense of hay and leather. Secret in there, dark and fragrant, with the soft seductive thunder of rain on the iron roof. A joy I was not to know.

"Vincent." She touches my arm rather timidly. "Can we go in there—Yvonne and I? There's something she'd like to talk to me about, privately. You won't mind, will you?"

I stare at her in cold despair, saying hoarsely, "You know it's forbidden. It's very dangerous. If anyone should find out—"

"No one will find out. You must stay here and watch, in case anyone should come. It would be very kind of you. We would be very grateful, wouldn't we, Yvonne?"

"Yes, very." Mrs. Meaghan turns her eyes to me with a look of grave sardonic courtesy. "I'm sure you realize, Mr. Bruce, what a luxury it is for two women to have a quiet confidential talk together, without open doors, or bars, or monitors. We are such weak creatures. I'm sure we shall find some way of repaying you."

"Yes, I know we shall," Lilith murmurs.

"You mustn't be too long," I mutter in a ruined, ravenlike voice. "They'll send a car for us if this rain keeps up."

"We won't. Oh, thank you, Vincent." She turns back for a moment, as they move away, to take my hand in a quick tender clasp and to whisper, "I love you." I stare at her with horror. They walk along the barn wall to the open door, holding their shoulders obliquely to keep within the curtain of water from the streaming eaves. I watch with helpless torment while they disappear into the dim wide arch of darkness.

There is a moment when the hideous delight of which I have written in my journal touches my heart with little filthy elfin fingers, and I find myself standing with averted head, listening, in an attitude of tense voluptuous attention. Then I drop my head, and after a moment, lifting it, stare out beyond the streaming eaves at the wet fields, listening to the roar of rain on the iron roof and crying quietly, like a child, my face contorted, remembering for some reason a summer afternoon long ago, before the war, when Laura and I ran for shelter under the wistaria arbor in her mother's garden in a sudden thunderstorm.

I do not know how long I have been standing thus—it has stopped raining, for the silver sheaths of water are no longer sliding from the eaves; only a gentle dripping, which pocks the red soil in a long pitted trench. The cloud-shadow has passed beyond the lake and the wet fields are glittering greenly in the sun—when I feel Lilith's hand on my sleeve and hear her murmured greeting: "Vincent, you're crying. Don't cry, dear." I turn suddenly and clutch her by the hair, shaking her savagely from side to side and shrieking in her face, "Slut, whore, dirty shameless bitch!" I fling her from me with all my strength against the barn wall. Her head and shoulders jar against it with a brutal thudding sound. She slides down, stunned, and settles limply on the damp ground. In a moment she lifts her hand and brushes back her scattered hair, staring at me with burning eyes. In a soft stark voice which seems both to bless and to condemn me she asks, "If you discovered that your beastly God loved others as greatly as he loved you, would you hate him for it? He shows love for none of you, and you worship him. I show my love for all of you, and you despise me."

Her words shock me profoundly—as much, I think, as what she has done. I stare at her in stupefaction, watching Mrs. Meaghan approach fearfully from where she has been standing against the wall and bend down, murmuring compassionately, to help Lilith to her feet. I offer no assistance; I do not want to touch them. Slowly, without speaking, we walk back through the bowed and dripping meadow grass toward the Lodge, my heart like a piece of carrion in my breast.

$\mathcal{T}$HREE DAYS later, in a cove of rocks, with the Potomac thundering beyond us and a fine spray of river-mist blowing over our bruised bodies, she paid me well for my ignominy:

¶ *THURS., AUG. 12:*

. . . I have never known such passion, such absolute abandon in her before. It was as if she were trying to redress the terrible humiliation she had forced upon me, or as if out of the monstrous service I had done her there had come a new intensity of love for me, a fantastic and triumphant joy which she must express with this wild, rapturous largess. It was the same with me. I never knew I was capable of such frenzied desire. It is very strange, it is terrible, that such a vile thing as that which happened last week could generate in us such a prodigy of passion. I can't think about this. I can't understand it. But I can submit to it, I can be a witness to it—like a beastly miracle. Afterward I could only touch her face, wide-eyed, in a kind of bewilderment, saying over and over, "Oh, Lilith, oh, my darling." She could not hear me because of the booming of the falls, but she watched my moving lips so strangely, laying her finger tips upon them as a blind person does, her face holding an almost afflicted look of bliss. Then I said to myself that I loved her utterly, that I would do whatever she asked of me, forever. And all the while those tons of water roaring down around us with dreadful, ungovernable power, like a renegade, deluging ocean. I could feel the ground trembling with their weight.

We bicycled home along the Old Falls Road, and she stopped

sometimes to pick milkweed pods from the tall bushes that grow along the fences, splitting the brittle brown husks open with her thumbnails and blowing clouds of silver flax out of them. Some of the little silken puffs of gossamer caught in her hair and clung there, trembling, like clouds of frozen breath, but I did not tell her. . . .

¶ *TUES., AUG.* 17:

How exciting it is to see her so openly contemptuous! This evening when we were walking home along Montgomery Avenue a woman came down the steps of St. Jude's, untying the scarf she had worn to cover her hair while she was praying. She looked very tired—a tired, anxious woman with some problem she could not solve, hurrying home to fix dinner for her family. Things of this kind always move me. I think I must have shown this in my eyes, for Lilith said, "You look as if you loved her, Vincent."

"It's very moving," I said. "Other people's faith is always very moving, I think." She did not reply, and I added rather abstractedly after a moment, "My mother believed in God, you know. She named me after a saint—the kindest of all the saints, she said. He gave his life to the miserable. She wanted me to be like him."

Lilith turned to follow with her eyes the retreating figure of the woman in the street, saying with sudden savage scorn, "Perverts, brute-lovers, worshipers of pain! The more he beats them, the more he lashes and scourges them, the more they worship him! Flagellants, race of degenerates! Haters of love!"

This, from her! Yet it was thrilling—and frightening, too—to see her eyes. She was silent the rest of the way back to the Lodge, but when I said goodbye to her in her room she smiled sleepily and collapsed onto her bed with a great ridiculous commotion, her arms and legs spread out—*plop!*—like a rowdy, cheerful child, turning her head to peer at me through the tangle of her hair and murmuring foolishly, "Good night, my saint."

316

. . . I knew it would happen again, of course. There was no reason to believe she would stop at one such piece of infamy.

Last night they both signed for the movies in Stonemont—but we did not go, of course. In a moonlit field beyond the railyards I stood sentinel for them again, with some hideous stray dog licking about my ankles all the while. I finally kicked it, in shameful, raging despair.

Those awful, fraught, degrading silences, when I have to walk back with them! And that woman's eyes, whenever I pass her on the floor—that unholy irony! It is more than I can bear. But I must learn to bear it, of course, because it will go on. There is nothing I can do. Some nights I lie awake until it is light, wondering what she will do next. I feel it moving toward some horrible, consummate piece of degradation which I shall be equally powerless to stop.

If I go on like this they will certainly begin to suspect on the staff. They have already noticed how haggard and preoccupied I am. Today Bea said she thought I had been working too hard, and asked if I would like to do shop duty for a week or two. A fine thing that would be—I should not be able to escort her, then! I must say I get a little sick sometimes of Bea's constant patronizing air. All the same, she is very shrewd, and I must make a greater effort to conceal my anxiety. And I must somehow try to sleep. I can never sleep any more; it is beginning to affect my health. Yesterday, for example, I distinctly heard that music—a thin, shrill sound, something like her flute—when I was playing croquet with Morrison. I set my mallet down and stood there, listening, like an idiot. It is only nerves, of course—the nervous strain I am under—but it's alarming, all the same. It can't be allowed to go on. And then there was that business about the soup, when I was having lunch in the cafeteria the other day. I knew suddenly, without any doubt whatever, that I must not eat it. It was unclean. Still, I am not convinced that my nerves were altogether responsible for this conviction; it is strange how intuitively one understands such things. Bob is a fool. Let him eat all he wants of it. No matter what state my nerves are in, I am sure there is someone on the staff who is not to be trusted. Nerves do not account for everything! It remains now to discover who it is.

¶ *WED., AUG. 25:*
More and more, water fascinates me. I have always had a love of water, but I have never before realized its great beauty and mystery. It is a much more compassionate element than air. Air does not properly cherish the things that have chosen to live in it. It is indifferent, even hostile, to them, I think. If you step off a ladder, or lose your footing on a cliff, for example, it lets you fall and be broken, or crushed. It does not swarm around you and sustain you, as water does, letting you down with so gentle, so solicitous, an embrace. And air does not have those wonderful rhythms; it blows fitfully and oppressively, disturbing and dislocating the things that dwell in it, all out of rhyme with their pulses and murmurings and metabolisms. It does not have that sweet ancient surge and withdrawal, that long comforting flow and ebb, like the blood's music, that lulls and ceaselessly, darkly rhapsodizes. It limits you, too—it lets you live in only two dimensions; if you are an air-thing you are condemned to stand with your feet on the earth, staring upward. You cannot take a great buoyant stride to the ceiling of the room in which you stand, or to the top of the tree above you, pausing there for a moment in a lingering, weightless escape from gravity. Birds can do this, of course—I think they are the only things that are truly at home in it—birds and angels, perhaps; not men. I think men are water creatures, really, who have somehow wandered out of their element.

I have a yearning to return and live in water. I would like to lounge and drift in it all night, assuaged, dreaming water-dreams. I would like to breathe it in cool delicious draughts and feel its

318

ceaseless, volatile caress upon my body. And I would like to dart through it with long silver friends, and visit coral castles, and stand swaying softly in their secret chambers. I would like to learn its languor and tranquillity—to endure the strange conversion of all things which it claims. I would live in the throat of a silent, chastened cannon, and study the transfiguration of rotting casks whose staves had fallen open like petals in a flower of resignation, and learn the beautiful apostasy of crumbling cutlasses and pious, shriven spears and gently, eternally, serenely rocking helmets, and still ships, and horizontal bones. I would understand and share their deep, grave beatitude, rolling and writhing forever in gentle epilepsies of devotion in the unending baptism of the sea. I would put on my green velvet mantle of renunciation and be redeemed with all the wrack and jetsam of the world. I would have the peace of things that have been evangelized by water.

I am going to buy an aquarium—one of those big oblate ones that they have in the ten-cent store—and fill it with little bright-colored stones and aquatic grasses and some of those tiny fishes—those slender vivid Siamese ones—and put it on my window sill. I think I will enjoy that enormously. Perhaps I will get some peace from looking into it. Perhaps it will help to still this dread I feel.

¶ *THURS., AUG. 26:*
I knew, as soon as the rocks and the fish and grasses were in, that I needed one thing more. A figure—a sovereign of some kind—for my water-world! And I knew immediately what it must be: the china fairy that we won at the carnival. I had to steal it, of course; she would never give it to me. She keeps it there on that shelf above her bookcase, in that weird little museum she has of my mementos: the skull, the red rosette, the china fairy. I had to be very stealthy, because she is so unnaturally observant; I think sometimes she is aware of every move

I make, every breath I draw, every gesture, even when she is turned away from me. So yesterday evening, just before I left her room, I invented this device:

"Did you know there was a tanager nesting by your window?"

"A tanager! Where, Vincent?" (Moving swiftly to the window seat.)

"Just a little above and to the right. I saw it this morning when I was coming up."

"Oh, where? I can't see anything." (Pressing her face against the wire netting.)

"Do you see where the water pipe is joined?" (Backing against the bookcase, giving a swift upward glance.) "There's a kind of hollow there, in the vines. If you look carefully you can see some wisps of straw."

I reached up quickly, clutched the doll and plunged it into the pocket of my jacket, moving hastily toward her.

She turned to face me, frowning. "I can't see anything. I think you are fooling me."

"Of course I am. It's almost September. The tanagers aren't nesting."

"Then why did you say that?"

"Because I love to see you get so excited."

"But you disappointed me. How silly you are. What a foolish kind of playing."

"Are you angry?"

"I am disappointed."

"But I invented it for you. If you can invent a world for me, won't you let me invent a little red bird for you?"

She stares at me somberly. "You are hateful, sometimes. Sometimes I don't like you at all."

I touched her hair briefly and backed out of the room, smiling at her petulance, clutching the doll in my pocket with feverish excitement.

So now the aquarium is just as it should be, ruled over by its tiny fairy queen. When I dropped her into the water the hem of her pink skirt caught on one of the rough rocks, so that she is hanging almost upside down in ridiculously regal disarray, her diaphanous dress already limp and raveling, her little sodden slippers falling from her feet in slow disintegration, her golden hair loosening and drifting in ruin, her painted features dissolving in a cloud of rosy dye. The Siamese fishes have become quite used to her (they were horrified at first!)—slipping across her dimpled hands, suspending themselves with curled tails in her shadow and nibbling at her glazed blue eyes and the glinting star of her tinseled wand, feeding on bright crumbs of her decaying majesty, which will, I suppose, eventually poison them.

I stare at it for hours sometimes, smiling with enchantment. It is most fascinating in the evening, when the light is very soft and the gold foil of her crown shines through the dark water with little burnished gleams of splendor, somber, sunken fire, something unquenched, ancient, royal, in which the sea abounds.

¶ *MON., AUG.* 30:

. . . Dread is not what I thought it was. I once conceived of it as a web woven of very delicate threads of some material as cold and fine as spun ice—and yet of terrible strength; for in spite of its delicacy, it so bound and ensnarled one that he could not move; he was held motionless, aghast, in a frozen skein of gossamer. But this is not true, at all; or I should say that it is only very partially true. Dread is a marvelously compound thing, far too complex for me to represent in any image. I could only set down words that I associate with it, that seem to be implied or included in its dark anatomy, or that cast faint, various-colored beams of light into its shadowy convolutions. It would be interesting for someone in a state of dread (I am well equipped for the experiment!) to make out such a list, very quickly, without pausing to consider or select. Here is one:

shrill
harp

burgeoning
hyena
lips
flee
roses
after
spume
blinding
stone
roses

It is useless, you see. A prescription from an amateur meta-physician! But taken constantly, I think, it would cure one of the malady of innocence.

Some day it may be interesting to remember the sequence of things that caused me to produce this curious recipe: First, clouds—blown into the air like the flaxen froth of milkweed pods by the breath of witches. And then the light lisping patter of her ballet slippers as she walks beside me along Montgomery Avenue, her head lifted to behold her clouds. A bee droning like a diamond drill against the panes of summer silence. A woman in a rocking chair on a front porch with a great book in her lap, reading to a little boy who sits on the wooden steps in front of her with his face in his hands and his heart in Arcady. A tiger moth floating over jeweled hedges, trailing pennons of vermilion velvet. Two cardinals, a kite string dangling from an elm, hot stone steaming where the spray from a sprinkler darkens it, the odor of verbena—and then, suddenly, rolling from behind a hedge with a charming old-fashioned gravity, as if from the pages of the *Hagerstown Almanacs* stacked up beside the wardrobe in the attic, a child's hoop (a wicker barrel band, really), bouncing over the curb, across the street, and falling with a quickening circular spin in the opposite gutter. A boy of nine or ten runs down the walk and stands in dismay at the curb, appealing to us while he plucks the buttons of his blouse in agitation. He is not allowed to cross the street, he says. But Lilith is. I allow her. She runs merrily across the black, elm-shadowed asphalt, bends down to snatch up the wooden hoop and rolls it back across the street with her finger tips, dancing behind it like a Druidess. She halts it at the curb and puts it over the child's head, tugging gently at the rim. He stands, delighted, yoked, in shy servility.

"If it were my hoop," Lilith says, "I would fasten ribbons to the rim, and they would flutter when it rolled."

"That's a good idea, ma'am. I never thought of that."

"And you could fasten little bells inside it, and they'd tinkle."

"Yes, ma'am, I could; but they'd cost right much."

"Then I must get them for you. Vincent, we have some money, haven't we? It can come out of my allowance."

Uneasily, although I can think of no specific reason to protest, I take a quarter out of the little purse in which I carry patients' spending money and hand it to her. She presses it into his palm, closing his fingers over it.

"There. But remember, it's only for the bells."

"Yes, ma'am. I sure do thank you."

"I'll come by in a few days. When? On Thursday, Vincent?" (Drawing a silent, apprehensive consent from my eyes.) "Yes, on Thursday—and see how you have fixed it."

"Yes, ma'am. I reckon I can get a half dozen of 'em with this, anyhow."

"But you mustn't forget to be here. I want to hear it tinkle."

"No, ma'am, I won't."

She lays her hand on his head for a moment, her smile fading while she looks into his eyes. We walk on down the street in a chafing, peaceless silence until I mutter churlishly, "I don't think you should have done that—given him money like that."

"Why, Vincent?"

"Children are selfish and . . . capricious, anyway. There's no sense appealing to the worst in them."

"Oh, I hate to hear that!" she says with defiant impatience. "You are all so terrified of children. I think you really hate them. You're so afraid of their purity, of their honesty, of their ability to love. They're the only ones who *can* love—truly—in your world; and it makes you ashamed!" There is a contempt in her eyes which scalds me, seeming, as it does, to include me in the alien and wretched category for whom it is intended. She stares down the street ahead of us, her face flushed lightly, lifting her hand in a moment to clutch her hair thoughtfully. She leaves her arm dangling there, her head bowed with its weight. "But to know that kind of love," she murmurs, "that pure unself-conscious, freshly minted desire. To possess a child—oh, that would be exquisite!"

I cannot speak. I do not even look at her. My face has gone pale, my hands cold, with a nauseous revulsion. We walk on down the street, our footsteps sounding oddly hollow on the stone—perhaps because I have the sudden dire impression that it is laid upon a vacuum; the blocks of cement are fitted carefully together over an enormous void.

This will be our next adventure in ecstasy, then! And I shall be expected to help her achieve it, of course! I thought I had already reached the depths of degradation, but it seems I have only begun. I am still a novice in the ways of joy! I cannot see any solution to it; I have become a kind of loathsome procurer for her. If I try to think about it rationally, my mind becomes a cauldron of hysterical remorse; if I abandon the effort—if I lapse into a wan, thoughtless despair—then I feel this profound, this indescribably complex, this sovereign dread.

When will it be? On Thursday? How will she manage it? Will she depend on some felicitous accident—like a thunderstorm— or is she planning it already? I wait in an abominable, fascinated anticipation of her ingenuity.

Lord, what is the answer? Is there no solution to this bestial dilemma but to submit to it? No answer. Stare into the bowl, smiling softly. Watch the flakes of tinsel drifting from her wand, the Siamese fishes nibbling her blind, soulless eyes, her rotting hair and decomposing dress falling slowly from her bright china body. Something true will be unclothed. Something indestructible will be revealed, and will remain.

On THE DAY after writing this entry in my journal I left the house immediately after dinner and, after walking for at least an hour through the darkening streets of the town, found myself, for the first time in many years, in front of Laura's house. It had certainly not been my conscious destination when I set out, and indeed until I turned the corner of Frietchie Street and started down the familiar stretch of sidewalk—recognizing suddenly the two great concrete urns on either side of a front walk, the white-painted tree stump on Mrs. Hagmeyer's lawn, the perforated kegs, with hens-and-chickens growing out of them like barnacles, that ornamented Dr. Davies' porch steps—I could not even have identified my whereabouts. But as I passed these long-forgotten landmarks which had punctuated so many of the summer-evening expeditions of my youth, I felt a sense of comfort come upon me, a quiet regenerate excitement, which increased as I approached her front walk, and flowered, as I stood there staring up at the lighted parlor windows and the familiar configurations of the gables and chimneys against the dusk, into a kind of lorn, nostalgic peace. It seemed quite unchanged. The huge wistaria tree in the back yard stood in its perpetual grieving grace, the arbor was full of the same scented shadow, the porch lattice sagged with its unabated burden of beauty. I could not have told the geraniums along the front walk from those of six summers ago;

perhaps they were the same. The glider was, surely, the same we had sat in while her father lay dying behind the windows of the huge old house, standing in its unaltered dark forbearance.

I wondered whether Laura was the same, too. I felt, in spite of the superficial changes I had seen in her on the single occasion when we had met since my return, that she was; and hoped, with a fervor that amounted almost to prayer, that I was not mistaken. I wanted to see her once again and be reassured of it—to hear her humorless talk, to watch her patting her plump moist throat with a white handkerchief, to witness her sober, diligent, invincible propriety, which I remembered like a rejected, long-forgotten blessing.

As if in answer to this rueful invocation the porch light suddenly switched on above the door, bathing the wooden floor and the front steps in an aura of amber-colored light; and almost immediately afterward the front door opened inward, revealing in its widening rectangle of illumination Laura's sturdy, indestructible silhouette. She carried a milk bottle in each hand, bending to set them down on the porch floor. As she did so I made a swift involuntary movement of withdrawal into the darkness, startled and—in spite of my nebulous desire to see and speak with her again—chagrined at being discovered in such a strange and unexpected attitude of apparent supplication. But I caught my toe in a crack of the sidewalk as I turned, and the sound of my stumbling made her raise her head. She stared into the darkness for a moment, her vision apparently impaired by the surrounding circle of light; then, catching sight of me at last, she stood up quickly and stepped out onto the porch floor, calling softly, "Vincent?"

"Oh, hello, Laura," I said with an idiotic attempt at casualness.

"Why, Vincent—my goodness, what in the world are you doing here?" She spoke with a hesitant, appealing modest quality of surprise, as if she might have sensed and respected my nostalgia.

"Oh, I was out taking a walk, and I just happened to be passing by."

"Oh. Yes, it's a lovely night, isn't it?" We stood for a moment in gentle embarrassment. "It's very nice to see you again. Are you in a hurry?"

"Well, I'm just out walking."

"We're just about to have our coffee. Why don't you stop in for a minute? Would you like to have a cup with us?"

"Oh, I don't want to interrupt your dinner or anything."

"No; we've finished dinner. We're just going to have some coffee in the living room. Why don't you come in? I know Norman would like to meet you very much."

"Well, if you're sure it isn't any bother. I'd like to meet him, too."

The last emotion in the world with which I would have expected myself to enter that house again—particularly on the occasion of my being presented to her husband—was the humble, redescending calm which I felt as I went up the front walk and mounted the wooden steps. Laura held the door open for me, saying as I passed her into the hall, "We just had a late snack tonight, because Norman has to go to the United Citizens' meeting in a little while."

"Oh, I see. Well, are you sure it won't hold him up, or anything?"

"Oh, no, we always have coffee after dinner, anyway."

While she switched off the porch light I stood uncomfortably for a moment in the hall, nodding and smiling rather foolishly through the open door at Norman, who, having arisen to investigate the intrusion, stood in the middle of the parlor floor clutching a newspaper in his hand and nodding back at me with vague affability. Laura guided me by the elbow into the parlor—a look of rapt anticipation developing on her husband's face as I approached him—and said in a voice of artificial gentility, "Norman, this is Vincent Bruce, that I told you so much about."

"Well, how do you *do!*" His strange, tense look of expectancy broke suddenly into one of joyful revelation as he thrust the newspaper under his arm and held out his hand to me. "My golly, we've been long enough waiting for this pleasure!"

I shook his hand rather weakly, muttering, "How do you do, Norman. It certainly is a pleasure to meet you finally."

He was a small man of about thirty-eight with a gray face, thinning ash-colored hair through which his scalp gleamed yellowly, and a manner which corresponded exactly with his gray, pained, avid and oddly resolute eyes.

"Vincent just happened to be passing by when I went out with the milk bottles," Laura said. "He's going to have a cup of coffee with us."

"Well, that's fine. Wonderful." He waved his newspaper at the sofa, retreating toward it invitingly while he spoke. "Come on and sit down, Vince, while Laura stirs us up some coffee. You won't be long, will you, honey?"

"No, I won't be five minutes."

"Remember my meeting."

"I don't see how I could forget it," Laura said in a soft, expressionless way as she moved to the door. Norman nodded wryly at her disappearing figure as he seated himself on the sofa, twisting his body toward me.

"Women and business," he said with confidential sufferance. "They just don't understand the importance of these civic things. A man spends an evening attending to his civic responsibilities, and they feel deserted."

"Yes, I guess they do," I said, smiling inanely.

"I've got a U.C. meeting at nine-thirty that's going to be a really decisive one for this town. We're getting up a petition to present to the town council. I don't mind telling you there's going to be some fireworks."

I stared at him with forged interest.

"You know that piece of property down back of Clark's Esso station? That big empty lot with all those oil drums in it?"

"Oh, yes. Yes."

"Well, there's been some pretty hot bidding for it, as I guess you realize. The biggest offer was from an anonymous group of investors who called themselves Ham's Enterprises. Well, we did a little digging around, and it turns out they're a bunch of Gentlemen of Color—can you beat that? I don't know where they got the money from, but there's talk they're being subsidized by some big national organization. They want to put a Colored People's Recreation Center, as they call it, in there—bowling alleys, dance floor, all that sort of thing. It was a pretty slick piece of work, I can tell you. So we're getting up this petition to rezone the place as residential; only way to get around it that we can think of. But I tell you, they're getting slick."

I ducked my chin, giving a little grunt of incredulity which I felt was expected of me, and settled back in the sofa, folding my arms and stealing a quick glance around the parlor, trying to reorient myself in it again. Its look of aggressive Victorian gloom seemed unchanged: the same dark overstuffed chairs and monolithic pieces of hewn mahogany; the same enormous sideboard, with marble top and mirrored back; and on the wall the same glass-covered print of "The Helping Hand" in which the same small boy—miraculously unchanged, miraculously innocent, for all his years of toil—grappled with the great oar in the immovable dory.

"Well, I guess you're mighty glad to be back," Norman said. "Laura told me she ran into you on Main the other day. How long have you been in town?"

"I got back around the end of March," I said.

"Must've been a great adventure. By golly, we're proud of you fellows. It's a privilege I didn't have, myself, and I can't tell you how I regret it. I tried, twice, to sign up, but I just couldn't make the grade." He tapped his slightly bulging abdomen, which yielded with an unpleasant rubbery resilience to his finger tips, saying with lugubrious pride, "Colon trouble."

"Oh, that's too bad. That's pretty unpleasant, I understand."

"I don't mind telling you there's times when I just don't know if I'm going to make it. I had a little piece of apple pie the other day—not any bigger than a shoe horn—and I was on my back for three days. It drains you."

"Yes, I guess it must."

"It's just a constant drain on your strength."

"Yes." I nodded solemnly.

"Now, my brother, he was more fortunate than I was. I've got a younger brother, about your age, who was in the First Marine Division. They were out in your part of the world, I believe."

"Yes, they'd just pulled out of the 'Canal when we moved in. They were a great outfit."

"That's the truth. They didn't come any better. Nick had a fine war record. Done fine since he got out, too. I guess he still had a little bit of wanderlust, so he tried his hand as a traveling salesman, and turned out to be a real natural at it. You know what line he's in now?" The pained, indomitable smile widened his gray lips; his eyes flamed with shallow fire behind their panes of anxiety. "Ladies' underwear! Now I call that a pretty unusual line for an ex-marine! That's what I say to him every time I see him: 'Nick, I never thought I'd see you in ladies underwear!' But, by golly, he's making us laugh on the other side of our face; you know what he made in commissions alone last year? Thirty-six hundred. Now, there's no joke about that!"

"No, there isn't," I said with a strained smile.

"My golly, it's amazing how these light lines are opening up. People are buying. Of course you've got to be in on the ground floor to get the good territories and develop them. But I wish I'd gone on the road myself, sometimes. It's a good life." He glanced stealthily toward the open door through which Laura had disappeared, and turned to wink at me. "In more ways than one."

I grinned with mock relish, and we sat in silence for a moment while I stared around the room.

"What kind of grass is that, in the vase there?" I asked finally.

"Hm? Oh, those. I don't know—pussy willows, or something, I guess. Laura puts them in there."

"She was always very good at arranging flowers."

"Yes, she's right good at it. Right good at it." He raised his head and stared at the open door for a moment, shouting suddenly, "Honey!" There was no reply. He waited, frowning with irritation, and then pushed back the cuff of his sleeve, staring at his watch dial and shaking his head. "*I* don't know, *I* don't know," he murmured.

Laura appeared suddenly in the parlor door, her face composed in a mask of habitual offended patience. "Do you have to shout like that, Norm?" she said. "You know Mother's trying to sleep."

"Well, I know, honey; but time's getting away."

"Once she wakes up she can't get back to sleep for hours. Keeping her up all night certainly isn't the best way in the world to get her into a good mood."

His eyes darkened with a look of hostile vitality. "Well, I don't think we have to go into that, honey. Now, how about some coffee?"

"I wanted to ask you, Vincent, if you'd like some little cupcakes with it. I just made some little blueberry cakes this morning."

"Oh, no thanks, Laura. I don't know if I ought to stay, really. I know Norman's anxious to get away."

"Not a bit of it, not a bit of it," Norman said with fiercely simulated protest, clapping his hand on my knee. "We want to hear all about you. Laura says you're over at the asylum. Is that right, Vince?"

"Yes, I am," I said, regretfully watching Laura disappear again toward the kitchen. "I'm working as an occupational therapist over there."

"Is that so?" His eyes became unpleasantly shrewd while he apparently estimated the importance of this profession. "An . . . uh . . . occupational therapist."

"Yes. We take patients out walking, play games with them and things of that kind. It's just a sort of glorified attendant, really."

"Oh, yes." He seemed both disappointed and encouraged by the modesty of this confession—disappointed, perhaps, by the degree of affability he had so far expended on me, and encouraged both by the thought that he would no longer be required to maintain it and by the relative superiority of his own position. This conclusion was supported by the faint but undisguisable tone of condescension with which he added, "That must be very interesting work."

"Yes, it is."

"Must see a lot of pretty funny stuff, working in a place like that."

"Well, yes, sometimes."

"I've heard it said that an insane person always attacks the one he loves best. Could you support that by any direct knowledge of your own?"

"No, I don't really know very much about it. I haven't been working there very long."

"I always thought that was a very unusual fact."

I was relieved to see Laura reappear from the hallway, carrying a circular metal tray on which there was a coffee pot, cups and saucers and a plate of blueberry muffins.

"I thought I'd bring some, anyway, in case you changed your mind," she said, setting down the tray and removing these objects to the coffee table in front of us.

"You'd better, Vince," Norman said, raising his eyebrows genially. "These blueberry cakes are Laura's supreme achievement. Isn't that a fact, honey?"

"Well, I guess some people would think so," she said softly.

For the next several minutes there was no sound but the clinking of teaspoons, the rattle of china, the gentle liquid throbbing of poured coffee and the rustle of paper napkins. The three of us stared with fascination, smiling in a paralyzed and painful way, while Laura performed the many actions which produced these sounds.

"Thank you very much," I said finally, when she had completed her ministrations. "I guess I'll try one of these after all, they look so good."

"That's the way to talk," Norman said. There was another extended silence, broken by the subdued sounds of sipping and munching.

"Vince wants to know what those grass things are in the vase," Norman said in a moment, waving his hand toward it, his voice oddly muffled by a mouthful of dough.

"Oh, they're just some sort of wild wheat or something that I pick," Laura said. "I let them dry, and then dye them with Easter-egg dyes. I think they're sort of pretty."

"Yes, they certainly are," I said, staring admiringly at the vase. "That's a very good idea."

"Did you think of that yourself, honey?" Norman asked.

"No. Mother's been doing it for years."

"Is that a fact?"

"How *is* your mother, Laura?" I asked.

"Well, she's pretty well. But she's not getting any younger, you know. She has so much trouble sleeping—that's the worst thing."

"Yes."

"Old people need so much sleep, and she's so cranky when she doesn't get it. Some days I just think she'll drive me crazy."

"Yes, they certainly need a lot of attention," I said.

"They certainly do. And most people don't realize that. Most people are so selfish and thinking about themselves all the time that they just can't be bothered with them. They'd rather let them die than give them a little bit of attention and happiness in their old age. I think it must be the worst thing in the world to get old and see everybody just sitting around waiting for you to die, so they can get whatever you have to leave behind."

"Yes, I guess so," I murmured, somewhat disconcerted by the quiet vehemence of this opinion. I took another mouthful of muffin, nodding with exaggerated appreciation. "These are wonderful, Laura. I think Norman's right about them."

333

"Yes, he's a very good judge of anything to eat."

"I am, but I suffer for it," Norman said, tapping his stomach regretfully. He lifted his coffee cup, drained it, and set it down with a heavy clatter that made Laura's eyes dart bitterly toward it. She reached across to center it in its saucer as he swung his arm out suddenly, baring his wrist and looking at his watch with an expression of gratified concern. "Vince, old man, I'm afraid you've caught me on a bad night," he said. "I'm going to have to run or I'll miss this meeting."

I stood up hastily, crumpling my paper napkin. "Yes, I've got to go myself," I said. "Maybe I can walk along with you."

"No, no. No need for you to move. You've got to finish up these muffins. The cat'll just get them if you don't."

"Well, she can use them," Laura said. "She's got a litter of kittens to bring up."

"I sure hope you come back soon, so we can have a real chat," Norman said, reaching across the table to shake hands with me. "It's been real nice meeting you."

"It certainly has," I said. "Thanks very much for everything, Norman."

"Don't you mention it. I'm mighty glad you stopped by. It's a pleasure I've been looking forward to for a long time."

"I have, too."

"Did you put the garbage out, Norm?" Laura asked suddenly.

"Oh. No. I'll get it when I come in." His eyes darkened again at the sound of her barely audible sigh.

She said in a wearily triumphant way, "That's the third night in a—"

"Well, I can't think of everything, honey, I can't think of everything. I've got more important things than garbage on my mind right now."

"Well, just leave it, then. You'll wake up the whole neighborhood if you try and do it when you come back."

He stood rubbing his hands together for a moment, his eyes drowsy with a look of smoldering mortification, saying finally in a quiet, cold, almost meditative way, "I'll let you know how that business tonight comes out, Vince; I think you'll be interested in that."

"Yes, I will. Thanks very much," I murmured. I stood while he went across to the door, taking a gray felt hat from the table as he passed. He paused to smile and nod at me from the hall. After a moment I heard the latch of the front door and through the open windows the sound of his footsteps receding along the concrete walk.

"I don't know how much business they do at those mettings," Laura said, "but they're certainly not in any pain while they're doing it." She looked up at me with a vacant, acrimonious expression of thought. "He wants to run for the town council now. Do you know anything about the council, Vincent?"

"No, I don't."

"I just wondered if you knew whether it was true that you have to be a householder to get on it."

"No, I don't follow those things very much."

"Oh. You see, the house is still in Mother's name . . ." She paused and smiled at me wryly. "But I guess you don't want to hear about my problems. Why don't you sit down and finish your coffee?"

"All right. I can't really stay very long, though, Laura. I've got some studying to do."

"What are you studying?"

"Oh, it's just in connection with my work. Some books I'm reading."

She stared softly into her coffee cup for a moment, reaching out to touch its handle with her finger tip. "I'm sure you'll make a great success of your work, Vincent," she said, looking up at me between the sentences. "I always hoped you'd find yourself some day."

I started to reply to her, but found that I could not speak, bowing over the coffee table and shaking my head slowly in a sudden hopeless spasm of grief.

"What's the matter, Vincent?" Laura asked.

I went on shaking my head, pushing crumbs around distractedly on my plate. We sat silently for a few moments, and I could hear the big mahogany clock ticking on the mantel. It ticked with a hoarse, imperfect sound, as if it were on the point of expiration, just as it had done ever since I could remember.

"You never got the clock fixed," I said finally.

"No. I don't know why it sounds like that. Did you remember that?"

"Yes."

"Isn't it funny, the things you remember?" She leaned forward across the coffee table and began to fold her paper napkin into diminishing triangles, creasing the edges of each fold carefully with her thumbnail. "Vincent," she said rather shyly, "how did you really happen to come by tonight?"

"I don't know, Laura. I just seemed to come here sort of by instinct. I guess I thought it would be nice to see you again. I wanted to see how you were getting along, and everything."

"That's very nice of you," she said gently. "I thought you'd forgotten all about me. Or that you might be angry at me, or something."

"No, I don't feel angry at you."

"Well, you see, I wasn't sure how you felt after Norman and I got married. I mean, I thought you might be . . . holding it against me."

"Oh, no, I don't feel like that, Laura. I guess when you find somebody that you just feel is made for you, why, you have to do something about it." I realized, as soon as I had said this, that it could be taken as the vilest piece of irony, and fell into a confused silence.

"It's a funny thing, I've been thinking about you, too," she said after a little pause. "I happened to see you downtown the other day; I guess that's the reason."

"Oh, yes, I remember."

"No, I don't mean that time when you said hello to me. I mean just the other day. You were with a girl."

"Oh."

"A blond girl, wearing dancing shoes. She was very pretty."

"Oh, yes; that was one of the patients. We bring them in town once in a while."

"Oh, one of the patients." I did not offer any further information, and she went on in a moment, "It's a funny thing: you know, I thought people were supposed to stop growing after they were about twenty; but it seemed to me that you must have still grown quite a lot. You looked much taller than you used to."

"Really?"

"Yes. I guess there're lots of things about people that you can't really see until you've been away from them for a while."

"Maybe that's true," I said somewhat uncertainly. We both sat staring at the dyed grasses in the cut-glass vase for, I think, a full two minutes, after which she turned to me with a rather arch and—considering the subject—incongruous effect of pleasant reminiscence.

"Do you know one of the things I remember most? That day when you killed the horse and came here all covered with blood and everything. I never saw such a sight in my life!"

I dropped my head, mumbling, "Oh, yes," and wondering for what barbaric reason she had chosen to remind me of this. "Do you remember that, Vincent?"

"Yes, I certainly do," I said, looking up at her somewhat reproachfully. "But I'm sorry you do, Laura."

"Why?"

"Well, I just think there are lots of nicer ways that you could remember me than that. It seems to me to be about the worst thing that ever happened between us."

She stared at me with gentle determination, her rather strained air of casual recollection changing slowly to a somber and candid one of revelation.

337

"I guess you thought I was pretty scandalized," she said softly.

"Yes. I know you were. I've never forgotten what you said."

"What?"

"Oh, it doesn't matter any more."

"No, tell me."

Her voice had an insistent, soft, crucial sound that seemed to mesmerize me; I stared into her eyes and found myself repeating—as if in an ultimate, defiant attempt to cleanse myself of an ancient, unhealed mortification—"You said, 'Don't, Vincent. It's horrible. I'll never do that unless I'm married.'"

"Oh, that," Laura said. "Yes, that's right; I did." She dropped her eyes to the table and sat quite still for a moment in a mild contemplative pause which gave to her next words—spoken with such appalling gentleness—a doubly shocking, utterly ruthless quality. "But I am married now, Vincent."

I made no reply to this at all: only a startled look of despair, which must have been unmistakable in its significance, for I remember the silence into which she suddenly fell—the bitter, hypersensitive silence of a woman who has critically and futilely exposed herself. I remember very little more of our conversation —indeed, there was not much more to remember; it was mostly humble and hesitant expressions of gratification on my part and brief acidulous acknowledgments on hers, all of them exchanged in a hasty, harrowing atmosphere of misery. She came to the front door with me in a severe, perfunctory way, and I remember that as she opened it the odor of wistaria from the porch lattice swept in about us on the dark summer air—an overwhelming wave of remembered fragrance that made me close my eyes and slightly bow my head in grief.

"Oh, that horrible vine," Laura said suddenly in a tense, trembling voice. I saw that she was crying.

"Oh, Laura."

"Goodbye, Vincent," she said, turning away and closing the door behind her.

. . . It is too late to sleep now; the sky is already getting a little bit light in the east, over the top of the Murchisons' roof, and it will be bright enough pretty soon to see whether there is a solid overcast—and whether this blessed rain is likely to continue all day. I think it will. It isn't falling like a shower; it's too fine and steady and cold, and that light in the east is very dim and gray— not like a real summer sunrise. Which means that I'll be able to go to work today, after all—and to see Lilith! Thank the Lord! I haven't prayed since Mama died, but when I heard the gutter pipe running over a little while ago I felt for the first time in years like offering a prayer of thanks. That's a strange thing. The rain betrayed me so expensively the last time that I never thought I'd be glad to see it again. It doesn't solve the problem, of course, but at least it postpones it for a while—for a good while, if I'm fortunate. Because if we don't go walking today there's very little chance that she will see the child again for a long time—even if she makes me take her past his house again, as I'm sure she will. But there are other children, and she'll make other plans; I have no doubt of that. Still, the rain—if it keeps up!—has given me the only possible reprieve that I can think of.

Very early this morning—just before that dream—I had re- solved not to go to work today. I would pretend to be sick (I had even decided upon my symptoms, and rehearsed them) and would have Grandma phone the Lodge and tell them I wasn't coming in. This was the only way I could think of to keep her from meeting the little boy as she had planned. It wasn't really satis- factory, of course; there was always the possibility that she would persuade Mandel to substitute for me, and thus not only be able to carry out her terrible intentions, but—which was almost equally detestable—be obliged to repay Mandel for helping her. This possibility was so agonizing that I don't really know if I would have been able to stick to my decision—but now I am saved! No one will take her for a walk; there will be no walk!

I may as well stay awake now, until it's time to get dressed. I don't think I could go to sleep if I did go back to bed. I'll try to put down that dream I had while I'm waiting.

I don't know what time it was—around three or four, I suppose. (I'd been awake all that time, thinking about what was going to happen today.) Then, when I'd decided that the only thing I could do was to stay home from work, I finally fell asleep in a kind of restless exhaustion. I *think* I fell asleep; I'm not really sure about it, because it seems to me that my eyes were open all the time, staring at the wall. I have this impression not only because of the starkness and clarity of everything I saw—more like that of a waking vision than a dream—but because there was a faint ray of moonlight shining on the gold seal of my high-school diploma which hangs in a glass frame above the highboy; and this darkly gleaming, circular, saw-toothed emblem seems to be super-imposed upon, or buried shallowly beneath, all the images of my dream. In every picture that I recall there is somewhere—in an upper corner, hanging from a lamppost, perhaps; illuminating an attic window; or behind his face, giving a deep golden beauty to his eyes—this disk of burnished radiance, like a sunken sun.

I could not have been asleep, or in this trancelike state of ex-haustion, very long, when suddenly I saw the streets of the town, as clearly as if I stood in them. They were empty and silent, with moonlight on all the windows, and the pale stone of the sidewalks glowing softly. I was at the corner of Main and Montgomery (not there physically; I did not appear in the dream; but it was this section of the town that I saw, as if projected on a motion-picture screen). I was looking down the dark street, out of town, toward the highway; and suddenly I became aware that there was someone approaching—a single figure, walking down the middle of the road into the town. A tall man in a shabby raincoat, whose torn hem flapped in a shadowy, silent way as he walked. (There were no sounds anywhere in the dream; he made no footsteps, the dark elms stirred soundlessly, everything happened in ghostly silence.) He wore a canvas knapsack, like an army musette bag, slung over one shoulder by a broad strap, and it banged heavily against his hip as he walked. As he strode, I should say, for he came down the street in a rapid and determined way, not like a stranger or vagabond, but as if he were familiar with the town and certain of his destination. As he came closer I felt a breathless, gathering sense of excitement. He paused once or twice, standing in the darkness of the elm branches that overhung the street, and looked for a moment at the silent house fronts. I waited, feverish with impatience, feeling a great sweet tide of hope and comfort begin to flow through all my veins, and yet almost unwilling for him to approach too closely, almost afraid to see his face.

In a few moments he had reached the corner, and I saw now that he limped a little, as if footsore from a long journey, and that his broken shoes were bound with tape. He stopped again under the darkened traffic light in the middle of the street and, raising his head, looked up past the windows of the drugstore toward Diamond Avenue. He was bareheaded; his long dark hair fell in a tangled glowing mass across the raveled collar of his coat, and the moonlight for a moment illumined his features fully. What a glorious joy and ease poured through my heart as I recognized my father's face! They were the same sorrowful, darkly beautiful eyes—but steadfast and triumphant—that I had seen in my mother's hidden photograph, the same sensitive, outraged mouth—but firm and enduringly tender under the dust of the highway and the weight of many unknown ordeals—the same fine forehead and delicately hollowed temples, made, it seemed, to withstand time itself with its nobility. I called out soundlessly, "Father! You came back! I always knew you would!" And it seemed to me that he must have heard me in some way, for a sudden beautiful smile curved his lips. "I always loved you, Father," I said in a voice broken silently by joy. "Even when I said I hated you, it was only because I'd never seen you, because I thought I'd never know you. I love you, though."

He stood as if listening, his eyes glowing with a deep golden radiance, and in a moment turned up Diamond Avenue and walked quickly to the corner. In front of the music shop he stopped and looked in through the dusty window at the moonlit dulcimer. I saw his lips moving slightly as he read the faded title of the yellowing songbook that lay beside it. He raised his hands, spreading his fingers on the pane. They were slender and beautiful. Clenching one, he raised it slowly and struck the sheet of glass, which shattered and fell in glittering fragments with a soundless ghostly tinkle on the stone. He reached in through the broken pane and lifted out the old glowing instrument carefully, turning it over and over and smiling at the shimmer of moonlight on the dark polished wood, his eyes so full of love that I realized suddenly the dulcimer was for me. It was the present which he would bring home to his son! I thought my heart would burst with gratitude and love. He cradled the dulcimer in his arms and began to pluck slowly at the strings, little feathery showers of dust drifting down from them through the moonlight as he did so. I strained to hear the tune, but the strings vibrated silently, making some spectral melody which darkened my father's eyes with somber absorption while he played. As I watched his fingers moving over the strings I saw that he had pierced his hand on the broken glass; there was a deep wound torn across his palm which bled onto the instrument, staining the gleaming wood of the cabinet. He seemed not to notice it until he had finished his silent sonata. When he had done so he put the dulcimer under his arm and, lifting his wounded hand, stared for a moment at the dark gash. He took a soiled handkerchief from his pocket and wound it about his hand; then, leaving a wet black pool of blood among the sprinkle of broken glass behind him on the pavement, he turned and walked quickly up the street toward my grandfather's house.

It was at this point that I woke out of my sleep—or trance, whichever it may have been—and sat upright in my bed, staring across at the faintly shining golden seal on the wall and smiling tremulously, my eyes wet with tears, a sense of peace and solace beautifully burdening my heart with a weight so unfamiliar that it was almost like a pain. I was still only half awake, confused with sleep, the images of my dream burning so freshly and vividly in my mind that they seemed to me like absolute reality. I swung my feet over the bed and leapt up, staggering a little in my haste and disorientation, and without pausing ever to put on my slippers or bathrobe I went out of the bedroom and downstairs through the dark house, feeling my way swiftly along the walls and balusters. There was only one thought in my mind—one radiant, eager thought: I must be at the front door to welcome my father home! He would be here very soon now—he must be halfway down our street already! Grandma had raised the parlor shades as she did every evening before she went to bed, and the room was softly illumined with moonlight; I trod quickly through the pale milky pools of light that lay on the floor and unbolted the front door hurriedly, hearing the strenuous sound of my own breathing in my nostrils. When I opened the door the street was as silent as it had been in my dream—it was so late that even the sounds of the night bugs had ceased—a circumstance which increased my confused, fervent faith. I stood for a moment staring out across the porch railings at the stretch of moonlit pavement, expecting at any moment to see my father's figure appear, walking quickly under the still trees. I held my breath, listening, but there was no sound at all. After a moment I stepped out onto the porch floor, feeling the smooth coolness of the painted boards under my feet, and called softly into the darkness, "Father? Father!" But there was no sound or movement. I stared with burning, anxious eyes into the shadows of the elms and hedges, waiting, feeling my joy wane slowly as the dream faded. Very gradually the reality of the silent summer night succeeded it; the coolness of the porch floor against the soles of my feet, the low shoals of cloud that moved toward the moon, the moist earthen reek of peat moss from Grandma's flower baskets, and, suddenly, the sound of a train whistle blowing far off for the crossing at Gaithersburg. With that sound my hope dissolved entirely and was replaced slowly by the same dull ache of desperation with which I had fallen asleep. I went back into the house and closed the door quietly, standing for a moment with my head bowed and my hand on the knob.

But I could not go back to bed. I began wandering around the softly lit parlor in a random, troubled way, as if there were something I had lost that I might discover there in the darkness somehow. I crouched on the floor in front of the sofa and ran my hands under all the cushions. I stood staring up at my framed medals, glinting darkly on the wall, and reached up to rustle the dried frond of palm leaf that was draped across them; I lifted the top off the old Chinese ginger jar and felt inside it with my fingers: dried rose petals that Mother had dropped into it, crumbling into flakes when I touched them. What was I looking for? I had no idea; but some idly desolate impulse made me search for half an hour, at least, in the still room. Then I came back upstairs and smoked a cigarette, lying on my bed in the dark, until I heard the sound of the water pipe running over. (It is stopped up with a sparrow's nest from last spring.) When I opened the window I felt this fine cold rain on my face and hands and saw the gray dawn light behind the Murchisons' chimneys. Since I have been writing it has increased considerably, and I can see now that there is a solid overcast—not summer shower clouds—which seems, thank God, to promise a day-long downpour. So I can get dressed now and go to work through the sweet rain, which seems to me to be falling for all the children in the world, making a cool shield of mist to guard them from desire.

*J* HAVE NOW, in these last few pages, to tell the consequences of this "reprieve" of mine. It is with them that I end this story. Then I will be able to put down my pen and close this shabby soiled copybook and—and do what? I can't think about that. I don't think I will ever fully realize that it is over until I have finished writing this account of it. Perhaps that is what has given me the strength to go on with it. While I write it is still alive, held together by the tensions of active memory; but when I close this book, what advent will there be to replace it? None that I can think of. Only an awful void. Let me keep it alive a little longer:

She is strange this morning. (I see her so clearly—although there is no sunlight and the room is dim—crouching at her window seat, her hands hooked in the wire, looking out at the dripping trees with restless intensity, turning back sometimes to stare at me, disengaging her hand from the netting and lifting it slowly with a wan look to clench the tips of her fingers between her teeth.) What is the cause of it? The frustration of her plans? More than that, I think: some profound unease. There is a fierce, musing vulnerability about her, like a cat cornered by vicious schoolboys. She picks at the hem of her skirt, her fingers soiled by charcoal.

"So we are not going walking?" she says.

"No. We can't walk in the rain."

"Are you glad?"

"Yes."

"Why?"

"I wasn't looking forward to it."

"What do you look forward to?"

"To you. Seeing you, touching you, loving you."

She watches the soft, rabid, shameless yearning of my eyes; never have I felt such desire for her.

"And nothing else?"

"No, nothing else."

"But you are afraid to make it perfect."

"Perhaps. It is enough for me as it is. I don't want it to—"

"What?" She watches me fiercely. "To corrupt others, is that it?" I lower my eyes, unable to withstand her scorn. "Fool. You don't deserve what I've given you. You have no taste for excellence."

There is a cry above. She raises her head, her eyes clenching slightly with suspense.

"Oh, God. He's starting again. He screamed all night. Who is it that screams like that above me?"

"I don't know. Mr. Davis, I think."

"Why don't you stop him? You don't know how terrible it is, all night. Why don't you do something for him? Why don't you kill him?"

"We are supposed to cure, not to kill."

"Are you?" She stares at me with bitter, mocking merriment. "Do you think you can cure me? Do you? Poor frightened Vincent. Can you cure this fire?" She doubles her fists and presses them against her belly, leaning forward and rocking her body, as if in agony. "Do you know what you have to cure? Do you know what I want?" I cannot meet the burning challenge of her eyes. "I want to leave the mark of my desire on every living creature in the world. That disgusts you, doesn't it? Poor, honorable Vincent."

"I don't have any right to be disgusted," I say.

"But you think it sinful, don't you? Terrible. If I were a poet I would want to do it with words, and if I were Caesar I would do it with a sword. But I am Lilith, so I must do it with my body. How it frightens you! Wretched, righteous fool!"

346

She leaps up from the window seat and prowls across the room, stopping in front of the bookcase, on which stands the broken skull. She has inserted the red rosette into its eyesocket, like a scarlet poppy. She stands staring up at it, clawing her hair with her curled fingers. I move toward her and lay my hands lightly on her shoulders, saying, "Lilith, I only want to—"

She starts violently and shrinks away from me, turning her head swiftly, her hair falling across her frightened eyes.

"Don't! Don't touch me! Your hands are so cold."

"Cold?" I lower my hands and look at them perplexedly. She stares, wide-eyed, through her scattered hair.

"Yes, cold. They feel so . . . dead. There was a rose in one of them, and all the petals blew away, like little flames. Why are your hands dead like that?"

I stand in silent confusion, feeling a chill of dread. She turns away from me, pacing across the room toward the window and then returning restlessly to the bookcase, staring up at the festooned skull.

"Why did you steal my doll?" she asks suddenly, turning to face me with blazing eyes.

"I didn't steal it," I murmur, my face burning.

She watches me for a moment with brooding scorn. "You're lying to me. And you say you love me. How can there be any love or trust between us, when you lie to me and steal from me?"

"I stole it because I love you," I say humbly, dropping my head. "I wanted to have something that would remind me of you."

She stands in silence; with bowed head I feel her eyes upon me.

"Have I shown you my paintbox?" she asks suddenly.

"Your paintbox? Yes, I've seen it lots of times."

"No, I mean my new one."

She moves to her desk and, opening the drawer, takes out a wooden box and brings it to me. It is made of cedar, or some rose-colored wood, its cover beautifully inlaid with chips of ivory, ebony and mother-of-pearl, in an intricate geometrical design. It has also four little feet of polished ivory and a tiny latch and hinges of brass. I turn it over in my hands, admiring it.

"Don't you think it is beautiful?"

"Yes."

"Open it."

I do so. Inside, it is divided into narrow compartments for her paints and brushes, the thin dividing strips of satin-smooth wood obviously fitted and glued by hand. There is a folded sheet of notepaper lying inside.

"You may read it, if you like."

I open the sheet of paper and read, in an ornate and devoutly executed hand:

*This is the birthday present I made for you, but I have not yet had the courage to give it to you. If you will do me the honor of using it when you paint, then I will be able to feel that I have contributed in some small way to the beauty that you bring into the world. I have not seen you now for eight days.*

W. E.

I feel a slight pang of indignation as I read the words.

"He asked Miss Brice to bring it up to me yesterday. Don't you think it's rather touching?"

"Yes."

She takes the box from me and lays her hand upon it musingly.

"He has nice hands. Not cold, like yours. I had no idea he could make anything so lovely with them."

"Yes, it's beautifully made." My indignation grows more intense, to something approaching active jealousy.

"I think it's quite touching. He's a sweet boy, really. I've been rather cruel to him."

"I thought you considered him a fool," I say, a little shamed by the strenuousness of my own voice. My breath is suddenly cool and shrill in my nostrils.

"Perhaps. But I don't think he will steal his gifts back from me, or lie to me. I think he is capable of trust. And I think he would follow wherever I asked him to."

"Yes, I suppose he would," I say bitterly. "I suppose there are many who would, if you don't care what kind of fools you have following you."

"I think he may be braver, and less of a fool, than you imagine," she says with gentle, infuriating calm. "I would like to know. I want you to take us walking together tomorrow."

My indignation breaks suddenly into a hot flood of outrage.

"And do you think I will? Do you really think I will?"

"Yes, I think so."

I stare at her savagely, my eyes feeling hot and heavy with rage.

"No, I won't. What do you think I am? Don't you think I have any pride at all?"

"I want your pride to be in me," she says, becoming suddenly more gentle. She inclines her head a little in a supplicating way, her eyes softening. "I want you to trust me, Vincent."

I feel my resolution ebbing slowly before her beautiful wild eyes.

"I can't tomorrow, anyway. I have to work on Third Floor. I'll be busy all day."

"Oh, that's a pity. I'll have to ask someone else to take us, then. Perhaps Mr. Mandel will."

She moves toward me slowly, her hands a little outstretched to clasp my head, her faint bitter-clean verbena scent enfolding me with fragile tyranny, like the climate of a dream. She takes my temples in her finger tips, bringing by forehead gently to rest against her breast. Whitest, most exquisite of all havens. Oh, white rose of the world!

"Vincent, I would cherish you so if you could learn to trust me," she whispers. "You would never have known such joy."

"I'll have to see," I murmur. "I don't know. You'll have to wait a day or two."

*I*N THE EVENING, as I walk down the drive from the shop, I hear the sound of a Chopin prelude wandering sweetly from the open windows of the Field House lounge. I stand for a moment under the wet trees, staring down at the wings of a drowned damsel fly, oars of iridescent filagree, floating in a dark pool at my feet. I listen to a few bars of the melancholy notes and then turn up the Field House path and enter the building. Warren is alone in the lounge. He sits in one of the overstuffed leather chairs in front of the open phonograph, tapping an imaginary keyboard with his finger tips, his long dark hair fallen forward to half conceal the look of mournful ecstasy on his pale, heroic face. He rises immediately when I enter the lounge and moves to the phonograph, offering to turn it off so that we may speak.

"No, no." I wave him back into his chair and sit beside him in another, listening. The late-afternoon sunlight enters through the western windows, casting soft yellow trapezoids on the papered walls; one of them is broken across Warren's chair. His hand lies in the light, and I study it while I listen to the music: the dark hairs blazing in the soft brilliance, the long fine fingers with their bitten nails and ragged cuticles. I imagine it touching her intimately, trembling. He will have just such a look as he has now—drowsy, avid, the absurdly doglike look of human ecstasy. The music rises in a grievous frenzy, then, after a stark pause, reaches its climax in three shuddering chords, like the stifled, sobbing moan she makes in love; and I see her clenching his hair to bring his mouth to hers.

"Isn't that wonderful? Isn't that a perfectly beautiful thing?"

"Yes."

I sit with closed eyes while he rises to switch off the phonograph, an attitude that he generously mistakes for reverence, for he says quietly in a moment, "It's almost more than one can bear. It almost seems like treason of a kind to come back from that world at all, doesn't it?"

"Yes." Idiotic man! I watch him settle himself in the chair beside me, tugging his trouser cloth from the crests of his knees and turning to face me with shy awkwardness.

"I wonder if Miss Arthur would like to hear them? I asked her once, you know."

"I don't know, Warren."

"I thought you might bring her over some afternoon. Perhaps you could ask her again; she may have forgotten about it. I'm sure she'd like to hear them." One hand goes nervously to his mouth; he retracts it instantly and couples his finger tips together to conceal them. His eyes plead with me. I stare into them and say with sudden deliberate malice, disguised by a solicitous hesitancy in my voice. "Why, I'm not really sure she would, Warren. I did mention it to her again, just this afternoon, and I'm afraid she seemed quite uninterested."

His face falls into a still, startled expression of dismay. "Oh. Oh, you did?" He lifts his joined hands and stares at them for a moment. "Oh, I didn't realize that. You saw her today?"

"Yes."

"I wonder if she mentioned the present I sent her? I asked Miss Brice to take it up to her yesterday. A paintbox I made her in the shop. I don't suppose she said anything about it?"

"Yes, she did, as a matter of fact."

"She did? Was she—did she seem pleased with it?"

"Why, that's rather hard to say." I drop my eyes evasively with just the proper expression of regret. "She showed it to me. I thought it was beautifully made."

"Thank you. Yes, I spent quite a lot of time on it. I found a book, you know, that tells how to do that kind of work. I thought she'd like to have something like that."

"Yes."

"But you don't think she seemed . . . particularly glad to get it?"

"I couldn't honestly say she did, Warren. I was a little surprised at her indifference; it's such a beautiful piece of work."

"Yes." He moves his head and stares miserably at the sunlit windows, an expression of harrowed resolution growing in his eyes. "I wonder if you would do something for me, Mr. Bruce?"

"Yes, of course."

"It would mean a great deal to me."

"I'll be happy to do anything I can."

"I wonder if you would tell me, absolutely frankly, what you consider her opinion of me to be?"

I pause effectively, spreading my fingers and studying them with quite spurious compassion.

"Well, you know, she's a very—well, a very capricious person, Warren. I'm sure you realize that."

"Yes."

"I don't think she's a type of person who could ever feel very sincere or lasting affection for anyone. Something she said today made me particularly aware of that."

"What did she say?"

"Well, there's no point in repeating it; it would only be . . . painful. But you can take my word for it that she's a shallow and very cruel person, really."

"I'd like to know exactly what she said. It's very important to me." He stares at me with a severe, carefully controlled look of desolate but dignified appeal. "You promised to be completely frank."

I look levelly into his eyes, capitulating at last, with simulated misgiving, to his demand: "She said, 'Just because I've tried to be nice to the poor fool once or twice, he seems to think he has some claim on me. He's a stupid, fawning creature, and I despise him.' "

I watch the sudden, swiftly deepening pallor of his face and the odd, involuntary working of his hands. His eyes have a diseased look of despair.

"I'm sorry," I say more gently. "You asked me to be frank, and I thought it might be better, really, if you knew."

"Yes. Yes. I'm very glad you told me. Thank you."

"I think it would be much better if you didn't have anything more to do with her at all. It can't lead to anything but humiliation, Warren. She isn't worthy of you."

"Yes. Thank you." He sits clenching and loosening his hands. His eyes close slowly with a look of great fatigue. I lay my hand on his shoulder and after a moment stand up.

"I enjoyed the music very much. I'd like to hear some more of it soon."

"Yes."

"I know it's very upsetting to you; but I hope you'll decide not to see her any more. I'm sure it's the wisest thing to do." He does not reply. I stand uneasily, looking down at his bowed head, and realize suddenly that I have no very clear idea of why I am doing this to him. Can it be that I honestly wish to do him good, to protect him from my own fate? It is possible, I think; for as I watch his silent suffering I am aware of a feeling of love for him which is very powerful—the feeling of devotion, of respect, of intensely shared distress, which one must have, I imagine, for a beloved brother. We are really very much alike. So much so that perhaps the bitterly humiliating things I have invented to say to him are a form of self-contempt, or even a way of preserving, however brutally, his mirror-image of myself from Lilith. I do not know, at all, and have no desire to inquire too closely. I go to the door, turning back briefly to say, "Thank you for the music, Warren. Good night."

He raises his head slightly, saying with difficulty, "You've always been very kind to me, Mr. Bruce. I hope you know how much I appreciate it."

"I wish I deserved it," I say, and go out into the rainy evening.

$\mathcal{I}$ HAVE COME to work early, as I could not sleep. There is no one in the shop yet. I let myself in with my key and set the kettle on the electric plate, standing at the window while I wait for the water to boil. It is a beautiful morning, clean and fresh, with an autumnal coolness in the air. Over Crowfields there are three buzzards drifting and soaring in the blue sky. The kettle squeals on the electric plate, the shop fumes with its fragrant smells of leather, wool and lumber. Exhausted by my dilemma, I stand in strangely sensitive acquiescence, accepting everything—all odors, colors, textures, temperatures—obediently, uncritically, with bemused felicity, enjoying my reduction to a kind of measuring instrument, my gracelike state of subjugation, so like that of innocence. In a moment the shop phone rings and I pick it up, saying rather stupidly, "Hello."

"Is that the shop?" It is Bea's voice.

"Yes."

"Vincent?"

"Yes."

"Oh, hi. Listen, is Greta there yet?"

"No, there isn't anybody here."

"Well, when she comes in ask her to ring me, will you? She'll have to take over this morning. I'm up here at Hillcrest, trying to help out about Warren. I'll probably be here all morning; they're trying to get his parents now."

After a short pause I ask in a frozen voice, "Why are they trying to get his parents?"

"Didn't you hear about it? Oh, God, it's awful, Vincent. He killed himself last night." There is a dreadful pause. "Vincent?"

"Yes."

"I'm sorry to spring it on you like this. I thought you would have seen someone this morning. It's shocking, isn't it?"

"Yes."

"Be sure and let Greta know."

"Yes."

"I'll see you at lunchtime. Bye."

"Bea," I say suddenly.

"Yes?"

"Where is he?"

"He's up here, in the clinic."

"Can I see him?"

"Yes. Do you mean right now?"

"Yes."

"All right. I'll wait for you at the desk, then. You'd better leave a note for Greta."

"Yes, I will."

I set down the phone and stare out of the window at the buzzards flying against the summer sky; how beautiful they are to observe—what grace and excellence, what indolent yet ardent loops and swift, spiraling descents, what long poised planes of shimmering, gliding flight, what delicately woven arabesques, all made in tribute to an unseen mound of carrion.

I write out a note for Greta and stand it up against the phone cradle; then, separated from the morning sunlight by my fine cool web of dread, like a moist, shining caul, I walk down the road to Hillcrest past the dew-dark mulberry trees.

Bea is standing at the desk in the broad, hotel-like foyer. She advances toward me as I enter, holding out her hands to me in a lovely gesture, intimate yet dignified, which makes me feel a wave of bitter affection for her.

"I'm sorry, Vincent. I know how fond you were of him."

"What did he do?" I ask.

"Oh, it's terrible. Are you sure you want to know?"

"Yes."

"He got a kitchen knife from somewhere—he must have brought it in from Stonemont, I guess—and held the point of it against his chest and then fell down full-length onto the floor." She closes her eyes for a moment and I feel her fingers tighten about my own.

"And he was always so afraid of getting hurt," I say. "Little cuts and bruises, and things like that."

"Yes, I know."

"When did it happen?"

"About four o'clock this morning, I think. Mrs. Larch found him when she was making her final check at five, and Dr. Donaldson said he'd been dead about an hour."

"I'd like to just see him for a minute. I never said goodbye to him properly."

"Yes. He's upstairs. Do you want to come up?"

"Yes."

We go up silently in the elevator and along the corridor to the clinic. A nurse opens the door to admit us to Warren's room. He is lying in a white metal bed, his face utterly drained of color, his long fine hands with their ragged nails resting on the sheet. I stand looking down at him impatiently; it is not his face I have come to see, but his wound. But Bea and the nurse are here—I cannot bare it before them, and there is no adequate pretext to be alone with him. Yet I want to see his wound. I feel that if I remember it exactly, and apply my mind to it forever, if I meditate upon it unceasingly, as long as I live, I can perhaps, in some small degree, atone. But I see that this is impossible, so I turn away from the bed, saying only, "I think you ought to cover his hands. He didn't like people to see his fingers."

"I will, Vincent."

She says goodbye to me at the door. "I don't think I'll get away till noon. You'll tell Greta to make up the schedule?"

"Yes."

"I'd keep this away from the patients until Dr. Lavrier tells me what to say. Some of the Field House people may have seen the commotion this morning, but I don't think any of them actually know. Just be noncommittal if they ask."

"Yes."

I leave Hillcrest and walk back to the Lodge with the sensation of being supported by some volatile and exotic element which swarms all about me and preserves me from collapse. I am sure I should fall face downward in the road if I were not supported by this mysterious atmosphere. Part of my resistance seems to be derived from breathing it, as well; for it is quite different from the air I breathed yesterday. It sends a bitter nourishment along my nerves with every breath I draw—little tingling flashes of inspired fortitude.

I have this peculiarity: very often, in moments of stress, I hear (I must actually invent them myself, of course, but the effect is that of hearing them) all kinds of sagacious voices clamoring within me, manufacturing epigrams, homilies, bits of abbreviated wisdom and advice of every description, abstract and practical, derived from my predicament; just as if there dwelt within me a gang of noisy aphorists who rejoiced at every such opportunity. I hear one of these voices now, repeating obstinately and pontifically: "You must fill yourself with the sky to bear the sky"; and I nod at this banality, much as a drunken man nods at the most abject platitude.

I must see Lilith immediately; this is the only certainty I have, and I am most crucially in possession of it. For what? Approval? Solace? Guidance? I think only to see her, to be aware of her tangled golden hair and wild violet eyes. Only the beautiful, unequivocal havoc of her presence can make this outrage congruous. Only by suffering the bewilderment of her beauty can I be saved.

I increase the pace of my strangely sustained walk to a mild trot, ignoring the O.T. meeting entirely as I hurry past the shop toward the main building. The elevator ascent of only one floor seems interminable. I do not stop at the floor office, but go directly down the corridor to Lilith's room.

I am aware, the moment I enter, that she has watched me approaching from her window, for she has risen to meet me and stands in the center of the floor, staring, her look of anticipation overshadowed by a totally foreign one of fear. She has drawn her hair back behind her ears in an oddly formal way, and stands stroking it with nervous abstraction. I close the door behind me and move toward her, recklessly ignoring the danger of an intrusion. She withdraws quickly—a movement which startles and pains me.

"What do you want?" she whispers.

"I want to touch you. Don't move away. Give me your hand."

She yields it strengthlessly, watching as I lift her hands and kiss them with gentle frenzy, murmuring, "Lilith, help me. Help me."

Her fingers are cool as porcelain; my lips tremble upon them.

"Vincent, what is it? Why are you trembling like that? They'll come in. What is it?" She clenches my hand suddenly with her own, her fingers hardening like stone. "Is Mother here?"

"Your mother?" I raise my head confusedly.

"Yes. I saw the ambulance. Is she here?"

"Your mother isn't here."

"But I saw the ambulance this morning, very early, hours ago. They came to get Ronnie, didn't they? They've taken him away." Her eyes have become dark with desperation.

"I don't know what you mean," I say. "No; they didn't come for Ronnie."

"But I saw them take him out, on a stretcher, with a white

blanket over him. So still. I was watching from the window. Why are you lying? You always lie to me."

"It wasn't Ronnie. I don't know who he is, but it wasn't him."

"It wasn't Ronnie? Are you sure? You mustn't lie to me."

"I'm sure," I say. "It was Warren."

"Warren?" She stares at me for a moment, her eyes wandering slightly as she struggles to solve some terrible inward complexity. "You said it was Warren. Oh, Warren. You mean that gentle one, with the beautiful hands. Who made me the box. Have I shown you my lovely box?"

"Yes."

"Oh yes, of course I did. And we're going walking, aren't we? You're going to take us walking."

"No."

"But you promised, Vincent. You said in a day or two. But you mean he's sick, don't you? Isn't that what you mean? When he's better, then."

"He's dead."

"Of course, he has another one of his colds. But when he's better you'll take us walking in the field where all those yellow flowers are. I'll lead the way, because I know the way best, and we'll walk in yellow joyflowers, perhaps even by the sea. On a special path I know, by the sunflower sea. Because you promised we could. You promised me."

"He's dead," I murmur with dull, brutal insistence, shaking my head in hopeless emphasis. Why does she feign this stupid bewilderment? Why will she not understand? She has promised to help me; she has told me of her strength and promised to help me when I needed it. I have most need of blessing now. I raise my eyes to hers with a ruined, hopeless look of supplication. But whose face is this I see? Not a splendid, triumphant queen's, but a child's—an anguished, terrified, lost child. I am suddenly stricken with fear.

"Lilith," I whisper, "don't you understand me? Don't you know what I've done? He's dead. He committed suicide."

"Oh, no. No, no. I don't understand what you're saying. You're lying to me."

"I told him you despised him. I said you called him a 'stupid, fawning creature.' I was crazy with jealousy. It was because I loved you. Don't you understand? You have to help me, Lilith."

She shakes her head with desperate denial, retreating from me toward the window seat, her face gone pale, her eyes enormous glittering jewels of dread.

"Oh, you mustn't! How wicked of you to lie to me! How wicked of you to say such terrible things!"

"I couldn't bear to think about what you wanted me to do. I couldn't stand it. So I told him those things. But it was right, wasn't it? It was what you really wanted me to do; I know it was."

"Oh, no, no. What terrible things you say to me! You think it was because I loved him, don't you? But it isn't true. That isn't why they die." She backs away from me as I follow her across the room, holding out her hands to fend me away from her. But I am filled with savage, importunate determination; I am hardly aware of—or else I desperately ignore—her frightened protestations. I clutch at her hair and clothing, as if drowning in the mysterious element which surrounds me.

"I've just seen him!" I whisper with hectic, half-forged exultation. "I've just come from his room. You should have seen how innocent he looked, lying there. Like a child. You would have been so proud of me, Lilith, because I've done what you wanted me to. You must say it. Say it! *Say how proud you are of me!*" I seize her wrists in my hands, but she sinks before me onto the window seat, her head dropping forward, her golden hair swinging from side to side in anguish.

"It wasn't because I loved him. It wasn't! It was because of that aspic on the glass plates down there in the garden; it looked just like blood. That was why he did it. I don't kill things I love. I don't! You're lying if you say that!" She moans softly, lifting one hand to tangle her fingers in her hair, her body gone limp with grief. I kneel on the floor before her, forcing my head into her lap, burying my face in the cleft of her thighs, taking her wandering hands to press them fiercely against my cheeks, mumbling soft, hysterical demands.

"And now you have to love me forever, because of what I've done for you. You see how much I love you? No one else would have done that for you. But I have. I'll do anything you ask me to, Lilith. Tell me what I must do now. Tell me."

"Oh, please, leave me alone. You mustn't say these terrible things to me. Leave me alone—please, please."

She goes on moaning comfortlessly, swinging her head from side to side in a restless, agonized way. My fear greatens suddenly, like a vivid, swiftly blossoming flower. I lift my head to look at her and rise quickly, fondling and stroking her with little cold nervous gestures of my hands.

"Yes, I'll go away now. I'll leave you alone. I know how tired you are. You have to rest for a while, and then I'll come back later." I murmur to her in a hurried, frightened tone of reassurance, my hands fluttering about her collar, her hair, her brow, half comforting, half beseeching, in little terrified caresses. "You'll feel much better after you've rested. We'll talk about it then."

After a moment she stops the restless swinging of her head and clutches her elbows, pressing her arms against her waist and shuddering silently. I stand stroking her head fearfully, bending down to touch her forehead with my lips. "Lilith, do you hear me? Will you lie down for a little while and rest? I want you to rest."

"What?"

"I'm going to leave you for a little while. I want you to lie down."

"Yes, please. But you'll come back? Do you promise to come back?"

"Yes, I'll come back. And I'll bring you something. Some flowers, perhaps. Would you like that?"

"Yes. A flower from that lovely field. A yellow one. Not a rose."

"All right. And you mustn't think about anything while I'm gone. Just lie down and rest. And then I'll come and bring you your flower. Do you promise?"

"Yes, I will." She lifts her head to me in a weary childish way as I leave the room. "There are some there that we crushed with our bodies; not those. You mustn't bring any of those."

"No, I know."

"And you will come back, won't you? Because I'm very frightened."

"Yes, Lilith."

I close the door and stand with my hand on the knob, staring down the hall. Its vast Arctic bleakness is broken by the sight of Miss Donohue, coming toward me in a white, frozen uniform which shrieks faintly with the sound of splitting frost as she approaches. At my appearance her look of casual greeting changes to one of professional acuteness; she pauses inquiringly before me, asking, "Is anything the matter?"

So habitual has my reflex of deception become that I do not require the pause of even an instant before my calm, succinct reply: "She's pretty upset. She saw them taking Warren out of Field House this morning in the ambulance."

"Oh, Lord; wouldn't you know it. I was afraid she might; she's up at all hours."

"Yes. I guess it gave her quite a shock. But she seems better now. I made her promise to lie down for a while."

"I'll have Dr. Lavrier come up; he may want to give her a sedative."

"Yes. You'd better check in on her from time to time. I'd stay myself, but I've got an O.T. meeting."

"I'll look in, in a minute. Thanks, Vincent."

"That's all right."

I go on slowly down the corridor, staring across the wastes which stretch out endlessly from Lilith's door.

$\mathcal{I}$ DO NOT know how I survived the remainder of that day; my memory of it is of that strange kind of possession which afflicts— or fortifies—one in moments of emergency. I moved through an interminable series of activities in a haunted, passionless way, directed by an intelligence and energy quite independent of my own. Gratified, but too distraught for admiration, I beheld myself performing my duties with a kind of frozen, expert apathy— addressing foreign faces, conducting foreign patients, my body animated by a remote competence, my lips producing involuntary and miraculously appropriate speeches from which my thoughts and feelings were separated in still isolation, numbed and pre- served in anxiety, as if in a cold liquor.

In the late afternoon I went into the meadow behind the O.T. dormitories and picked a handful of primroses for her, bunching them together in my hand and twisting a strip of vine around their stems to form a little bouquet as I carried them to her room. I found her much calmer. She had drawn the curtains across her window and lay on her bed in the dark, staring up into the dusk of the room.

"Vincent?" she asked as I entered.

"Yes. Were you asleep?"

"No. I was only thinking—remembering. I was afraid you wouldn't come. I've been waiting such a long time." She took the flowers from me with a murmur of pleasure as I approached her bed, cradling them in her hand and holding them lightly to her nostrils. "Ah, you remembered. Thank you, Vincent. Are they yellow? I can't see them, quite."

"Yes. They're primroses."

"Primroses, from our field. How sweet of you. Witnesses of our joy. And, you see, they're not blemished: so fresh and bright. Aren't they, Vincent? I know they are."

"Do you want me to open the curtains? You can see them better."

"Oh, no; the sun is too bright. It seems to scald my eyes. What makes the sun so bright today?"

"I don't know. Sometimes it's like that in the early fall."

"In the fall? But it isn't fall yet; it can't be fall already. Oh, then you'll be going back to school!"

"I'm not going to school."

"You're not going to school?"

"No. I'm going to stay here with you. All winter. Always."

"Will you? Do you promise?"

"Yes."

"And bring me flowers? All winter? Where will you get them?"

"I'll find them. In our field, perhaps."

"Yes, I think they'll bloom all winter there. Even in the snow. Because we've warmed the earth forever with our love. Haven't we? We're the ones who keep it warm, not that horrid sun."

She lay quietly, brushing her lips and nostrils with the bouquet, while I bent above her, stroking her hair.

"What were you remembering?"

"Oh, all sorts of things I haven't remembered for years. A tea-cup falling on the floor in the sunroom because of something I said, and everyone staring; Cousin Priscilla's kimono, with those gold dragons embroidered on it, all wound around her breasts, as if they were suckling her; the sound that tires make on gravel, very late at night, underneath the rose arbor; and the pier at the bay, with dried fish scales stuck to it, and all the initials cut into those old pale boards—all those summer loves. Terrible things. Why do I have to remember such terrible things?" She pressed her face against my forearm with a gentle, fearful movement, staring into the darkness. "I try not to think about them, because they frighten me; but they keep coming back. They're beautiful but frightening, like knives wrapped in silk—lovely, soft, scented silk, with knives inside. What must I do to keep from remembering them?"

"You can work—do some painting, or play your flute, or compose."

"Yes, I must do that, mustn't I? I must work very hard on my language. There are so many words I have to put into my vocabulary. What do you call it when someone is afraid of beautiful things—of light? Luxophobia? No, there isn't any word for that in English, is there? I should think there would be. There are so many things I haven't found a word for yet." She turned to look up at me and stretched out her hand to lay it lightly on my face. "And, Vincent, I don't want to make you angry. I don't want you to be miserable and say terrible, angry things to me again—so when Warren is better I'll give the box back to him and won't see him any more. Will that make you happy?"

"Yes." I laid my finger tips lightly across her eyelids. "Don't talk any more now. Go to sleep."

"I'll see him just once more—to give the box to him—and then we won't need to talk about it any more. I won't ask you to take us walking again. He'll be better soon, won't he?"

"Yes, I think so. We'll talk about it later."

"In the morning? Will you come back in the morning?"

"Yes. Go to sleep now, and I'll come back in the morning."


𝒯HE NIGHT that followed was full of terrible livid dreams, imposed upon the darkness out of which they rose like jewels lying on black velvet, and in which Warren's face appeared in a score of tormented images, sometimes drowned and bloated, drifting whitely in fathoms of dark water, sometimes bruised and disfigured with blows, the mark of my knuckles printed brutally across his swollen lips. In one—the last of all, for I was startled into wakefulness with it just as the windows were growing pale with dawn—he appeared miraculously resurrected, in a robe of rotting and verminous sable, with a makeshift coronet of tinsel on his dark hair, clutching a broken, rusted sword in one hand and sitting in state beside Lilith at the end of a great narrow hall down which I advanced in trembling anticipation while they beckoned to me, chuckling, with foolish, feverish gestures of their hands. It was just as I knelt before them to receive the touch of peerage on my shoulder that I awoke, shivering, in an icy ague of excitement, my hands pressed in homage to my breast.

*H*ERE IS the last scene of all:

I walk quickly, still full of the cold fear in which I have awakened, under the avenue of poplars toward the main building. I must stop to see Lilith for a moment before I attend the morning O.T. meeting. The shrill, ugly anxiety which animates me is controlled by my attention to the silver trails of slugs upon the pavement. The morning shift is changing and the elevator is busy; I walk up the emergency stairs, oppressed by the chill reverberation of my heels in the tiled shaft. I unlock the metal door of the stairwell and walk quickly down the morning-quiet corridor to Lilith's room. I knock at her door twice in my usual pattern, standing with tightly clasped hands in sudden desperate impatience. Will she never reply?

I knock again, more loudly. Silence. Can she still be sleeping? Nonsense; she is up every morning at dawn. There is something the matter. I turn the handle, push the door inward and stand peering about the sunny room. She is not here! A lattice of triangulated shadow lies across her desk, which has an appearance of disarray. A bottle of scarlet dye has been overturned, spilling across the pages of her open Gospel and making a ghastly stain upon them. A sheet of gold leaf has fallen to the floor and stirs with a tinsel whisper in the draft. The horse skull lies beside her loom, broken into many chalky fragments. The red rosette is ripped apart, its crumpled satin ribbons tangled about a chair. Raising my head, I see that the motto on the wall above her bed has been defaced, the great letters blacked out with fierce strokes of charcoal. How silent it is—how desolate! "Lilith," I say softly. (Perhaps she is hiding under her bed.) There is no answer. After a moment I turn and leave the room, walking down the hall with frantic haste. In the floor office Miss Donohue is filing the night attendants' reports. I stare at her somewhat wildly as she turns toward me with a look of consternation.

"You look awful," she says. "What's the matter, Vincent?"

"Lilith," I demand. "Where is Lilith?"

"She's gone, Vincent."

"What do you mean?"

"She's on Fourth. She went all to pieces last night. They've just taken her up."

"She's on Fourth Floor?"

"Yes. Completely out of contact, I guess—from the report. I didn't see her; they took her up just before my shift."

I stare bleakly, plucking at the buttons of my jacket.

"Do you think I could see her?"

"I don't know. She's probably still in isolation, but it's worth a try. Why don't you go up?"

"Yes. I will. Thank you."

I take the elevator up two floors, standing very still and erect in a formal, almost military attitude of sufferance, as if awaiting inspection. When I open the door the squalor of the fourth floor assaults me in a wave of noisy, odorous babel. I move down the corridor among the stealthy, stupefied, hilarious or mimicking women, each of them a derelict parody of Lilith's careless, wanton loveliness. For the first time I feel revulsion toward them.

When I enter the floor office Miss Jackson nods at me briefly; she is a very businesslike, rather distant nurse.

"I hear they brought Lilith Arthur up last night," I say.

"Yes. She's in isolation."

"How is she?"

"She's quieted down some, but she's still way out of contact. I think she's pretty bad."

"Could I try to talk to her for a while?"

"If you like. You've had a good bit of success with her, haven't you?"

"I get along with her pretty well, yes."

"Well, go on back if you like. Brewster's on duty back there; he'll let you in."

"All right."

I go down the hall to the two isolation rooms at the end. An attendant stands outside them, peering occasionally at their inmates through the tiny slotted window at the top of each metal door. He smiles and says hello to me. I hear my voice asking with determined casualness, "Which one is Miss Arthur in?"

"Number Two. Are you going in?"

"Yes. I'm going to try and have a chat with her."

"Okay. I hope you enjoy it." He grins and, after peering through the window for a moment, unlocks the door cautiously, blocking the exit with his body as I enter. The walls and floor of the room are padded with canvas and there is only a single small, barred window, set high in the outer wall. Lilith stands staring up at it, her hair burnished darkly by the narrow ray of light it casts down through the dimness of the cell. She turns quickly as I enter and backs away from me into a corner, her eyes terrified.

"Oh, no!" she says in a soft stark voice. "You mustn't come in here with those hands. How horrible to have dead hands! You must take those hands off before you come in here!" She stands divided from me by the sloping plane of light, her shoulders pressed against the canvas padding, her hands lifted and held against her mouth.

"Lilith," I whisper, "I'm Vincent. Don't you know me?"

"Oh, no, don't! Don't come near me, please! You mustn't touch me."

"I'm Vincent, Lilith," I repeat desperately, imploringly.

She stares in confusion. "Vincent?"

"Yes. You know me. You love me. You're not afraid of me."

"But then why do you have those hands? Those are his hands. I know they are. I saw him clutch that rose with one of them, when he was dying. So tightly. Crushing it into a little ball. As if it might be the thing he wanted. There was something he wanted to hold, all his life. But then his fingers shivered and he let it go; and all the broken petals blew away out of his hand. They were exactly the color of fire."

"Lilith, look at me," I say, moving toward her and holding my hands up into the ray of light that falls from the high barred window. "I'm Vincent. These are my hands. I held the lance for you with them. Don't you remember the tournament?"

"No, there wasn't any lance. It was a rose." She stares at me with somber, hectic excitement. "You think it was an accident, don't you? That's what they said it was. But it wasn't an accident. I know because I saw him jump. Nobody ever knew that, but I did. I never told them. I was standing at my bedroom window combing my hair to come down for lunch and I could see him all the time. Penelope set the glass table on the terrace and there were big red blobs of aspic on the plates. Horrible. He was standing at the edge of the sundeck with his hands on the rails, looking down at them. He didn't slip, or fall, or anything, like they said. He just tightened his hands on the rails and then closed his eyes and jumped over them. Don't you believe me?

You always want me to tell you things and then you don't believe me. But I saw him. He fell down through the sunlight and it made his hair blaze, as if it were on fire. Like Icarus. And I was the sun, I think, because that's what he called me sometimes: *Soleille*. Like he did on the *Ile de France* that evening when we were standing by the deck rails looking out at the sea when we were coming back from Paris: *Soleille*. And then he ran the tip of his finger along my ear."

She turns her head slowly and looks up along the shaft of sunlight that falls into the cell.

"Lilith, please," I say softly.

"He hit the iron pipes of that rose arbor underneath on the terrace. That's what broke his back, the doctor said. And then he just lay there staring up at the sky, all spread out and shivering, among the roses."

Her face falls into a weary look of pain. She closes her eyes and bites her fingers, shuddering.

"Lilith, listen to me, please. I have to tell you what I've done. You can't leave me now. Lilith, please."

"What? What do you want, Doctor? You always want me to tell you things. Don't you know enough about me?" She raises her eyes to mine, smiling slyly. "Did you know I made them up sometimes? I do, lots of them. But not that about Ronnie. I saw that. I couldn't make up anything as terrible as that. And shall I tell you something else? Something worse? Oh, there's much worse. You'll make little disgusted faces, like Mother does. Perhaps I ought to make you a cup of tea first, so you can stir it sadly and silently, with that look of suffering, clicking all those little jet things on your collar with your fingernail. Or tell me about Cousin Priscilla's virtue, which earned her the Junior Vice President of the Corn Exchange, or some damn thing. Only I know she sat on the subway once all the way to Van Cortlandt Park, because she didn't want anybody to see that stain on her dress. The Shame of Eve, she called it. Cousin Priscilla's vocabulary was just as extravagant as her virtue. But *she* wouldn't have made Mother suffer like that. She suffered so much; ever since that time at the beach cottage on the bay when she caught me standing on the hamper to look over the top of the shower stall when Ronnie was taking a shower. All salty and sticky when he tackled me while we were chasing the ball, with a little line of white rime running along the brown skin on his arm. Oh, that taste of hot brown skin and salt, and the way his hair got all sticky, and you could see the down on the tips of his ears when we were playing the pinball machines in the evening, when we walked in to Rusty's barefooted along that sand road that smelled of jasmine in the dark. I don't think she really knew anything; she just suffered and tapped her beads and stirred her tea. Even when I came out of the room she didn't really know anything. She couldn't have. When I said, 'Mother, I want to be alone with him for a little while,' she just stood there by the piano with Daddy stroking her hair, and those jet beads going click-click-click, as if maybe I'd come in too late from a dance or lost the aspirin bottle or something. So I went in and closed the door and locked it, turning the key very hard, so she would be sure to hear it. Then I went and sat by his bed and laid my hand on his cheek. His skin was still warm, and he was so beautiful. All the pain gone out of his mouth at last, and his face so still. He was only nineteen. His hands were brown from the beach, with a little band of white around his middle finger, where she had taken his ring off. Oh, why did she do that? She knew I wanted his ring! They were still limp and warm, and with that same look of yearning. I even thought they were trembling a little, as if he knew it was the last time we would ever be together; the way they trembled when he brushed the sand out of my eyes when we fell down there in the tall sea grass on the dunes when he tackled me, brushing my eyelids so softly with his finger tips. His voice trembled, too, when he said, 'Oh, Lil, did I hurt you?' He thought he had hurt my breast, because I was holding it; but it was only because I had to hold my heart suddenly. I turned his hand over on the sheet and his fingers curled up a little. They looked so empty, so hungry. So I unbuttoned my blouse and made my breasts naked, and then I leaned down over him and put my breast into his hand, so he could hold it at last, the way he wanted to there on the dunes—the way he always longed to. But I felt how cold his hand was suddenly, and that was when I really knew that he was dead."

Her face has grown quite still with a strangely beautiful look of austerity. I stare at her in terror, utterly forsaken, reaching out toward her with trembling, destitute hands.

"Lilith, come back! You mustn't leave me now! You have killed me. Lilith come back to me!"

"So you can have two roses," she says, raising her eyes to mine gently. "A white one and a fire-colored one. They are both here somewhere."

"Lilith," I cry softly, "please come back. Please, please, please."

She comes toward me, smiling, the bar of sunlight striking her a sudden dazzling blow as she moves through it. "Yes, I will. I'll come back to you. And you won't jump this time, will you? You won't be afraid any more, because I've taught you not to fear."

$\mathcal{L}$ILITH never recognized me again. I spoke to her twice more, but each time she was more confused and remote than before, and her progressive deterioration was more than I could bear to witness. I stayed on until she left the hospital, in the desperate hope, I suppose, that she might be restored, that I would come some morning and find her in her room again, with her loom and manuscripts and paints, playing her flute or studying the sunlight with her prisms at the window sill; but I knew, really, that she had gone forever. When she left the hospital I went up to the second floor—I could not say goodbye to those blue, uncomprehending eyes—and from the windows of the common room watched the black limousine carrying her away. She was seated in the middle of the rear seat with an attendant on either side of her, so that I could see only the barest flash of her yellow hair inside the car as it turned out of the shadows of the poplars and into Montgomery Avenue. When I turned away from the window I saw that Mrs. Meaghan was standing in the door.

"Has she gone?" she asked.

"Yes."

"I have her prisms."

"How did you get them?"

"There was a good deal of confusion when they took her upstairs. I simply walked into her room and took them off the window sill."

"I see."

"I thought you might like to have one."

"Yes, I would, very much," I said.

She took one of the triangular crystal prisms from the pocket of her skirt and handed it to me.

"I thought, for us, they would be particularly significant."

"Yes. Thank you very much." I closed my hand upon the crystal, staring at it. "It feels quite warm."

"Yes, I've been using them." She smiled at me in her allusive way. "I have always been intrigued, as she was, by the number of colors it takes to make up what we call pure light. She loved the vividness of primary colors—of violet, particularly."

"It was the color of her eyes," I said.

"Yes. Violet is a beautiful color."

I put the prism in my pocket and said again, "Thank you very much."

"I suppose you will be leaving shortly?"

"I don't know. I really don't know what I'm going to do."

"I see. Good afternoon, Mr. Bruce."

373

"Good afternoon."

Shortly after her relapse Lilith was removed, at her parents' decision, to a European clinic, for treatment by a Viennese physician whose combined drug-and-analytic technique was at that time enjoying considerable publicity. Her departure from the hospital added less to my desolation than might be imagined, for I had come to realize, as I say—although scarcely permitting myself a conscious realization of the fact—that she had already left me forever; and whatever hopes I may have had for her recovery were tempered, I think, by my remote but certain knowledge of the dilemma which would have attended it. For how should I have behaved if she had been restored to me? It must have been evident, in spite of my sense of loss and destitution, that I could never have resumed my relationship with her. I have even asked myself—having read enough in these succeeding years to be able to imitate, at any rate, the manner of the wise—whether her destruction was not my own wish and, in an abominably involuted way, my own achievement. I say these things now, from the security of almost fifteen years of perspective—and yet I do not wish to give a false or pedagogical impression of my liberation from her, or of my present independence or piety. To the latter I have, of course, forfeited all claim forever; and as for the former: liberation, in such an absolute and final sense, is something I never experienced from Lilith—either when she left the hospital or when I heard from Bea, many months later, after I had resigned my job, of her death. How, indeed, should I behave today if, leaning from my window some summer evening, I should see the flash of her yellow hair among the maple leaves beneath, or if, walking past the Lodge—as I often do on my way home from the tavern—I should hear the sound of her flute drifting out among the willows? Yet these are questions upon which I have come to realize that it is useless to speculate; for Lilith is gone, and they can never be more than rhetorical now. They might be asked, with as much hope of a pertinent reply, of anyone, and have no true significance. What alone has significance for me is that I have survived, and preserved my will and reason sufficiently to make at least a partial atonement.

I tried desperately for a while to continue with my work when she had left the hospital, feeling that by doing so—by dedicating what remained of my life and energy to these people—I might make the feeble beginnings of an act of expiation. But I knew within a very few days that this was impossible. The loneliness of the place without her presence, the constant reminders of her (that would bring me, staring sightlessly, to a halt, lost in anguished memory), the daily contact with the people whom I had betrayed, the constantly revisited scenes of my ecstasy and treachery—all these made it impossible for me to perform my duties with competence, far less with devotion. I was incessantly anxious and distracted, and had lost as well—as I came to realize very soon—all faith in my ability to help them. It was Bea herself who suggested that I should "take a long rest" and Dr. Lavrier who supported the suggestion. No explanation was necessary; the disaster to the two patients for whom I had had such obvious affection seemed reason enough for my incapacity. I do not honestly believe they ever suspected any other; nor have I ever offered any—except here, in these pages. I was to return, at any time that I felt sufficiently recuperated, to take up my duties; my job would be held open for me. Both were particularly solicitous that I should come to visit the Lodge whenever I wished; they would always be delighted to see me.

I think Bea realized, when I said goodbye to her, that I would never return to work there. She always seemed very pleased, however, when I accepted, as I frequently did, her latter invitation. There was a period when I went as often as twice a week, to drink coffee and chat for a while in her office, although my visiting her was only a pretext. I went really to sit on the veranda for an hour or so, as I invariably did when I had left her. I was almost always alone there, for it was seldom used by patients, and in the cool gloom of its eternal submarine season I felt curiously at home. It was particularly lovely in the fall, because the poplars had begun to change their color, and all along the drive I could see the great yellow leaves falling slowly through the autumn sunlight. I would sit in a wan trance of memory, recalling with sudden excruciating vividness snatches of our conversation or fragments of scenes that we had played out together, and occasionally, out of habit, feeling for the tendril of vine that she had slipped onto my finger while we were sitting there. (It is gone now; I lost it long ago.)

It was on one of these visits that Bea told me of her death. She had managed, during a walk about the grounds of the clinic where she was hospitalized, to slip away from her attendant, and in trying to escape apparently had drowned in the waters of an Alpine lake which bordered on the estate. I say "apparently" because, however probable, this can only be assumed; for although her discarded clothing was found among the rushes of the lake shore, her body was never recovered. This—or so Bea explained it to me—was due to the extreme depth and precipitousness of the mountain lake beds.

I cannot truly remember what I experienced on hearing this account; not grief—in any conventional sense, I think—nor credulity, nor yet, as I say, that sense of finality, of liberation, which one might well have expected such news to invoke. Perhaps it was the ambiguity of her death that prevented me from experiencing this latter, for she was as enigmatic in that as in all things. I do remember the added fascination and sense of portent with which, for a long while afterward, I would stare into my aquarium in the evenings, watching the watery disintegration of the fairy doll. Several weeks later it blew off the window sill one night in a thunderstorm and shattered on the porch roof underneath. For a long time all that remained were a few chips of broken glass and a wisp of tinsel, glittering among the black twigs in the gutter pipe; now these are gone as well, washed away by the torrents of many springs. (I have only the crystal prism and the blue scarf we raised above the tournament; they are folded away, I think, somewhere among my things in a wicker

376

hamper in the attic, although it is years since I have taken them out or seen them.)

How have I endured? By what premises and through what undertakings, since Lilith's death, have I earned the will, the strength and the privilege to exist? Only by these: by restoring the devotion which had existed between my grandfather and myself, and by the writing of this book. I could wish that they were more than two in number and more expressly sacrificial in nature; and yet, men who have the fortune to work out their salvation have few pretensions in the matter. I can say that I am alive and sane with the knowledge that to list these as achievements would speak little for one's humility or the quality of one's contrition, unless one had experienced despair.

There was a time when I was greatly inclined toward some directly religious method of redemption—through prayer, or meditation, or service in some holy order; but having neither a monastic nor a truly contemplative nature, I must have foreseen, I think, the futility of such a measure on my part. For a long time—almost a year—I could do nothing. I used to wander about the streets of our town in a stupor of grief, peering into shop windows, loitering in alleys, sitting for hours on the Lodge veranda or musing on the courthouse lawn, across the street from the statue of the Confederate soldier. These last two localities were, during this period, the poles between which my life—if it can be called such—seemed to alternate. From my long reveries on the veranda I would drift down through the evening streets to the courthouse lawn, to stare with a kind of slowly growing, inarticulate agony at the sculptured bronze-and-granite fortitude of the shabby Rebel soldier.

One evening while I sat staring at it from the retaining wall my grandfather crossed the main street to the narrow island on which it stood and paused for a moment directly beneath the statue, waiting for the traffic to subside before he proceeded across the intervening pavement. As he did so the shadow of the soldier fell across his figure in the low evening light and fitted him so exactly that I felt my heart—I do not know how else to say it—awaken. There was something so miraculously picturesque in the way their two forms coincided—the shadow of the slouch hat matching so precisely his own frayed Panama, the empty scabbard extending at the identical angle as the Malacca cane which he held thrust beneath his arm, his foot placed forward to the curb in the same indomitable attitude as that of the booted infantryman above him—that I seemed at last to recognize him, to see revealed some long unrequited aspect of his own tattered humanity; and my heart cried out to him.

That evening after dinner I went into the parlor where he invariably sat waiting for my grandmother to join him, an unread newspaper lying folded in his lap and his clasped hands resting heavily upon it, tapping together the tips of his thumbs while he stared sightlessly across the room. I asked if he would like to play a game of cribbage. He looked at me in a startled, somewhat suspicious way and said hesitantly, "Why, I don't know . . . well, yes, I would, Lad. It's such a long time . . . I don't know how well I'll play. But yes, I'd like to very much."

It was in this way—not so much through any calculated course of redemption on my part as by the augury of that image of my grandfather, clothed in heroic shadow—that I began the slow and painful but quietly joyful task of restoring to the old man the love and self-respect which I had so long denied him. I cannot help believing that there *was* augury in it—that I was by this means led to see how sovereign for me were the responsibility and privilege of redeeming the single human situation to which my initiative and faith were indispensable. It was more difficult than might be imagined, for we had been long alienated, and in spite of our mutual wish to recover the relationship we once had shared, we had grown to resent and suspect each other in many things. There was, as well, in all of our approaches toward each other, a painful, confessional quality of abasement (for we both were guilty) and the sorrowful bitterness which exists between

378

proud and sentimental people in such circumstances. Yet, through unyielding perseverance and by small means and great, I managed to renew in him, over the years, the conviction of my love and respect which has permitted him to live out his years in peace and dignity.

Perhaps my most productive measure was the offer I made, a few months later, to work with him at the tavern. I have never known exactly what my grandfather's opinion was regarding my resignation from the Lodge. My distress must have been evident to him, and he cannot have failed to draw conclusions from it; yet never once, during the long period of my indigence, did he question me or make a comment of the least direct kind upon it. Whether this was through tact or by reason of our growing estrangement, I do not know; but I am inclined to believe that it was, rather, from fear that I would leave home. I think he was always afraid that I would desert him, as my father had done, and abandon him and my grandmother to a bitter, childless age, each dreading the other's death and the utter loneliness that would follow it. I am supported in this conviction by the memory of his face when I asked him, during one of the regular evening cribbage games which we had by this time reinstituted, if he thought there might be a place for me at the restaurant. I was on the point of repeating the question—for he sat so still, staring at his cards as if absorbed completely in the play, that I thought he had not heard me—when he raised his head slowly, his face filled with an expression of such profound and long-unfelt joy that it gave to his eyes and features the effect, almost, of resurrection.

"Why, Lad, there is always a place for you, if you want it," he said; and after a considerable pause he added softly, "I never realized—I always thought you had such a distaste for the work, Sonny."

"I used to, I guess," I said. "But I used to have all kinds of false pride."

He lowered his head again and paused a moment further, shifting and studying the cards in his hand before saying humbly, "Well, I guess you come by that honestly enough, Lad."

From that time onward, with slowly dissipating embarrassment and slowly growing pride, we walked to work together every morning through the coolly stirring streets to the old tavern at the outskirts of the town, where I applied myself with grateful resolution to learning the trade he had so laboriously established and which, one day, he had so fervently anticipated bequeathing to his own flesh. I did have, indeed, a distaste for the business—the kitchen, with its smells of blood and boiling food and its huge hanging quarters of dismembered meat, often used to make me reel with nausea—but this I welcomed, for it gave at least a semblance of penance to my labor and saved me from a suspicion of felicity in it. As he grew older I took over a greater and greater share of his responsibilities, until, after several years, he gratefully relinquished them entirely and, except for an occasional bustling and cheerful visit, took to spending his days at home with my grandmother, exchanging idle, ruminative conversation with her on the front porch, playing chess by correspondence and, in fine weather, tending an herb garden in which he took great pride. After her death, which occurred about five years ago, the emptiness of the house oppressed him, and he began again accompanying me to the tavern in the mornings, as he still does. He is a very old man now, and sits most of the day among the gleam of his copper scullery-ware in an old black leather armchair which I have had placed for him in a warm corner of the kitchen, from where he watches the activity with comfortable vigilance, drowsing occasionally, waking at noon to eat a cracker and a bowl of warm soup, looking forward with patient content to our slow walk home together through the dark streets and our evening cup of tea and game of cribbage. I suppose I shall continue keeping the tavern when he dies, as I know he wishes me to. I shall never marry.

If by devoting myself in this way to my grandfather I have

managed largely to endure, I owe as much, if not more, I think, to the other thing which I have mentioned: the writing of this book. How I first conceived of such an undertaking I cannot remember; perhaps it originated as a barely conscious impulse to confess. If so, it is one that grew in intensity and complexity over the years until it became a passion (whether moral or aesthetic I do not know, and I feel I have relinquished the right to an opinion as to how far the two may be analogous). I know only that I came to realize that I should never rest until I had created something formal, some shapen thing, from my experience. To this end I read incessantly. Outside of my work and my attentions to my grandfather, it became my single occupation, my single diversion, my single consolation. I must, in a dozen years, have read five hundred books, studying their manner and their matter with equal assiduity. Through volumes of theology, science, philosophy and fiction I worked my indefatigable, often exalted, often chastened way, searching out whatever wisdom and comfort I had the wit to discover in them and applying myself to those elements of composition only by means of which can literate records of experience be made. If there was little penalty in this for me, there was much in its application; for the writing of this book has been far from an easy or a comfortable task—indeed, there have been times when, if to renege in it had not threatened me with far more critical discomfort, I do not know if I should have found the courage to persist. Yet, it is written at last; and in completing it, have I found the peace that I anticipated? I have come as close to it, I think, as I am ever likely to again. This is not to say that I confuse peace of so humble a degree with virtue or fulfillment, or that I believe my repentance to be perfect, for it can never be. And yet I exist; for along with many lesser vanities, I have lost the hunger for perfection.